A NOVEL

PROPOSITUM

SEAN P. CURLEY

Wasteland Press

www.wastelandpress.net
Shelbyville, KY USA

Propositum
by Sean P. Curley

First Printing – September 2012
ISBN: 978-1-60047-762-1
www.seancurley.me/propositum

Edited by
Emerald Editing
http://emeraldediting.com

Printed in the U.S.A.

0   1   2   3   4   5   6   7

For

Burton Mack
Bart Ehrman
Alva Ellegard
Hyam MacCoby
Leonard Shlain

Giant Shoulders, One and All.

Acknowledgements

This book would not have come to fruition if it were not for two outstanding people.

First is my daughter, Caitlin Curley, in her professional role with Emerald Editing. Her diligence, attention to detail, and willingness to point out my faults is nothing less than astonishing. This book owes its quality to Caitlin. Second is David Gerring who stood by me and encouraged me through the years of research, doubt, success and failure. He never wavered in his belief in the story and in my ability to craft it.

My deepest appreciation goes to both of these fine people.

Additionally there were dozens of friends and family members who helped by reviewing the book and offering valuable suggestions. My heartfelt thanks go to each of them.

Table of Contents

Rough Historical Outline

722-200 (BC)	Jewish Diaspora
159-152	Teacher of Righteousness is High Priest
31	Augustus' reign begins
14 (AD)	Augustus' reign ends; Tiberius' reign begins
36	John the Baptist (preacher and ascetic) put to death by Herod Antipas
37	Tiberius' reign ends; Caligula's reign begins
38	Theophorus ("God Bearer") born; he will later be Presbyter (Bishop) of Antioch
40	Caligula declares himself a living God and requires all provinces to worship statues of him; Judea refuses and tears down the statues; Caligula dispatches the army
41	Caligula is assassinated, ending the crisis for Judea; Claudius becomes emperor
42	Paul's trip to Jerusalem; he obtains permission to be the preacher to the Gentiles
44-46	Paul's first missionary trip with Barnabas
49-50	Paul's second missionary trip with Silas
53-57	Paul's third missionary trip with Timothy
54	Claudius murdered by poison, Nero becomes emperor
58-60	Paul arrested in Jerusalem and imprisoned in Caesarea
60-61	Paul travels to Rome
61-63	Paul is prisoner in Rome
63-67	Paul free, expanding Roman community
66	Jewish population rebels against the Roman Empire
67-68	Paul again imprisoned
68	Nero's reign ends
70	The year of the four emperors
70	Vespasian's Reign begins
70-72	Roman legions under Titus reconquered and destroyed much of Jerusalem and the Second Temple

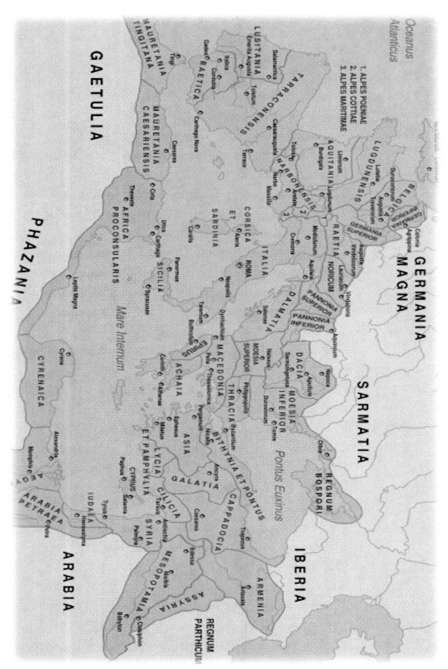

Map of the Roman Empire

Map of Iudea (Judea) Province

Map of Jerusalem

PART ONE

Permission

I. The Proselytizer (30 AD)

"A good tree does not bear rotten fruit; a rotten tree does not bear good fruit. Are figs gathered from thorns, or grapes from thistles? Every tree is known by its fruit"

- The Book of Q

They were nothing alike, the two of them, but maybe that was for the best. Proculus, an ex-senator and devoted believer in the Roman Republic, was intelligent, successful, confident, stalwart, and above all, a visionary. Saul, the current object of Proculus' ponderings, was studious and devout, but was also stubborn and somewhat delusional about his own abilities. *Nevertheless,* Proculus thought, *he may just be the one person who can help save the Republic.*

Proculus was walking a convoluted path. The twisted trail in the woods behind his villa in Antioch offered a respite from bustling people and was one of his favorite places to think, especially in spring. He came to his beloved spot, where he had built a bench of stone and Shittah wood to overlook the small lake in the hills named Lake Yosef. He admired the calm glistening surface, and turned his mind to the failing Roman Republic. It was clear to all who would open their eyes that the Republic was dead and an insidious Empire was consuming it. What people could not comprehend was the impending war with Judea.

He heard birdsong and smiled, enjoying temporary relief from his gloomy thoughts. He could barely feel the sealed scroll in his hand as he breathed in the fresh air and the sweet smell of acacia. He stood erect with his folded hands behind his back and his fingers worrying the message from Saul. He hadn't even bothered to unseal it before heading to the woods. The content was not what was important. *Could it be this simple? Could this son of Aharon be the proselytizer we need?*

Proculus finally opened the letter and skimmed it to find that Saul was planning a trip to Antioch and wanted to visit. That would give Proculus a chance to explore his ideas with the young Jew, even if he would have to do it in private, away from the prying eyes of servants. *I'll have to be very careful about what I say to him.*

Proculus left the lake and continued up the trail as he thought back to their most memorable encounter. Saul was a young man just accepted to the Pharisaic school in Jerusalem; the only school for Jewish scholarly studies and dedicated to that sect's intellectual interpretation of the Torah and Jewish law. His proletarian parents, Aharon and Ruth, were friends of Proculus' and they were both justifiably very proud of the young scholar. It was no easy task getting into the elite school for the Pharisees. Proculus remembered thinking at the time that he had doubts the boy could make it. But he was a devout Jew who had studied the written and oral histories and seemed quite motivated.

As it turned out, Proculus had been right and the school discharged Saul midway through the program. As far as Proculus knew, Saul's parents had not heard from the failed student since his release.

Proculus came upon a fork in the trail and had to decide whether to take the long route around or the shorter one on the right that headed directly to the villa. He went left.

The question at hand was whether Saul could be the proselytizer they had been looking for. Proculus and Maximus, his best friend and cohort, had failed twice before with potentials and there was little time left. If they did not find a suitable person soon they would be too old to bring their plan to fruition.

Saul did have the right temperament – that overinflated view of himself – that meant he might be able to become a notable speaker and he did know Judaism and Judaic law well enough. He had also been somewhat shunned by the Pharisees, which might help him accept new ideas. The real question was whether he had gotten over being so devoutly Jewish. Proculus followed the circuitous path back to the villa hopeful and anxious.

* * *

Nine days later Saul arrived at Proculus' Villa. It had been a long and dusty trip, his muscles were sore and his energy drained, but he wanted Proculus to know he was in town. He hesitated twice walking up the path to the front door and stood, unsure of what he would say or how they would greet him. His eyes flitted back and forth nervously and he ran his hands through his thinning unruly hair. He shook his hands out as if wet and stretched his neck in an attempt to relax. He then took a deep breath and knocked.

A servant invited him into the house where he found Proculus' wife June approaching. Saul frowned as he wondered what pleasantries he would have to exchange with the woman. She must have interpreted his reaction correctly because she immediately led him to the library where Proculus was working.

The library hadn't changed much since he'd been there years before. Two plush chairs covered with purplish leather sat next to a small round table. Most notable, however, were the shelves of scrolls and books, rare objects since they took so long to replicate. Proculus sat comfortably behind the desk.

From when he was a young boy and Proculus a senator, Saul had been intimidated by the man. The few times he saw Proculus on visits to their home in Tarus, he appeared to be an imposing figure who seemed to command attention and obedience by his mere presence.

Saul observed him from the doorway. Proculus was taller than Saul's average height and the man's upright posture made him look taller still. He had short neatly kept curly black hair and dark penetrating eyes. His waistline had thickened over the years though he wasn't unfit. The desk he sat behind was made of fine mahogany and held some papers, a quill, and a few unlit candles.

The best memory Saul had of Proculus, and the one that always returned when he saw the man, was when he had won the scholarship to the Pharisaic school. Proculus had given him a scroll with notes on the Jewish Oral tradition written down by Gamaliel himself. It was still one of Saul's most prized possessions.

He was shaken from his reverie when Proculus stood and smiled at him, "Welcome Saul, it has been too long."

He didn't smile back; he was always a little nervous around Proculus and his situation with his parents made any interaction with their friends difficult. He replied, "It has been too long, sir. My duties keep me traveling."

"I have heard about those duties, I cannot imagine they are pleasant."

Saul looked down, mildly ashamed, "No, but someone has to enforce the laws and I am... found useful."

June asked, "How are your parents, Saul?"

The two men looked at her as if they realized for the first time she was still in the room. Saul blushed and stammered a response, "I, um, have not spoken to them. Not since I left the school." He avoided their gazes and stared at a set of elephants carved out of ivory on the shelf behind Proculus. June must have seen how uncomfortable she made him since she quietly backed out of the room, bowing. He was thankful she had left. A woman's presence was never comfortable and her pushing him about his parents hadn't helped.

Proculus turned back to Saul, but before he could say anything, Saul interrupted him, "I'm sorry, but I can't stay long." Proculus raised an eyebrow. "I have friends I must meet and I need to arrange a place to stay. I just wanted to stop by quickly to tell you I had arrived."

Proculus replied, "As you wish, but I hope we can spend some time together while you are here. Your parents would like to hear how you are doing and I am sure you want to hear about them, even if you are not ready to see them yet."

"Yes, of course. I'll call on you within a few days."

Saul turned to leave and Proculus followed him out of the library. As they made their way towards the front door, June joined them. "Are you leaving already Saul, I thought you might stay for dinner."

Saul blinked in surprise and then frowned at June, trying not to be offended at the offer, but a little shaken nonetheless. *Why would she ask such a question? She knows I won't eat with Gentiles.* He laughed a little, nervously, before he caught himself. "No, thank you, I must be going now," and he hurried out the door.

* * *

Once Saul was outside and the door closed, Proculus turned to June. "I am surprised you offered that already; you know he had to say no."

"True, but I thought he should say no now and then if you do convince him to be this evangelizer of yours, he may accept if asked again and that will say much."

Proculus was nodding as he considered June's reasoning. "Well, let us hope he's the one and this works. He seemed to make excuses to leave... Maybe we made him too uncomfortable to stay, so if he is not back within a few days, I may need to approach him."

They started to withdraw back to the library and June said, "You know, one of the mistakes you made with Marnie, was that you didn't take him through a progression. From being a devout Jew to being willing to convert Gentiles, something most Jews don't agree with." Then, after a pause, she added, "You need to take it slow and let him see how to counter the old traditions one at a time."

"Perhaps, but we do not have enough time to be overly sensitive. We have to begin soon if this is going to happen in our lifetimes."

"Yes, but pushing too hard and losing him won't make it happen any faster."

"Saul will be back within a few days and we can start the more important discussions then. I implied we have news about his parents and he will not ignore that."

* * *

Saul returned to the house two days later feeling rested and more composed. Proculus led him to the garden table as a gentle wind caressed them under a cloudless sky. A servant brought watered down raisin-wine and then left without a word. Proculus never even glanced at the woman, though he did seem to nod at a different servant working in the garden and the man put down his trowel and left.

Saul was nervous and forgot about pleasantries. "Do you have word of my parents?"

The corner of Proculus' mouth raised in a slight grin. "Yes Saul, they are well. Your mother continues to be involved in temple."

"How about Father?"

"He was just recognized at synagogue for his contributions and I know he continues to fight for the rights of Jews in Rome. I also heard that a friend of his there in Tarus named his son after your father. I do not need to tell you how unusual that is or how much of an honor."

Saul leaned back in his chair, closed his eyes, and sat silent, relishing the idea of his father doing well. After a few moments, he opened his eyes. "And how is his business?"

"Still trading, although I have heard that he does not travel as much now. He has hired others to do that for him and his business grows. He is importing dyes now as well and that has proven quite profitable."

Saul glanced around the garden. The spring flowers were in bloom and he could smell jasmine and other flowers. A limestone wall, about the height of a man, surrounded the courtyard and was mostly covered by climbing vines. Fruit trees and flowering shrubs filled the enclosed area, along with a small shallow pond at the far end where birds were splashing and preening.

Saul's attention returned to the conversation as Proculus said, "He would love to see you again, Saul."

Saul immediately became distressed, his eyes pleading. He struggled with the possibility of having that conversation. When Proculus didn't say anything more he answered resignedly, "You know I can't. Not yet."

"Why not yet?"

Saul stammered, "Because, well... my father loved the Pharisees and now I'm," he had trouble even saying the word, "persecuting them. I'm the exact opposite of what he wanted."

"You do not know that Saul and if I remember correctly, you were the one who wanted to be a Pharisaic scholar." Then with a little more compassion in his voice, he added, "It is true that he tends to disagree with the aristocratic Sadducees and their deference to Rome and Hellenistic ideas. But that does not mean you had to become a Pharisaic scholar to please him."

That mollified Saul somewhat, but he kept his head bowed. "Saul, let me ask you this: How do you, you personally, feel about working for the Sadducees as an enforcer?"

Saul's eyes brightened at the distraction as he answered, "It troubles me. It's work and I'm thankful for that, but it isn't what I was taught and certainly isn't anything to be proud of."

"Then why do you do it?"

"It's work," he repeated, simply.

"That is not an accurate answer. You know you could do other work."

"I guess it makes me feel better when I get back at them for kicking me out of school." His eyes darted down and his face warmed. *Why am I so honest with him? It's like he has some magical power to make people tell their inner secrets.* Saul was mad enough at himself that he stood up and walked away from the table towards the pond causing the birds to flutter away. After getting some distance from Proculus, he began to wonder why Proculus was asking these questions. *Is this just to convince me to talk with Father? Or is there some other motivation here? Why should he care if I support the Sadducees?* To Saul's knowledge, the senator hadn't shown a preference for any of the Jewish sects in the past.

Proculus stayed sitting while Saul perused the flowers. After a couple of minutes, Saul returned and offered, "You have a truly beautiful garden here."

Proculus laughed. "That would be our servants Rebekah and Daniel." Then he became serious again, "Saul you do not need to be ashamed. You spent most of your youth studying to get into that school. You understand their laws better than most people I have met, including some who graduated." Saul felt the back of his head tighten at the praise. He recalled the school and his eyes quickly narrowed as his lips tightened into a line. He became pensive and mumbled, "I've been having dreams lately where I'm doing evil things to Pharisees and then they turn out to be good people and, well, it's disturbing."

"I'm no reader-of-dreams, but maybe you should consider seeing your parents again. They would love to see you and they are not the kind of people to think negatively of you."

So he is just trying to push me into seeing them? "Maybe," was all he could say.

After an uncomfortable silence, Saul changed the subject. "I've often wondered why you retired at such an early age. You were one of the youngest senators ever and could have gone far. May I ask what happened?"

Proculus glanced to the side as a series of emotions seemed to cross his face. Saul thought he saw hope, pride, frustration, disappointment, and even regret in Proculus' face. He wasn't sure he would answer, but after a minute, Proculus looked directly at Saul. "Did you know I was married once before, to Cæcilia Aelius?"

"Yes, I might have met her once at my parent's house."

"Possibly. In any case, she was the more politically inclined of the two of us. My parents were wealthy and she came from an aristocratic family with influence. I was young and eager to make a difference and the marriage seemed appropriate."

Proculus hesitated, his eyes blinking and sad as if a dark memory had invaded his mind. "She was also a sickly woman and never really recovered from a serious bout of malaria. When she died, I decided to leave politics. I had come to respect and appreciate Judea and its people. So I sold my estates and moved here and this is where I fell in love with June."

"Why Antioch?"

"Its diverse population, proximity to a busy port, and that it is one of the largest cities in the Emp... Republic."

What was he about to say? It isn't like Proculus to misspeak.

June came into the garden then with a note for Proculus. "This just arrived and I thought you would want to see it right away."

Saul took a longer look at her, curious after hearing Proculus say he had fallen in love with her. She was Jewish by descent, but had taken up Gentile ways with Proculus and had even changed her name to Junious. A somewhat robust woman with long reddish hair and hints of gray, she had an elegant look to her, but what disturbed Saul most was her penetrating eyes that seemed to read a man's soul. It was difficult to be in her presence for long. *She eats with Gentiles!*

June left and Proculus opened the note and read it in silence. Saul could see his face becoming heated and foreboding as he read, but he knew it wasn't his place to inquire. When Proculus was finished reading he folded the note and tossed it onto the table, looking into the distance in contemplation.

Saul asked, "Is everything all right?"

"No, not really." Proculus pulled his attention back to Saul. "This is something not many people are aware of, but the Roman Republic is dying."

Saul's head went back as if slapped, his mouth opened slightly, and he blinked. All he could manage to say was a stumbling "What?"

"What I mean is that it is turning into an empire, rather than a republic. The change began back with Augustus, or maybe even before, with Julius Caesar, but it will, eventually, be the downfall of Rome and it… irritates me."

"As much as I hate Rome and think it needs to burn, what you are saying is difficult to imagine. What enemy could possibly challenge them?"

"It will not be an outside enemy, at least not initially. It will be the weakness of the Senate or in-fighting or even civil war. It will be the generals vying for control of the government and a senate too weak to stop them."

"But," Saul spluttered, "they seem so… solid, so untouchable, and Tiberius Caesar seems to have total control."

"I know it seems that way and few understand the problems, but they exist and they will grow. My bigger concern at the moment is how all of it will affect Judea."

Now Saul became apprehensive and leaned forward in his chair attentively. *What could he be thinking? Has he just become a paranoid old man? And why wouldn't the failure of Rome be a good thing for Judea?* "How do you mean?"

"There has always been strife between Rome and Judea. They are a relatively new province and they still see themselves as the chosen ones. They cannot fathom Rome as their masters."

The 'chosen ones' phrase vexed Saul and he let it show. But before he could say anything, Proculus continued, "I know what you are thinking Saul, hear me out.

"Judea is the only province that is allowed to skip paying taxes once every seven years. I know the sabbatical has religious origins and Rome honors local religious customs, which is why Judea has been allowed to suspend taxes during that time. But there are Romans who grow tired of the special treatment. Imagine what happens if one of those becomes Caesar? Since so much power is in the hands of one person, he can just order the Jews to pay, whether or not they are planting and harvesting that year. Just imagine what that would cause."

Proculus' voice grew more urgent, "And what of the Caesars proclaiming their predecessors to be Gods and wanting us all to worship them? We have already seen that cause strife. Did you know that some people wanted Tiberius to proclaim himself a living God and build temples in his name? Thankfully, he refused, but one of them will do so and what happens when they require the Jews to worship them as a God? It will happen and you know how the Jews will react. They will refuse and that will lead to war between Judea and Rome and that is, well, that is unthinkable."

"Truly? War? I know there's disagreement, but not to that level."

"No, not yet, but that is because Tiberius is a reasonable Caesar. What happens when we get an unreasonable one?"

Saul shook his head, "That's impossible to plan for."

"Possibly, possibly…," Proculus mumbled as his intensity subsided and he relaxed into his chair. He seemed to drift into deep thought.

After a few minutes where both men sat thinking, Saul spoke up, "I should be going."

Proculus frowned, "Oh, will you be coming back to see us before you leave Antioch?" There was a hint of anxiety in his voice that troubled Saul. *Does Proculus want me to come back or not? What is he not saying?*

"I don't know, I'll try to," and he stood to leave.

* * *

After he was gone, June came out. "Well?"

"I do not know. I was able to tell him about the problems with Rome. He has some of the right makings, but he may not be able to accept that there is a real threat, or that he will be willing to help do something about it." After more consideration, he added, "If he comes back before he leaves town, then we have to present the idea to him." Proculus picked up the blank piece of paper, handed it to June, and added, "Thank you for bringing that in; it was perfect timing, though I was surprised you did not write something on it so I would not have to hide it so obviously." He smiled and June giggled.

* * *

Over the following days, Proculus became demonstrably agitated with terse responses to June and the servants, and an inability to sit still for long. Saul had been gone almost a week and it was approaching the day he had said he would be leaving town. Proculus noticed June keeping her distance and was thankful even as it exasperated his agitation. There were few prospects for what he had in mind and he had built Saul up into a real possibility. June had even suggested they consider a way to force a meeting before Saul left town.

On the day before Saul's planned departure, he finally arrived at Proculus' house. Proculus had been away on an errand when Daniel came running up out of breath and told him Saul was at the villa. It was early evening, just after the final meal. Proculus dismissed the errand and rushed back.

He took a few minutes to get his breathing under control and wipe some of the perspiration away before entering the library. He looked in to see Saul standing at the shelves of scrolls and books. The man's dark complexion and long nose made him look distinctly Jewish. He had clean but ruffled hair and a freshly trimmed beard. Proculus advanced through the door and Saul turned to greet him. The two men exchanged small talk about Saul's activities in Antioch and then Proculus sat in his chair, looking into Saul's vague blue eyes, and leaned back waiting for him to initiate the real conversation.

Saul looked intently at Proculus. "I've considered this a great deal. It's been hard to concentrate on anything else. But I know you well enough to know you have a plan. It was one of the things my father used to say about you. I clearly remember him proclaiming, 'Proculus is a visionary. He's always looking to the future and he always has a plan.' So I may not agree with what you've said, but I am curious. What's your plan?"

Proculus was surprised at how accepting of the situation Saul seemed to be, but maybe it just seemed that way. He decided he still needed to be careful. "Yes Saul, there is a plan, at least a vague one. It will take a long time to come to realization and, as you probably guessed, I could use your help."

Saul leaned forward in his chair. "Yes?"

"The idea is to spread Judaism so far into the Roman Empire that war would be unthinkable. People link Judaism with Judea and if we can spread Judaism, we protect Judea."

Saul turned and seemed to look at some scrolls behind Proculus left shoulder. He replied, "You mean to try to convert Gentiles to Judaism?"

"Yes, exactly."

"That won't be easy. The laws..."

"Which is why I need your help."

Saul relaxed into his chair. "You want me to find a way around those laws."

"Precisely."

Saul's eyes flicked back and forth and he rubbed his neck. Proculus waited patiently. Saul said, "There might be some who would favor such a move. We will need to use the Essenes. Their founder professed universal availability to the Kingdom of God. I haven't studied them much, but I think their teachings might support this."

Proculus could hardly believe his ears. The writings of the Essenes were part of the inspiration for this plan and were at the heart of every idea he had for converting the Romans. He was also elated that Saul had used "we" since it implied he had already decided to help, even if he had not realized it yet.

The two continued to talk until darkness consumed the sky and Saul realized he had to leave in order to be safe. As he stood up, he sighed. "It's a nice dream, but I don't see it really happening. The Jews would never change their laws and without that, we cannot convert the Gentiles.

Proculus wasn't giving up though, "Saul, would you consider extending your stay in Antioch so we may discuss this further? It is possible and I would like the chance to convince you."

Saul cocked his head and opened his mouth to say something, but hesitated. Then he relented, "I can do that Proculus. Let me make plans for some place to stay. I'll be back in a couple of days to continue this." He turned and left as Proculus looked on intently.

II. The Vision (30 AD)

"Those who cry are fortunate for they shall also laugh."
                                                          - The Book of Q

Proculus spent the next two weeks with Saul, as time permitted, discussing various Jewish sects. They both knew the Pharisees and the Sadducees well, but the mysterious Essenes were elusive and few knew much about them other than they were diasaporic and followed the teachings of a long-dead high priest known only as the Teacher of Righteousness. They also discussed what it would take for the High Council to allow them to openly convert Gentiles. As Proculus knew they would, they concluded there was not enough information to convince the Sanhedrin in Jerusalem. What was most significant, however, was his appraisal of Saul as a proselytizer.

On their fourth such meeting, Proculus decided to take the next step. He had spent most of the previous discussions explaining to Saul the intricacies of the Roman Empire and exactly why his predictions were likely. With this meeting, he had Saul come after the last meal of the day and had a flask of good wine waiting in the library for them.

Rebekah led Saul to the library when he arrived, but left the door slightly ajar. Saul glanced at the open flask of wine on the desk. "What's this for?"

Proculus' hands came together under his chin as his forehead crinkled in concentration. "We have talked a lot about the Essenes and others and about the tact we might take with the Sanhedrin. However, I still see doubt in your mind and I think I know why."

Saul grimaced and leaned back in his chair, but stayed silent.

Proculus reached down, poured two cups, and offered one to Saul as he noticed a lock of hair that had fallen in front of Saul's left eye. *Sometimes he appears so young.* "We have only discussed the first part of this plan. You see, after we get permission to proselytize, then we have to have a speaker for the new sect go out among the Gentiles of the Roman Empire to establish communities and teach them new ways." Saul was scowling, so Proculus added, "We need to create a separate sect, Saul."

The scowl remained and Proculus' eyebrow went up in a prompt. "Why wouldn't we just join with the Essenes?" Saul asked.

"Initially that may be the most reasonable approach, and at a minimum we need to learn more about them, but they are reclusive and are seen by mainstream Jews as outcasts. We need to use their ideas, possibly enhance them, and work with the existing synagogues or this will take centuries.

"You know that most Jews outside of Judea do not care about the various sects within Judaism; they are all collectively Jews. And so shall we be. Only we will have permission to convert Gentiles with new ideas and rules that enable and encourage conversion." There was a lot more to it than that but he was not about to go too far with Saul like he and Maximus had with Marnie.

Saul rediscovered the wine in his hand and held up the glass, appreciating the patterns of swirling blue and green in the stonework. He asked again, "So, what's this for?"

Proculus laughed and touched Saul's cup with his in an informal toast. "Because, I think you and I understand each other and are heading down a path to form something better."

"I haven't agreed to help you."

"Indeed. However, I think you will."

They both took a drink and Saul commented, "This is fine wine; I don't often get to taste any this good."

"It is one of the finest, called Falernian, and comes from a viticulturist associate of mine in Rome."

The two schemers spent hours drinking and discussing what types of people would be best to travel the empire and build up Gentile-friendly communities. Eventually, Proculus changed the subject. "You know Saul..." June interrupted them with a replacement flask of wine. This one was lesser quality, but Saul didn't seem to notice as he reached out and poured. June left quietly. Saul stared at her silent withdrawal, eyes squinting. "You were saying?"

"Just that you might not be aware of this, but I was at your naming ceremony."

Saul's eyes went wide in mild surprise, "No, I didn't." He sat the cup down with a look that seemed to indicate he was done or at least wanted to concentrate on this new topic.

Proculus relaxed into his chair to tell the story. "I remember your father was so proud that day. He and your mother were young and just starting their family. They had had trouble conceiving, so you were, in your mother's words, 'a magnificent gift from God.' Ruth was still recovering because the delivery had been quite difficult; in fact, the attendant was not sure she would survive, but she did and there you were. I remember her sitting in a chair, at the naming, holding you while your father tried to stand still behind her, but he was so excited he struggled to stay in one spot. During the ceremony, I could see tears in his eyes.

"I also remember that, before you were born, they had a hard time finding a name for you. They struggled for months because the only names they liked were already in use by living relatives. Then, just weeks before you were born, your paternal great uncle died and he had been a kind and devout man and your mother and father knew they had found your name."

Saul interrupted. "How is it that you were allowed to attend? Not being Jewish…"

"Normally that is true, however your father is a respected leader and away from Judea the communities tend to bend the rules a little. I was allowed to stand just outside the room, with the doors open so I could see and hear the ceremony." Then he added with a smirk, "So in reality, I was not actually in the room when the ceremony occurred."

Saul sat back in his chair, with his face relaxed and his eyes glistening, looking up at the ceiling. After a few moments, he mumbled, "Maybe it is time for me to see them again." Then he shook his head and refocused on Proculus.

Proculus watched Saul in silence as he seemed to be looking inward and then brought up the story he had been planning to tell Saul all night. "I also saw you give a speech when you were ten and getting ready to go to the Pharisaic school."

Saul examined his near-empty cup as his shoulders slumped. Proculus ignored the look of dejection and continued, "It was in front of the congregation again and because it was not a religious ceremony, there were a number of gentiles there. Cæcilia was in bed ill, so I was standing with your father.

"The entire town was swollen with pride to be having one of their own accepted into the school; well, at least the Jewish quarter of the town. There must have been three hundred people. I remember there were so many that they did not fit into the synagogue. Some of the latecomers were quite disappointed.

"I really expected you to be nervous, talking in front of all those people. You walked in with your head down. I recall thinking 'this could be embarrassing,' But you seemed to gather your strength, walked to the front with your head upright and proud, and stood on a small platform they had placed there for you. You lifted your head, took a deep breath, and spoke with confidence."

Proculus could see tears welling in Saul's eyes and was pleased at the emotion. He touched cups with him again for a distraction and Saul ran his sleeve across his face. Then he drank the remaining wine in his glass. Proculus poured another and continued, "Your parents were beaming with joy." His voice got a little quieter, "You were their only child and there was no telling if you would even make it to adulthood, let alone achieve something, and even being accepted into that school is quite an accomplishment.

"What was most impressive about your speech, in my opinion, was that you had no notes or queues. You spoke for about ten minutes, unwaveringly and intelligently. You brought in scripture, oral stories from Abraham, and you were modest and appreciative. I remember thinking that I had heard speeches from senators that were not as well thought out, appropriate, or articulate as yours." Proculus wondered if Saul remembered just how nervous he really was giving that speech.

June came in quietly, placed another flask of wine on the desk, kissed her husband goodnight, and withdrew. Proculus knew Rebekah would be watching from the door and would bring in more flasks as needed.

The night continued and the conversation degenerated. Long stretches of silence fell between the two without either of them noticing and when they did talk, it was only partially intelligible. The men stayed that way, becoming increasingly incoherent, until they noticed the night being swept away by dawn. When Saul noticed the brightening day, he stood to leave but fell back into the chair. He concentrated, gathered his strength and this time made it upright. Proculus had been wondering how long it would take, but he did not want Saul to walk the streets at night, so he had not pushed. Saul staggered to the door, managed to mumble something that Proculus guessed was 'farewell,' and left.

Proculus came out of the library to find June already awake with the household staff preparing for the day. She smiled at her tired and inebriated husband. "You need to get to bed."

"What makes you say that?" Proculus replied sarcastically with a half-smile as he struggled to remain upright. "Wake me if you hear from Saul, otherwise let me slumber."

* * *

Saul staggered home, spending almost an hour trying to find the place where he was staying. He knew it was near the south side synagogue, but he'd only been there a couple of days and wasn't sure which house it was. The sun was a hand's width up in the sky when he sobered up enough that he was finally able to recognize the house. The couple was awake and gave Saul a disillusioned look as he made his way to his room without a word. Saul avoided their stares as his face flushed. *At least they don't have children to see this display.* He collapsed onto his bed, asleep.

Saul found himself on the road to Damascus in what seemed to be the predawn hours. Traveling here made some sense to him since that was where he had been heading when he had stopped at Antioch. However, it still felt all wrong; he had this terrible sense of loss as if he hadn't a friend in the world and yet he was traveling with two other men. He looked over at them and realized he had no idea who they were and they didn't seem interested in him either.

A butterfly, with white wings and patterns the color of moss, flew past him and he cocked his head in wonderment; what was a butterfly doing out here where there was no vegetation except some scrub brush?

Then, he wondered what had happened in Antioch. He didn't even remember leaving and couldn't recall whether he and Proculus had come to any kind of resolution or what the plan was. He stopped and looked around realizing that this was the road from Jerusalem to Damascus, not from Antioch; how did he get here?

His supply donkey stopped with him and then the two fellow travelers stopped to see what the problem was. At that point, the sky began to brighten, but not like a sunrise. Instead, the entire sky brightened at once. Saul could see it and his forehead crinkled in concentration trying to figure out what could cause such an event even as he realized the other men didn't seem to notice.

The brightness coalesced to a single point that seemed to center half way up the sky. "That appears to be directly over Jerusalem," Saul said aloud. The two men turned towards Jerusalem, but didn't appear to react to the light.

The light began moving directly towards Saul; he wasn't sure how he knew this because it's apparent size stayed the same, even as it got closer. He was, nevertheless, positive it was heading straight for him.

As the light settled into a position directly in front of Saul about twenty feet away, Saul noticed his two companions go into a stupor, not aware of the light or, apparently, anything else as they continued to stare in the direction of Jerusalem. The light concentrated its obvious and intimidating power on Saul and in a loud deep voice spoke stridently, "Saul, why are you persecuting my people?"

Saul fell to his knees in supplication. The butterfly that had been flitting about fell dead right in front of him and he looked around to see what had killed it. Then he saw another butterfly, but as he noticed it, it too fell dead on the sand. And then another and another, and then hundreds all around him. Saul gave up trying to figure out what that could possibly mean and returned his attention to the strange talking light. He had no answer to its question, so instead he stammered a question of his own, "Who... who are you?"

"I am The Teacher, Saul. You have been persecuting my people and you must stop."

"I know, I know. But I persecute the Pharisees more." As soon as he said it, he realized how wrong it sounded.

"It matters not; they are all my people. You must stop."

Saul began to feel all the pains of the people he had been persecuting and remembered all the wrongs he had committed in his effort to exact revenge upon them. He began to cry.

The presence let him empathize and then said, "Saul, you must travel among my people, the communities of my followers. Go as a student and learn their ways. They will accept you and teach you the path to the Kingdom of God. You will take their message to all the peoples of the world. Saul, go and save my people.

"The One True God has spoken." The light vanished with a popping sound that startled Saul and woke his two stupefied companions.

Saul looked around for the dead butterflies, thinking they might be proof of what had happened, but they had all disappeared.

Saul woke up soaked in perspiration and trembling. The dream had been so realistic that he had trouble orienting himself. He sat up on the straw covered cot and struggled to contain his shame and contrition. He stood up to head back to Proculus' house, but became instantly dizzy and fell back to his bed. With a concerted effort, he was able to stand, throw water on his face from a bowl near the bed, and leave the house. He tried to run but that proved impossible so he walked, as quickly as he could.

When he arrived, Rebekah called to June while Saul waited. He was wearing the same disheveled clothes, now with bits of straw on them, and he stank of perspiration and too much wine. When June saw him, her eyes brightened and she let him in immediately. She told Rebekah to fetch a steamed cloth to freshen his face.

She left Saul sitting in the foyer and headed towards the bedrooms. On the way, she passed Rebekah, took the steamed cloth from her, and told her to fetch another one for Saul and to lead him to the library when he was ready. She then disappeared, presumably to find Proculus.

* * *

Twenty minutes later Proculus entered the library refreshed, but moving slowly. Saul hesitated and then, before Proculus could even sit down, blurted out in an excited voice, "I had the most realistic dream, more like a vision, I had to come tell you about it."

Proculus' eyelids were half closed and his mouth was hanging open as he stared at Saul.

Saul ignored Proculus' fatigue and continued, "It was The Teacher of Righteousness, telling me that I had to spread the word about his teachings." After rethinking the dream, he added, "Well, he really said that I should travel among his followers and learn about them first, as a student I think, and then I should spread the word about the Kingdom of God."

Proculus said, "I have thought for a while now that you were the right person for this role. It was just a matter of your confidence." He took a few breaths and blinked to clear the sand from his eyes. "Why don't you tell me all about this vision of yours, from the beginning?"

Saul went through the entire dream, though he left out the bit about the butterflies since that seemed irrelevant.

"Interesting," Proculus said introspectively, "The Teacher had a set of disciples that spread out around the Republic and they established communities of followers. We know the location of some of them. It seems like the appropriate course is for you to travel among them to learn about their ways and their teachings.

"The part about 'The One True God has spoken' is rather unusual. Does it mean that God told The Teacher to tell you this or that The Teacher is God or that the light represented both?" Proculus leaned back in his chair and stared at Saul. He concluded, "Saul, this is truly astonishing. We have the makings of a plan that can accomplish what you and I have been discussing and now it appears to have divine sponsorship as well."

They both sat for a while, the energy draining like rainwater as the long night caught up with them and the adrenaline ebbed. Proculus offered, "Please lie here and get some rest and I will go back to bed and do the same. Then, in a few hours when we are rested and more alert, we can discuss plans."

* * *

The two men slept until early afternoon and then took their time refreshing and drinking plenty of water. They sat down in front of Proculus' desk where he had a map of the Roman Republic spread out. Saul leaned over it with interest. As he opened his mouth, Proculus interrupted.

"Before we look at the map, we should talk about next steps."

Saul leaned back in his chair, apparently confused. Proculus saw he was let down, but it made no difference. "First, you will need to resign as an enforcer of the Sadducees. You should not just disappear as they might send people to look for you. You have to give them some reasonable explanation."

Saul offered, "That's easy enough; they already know I'm not happy. I can simply tell them I've found work here in Antioch and they'll believe me.'

Proculus smiled and added, "It is somewhat true if you look at this as work for me.

"Next, I have a servant, Daniel, whom I have asked to travel with you. He is literate, can write to me about your progress, and can help in sundry ways. You can think of him as your servant, however he is a freedman, not a slave, and do not treat him as one. He is away right now or I would introduce him.

"We should also talk about timing, but that may depend on where you go, so I will save that until we discuss the route."

"I want to get going right away."

Proculus appreciated his enthusiasm, "Yes, but depending on where you go it may be easier to start in spring or fall. It is spring now, so heading north into Cappadocia would make sense and there are some other reasons why that is a good start. Moreover, this exploratory trip could take a pair of years, so we should not rush."

Saul appeared frustrated, but Proculus continued, "We also need to discuss your goals for the trip and possibly the position you should take."

"I thought that was... I'm to be a student and learn The Teacher's ways through the communities his disciples left."

"Yes, but part of that is to make sure you do not attempt to preach yet and, more importantly, you should not mention the vision." When Saul's mouth became a tight line, he added, "At least not yet. People do not know you as a prophet or even as a follower of The Teacher, so for them to hear that you received a vision, especially when none of them have, would make them see you as a fraud."

Saul looked down and Proculus sat silent, letting him think. "I understand that; I'll keep the vision to myself... for now," he said.

Proculus examined the map. "These circles are where I have heard there are communities of Essenes. The ones I am most sure of are in Cappadocia, Mesopotamia, and down in Egypt."

The two studied the map for hours talking about various routes Saul could take and where they might find Essene communities. In the end, a northern route proved most appropriate because they knew there was a community in upper Cappadocia somewhere and Saul knew an Essene couple, who had moved to Trapezeus. They could also travel through Caesarea, which was not a place Saul could linger since he had spent time there persecuting the Pharisees, but they could resupply.

* * *

Saul realized he hadn't eaten since the evening before and that he was famished. He said so and the two men agreed to meet the next morning to continue their discussions. They left the library and June saw them. She walked up and pleasantly asked, "Saul, will you join us for a meal?"

Saul blinked in shock, taken aback at her effrontery. *Why would she ask me that again?* He started to object, "I..." and then stopped. Eventually his mission was going to be to go out amongst the Gentiles, eat their treif food, and convert them to Judaism. He was going to have to bend the Abrahamic rules, the covenant, in order to do that and it would probably start by eating non-kosher foods with gentiles.

He looked back and forth between Proculus and June a few times, but their faces were blank, almost accepting. Finally, he answered, "Certainly," though it pained him to do so.

As Proculus and June walked toward the kitchen, they touched their fingers gently together.

* * *

Preparations for the trip took three days. They acquired two asses to carry supplies, two horses that were young enough to have the stamina for a long trip, and enough nonperishable food stuffs to last them through the first leg of the journey. Proculus also gave them a bag full of denarii each, commenting that it would not last the entire trip, but might last a year or more, especially if they could augment it by working whenever they stopped for a long period. Finally, Saul and Daniel were ready to leave on their trip. Daniel was saying a heartfelt and tearful goodbye to Rebekah, while Saul, Proculus, and June were laughing and joking animatedly.

After they left, Proculus retired to his library to write a letter to Maximus, his most trusted friend, and the only other person who knew the full extent of the plan. Maximus would be surprised and a little chagrined that he had not been here to meet Saul himself, but he trusted Proculus.

They were also going to have to start considering Tiberius Caesar. The High Council in Jerusalem would never agree to the plan, let alone recognize a need for urgency without significant contention with Rome. Tiberius was just too evenhanded and the council would never be convinced of the looming dangers Rome represented. The Jewish leadership had to feel threatened in order to approve of the changes.

Somehow, Tiberius' reign would have to end.

III. To Rome (36 AD)

"Do not carry money, bag, sandals, or staff; and do not greet people on the road"

- The Book of Q

Six years had passed and Proculus was becoming increasingly worried about the lack of progress. It was early fall and he was again wandering the paths in the woods behind his villa fretting about the situation. They had decided to take time for Saul to visit some of the isolated tribes of the Essenes while they waited for Tiberius' health to worsen. However, all these years later Saul was still traveling and Tiberius' was still emperor. *We cannot let this go on.*

Proculus usually enjoyed the sounds of nature, the crush of leaves and twigs under his feet, the soothing earth tones of the fallen detritus. Today, however, the circuitous path in the woods and the compression of life all around reminded him of how mired the plan was. They had to do something to get this propositum moving again. The issue was not Saul, but Tiberius. He could recall Saul at any time, but something had to hasten the end of Tiberius' reign.

He sent word for Maximus to join him in Antioch.

* * *

Many weeks later, in late fall, Proculus received a runner who informed him Maximus would meet him that very evening at sunset. He was preparing to leave when June came to him in a rush. "Proculus, dear," she said in a breathy voice, "you have another letter from Saul."

He smiled. "This one will have to wait. I must meet Maximus at the Rock Rest for drinks and some quiet conversation."

June frowned. "When did he arrive and how are he and Curia?"

Proculus immediately realized his mistake. June would have expected Maximus to come for dinner at their house and she would want to hear all about Maximus' precocious daughter. "I do not know his plans as yet. He just arrived." He could see the answer was not going to satisfy her. With a sigh he added, "We just want to discuss affairs in Rome and knew you would not be interested. I shall invite him to dinner tomorrow night so you can hear all about the two of them."

She glared, but seemed to relent.

* * *

While waiting for Maximus at the famous tavern Proculus perused the interior. His nostalgic love for the old place stemmed from a combination of unique wines and beers from around the Republic and a personality that could only come from an establishment existing for many decades. It was like an old, worn blanket that comforted with its mere presence. There were impressive displays of trinkets from Egypt, Mesopotamia, Spain, Gaul, Asia, and, of course, Rome. One of Proculus' gifts sat on a shelf at eye level behind the center of the bar. His gaze fell on the little statue of Augustus Caesar as he recalled the years he had spent in Rome.

It had been a prosperous time when he was a young senator trying to represent his people the best he could. Proculus came from a family with strong Roman lineage and many considered him an *old roman*, someone dedicated to the idea that the power of the senate and the republican form of government was paramount. He recalled the time when he believed the Roman Republic still existed. The Republic had survived for five centuries, but in the end, had failed. That had become all too obvious to anyone intimate with the internal political maneuverings. Marcus Tullius Cicero was arguably the last true Roman politician, and that was back when Julius Caesar came to power. *Oh, if either were around today, they would be ashamed at what the Republic has become.*

Movement interrupted Proculus' reminiscences. The Rock Rest's owner, Josephus, approached the table. "Hello senator, we haven't seen you here for a while," Josephus said casually. "It isn't often you frequent our lowly tavern," he added with a smile.

Proculus returned the smile with a jest. "Yes, it is a burden, but I wanted to remind myself of how the unfortunate live." *Why does he still call me senator? I gave up that post years ago.*

Josephus sat down, as was his habit with many guests. He seemed to know them all and had a talent for making people comfortable with friendly and unimportant talk. Proculus always admired the man. Maybe it was because of that very ability to be comfortable with anyone, despite their difference in positions or social level. It certainly was refreshing to have the honesty of this unassuming tavern-owner. "How is June?" Josephus inquired.

"She is spending a lot of time in the garden and helping out at Temple of course. She keeps busy and seems content."

"As it should be. Well, what can I get you to drink?"

"How about some mulsum?" Proculus responded. "And Josephus, Maximus Octavius should be here shortly, we will need privacy."

"I understand senator; I hope everything is fine in Rome."

He responded a little too quickly. "Yes, of course, it is just a private matter." He turned, ending the conversation.

Proculus returned to considering the tavern and its long history. It had seen so much diversity. Antioch had been a cultural center of the area for many years, so the tavern enjoyed varied clientele including numerous senators and a few Caesars. Even Julius Caesar had overnighted there. Josephus did a remarkable job retaining the antique personality of the tavern while catering to the frequent traveler.

The only aspect of the Rock Rest that bothered Proculus was the smell. It was some combination of too many oils rubbed into the tables, sweat from the multitude of patrons, and the faint but disturbing hint of urine. It was difficult to ignore. Nevertheless, the dark woods, comfortable seating and semi-private alcoves made it an appealing place to meet.

Maximus came through the door. He was a hard person to miss given his size and natural stature. A military man, ex-centurion from the I'st Germanican Legion, he still carried himself in the unyielding stance of a professional soldier; upright, composed, even rigid, but ready for... anything. He just as obviously expected obedience and few would consider otherwise. He still wore shoulder-length brown hair, though it was turning gray at the temples, and had hazel eyes that seemed to absorb all of his surroundings at once. His face was squarish with a strong jaw and high cheekbones that made him look even more formidable.

The old camaraderie and friendship Proculus felt with his life-long friend always brought a wave of relaxation as if the world were a safer place. Maximus was the one person that Proculus trusted with his life and, even more importantly, with his plan.

Proculus waved to Maximus as the dim light was making it hard for the ex-soldier to see. He motioned for Josephus to bring a second drink.

Maximus shook Proculus' hand as he sat at the table and held it an extra breaths-worth in warmness. He was tired from the trip, but his handshake was firm and definitive, as always, and it was clear that he was as excited as Proculus was to talk about Rome. "How was your trip?"

"Fine, the sea voyage in fall is always pleasant and the winds helped us make good time. How are you and June?"

"The same." They smiled at each other in silence as they both had little need for small talk.

Maximus' muscular arms opened up as he leaned forward. "Tell me how Saul has been doing these past few years. I read your letters, but I want to hear it."

Proculus' mouth formed a small grimace that Maximus either ignored or missed. *Apparently, we have to talk about Saul before Rome.* He sighed and began, "He is progressing. He has learned a lot while traveling among the Essenes and his confidence is growing. It is almost time for him to approach the council, but that depends a great deal on what is happening in Rome."

"Are you sure he can do this? The man I spent time with couldn't convince a fool."

Proculus smiled at the typical Maximus question. "His preaching ability is not the worst problem we have. For years, he was persecuting the very people we want him to preach to and they are still scared and distrustful of him. In fact, his life may be in danger in some communities and especially in Jerusalem. He also will not be able to stand up well in a debate to a serious Pharisaic scholar. If he argues with them, it will be embarrassing. We will need to keep him preaching to the Diaspora communities. He may get overconfident and try to debate with some of the scholars either in Jerusalem or when they happen to meet in the communities."

"Then the plan is to travel areas of the Republic away from Judea? I'm assuming you will want me to travel with him, at least at first, to protect him. What do you want done if Saul tries to confront Pharisees? How overt do you want me to be?"

"Initially he will mostly be practicing, but yes, it would be best if you were there with him and that will indeed be away from Judea. You will need to try to find out if there are any scholars in the community when you first arrive and then make sure Saul does not meet them. You will not want to be obvious. Saul would get suspicious if he knew you were keeping them apart as he grows in confidence, perhaps we can let him attempt a few debates with some of the less skilled scholars, but that may be years away. If you need to protect him from harm, you can be as blatant as need be. You may want to make use of that. The impression that someone is protecting him will increase his reputation and bring more people to listen to his preaching. If it does not happen naturally, you may even want to stage a few disruptions."

"I suspected as much. Where is he now?"

Proculus had to recall the various letters Saul had sent him over the last few years while traveling. "He has continued to visit some of the Essene communities." Maximus cocked his head at the mention of Essenes. "The Jewish sect founded over a century ago by *The Teacher of Righteousness*. They seem the most aligned with what we are attempting to do."

"In any case, he has learned a lot from their followers." He was going to go into more details until he realized they did not really matter to Maximus, at least not yet. "He is in Egypt, mostly around Alexandria, but traveling to some other communities. It is time for him to return, but that depends on your news from Rome. How fares Tiberius Caesar?"

Maximus' brows furrowed in concentration but he did not appear concerned. Proculus knew that was as close to positive as Maximus could be. "Tiberius can't be far from death and if he isn't, there are quite a few people who would help him along. The better news is that he seems to have narrowed the field of possible successors down to Gaius Germanicus, or Caligula as he likes to be called, and his blood-grandson, Tiberius Gemellus."

"I know Caligula. Tiberius actually adopted his father, Germanicus, who died here in Antioch. Caligula was a reasonable general, but sadistic." Proculus recalled Caligula as a leader of men. "He may be just the kind of Caesar we need. I do not know much about Gemellus; I met him once, but it was just in passing and it was many years ago. What is your impression of him?"

"He had a troubled childhood; his father was killed when he was four, probably by his mother and she was put to death for plotting against Caesar. However, Tiberius took to him many years ago and the imperial favor helped his career. He was never in the military, but he is a reasonable leader if a little naive and too kind-hearted."

"That does not sound like the right sort of person. He would be more likely to protect and nurture instead of causing the disruption we need. Do you know which one Tiberius will choose?"

"There's no way to tell. Tiberius hasn't been forthcoming on his views of a successor or if he supports the move to an empire. He may have a peculiar notion that having co-emperors could help to bring back some of the power of the Senate. If he really names both, it will just cause confusion; we can't be a Republic again, it's too late for that."

"I agree, there has to be a single emperor, and for our cause, it probably needs to be Caligula, not Gemellus. At least that is my impression. I think it is time for me to make a trip to Rome. We can evaluate these two potential Caesars and if your impressions are correct, perhaps we can work together to ensure Caligula becomes the new emperor... and soon."

Proculus leaned back into the padded leather back of his chair, contented that the plan was progressing. "How is Curia? She must be fifteen by now, are you looking for a husband yet?" A smile escaped his lips, knowing that Maximus would not relish that task and that it would be difficult with no wife to help.

"She's good; high spirited, bright, and much more of a politician than I am. She also has a strategic sense. She would have made an exceptional general if only..."

Proculus leaned forward on the table. "How much does she know about the plan?"

Maximus' eyes narrowed and he stared at Proculus for a few seconds before responding. "She knows we believe in the Republic and that we think the Empire is doomed, and she agrees. She also knows we are working on something to try to save it, but she doesn't have any details. And she knows we favor the Jews, but not why. So she has hints and she is a very bright girl, which means she has some suspicions that are probably accurate." More emphatically, he asked, "Why do you ask, Proculus?"

"Because, it might be valuable to have someone in Rome watching our interests..." He noticed the concern on Maximus's face. "Just as an observer. You will be traveling with Saul, possibly for years at a time. We need to have someone we trust in Rome who can tell us when significant events happen. I cannot think of anyone better."

"I don't want to put her in harm's way and there are other people we could use."

"Possibly, but any you trust as much as her?" When Maximus did not reply, he added, "Consider it and we can speak later." *He will come around in time.* They grew silent and finished their drinks in relative contemplation. The plan was progressing, Saul was out learning about the communities, and Rome was degenerating as expected. A few more nudges and events would begin to fall into place.

Proculus concluded, "Oh yes, June wants you at dinner tomorrow night and, I am sure, will want to hear about Curia. I will also have to tell her that I will be making a trip to Rome. She will not be happy."

* * *

"Hello Maximus," June said warmly, "it's been too long." She hugged him and gave him a kiss on the cheek. Proculus saw how uncomfortable Maximus was. They had talked before about how June unnerved him. He had told Proculus that she had a way of looking into his eyes that made him feel like she could read his mind. Proculus had agreed that would not be welcome.

"Yes it has June. It's good to see you too."

"Come in, we have dinner prepared and you have to tell me all about Curia. Have you been able to find her a husband?"

Proculus and Maximus exchanged a knowing look. Maximus hadn't answered the question when Proculus asked at the tavern though they knew that June wouldn't let it go. "No, I haven't found a husband yet. It's, well, difficult with a spirited, intelligent girl like Curia. Suitors are too easily intimidated. The ones that aren't overawed are married or bullies. It's even more difficult trying to do this myself along with all my other responsibilities."

"Well, perhaps I should make a trip to Rome and help out," she laughed, half joking, and started to turn away. She then turned back and added more seriously, "It has been a long time since I've been there and I'd love to see her again."

Proculus and Maximus exchanged thoughtful looks, again. They had known each other for so long that agreements could be made with a glance. Proculus said, "I think that's a splendid idea. It's a nice trip this time of year. We were just discussing the need for me to go back to Rome since it appears that Caesar is... fading. We can all go together, though you do understand that we may be there for several months, probably until spring when the winds favor an easterly return trip."

June considered the ramifications of being gone for so long. "Yes, Tamar can manage things here for the winter."

Proculus smiled and his hand reached out affectionately to touch June's shoulder. "Then it is settled. Arrangements will take a few weeks. I must send letters to friends in Rome, letting them know that we are coming. They may be able to help us find accommodations. Maximus, you should take care of the arrangements for the trip itself, and June you can get the estate ready for an extended leave."

"Do you know who the next Caesar will be?" June asked, somewhat interested.

Proculus answered, "Not for sure, but it appears it will be either Gaius Germanicus or Tiberius Gemellus. They are both competent, though Gaius has military experience and Gemellus does not." Maximus raised an eyebrow at the answer.

June looked back and forth at the two men for a moment before dismissing the exchange. She turned and led them towards the dining room.

* * *

Three weeks later, they were ready to leave on their trip to Rome. Proculus had decided that he wanted to stop by Tarus to see Saul's father, Aharon. Maximus arranged for travel by boat from Seleucia Pieria to go directly to Tarus. They would then travel by carriage and horse to Rome. They decided to include Daniel's wife Rebekah in the trip since she was lonely while Daniel was traveling with Saul and she had never been to Rome. She was also a competent woman who could help June with some of the more mundane tasks.

The eight-mile trip to the port city was uneventful. They arrived to find the Pulchra Viator and men loading its belly with grain. The merchant ship was a three-thousand-amphora vessel with two masts and twenty-eight oars. Maximus had reserved the small cabin for the senator and his wife, as well as Rebekah, while the crew and he would sleep in the open. Unfortunately, there were delays with some of the cargo and the boat did not leave Seleucia Pieria until the next day. The three resolute travelers settled in and then met on the deck to watch the coastline slowly recede. Proculus thought it was like watching a loved one fade away and he felt a hint of regret at leaving his comfortable home. *Into the lion's den we go.*

June leaned on the railing as she stared at the rippling, dark blue waves. "How long will this trip take Maximus? In the past we went straight to Rome by boat."

"Eight to nine weeks all told with the last few on land," he replied.

"Why not take another boat to Rome?"

"There wasn't one available in time."

"Well, we'll have plenty of time to talk about Curia. What are your expectations for a husband?"

Maximus' arms crossed as he studied the synchronous oaring below them for long enough that Proculus began to wonder if he was going to answer her. "You know, that is difficult," Maximus finally answered. "I know I want her to be fulfilled, but I also know that she could be a tremendous help to someone's career and that she's happiest when she's challenged. What is difficult is finding someone who can make her happy and challenged and who wants to deal with a spirited girl like her." Maximus' intake of breath hinted at humor. "She could certainly use a mother's influence."

June's forehead creased as she inspected some fishing vessels in the distance. Proculus wondered if she might be recalling her own childhood. She and Curia were alike in many ways.

"What about the career? Do you want a soldier, a politician, or do you have something else in mind?"

"I don't really want her to have the life of a soldier's wife. A politician would be good and she could really help the career of one. But I wouldn't want her too close to Caesar's line as they tend to get wiped out at times. I could see a philosopher or a lawyer; I know she reads Marcus Cicero, even at her age, and I find him boring at best."

"Do you have other characteristics in mind? What about age or temperament?"

"It should be someone relatively young, but with a promising career. He will need to be strong and capable or he won't be able to handle her. But I want him to treat her well, of course."

Proculus had been quiet during the entire conversation as this was something, mostly, between Maximus and June. He finally spoke up, "It would be worthwhile if you found a citizen, and one with some land and wealth." Both June and Maximus quickly turned to him as if they had not understood.

"Why do you say that, dear?"

Proculus hesitated while his eyes darted between the other two. He had spoken too quickly and he knew it. "Well," he improvised, "it just seems that a girl of her caliber would be happier and would accomplish a lot more if she was in Rome and had access to resources."

Maximus seemed to accept the answer, but he knew of Proculus' intentions. June's eyes narrowed and her lips puckered for a moment, but then her face relaxed.

* * *

The winds weren't as favorable as expected so they arrived in the port city of Tarus just over four weeks later. As nice as the sea was, they were all tired of the constant motion and June had expressed discomfort with the unending queasiness.

The Pulchra Viator maneuvered into the quiet semi-circular inlet. The dark waters were calm and the seaweed parted at the boats onslaught. There were outcroppings of lava stone to the north and open beach to the south. Off the port bow, they could see Aharon waiting for them at the dock. *How could he know of our exact arrival?* Aharon saw June and he waved enthusiastically. Proculus had written that he and Maximus would be coming, but neglected to mention June and had not specified an exact date. He knew it would be a pleasant surprise to Aharon and Ruth. Once they docked and disembarked, they exchanged pleasantries and then set out on foot towards Aharon's house.

Aharon was a short man with thin gray hair on the back half of his head. He tended toward the portly side and, Proculus noticed, had begun to slouch in his advancing years. He gave the visitors a running tour of the city and its history. "Did you know that the story goes that Tarus was founded by the son of Poseidon? His name was Partheniae and Satyrion was his mother. She was a nymph in this area. Tarus has been a major trading city since the time of the Greeks."

The three visitors smiled. Proculus loved Aharon's enthusiasm about his city, but he was not particularly interested in its mythical formation. Aharon's zeal was contagious though and the three began to ask questions about the city and its buildings. At the theater, they heard that it was the home of Lucius Livius Andronicus, the father of Roman drama and epic poetry. He had translated many of the Greek plays and some poetry into Latin. Maximus must have had enough of the trivia as he excused himself after they passed the theater.

The walk to Aharon's house went by more quickly than expected because of the distraction of the tour. When Ruth saw them approaching she came out and greeted them with special exuberance for June. Ruth was even shorter than Aharon, but her gray hair was long and well kempt and her eyes glowed with excitement and a hint of mischief. Seeing her again, Proculus remembered how animated her hands were when she spoke. She and June soon disappeared into the house and left the men to fend for themselves. Rebekah followed the women at a respectful distance.

"How long will you be staying?" Aharon asked.

Proculus replied, "Unfortunately, just a couple of days; we need to get to Rome. Maximus arranged for the trip already. He just has to pick up supplies."

Aharon welcomed them into his home and showed them their rooms. The house was small with only the one extra bedroom. Ruth was meticulous about keeping the place neat and everything seemed to be in a precise location. Living so far from Judea and among so many Romans, the couple had no issues with Gentiles staying in their house or eating meals together, especially since Ruth would prepare food properly.

The two couples had a pleasant meal together and then adjourned to the porch for a quiet evening of conversation. When they were relaxed, Aharon finally asked the question that Proculus knew was coming. "Please… tell us, how is Saul doing? We haven't heard from him in so long, it troubles us." Ruth agreed with a nod and a hopeful smile.

"Aharon, Ruth, I have to tell you, I think he is finally starting to heal." He knew it was a stretch, but Saul was at least headed in the right direction. Proculus could see the relief on both of their faces. "He has finally quit persecuting the Pharisees and is no longer aiding the Sadducees. He is on a journey of discovery around the Empire to reconnect with the Pharisaic Judaism he loved as a child and to come to understand the Essenes. He is finally becoming more accepting of other peoples and ideas. He still feels guilty about who he became, but once he is happy with himself again, he may come back to you."

June added, "You know that Proculus and I will encourage him and will work at getting him back here to Tarus and to you two."

Aharon and Ruth smiled at each other and leaned back into their chairs. As their fingers relaxed their tight grip, Aharon reached across to hold Ruth's hand. The distance between them and their only son was a loss too painful to bear. It was unusual to have only one child, but luckily, theirs survived into adulthood and was a good person with a lot of potential.

The four continued talking of Saul, Antioch, the Roman Republic, and anything else that came to mind until late into the evening. When Proculus and June were too tired to continue, they finally retired to bed. It was a welcome sight after weeks in cramped quarters on a boat that rocked continuously.

* * *

Early in the morning two days later, right on schedule, Maximus arrived and informed Proculus that everything was set and they could leave for Rome at any time. They gathered their baggage, said goodbyes, and left with Maximus for the stables. Proculus and Maximus were on horse whereas June and Rebekah were in a small carriage with a packhorse trailing behind. The land trip to Rome would take them almost three weeks. Proculus was glad to have Maximus on the trip. He knew the route well and the places to stop along the way. The road was not always safe, but he could handle that as well.

After they had been traveling a while, June asked, "Maximus, tell me, why are you wearing your military insignia and sword?"

Maximus broke from his reverie and shook his head, apparently trying to focus. "It's called a *gladius*." Then he grew serious. "Even though we are on the mainland of Rome, the roads are not always safe. A few civilian travelers along the road might be easy prey, but someone with a military escort, even of one, would be a challenge for any would-be thieves."

Later that evening, still an hour from the small town they would stop at for the night, they came across half-a-dozen rag-tag men standing about twenty paces from the side of the road. The men didn't say anything as the travelers passed. June tried to smile at them, but they just stared, blank-eyed, back at her. She shrank into her seat at their stares. After they passed, she asked Maximus who they were.

"Remember our talk this morning of would-be thieves?"

"Yes," she answered hesitantly and then said "Oh..." She quickly turned back to see the group still standing there in the distance and still staring in their direction. After a few moments, she asked Maximus, "Why aren't they arrested or dealt with by the military?"

"The military doesn't have time to stop and deal with local bandits on their way out, and on the way back they are too war-weary to care. The local prefect might deal with them if they got out of hand, but as long as they stick to harassing the unwary, it tends not to be worth it. If the prefect sends a unit, the thieves would just melt into the local community. It takes a serious effort by someone that understands tactics to catch them and then as soon as diligence wanes, they reappear. So it's easier to let them be as long as they don't cause too much trouble and don't go after anyone important."

Proculus overheard the exchange and was glad of it. June would come to appreciate Maximus' talents. She never had understood the friendship between the two men. He had told her of some of the things in their past that tied them together, but he knew she still felt their relationship was unusual.

Happily, there were no more strangers standing by the side of the road on the trip to Rome.

IV. Curia Octavius (36 AD)

"Ask and it will be given to you; seek and you will find; knock and the door will be opened for you."

- The Book of Q

Nineteen days after leaving Tarus their small caravan came through the Seven Hills of Rome. June had not traveled through Rome from this direction, so Proculus pointed out the important monuments and structures. They marveled at the Mausoleum of Augustus and were duly impressed with the efficacy of the many aqueducts. June laughed at the opulence of the bathing complexes as Proculus commented on the accumulated knowledge in the libraries. The residences they passed ranged from small shacks to countryside villas and the opulent imperial palaces on Palatine Hill.

Proculus had arranged to stay at the villa of Senator Duccius who was leaving for the latifundia he maintained in Spain. The villa was a fine estate made of whitewashed pozzolona concrete that contained a dozen rooms including a library and a large open room for entertaining. There were stables in back and the kitchen fires were on the outside away from the living areas. Slaves were in attendance and there were plenty of bedrooms for guests. It was also central enough to allow the three of them to accomplish their work. They had most of the winter, as the winds would not favor a trip back to Antioch until spring. They settled into the villa and had a quiet dinner and drinks on the veranda. For Proculus, it felt like a respite before the ensuing turmoil he knew they would face. The quiet, subdued evening was antithetical to the pace they would have to set.

Maximus disappeared early the next morning to get an update on the situation with Caesar and to let his network of contacts know he was back.

Proculus and June went to the marketplace with a number of Senator Duccius' slaves in order to obtain supplies. June was surprised at Proculus coming along, but he explained that it would be best to give Maximus some time to work out the current situation before setting out to meet with senators and politicians. Maximus would provide useful information that he would need to sound credible.

The two spent the day preparing the Duccius residence for an extended stay and relaxing. They were both still somewhat tired from the trip and were glad for the break.

Maximus arrived early that evening. They sat in the library listening to the sounds of the meal being prepared. "The physicians say that Tiberius is not likely to live the winter. He is almost seventy-seven years old now and is fading. He's still staying south in Misenum with Caligula and Gemellus in attendance along with his usual retinue and a collection of imperial physicians. Both Caligula and Gemellus seem to have given up all political duties in lieu of gaining Tiberius' favor. I doubt it will work. Tiberius has been unclear on a successor since he became Caesar. My impression is that he understands there is no good leader available. He also wants us to return to a Republic and hates the idea that there is an emperor at all. Most people I talk to believe he will appoint both Caligula and Gemellus as co-emperors, as foolish as that sounds."

"How can we have co-emperors? What happens when they don't agree?" June asked. Proculus was surprised at the interest though not at the political naiveté.

Maximus uncharacteristically answered in full, "Partly, Tiberius just can't make a decision. He was good in the field when the decisions were tactical, but when they became political and when Caesar Augustus tied his hands by telling him not to expand the Empire, any ability at decision-making vanished. In reality, one of Caligula or Gemellus is likely to strike first, have the other killed along with any potential heirs, and assume dictatorship. At least this will give us the most decisive emperor of the two and that may have occurred to Tiberius, but I doubt it. More likely, he's just fooling himself about the potential vigor of the Senate and their ability to step up and take control, and about Caligula and Gemellus cooperating."

Proculus sat listening to the exchange. There were no surprises, though it was good to hear that Tiberius would last long enough for them to be able to affect the outcome. If he passed too soon, there may not be time to prepare. He also noticed how Maximus put Caligula first whenever listing the two; he was quietly intimating who he thought was the best choice. He had also neglected to tell June just how far the killings might extend. The effect on June would be interesting to watch; she was observant, but she would not believe Maximus to be so shrewd. She would probably not catch on that it was intentional.

He said, "Tomorrow I will visit the senatorial baths. The support of the senate is not required, but it could help the successor. Maximus, you should try to determine if either Caligula or Gemellus is planning anything overt. My suspicion is that they are not if they are still trying to gain favor. That implies they believe they can win the appointment without bloodshed."

There was a pause in the conversation. Proculus deliberated the ramifications. *What if they both became Caesar? Could we precipitate an assassination? What if Gemellus is cleverer than we think and acts quickly? If that happened, we may be stalled for years.* June interrupted, "So when do I get to see Curia?" she asked with a smile.

Maximus fidgeted and avoided looking at June's questioning eyes. "Actually, she left on a trip to Alexandria and won't be back for a few months… sorry." June's eyes grew large and her mouth formed a small oval while her head went back in shock. Then she saw the smirk on Maximus' face, narrowed her eyes, and slapped him on the shoulder just as Proculus and he couldn't hold it in any longer and laughed aloud. Then Maximus admitted, "I asked her to meet us here for dinner tonight because I knew you would want to see her right away." His mouth turned down in a grimace. "You know, it's been a few years since you've seen her; she has matured a lot since then."

"I can only imagine…"

Moments later Curia arrived and Proculus and June were indeed both surprised when she entered the villa. She had become a young woman since they had last met and was taller than June was and almost as tall as Proculus. She was also quite attractive in a serious, studious way. She had an oval face with eyebrows that turned up, straight, shiny, black hair that went down to the middle of her back, and dark eyes with a deep-blue calmness to them that established her intelligence. She was also trim and stood erect, much like her father. She wore a traditional stola of a light blue with a darker blue palla that contained a hint of aristocratic purple. The entire impression was imposing, almost intimidating, especially from a young woman.

It had been a number of years since Proculus or June had seen her. "Close your mouth dear," June mumbled to Proculus. "Hello Curia, you have to forgive my husband. You've grown into a beautiful woman and we still remember the rambunctious girl." They gave each other a perfunctory hug and kiss and Curia shook Proculus' hand.

"It's great to see both of you again as well. I was thrilled when Maximus told me you were here."

"Why don't you and I find a quiet place to chat and let these two men talk more politics?"

* * *

Curia looked between her father and June. She would rather talk politics than have a 'chat' with June who would probably only want to talk about finding a husband. That seemed to be the only topic people wanted to discuss lately as if it was the only thing Curia should be thinking about. She wasn't even sure she wanted a husband; she certainly hadn't found an eligible one that she respected. She wanted to spend more time with the enigmatic senator. Her father had spent much of his life in service to the man and she knew little about him. Her memory was of an imposing figure from years ago that caused her insides to flutter whenever she recalled it. Grudgingly, she followed June into a sitting room and looked back longingly at the two men. Both faces appeared empathetic though with a hint of humor at the corner of their mouths.

When Curia got into the other room, she let June know her opinion. "I know what you want to talk about and I'm tired of hearing how important it is that I find a husband. I mean, really, men are pigs and they treat women like slaves. Why should I even want a husband anyway?"

June grinned.

She's condescending, Curia thought. She promised herself she would remain obdurate.

"What do you want, Curia?"

It was a simple question, but wasn't what Curia expected. "You mean in a husband?

"No, I mean what do you want in life?"

That made her pause. *What is her point?* "Frankly, I want to be a lawyer or a senator, but that doesn't seem possible."

"Why do you want to be those?"

"Because... they accomplish things. I really want to do something important and I think I can."

She must have raised her voice too much because she noticed both Proculus and her father look up at her from the other room.

"I think you're capable too. What will it take to accomplish something important?"

She pondered that for a moment, "Reputation and money."

"That's very perceptive of you, and I agree. Your father has a great reputation, and some money. But his reputation is for his military acuity, and I doubt he has enough money to accomplish what you are after. Do you agree?"

"Yes, but that doesn't mean I can't get the money or that I can't build a reputation."

"True... How?"

That stopped her, again. Nobody had ever queried her like this. She was used to being the one doing the pushing and being the only one that believed she could do it. Having someone believe in her, but pushing her for specifics was not something she was prepared to handle.

Proculus and Maximus were still in the other room, apparently talking, but Curia had the impression they were listening to the conversation. She turned her back to the door.

"Well... um... I could write, or, or, I could assist some other lawyer."

"Yes, but writing won't get you the exposure or income for many years and most successful writers go out and experience life first and then write. Besides, if we are being honest, not many Romans would want to read a female writer. As for assisting someone else, shouldn't you lead instead of follow and how exactly will that earn you enough money to be able to accomplish anything?"

Getting her confidence back some she responded, "You seem to know so much, what do you think I should do?"

"You need to be in a position where you have money without having to spend the time earning it and where you can apply yourself to whatever endeavor is important to you. Eventually you can turn this into writing. Personally, with your knowledge of politics, you should write about the state of the government and the degradation and decadence of the Senate. You might just be a voice for change if you positioned yourself correctly." Curia's eyes lit up at that. "Curia, you have to recognize that all of this would be easier if you married someone with some money and a house full of slaves. That would free you to work on important matters and would give you the resources you will need."

Curia's shoulders dropped. *So this is just about marriage.*

"Don't look so glum. You knew the direction of this conversation. And don't get so fixated about men being pigs. Many of them are, but that just means you haven't met the right one. No offense to your father, he doesn't really know how to look for someone that is right for you. He has done a wonderful job raising you alone since your mother died, but he is not a mother and doesn't understand a daughter. Let me help. Give me a chance to see if I can find a man who isn't a pig, and who would love to have a spirited, capable woman like you and, most importantly, doesn't mind you succeeding. We might even find someone that you really want to be with."

Curia looked at her, trying to see in her eyes whether or not she could really make that happen, and decided that she didn't really have a choice and maybe, just maybe, it would be worth it. June was right that the appropriate husband could open up possibilities.

"All right June, but don't expect me to be enthusiastic about it."

"Of course not, dear. Just be yourself and we'll see what happens."

* * *

The next two months were a busy time for all of them. Proculus had to listen to June complaining that the Roman men really were pigs as Curia had said. Internally it pleased him because he knew June thought more of him because of the comparison. She had actually called him an aberration during one of their discussions. More than once, he had to convince her to keep trying when she despaired.

Proculus was spending his time ingratiating himself into the lives of various senators. They still recognized him as a stalwart figure and one of the few Roman experts on Judaism and Judea. In late winter, they asked him to give an open lecture to the Senate on the situation in Judea, a summary of the dangers in the area and the potential for improvement. Antioch had become the third largest city in the Empire, next to Rome and Alexandria, so Proculus understood the importance of the area, as did the Senate.

The day arrived for his talk to the Senate. The building was a large, formidable structure of stone with multiple layers and a slanted, tiled roof. The structure was designed to impose fear and trepidation on any non-Roman and it proved successful. Proculus had invited Maximus and Curia. He arrived at the Senate in his best robes with purple and gold accents, indicating he was of the senatorial class. He also had an ancient clasp that designated patrician lineage. Old friends and a few enemies welcomed him as he looked around the chambers to count the number of senators that had elected to hear his speech. However, when he realized Maximus and Curia were nowhere to be seen he stopped counting. Then, he was surprised to notice Gaius Germanicus. He walked straight up to Caligula, "I am surprised, and honored, to see you here Gaius."

"Please Proculus, call me Caligula, and I wouldn't miss this. Caesar has spoken kindly of you and Judea is an important province, although one that may need a firm hand."

Proculus cocked his head, taken aback. "I do not disagree, though we must be careful as they have a lot of support around the Republic and are a fierce people."

"Fierce, ha; they cannot stand up to Rome and shouldn't be so ignorant. They have to live as Romans do."

"However, Rome has had a long policy of letting subjugated people live as they will as long as they pay their taxes."

"That's just it; they aren't paying their fair share of taxes. We are letting them get away with more than any other people and there is no reason to treat them specially."

They both glanced around at the diminishing noise. It was clear that the Senate was ready for the speech to begin. Proculus nodded his head to Caligula as he departed. "I hope the speech is valuable and that we can spend more time together while you are here in Rome."

"Of course…," Caligula answered hesitantly.

Proculus followed a pair of administrators to the open area in front of the curved row of seats that formed into a small stadium. Roughly, one-hundred and twenty senators were in attendance; a significant number this being an optional assembly. As he turned, he saw Maximus and Curia enter the spectator area from the rear. They would be behind him as he faced the Senate, but they would be able to hear him clearly enough.

* * *

Curia leaned forward intent on hearing every word.

"Esteemed colleagues, senators and patricians," a pause, "and those of you just pretending," he began with a smile and received subdued laughs from the audience. "Thank you for honoring me today with your attendance and a special thank you to Gaius Germanicus, our next Caesar, for making the trip from Misenum." Proculus gave a slight bow in Caligula's direction.

Curia turned to Maximus and asked quietly, "Did he really just offer his support to that corrupt swine?"

Maximus smiled and grimaced at the same time. "In a way, but he will support Gemellus as well. It doesn't really matter who is supported, it will be Tiberius' decision. All Proculus did was get himself closer to Caligula, which could prove useful in the coming months."

Proculus continued, "The topic today is Judea." He perused the audience and continued, "However, we cannot look at Judea without looking at Judaism. Specifically we must recognize Jerusalem as the center and the symbol of an ancient and widely dispersed people.

"The Jewish people have a history longer than Rome's."

Curia commented, "That will surprise these senators who believe the world began with Romulus and Remus."

Proculus continued, "Yes, they can trace their roots back to before the time Rome was founded. More importantly, in all that time, they have had a singular vision, an expectation... an expectation of greatness and of an ultimate union with their One True God. They believe their homeland, and in particular Jerusalem, is the land of God's chosen people and no amount of conquering or cajoling has dissuaded them. The Jewish people have been conquered three times in their past and each time they spread out to the surrounding lands and then returned when they could. The Assyrians under Shalmaneser V conquered them over seven centuries ago and then Nebuchandnezzar II conquered them one hundred and forty years later.

"However, by two hundred and fifty years ago many of these *diaspora* families had returned and rebuilt their prized temple and lived in self-governance until Rome formally acquired the area thirty years ago."

He took a drink from a cup of water. "The wise Caesar Augustus made a practice of respecting conquered peoples and the same was true for the Jews. We have respected their right to practice their religion, including their *sabbatical*, which says that they must not work or even plant the fields one year out of every seven. Therefore, we do not require taxes once every seven years. They are the only people in the Republic who are allowed to periodically forego taxes."

There were murmurings from some of the senators. Proculus waited for them to subside.

Curia said, "You would think they would know that already." Then she turned and whispered conspiratorially, "Is he trying to incite this Senate against Jerusalem?"

Maximus didn't answer right away, which made Curia wonder if she had broached a sensitive subject. "Perhaps just a little, but for good reason. We'll talk later."

Proculus went on, "However, Antioch is the third largest city in the Empire and some of their structures in Jerusalem, like Herod's Temple or what the Jews call the Second Temple, rival Rome's." Multiple senators vociferously baulked at that. "These are a proud people who are not likely to ever become "Roman" because they are too sure of their own birthright as the chosen people of the One True God. On the other hand, it has only been two generations since we acquired the region and there are still people alive today who remember Jewish independence. We have to keep a careful eye on them and have a strong, Roman, governor in place to ensure allegiance."

Curia raised both eyebrows at that. "He has to know that a Roman governor will just cause discontent in Jerusalem." Maximus remained silent.

Proculus continued with statistical detail, but it was clear that he was through with the substance of the talk. Maximus and Curia stayed for a while, but when it was obvious the speech was winding down, they made their way out of the building. "Do we not have to wait for Proculus?" Curia asked.

"No, he's going to meet us for lunch in an hour or so. He wanted to stay behind to see if any of the senators had questions. It's common after a short speech." They made their way through the marketplace while Curia reviewed what she had heard. She knew she had to wait for Proculus to explain the meaning of some of it. These two seemed to be manipulating the Senate. *But to what end?*

* * *

The three of them met at a small outdoor eatery and found a table where they could talk without being overheard. Curia noted the seriousness of the men. It bordered on apprehension. Something momentous was happening and they seemed to be including her. She beamed with excitement and curiosity, but held her tongue.

They sat down, ordered, and said… nothing, and then she realized they were waiting for the waiter to depart. Then, Proculus looked at Curia. "What did you think of the speech Curia?"

She was well aware that this was some kind of test, but all she could do was answer honestly, because she had no idea what kind of answer he was after. "It seemed like a nice, though terse, summary of the situation in Judea, but I was surprised at a couple points you made."

"Oh… Which ones?"

"Well," she began hesitantly, "the apparent backing of Caligula was a little disturbing, but the bigger concern is why you seemed to be pitting the Senate against Jerusalem." She looked up at him inquiringly.

"Those are both good points Curia," Proculus smiled. "In fact, they are the two main things I wanted to accomplish in giving that speech. The rest of the speech had little to no meaning and was just to fill the time. Why do you think I wanted to make those points?"

Curia had to gather her thoughts. *What is he after?* "Backing Caligula makes some sense if you already have reason to believe he will be the next Caesar. It's troubling because he is such a decadent, immoral person, that I have trouble seeing him as Caesar. We need another Augustus, not a wretched pig like him." She had tried to keep to a more sophisticated language, but the word *pig* always seemed to come to mind when thinking of Caligula.

"And what of Gemellus? He is the only other person Tiberius is considering as successor."

"He seems a little soft, but he is fair and he treats people well. He is also a lot more moral than Caligula. He isn't Augustus either, but he is better than Caligula."

"That depends on what Rome needs right now and what is best for Rome in the future." Proculus looked at some pigeons on the ground and then turned back. "What would happen if both were named as co-Caesars?"

Curia's mouth turned down in a frown. She was pretty sure she knew what would happen. "One of them would have the other assassinated within the first month and we would again have a single Caesar."

Proculus stopped asking questions and looked directly at Maximus, questioning him with a single raised eyebrow.

Despite Curia's namesake and her propensity for blurting out questions, she stayed quiet, even obsequious. She could see some decision was being evaluated by her father from the downcast eyes, tight jawline, and deeply creased furrow. She rarely saw him this indecisive, so the decision must be a difficult one for him, and it was an indicator of just how momentous this situation was. It was just as clear that Proculus had already decided and that he was deferring to Maximus, which was, frankly, unheard of. She couldn't stop herself from looking back and forth between the two even while keeping her head slightly inclined.

Finally, Maximus looked up at Proculus and gave him a slight, almost imperceptible, nod. Proculus turned immediately to Curia. "To explain these things, we have to talk you through the real situation in Rome and what your father and I are planning. However, right now, only the two of us know about this plan and if we tell you, then you have to swear to us that you will never tell anyone else unless your father and I agree. This is something that June does not even know Curia, so you can see how critical it is to keep it to ourselves for the time being. If you marry, then you will not be able to tell your husband. Also, and this is even more important, you have to understand that what we are doing could become dangerous. You may have to do things that could get people, or you, killed."

Curia saw her father cringe at that.

Proculus put the ultimate question in front of her, "Are you sure you want to be a part of this *propositum*?"

Curia frowned in concentration and wondered what exactly it was she was getting into. She knew, however, that this had to be incredibly important for Proculus to be asking this. Her arms tingled as she sat rigid. She trusted both of these men totally and if they needed her, then being afraid wasn't going to stop her. *How bad can this really be? Could I really kill? Could they really involve me if they thought I might be killed? I have to know. I have to.*

Enough thinking. "Yes Proculus, I do," she said with as much confidence as she could muster and was surprised, and pleased, at how calm and confident it sounded. Now that that was out, she was excited to hear the details of this plan. She leaned forward and looked up expectantly.

A man walked near the table. The two men bent to take a drink.

Proculus laid out the situation with the Roman Empire. Curia had heard her father increasingly refer to it that way, so she wasn't surprised at the idea. However, she was surprised at how far it had gone and that Proculus, the wisest person she knew, considered it all but a lost cause. Luckily, she knew quite a bit about Judaism and Judea, so he didn't have to explain them in such detail.

"So, Curia, the idea is to try to merge the political concepts of the Republic with the religious governance of the Jews. To do this, we are going to try to turn much of the Empire Jewish. The old Gods are a travesty, especially since the Caesars started becoming Gods. We think many Romans would be willing to practice Judaism if they understood more of the Jewish religion and if the Jews would relax on some of their requirements." He added in a quieter voice, "like requiring grown men to be circumcised."

"That's an enormous task; you would need an army of Jews to go out and preach."

"Less than you would imagine. There are Jewish communities in most of the main cities in the Empire, at least any that are on Mare Internum. We have proselytizers, as they are called, ready to go out and work with the communities to spread the word. What is stopping us is the Jewish laws of conversion, and the leaders in Jerusalem control those.

"The difficulty, and the reason we need to be delicate, is that we need to cause enough strife between Rome and Jerusalem that Jerusalem becomes afraid, but not so much that there is any open conflict between the two. Then we should be able to convince the leaders in Jerusalem that converting the Gentiles to Judaism would help their position. Since they do not really care that much about the Gentiles they should see that it can only help. That is the reason for the antagonistic elements of the speech you heard."

"Both sides would hate you if they knew what you were doing."

"Yes, but they will not find out. Only the three of us know. Even the proselytizers do not know any of this; they only know that they are waiting for approval from Jerusalem to try to convert the Gentiles. June does not know... she would never understand us pitting Rome against Jerusalem. In fact, she would not even understand how I could have invited you to the speech without inviting her, so you should not mention the fact that you were there."

"Then, why are you including me in this conspiracy?"

"I hate to call it a conspiracy, but it really is not far from the truth." Proculus looked around at patrons a few tables away.

To Curia's surprise, her father spoke up, "The main reason is that I will need to travel with the lead proselytizer, if we can call him that. And while I'm away, we need someone here to monitor what is happening in Rome. There is likely to be some political maneuvering here over the next few years as we expect leadership to change at least a couple of times. There may also be things you can do to help move the situation in a particular direction. For instance, we may want to assure a particular Caesar is chosen between Caligula and Gemellus."

"But I thought you said that Tiberius would probably proclaim both to be co-Caesars."

"But, as you said, only one will ultimately be Caesar."

Curia looked around to make sure nobody was listening and then exclaimed, "Are you seriously suggesting that you might aide in the assassination of a Caesar?"

Maximus hesitated and Proculus answered. "It probably will not come to that. However, if it did come to that, do you not think it would be acceptable and even appropriate if we are trying to help save the Republic?" Proculus looked at her expectantly.

Curia considered that for a full minute before answering. "I can see that it could be useful. However, you are talking about murder based on speculation of something you are trying to make happen in the distant future."

"True, but you know that one of them will do it anyway. Is it really so bad that we help choose which one? Also, you said yourself that neither one of them is anything like Augustus. I would contend that, whichever one becomes Caesar, he will not survive more than a few years. Perhaps at that point, and after we have motivated Jerusalem to relax their conversion laws, we will find a more appropriate emperor."

"So what can I do?"

"You may hate this answer, but the best thing you could do right now is to find the right husband."

Both Curia and Maximus raised their voice and exclaimed "What?" at the same time.

Proculus smiled. "You will need to build a network of people to keep you informed about what is happening. I doubt that you can utilize your father's network; they just are not the type to consider a young woman a confidant. The best and fastest way is to marry someone with good standing and important connections; someone in politics and someone with money. I know that sounds harsh, but it is not uncommon to marry for business or political reasons."

Maximus and Curia spoke at the same time, complaining about how insensitive Proculus was. How he couldn't be seriously suggesting Curia would marry someone just to promote the plan. Proculus held up his hand to quiet them down. "I am not suggesting that you find some hideous husband you cannot stand to be around. Just be cognizant of what we could accomplish with the right sort of husband. What I described is exactly what June would probably look for anyway, so it is likely that your choices will include a number of men who fit this profile."

Curia was still aghast at Proculus' suggestion, but she was too stunned to argue the point rationally, so she acquiesced for the moment.

In the lull, Proculus continued, "The other thing you can do is get as familiar as possible with the real political situation. Your father can help you; he has more connections and therefore knowledge of the politics in Rome than most in the Empire. You should make sure you understand the idiosyncrasies in the Jewish situation. You understand the Jews and Judaism reasonably well, but you have not thought through what it means to combine that with a republic, or what it would mean for the average Roman to become Jewish."

The three continued with small talk; Curia was still upset with Proculus and she could tell her father was as well. *It's just so… presumptuous of him.*

V. Gaius Julius Caesar Germanicus (36 AD)

"Everyone who glorifies himself will be humiliated, and the one who humbles himself will be praised."

- The Book of Q

Proculus made himself scarce for a few days while he let Maximus and Curia absorb the conversation and come to terms with Curia's new role and the sacrifices that might need to be made. He knew they would come to understand his comments and may even agree with them.

Then he received an invitation to visit Caligula's estate for a meal and, surprisingly, a special request was included to come early to talk privately. That could be very good or it could be a problem. There was no telling what Caligula had in mind. Proculus knew he would have to go and that there was no way to take someone else since that would offend Caligula.

The next evening, precisely one hour before dinner, Proculus arrived at Caligula's estate in Rome. The style was similar to Duccius' villa, but it was twice the size and the furnishings and decorations were lavish. The attendant immediately escorted him to the changing rooms for the baths that Caligula maintained. Unlike many politicians who enjoyed public baths for the socializing and interaction, Caligula tended to prefer private baths for reasons that would soon become obvious.

Proculus removed his clothes and donned a robe offered to him by the attendant, who then led him into the bathes. Upon walking in, myriad erotic images and sounds assaulted his senses. There were twelve alcoves surrounding a large rectangular central bath. Proculus did not even notice Caligula staring at him from the far side of the bath as all his attention was pulled to the alcoves on the sides of the bathhouse. Each contained one or more naked people who were fondling each other, or themselves, sexually. They were culturally diverse including some who were obviously from Africa. Every one of them was exceptionally attractive. There was a musky, sweaty smell in the air. Then he noticed the far side where there was one alcove with two men and another with a man and a boy. He had heard about the decadence and debauchery of Tiberius and Caligula, however he had never experienced it directly, especially in such a blatant display. Living with a Jewish wife and in a community with a strong Jewish presence had made Proculus accustomed to a higher moral standard. This display was offensive and disgusted him. But it also... aroused him deep inside stirring passions he had not felt for many years. He quickly submerged into the bath to hide his reaction.

Caligula clapped his hands twice. That brought Proculus' attention back to matters at hand, but it also started every one of these *distractions* into motion. They began copulating or masturbating, as the case may be. Slowly at first and then with increased vigor as Proculus tried to make his way to where Caligula relaxed against the far wall of the bath. Proculus had felt he couldn't be any more offended. Clearly, Caligula was testing him to see if he could stomach the situation. Proculus swallowed his feelings about the display and kept advancing towards Caligula. *The retched pig – Curia was right about him.*

"It's invigorating isn't it Proculus?" Caligula asked with a mischievous smile. He was a tall man with a thick muscular neck, sunken smoke-gray eyes, and a triangular face with a broad forehead. He was mostly bald on top, but had large patches of body hair, which was why many people risked calling him a goat.

"Disturbingly, it is," Proculus replied a little too honestly. He realized at that point that he had to get control of himself. The erotic environment with shocking visuals, loud moans, and enticing smells confounded him enough that he wasn't paying attention to the powerful man in front of him. That was dangerous. "I have heard about your interest in sexuality, but I have never seen such a display." *A reasonable recovery.* He looked at the water and tried to ignore the alluring sounds. Caligula must have given some hidden signal at that point because the slaves slowed down– without climaxing Proculus noted – and then went back to the fondling they were doing previously. Caligula probably enjoyed keeping them at a high level of excitement at all times. *How frustrating that must be for them.*

"Your speech about Judea was good. You presented valuable information without a lot of obfuscation or extraneous information. You also clearly put Rome first, which is difficult for someone who has lived in a province as long as you have."

Proculus was still finding it hard to concentrate in this environment, but he did his best. "Thank you Caligula, I always have the interest of Rome in mind," which was completely true, but for Proculus, that meant in the long-term and not necessarily the current generation, or leadership.

"Do you think Judea will need to be taught a lesson?"

Proculus had to be careful because the timing of any lesson was critical. "Perhaps at some point they will, but that will not happen under Tiberius Caesar."

"You and I both know that Tiberius won't last long."

There was no point in acting shocked by this statement, "Of course, but we do not know who his successor will be... do we?" He asked pointedly.

Caligula chuckled. "At least you didn't falsely deny Tiberius' condition. No, nothing is for sure. He seems to think he can appoint both Gemellus and me as co-emperors. That would be a travesty. We are very different people and, as much as I love Gemellus, we won't be able to agree on any one course of action. Every time Rome has tried multiple leaders, one has eventually ruled." This was a not-so-veiled threat by Caligula regarding Gemellus and was exactly what Proculus expected, though he was quite surprised that Caligula would openly admit it.

The best approach, Proculus thought quickly, was probably to ignore Caligula's blatant statement, "Judea will not be your most difficult issue. The military is fat and restless from years of inactivity, but they are all well aware of Augustus' belief that we have reached the maximum extent the Republic can handle without collapsing. Somehow, you will have to get the military busy without expanding too far. You also have a Senate that is becoming more of a burden and less useful." Proculus knew that all of this was true and that it was exactly what Caligula would want to hear because he would want more power for himself. Expanding the Empire and diminishing the Senate both helped to achieve that goal.

He added, "The people also need to see their emperor. Tiberius has been too long absent and people need the ceremony and extravagance of Caesar to feel like we are still rulers of the known world."

"You are bold to be so forthright."

"Only here in private and I am sure you already knew of these issues."

"True enough. However, few senators would be honest with me." After a moment, he went on, "I do know the problems of the Empire well Proculus, and these will not be difficult issues to solve. The people will see me and love me a great deal more than Tiberius." Caligula's arm raised and his hand flipped in an odd motion that Proculus could not interpret.

To Proculus, Caligula was too confident in his ability to satisfy the fickle Roman populous, but he was not surprised and it did confirm the speculation by some that Caligula was deluded about his own abilities. Unfortunately, he was concentrating so hard on the conversation and ignoring what was happening around him, that he failed to notice the woman headed their way. He finally sensed her approach, probably more from the stares of the sex-slaves than from any motion or sound from her. She was astonishingly beautiful with long silky black hair. The curls cascaded over her white skin and down her back. She had brilliant sparkling eyes of an indeterminate color, a slim athletic figure, and full breasts that were halfway submerged at the low point of her stride and fully in view when she undulated with the flow of the water as she approached.

She waded right up to Proculus with confidence until her mouth was inches from his. Her nipples were lightly caressing his chest and her legs were delicately straddling his right leg. The tickle of pubic hair on his thigh made him extremely uncomfortable... and aroused. Proculus was at a total loss as to what to do. He didn't want to offend Caligula and he was too entranced with this goddess to even think of moving. She was flowing sensually up and down his body, lightly caressing his lips with hers, letting her erect nipples trace patterns on his stomach and chest while her *debent* rubbed against the length of his upper leg. His erection was becoming difficult to hide, especially when it broke the surface of the water. Each time it came into contact with her stomach, intense tingling consumed his body and mind.

Finally, he came to his senses, placed his hands on her shoulder and gently pushed her away. "You are truly a stunningly beautiful woman and I'm sure any man would give a great deal to be in my position, but... I... can't."

The woman glanced at Caligula who nodded towards the exit. Looking a little dejected, she turned and ambled away with the same sensual gait. Proculus tracked her all the way across the large bath and watched the bulge of her breasts and the sway of her hips as she left the water. He was still uncomfortably erect and feeling guilty.

Caligula was quiet as Proculus tried to contain his reaction and finally, after some minutes, he gained enough composure to realize Caligula was still there. "I am sorry Caligula, I really do not mean to offend you, but I have chosen to be with just one woman and I must live by my commitments and by my own standards. It is the basis of my honor."

Caligula smiled and slapped Proculus on the shoulder. "Don't worry about it Proculus, I really had no idea how you would react to that, but I was curious to see. You would be a formidable person here in Rome, though I would worry about your ambition. The fact that you are retired and living far away, and that you are honest and honorable makes you a person I want to know. Please, let us get ready for dinner where I will introduce you to some of my friends."

As they advanced across the large bath, Caligula added, "If you can call them that…"

* * *

Curia arrived later that evening, greeted June and without even a glance at Proculus headed into the library. Proculus had leaned forward quickly as if to rise, but then held his position and stared their way. Curia noticed June had not moved and stood looking back and forth between the two of them. She turned and said, "Are you coming?"

June said nothing and followed. Once in the room she asked hurriedly, "What is going on between you and my… Proculus?"

Curia hesitated because she knew very well who was most important to June. Then she decided to tell June because she might be able to talk some sense into her husband. "I don't like how he insinuates himself into my life. He seems to think he has the right to tell me who I should marry and why."

"You know, Curia, he thinks of you as a daughter. He never had children of his own and he is very close to your father. He probably is just concerned that you have a fruitful and fulfilled future."

"Maybe…" She realized that she couldn't tell June the whole story and so her being upset wasn't going to make a lot of sense. She decided quickly to back off.

June's lips tightened at Curia's indecision. "Well, we can ignore him and just find the right husband for you. How does that sound?"

Curia beamed. "That sounds great." She realized she should pay attention to how June handled Proculus. Growing up without a mother around meant she hadn't seen that interaction in her own parents. June seemed so happy and she made it all appear easy.

They sat down and got comfortable while one of the servants brought in some food. "I have to tell you Curia that you were right when you called Roman men *pigs*. I've talked to hundreds of people and met with dozens of men and so few of them are moral or have any honor that it's hard to understand how Rome has come to rule the known world. Still, I was able to find a few, actually seven, that were a combination of the right age, temperament, and attitude and who seemed like decent people." She laughed a little. "Of course I have my favorite, but I don't want to influence you, so we will just go through each of them and what they are like and you can tell me who you would like to meet. I can arrange a brief casual introduction."

Curia was nervous. She didn't believe in this kind of arranged matchmaking and was sure she could find a husband on her own. However, she had to admit that it hadn't happened yet and she was getting old enough for it to be a concern. Logically she agreed June could help and she accepted that, especially with her father's insistence. *It still feels wrong.*

"Let's begin," she said, hesitantly.

June proceeded with going through the list and explaining some of the salient attributes of each man. Curia was impressed that June could do all this from memory. Clearly, she had done a lot of work and she had taken their talk seriously because each of the men did indeed sound reasonable. They agreed on starting out meeting two of them, separately of course. Curia didn't know what to base it on because they all sounded acceptable, and she really didn't know what was important to her, so she chose the two whose names appealed to her, Quintus Scaevola and Decimus Balbus.

June's mouth dropped open slightly at Curia's choices. *Those weren't the ones she expected.* "Interesting choices, Curia." It seemed to Curia that June was struggling with how much to tell her. She must have decided to keep her opinions to herself because she added only that they would start with Decimus.

Three days later June and Curia went to the home of the late importer Balbus. His son Decimus along with his widowed wife and two daughters still occupied the moderate residence. They had decided a surprise visit was better than something planned with all the expectations and nervousness that might bring. This way they could have a short chat without any pressure and Curia could simply meet Decimus.

Unfortunately, their careful planning didn't turn out well. Decimus was away on business. Curia was able to meet his mother and one of his sisters. It was pleasant enough, though Curia felt nervous the entire time. The mother seemed a little protective of Decimus and that might be hard to handle in a marriage of this sort, especially with Decimus being the eldest son. She also refused to let Curia talk privately with Decimus' sister.

They decided to return the next day for a more planned visit and where they could ensure Decimus was there. They arrived in midafternoon. Decimus' sister, Charito, met them at the door and escorted them to the sitting room where they found Decimus. Charito then stepped back to the corner of the room to observe. The man stood when they entered and greeted them pleasantly enough, though Curia thought it would have been better if he had met them at the door. He knew they were coming; to send his sister seemed demeaning. Except that she didn't know of any Roman man who would do that, so maybe she was just being harsh.

June proceeded to introduce them. "Decimus, this is Curia, daughter of Maximus Octavius; Curia, this is Decimus, son of Opiter Iulius Balbus."

"It is an honor to meet you Decimus." Curia opened with a pleasant, if a little formal, greeting.

Decimus smiled at Curia, "And it is a pleasure to meet you Curia. You have an interesting name; have you lived up to the namesake?"

"Many, including my father, think I am too curious. I tend to be interested in many things. I hope that doesn't bother you." She realized the last statement was too ingratiating and she decided to stop there before she made a fool of herself.

Decimus concentrated for a moment. "I may have heard of your father. What sort of things are you interested in?"

"Uh…" she had to think fast. On the one hand, it was true that she was interested in many things and maybe she should just be forthright about it and see how that affected Decimus. On the other, few Roman men could handle a wife who gets involved in his business or his affairs. She decided to just be honest and see how he reacted. "Politics, philosophy, history, business, various types of people in and out of the Republic." She decided to add, partly for June's sake, and partly because it might help with her new role within Proculus' plan, "especially the Jews. Then there is science, astronomy and even a little math and some medicine. So I guess, yes, you could say I am a very curious person." She smiled hesitantly wondering how he would react. She could see Decimus' sister in the background, somewhat aghast. Unfortunately, she couldn't see June's expression from her angle.

"And where do you see all of those interests leading you? Wouldn't having so many mean you wouldn't become expert at any one?"

"I don't really need to be an expert at any one of them and I don't see them leading me anywhere in particular. I am just interested in them and so spend time trying to understand. The breadth of knowledge should help me in whatever endeavors come my way." She decided it was time to take the attention away from her and put it on Decimus where it belonged. "What are your interests Decimus? I mean besides your father's import business."

"Well, most of my interests are around the business. Of course, these include management, accounting, foreign affairs, politics and others. However, I'm only interested in those things insofar as they impact my business." Decimus had grown serious and stood more erect as he spoke about his profession. It impressed Curia, but she thought it was somewhat narrow in scope.

"Do women fit into that picture at all?"

"Oh yes, in many ways. We have several women working for us. Of course, few of them are married and we have to be careful with the type of jobs we let them do." Decimus narrowed his eyes.

Curia's eyebrow rose as she questioned Decimus' opinion of women. *He wouldn't expect me to work or help at all.*

An uncomfortable silence ensued. Curia felt June start to step forward and then retreat again.

After the moments of awkwardness, Decimus' sister stepped in and asked if they wanted something to drink. The would-be couple looked at her as if she were an intruder and then realized how timely it was. Decimus answered for them, "yes." When the drinks came, Decimus silently took his first followed by the women who each thanked Charito for the drinks. The conversation turned civil if impersonal. *This won't work.* There wasn't a lot of reason to prolong the suffering. June asked their leave after a short while and the two made their way towards the Duccius residence.

"Well, that was awkward," Curia blurted once they were far enough away from the Balbus mansion to be sure she wouldn't be heard. "At least we were able to escape."

"I think you will find with each man we meet that you will pretty quickly either like or dislike him. They each have strong personalities or I wouldn't have even considered them. That means you will see right away how close of a fit it is. We should be able to visit a few of them in quick succession and then come back to ones that seem to have potential."

"And what happens if none of them seem to have potential?"

"We'll walk that road if we get to it." After a pause, June added, "You have to remember, I'm not one to suggest that you *settle*. This is too important and it is a life-long decision. You should not only be comfortable with the person, you should be happy to be getting married."

"That'll be the day..." Curia mumbled.

June ignored her remark.

* * *

Four days later, they met with the second candidate. In this case, a servant met them at the door, but Quintus Scaevola was right behind her. The Scaevola name was an honored one that came from a Roman hero named Gaius Mucius

Scaevola. There had been no less than four Consuls and one Governor, of Sardinia, in their family. Quintus had a regal, though relaxed appearance. As he approached the door, he politely told June he would show them in. June said, "Quintus, you surprise me, meeting us at the door like this. May I introduce Curia, daughter of Maximus Octavius?"

Curia was a little in awe of Quintus, which wasn't a common feeling for her. Partly this was due to the long history of his family, but also he had accomplished a great deal while still young and, as it turned out, was good looking with black curly hair, prominent cheekbones, sky-blue eyes, and broad shoulders. He was obviously quite fit. What struck Curia most, however, was a presence he had about him. He had a stately composure, but seemed at-ease with himself and, more importantly, didn't seem at all pompous. She found herself liking him, even before he answered June.

"It's my pleasure meeting you," He said with an open smile. "Let's proceed to the reading room." As they walked, he continued talking to both of them in a friendly, open way. "I know of Maximus Octavius, he has a reputation as an honorable and capable soldier and many call him one of the few true Romans left. I also know of your husband Proculus. In fact, I met him on two occasions, though I don't know if he would remember. He too is a principled man and Rome has diminished with his retiring to Antioch."

As they entered the reading room, Quintus' sister Ionnia met them and a servant brought in food and drinks. It was all very pleasant and efficient. Ionnia stayed, sitting next to Quintus on the sofa. It was such a different atmosphere than the Balbus house that it surprised Curia and at the same time put her at ease.

"So this is Curia," he turned towards her with an interested look and one side of his mouth turned up in an odd smile. "I've heard a little bit about you, but nobody told me you were beautiful."

Ionnia slapped Quintus on the leg and spoke up quickly. "Oh, Quintus! You're going to embarrass her. Don't let him bother you Curia; he does like to have fun with people."

Curia felt at ease answering her. "Don't worry about me, I don't embarrass easily. Quintus will have to work harder than that if he is going to get to me."

They all laughed as Quintus said, "Excellent! A challenge; I accept."

"May I ask how you know of my father?" Curia asked before anyone had a chance to continue a conversation about her.

Quintus became more serious, but still relaxed. "He is well known in the Senate and by most of the military commanders as well. The only people I could find who said anything negative about him were not people I associate with. By all accounts that matter, he is an upright and honest person who truly has the Empire's interest in mind."

"You use the term Empire openly and to people you hardly know."

"Well, we are among aristocracy here and we all know that the Republic no longer exists, even if the people think it does. Do you not agree?"

"Oh I agree. It's just that many people are afraid to say it, even if they know it to be true."

Ionnia giggled, "That has never been a problem of Quintus'. He says whatever comes to mind. I've tried to teach him how to think before he speaks, but it just doesn't work."

"So what kind of career does a person with an unfiltered mouth have?" Curia asked smiling with the rest of them.

"A politician, of course, just not your everyday one. I'll never become Consul, but then anyone who might is in danger from Caesar. I did a tour in the military and found it invigorating, but not something I want for a career. My father, as you probably know, is a lawyer. He and my mother are both vacationing in the south or they would be here to meet you as well. I have a fairly diverse background and I want to do what I can for Rome. I work with the Senate as best I can for the good of the people.

"What about you Curia, what do you want to do with your life?"

Curia had a lot less problem opening up to this unassuming and clearly self-confident man than she had with Decimus, who seemed to feel the world was there for him. "The same as you I guess; I want to do something useful for the Empire and something important for humanity. I also have a diverse background and love studying almost any subject."

Curia had a hard time believing how pleasant this was. She felt like she could talk forever. June seemed to have other things in mind. She spoke up, "Thank you for seeing us today." As they stood, she added, "Perhaps you would like to come meet Maximus at the Duccius residence where we are staying?"

Quintus seemed not only pleased with the idea of another meeting, but also thrilled at the chance to meet Maximus Octavius.

This time as they walked away, Curia was quiet, even contemplative. June remained silent, walking beside her.

Finally Curia spoke up, "You know what really upsets me? Quintus is exactly the type of man Proculus wants me to marry. If something does work out between me and Quintus, then Proculus will think...," she hesitated "well, I don't know what he will think, but I don't like it."

June replied simply, "Let's meet a few more of the men on my list and we'll see what happens."

"This time, you pick the next three. You clearly have good taste in men."

* * *

It took three weeks for four more meetings to take place. Although they were fine men with good attributes, they weren't Quintus and the meetings only resulted in Curia becoming more convinced that Quintus was a good choice.

"Curia, you will have to be careful to not count on Quintus as the only option." June admonished. "There are many barriers to this working out between you. You should keep your mind open and consider some of the others."

"I know, but it's difficult when everything seemed so right with Quintus. I'm nervous about this meeting with my Father. He can be overbearing at times and he is very protective. I don't want him to scare Quintus away."

"Don't worry about that. If Quintus is so easily scared then he isn't the right man for you anyway." They both smiled at the mild accolade.

Proculus walked through the door just then, which surprised both the women because he was supposed to be out for the evening. June opened her mouth to complain, but Curia spoke first. "Proculus, what are you doing here. You were supposed to be gone all evening."

"My dinner meeting with Senator Strabo was canceled." He looked back and forth between the two. "Why are you upset with my presence?"

Curia hesitated because she didn't want to offend Proculus. She glanced at June who was obviously letting her handle this. "It's just that we have a guest coming over for dinner to meet my father and, well, when you are around, he tends to defer to you and we can't have that tonight."

Proculus looked again back and forth between the two and then settled on June's face who appeared to be agreeing with Curia.

"Well, there are some other people I'd like to see to try to set up a meeting with Gemellus; I will just make some surprise visits. How long do you want me to stay away?"

"A few hours should be plenty, and… thank you, I appreciate this." Curia answered politely.

After starting to walk away, he turned back. "May I ask the name of this gentleman?"

"His name is Quintus Scaevola."

"Hmm," Proculus reflected, "I know that name."

"He says he has met you twice, but he didn't think you would remember."

"I do remember, but I cannot quite picture his face. If I am recalling correctly, he seemed a capable young man and was from a good family." After another pause, he added, "Have a nice evening."

Twenty minutes later Quintus arrived for dinner. He was dressed well, but not formally and had brought flowers for both Curia and June. When they entered the library, June excused herself to help prepare the evening. It was clear to everyone that she wanted Curia and Quintus to spend some time alone before Maximus arrived.

Maximus was a half-an-hour late and had to spend time cleaning up. It was apparent that he had been exerting himself in some way, not that Curia wanted to ask how. He finally strode into the reading room with June in tow. Curia and Quintus stood up immediately and were apprehensive about the introductions. It didn't help that Maximus was so overpowering with his sheer size and his militaristic bearing.

"You must be Quintus." Maximus shook Quintus' hand. "Curia has told me about you, as has June. Your family is a principled one, if a bit aristocratic for my taste."

Quintus raised an eyebrow at the aggressive statement, but handled it with ease. "We can't decide the family we are born into, all we can do is the best with what we are given." He smiled.

Maximus smiled as well and the atmosphere in the room palpably eased.

The dinner went well with general discussion of politics and the state of Rome. They had similar philosophies about the fall of the Roman Republic and what it meant to the people.

When Quintus left, Curia put on a coat to walk with him and June asked a servant to follow.

"Ionnia had said you couldn't filter what you say, but I thought you were very reserved with my father tonight."

"She exaggerates. I bend what I say based on who I am around and I didn't want to offend your father at our first meeting, so yes, I was on my best behavior. Does that bother you?"

"Not at all; I just want to make sure I know the real Quintus."

"That may be difficult. There are multiple versions of me: one for the Senate, one for family, one for the public, and a private one. There may be more..."

"I'd like to get to know the private one someday."

He hesitated, "Perhaps, someday, you will."

"Well, I should be getting back. I really enjoyed our evening and I hope we can get together again soon."

"Certainly, I would like that very much."

VI. Tiberius Julius Caesar Augustus (36 AD – 37 AD)

"When someone said to Jesus, 'Let me first go and bury my father,'
Jesus replied, 'Leave the dead to bury the dead.'"

- The Book of Q

Proculus was finally successful in arranging a meeting with Gemellus. Unfortunately, the prospective Caesar was still near Misenum, in the port city of Arecii, so it would take travel to reach him. He left early the next morning for the three-day trek, thankful that he did not have to cross Mount Vesuvius because of the harsh terrain.

He arrived late in the evening and decided to stay at a local inn as not to bother Gemellus late at night. The following morning he went to the residence of Tiberius' grandson.

A servant met Proculus at the door and directed him to a sitting room. It was an ornate, pleasant residence and kempt. It also had little of the decadence and debauchery that Tiberius and Caligula demonstrated. The only display of sexuality was some risqué statutes placed on columns around the large entry room. The most explicit pose was a headless man frozen in a perpetually frustrating position with his hand on his erection. The sitting room held a few books and scrolls on the shelves and some tasteful statuettes, but was otherwise sparse. Proculus noticed that the trinkets were from distant lands. Gemellus must have either inherited them or obtained them as gifts since it was known that he had traveled very little outside of Italia.

Proculus waited for over an hour. He was beginning to wonder if Gemellus had something against him or if he just liked to make people uncomfortable. Finally, Gemellus came through the door and greeted Proculus pleasantly, but did not apologize at all for the delay. It seemed expected that

Proculus would be willing to wait all day if needed for a chance to meet the man.

Back when Proculus was a senator, he had met Gemellus a couple of times. Gemellus had grown fat and pompous in the intervening years. His hair was longer and bound with expensive clasps. He had an upturned nose and bulky straight eyebrows. He was wearing a toga with purple trim, as if he was of the senatorial class, which certainly was not the case. He might become Caesar because of his genetic link to Tiberius, but he was no senator.

"It has been some time since I've seen you Proculus; aren't you retired now?"

"Yes, however I still like to do my part to further the interests of the Republic, especially when it involves the Jewish people." He had heard from multiple senators that Gemellus seemed to believe Rome was still a republic.

Gemellus spoke in a rush with his eyes darting around. "I heard about your speech to the Senate. It seemed to be a success. I know a number of senators gave you praise for it. I've also had a number of friends tell me I should accept this meeting request of yours. However, I have no idea what it is about or why I might want to meet with a retired senator from Antioch. Nevertheless, I don't lightly dismiss these friends. So why is it I'm meeting with you?"

Proculus was a little astounded at the pretentious attitude of Gemellus. *It is not as if he is Caesar yet nor am I his slave.* "I would hope that it would benefit both of us. The more you know about the various people Rome rules, the better you will be able to lead them. The Jewish people are widespread and they have a lot of influence on the Romans in those communities."

"And what is in this for Proculus?" Sweat glistened across Gemellus' forehead.

"Just the hope that I am able to offer help to my people…"

"Let's be honest Proculus," Gemellus said with a rising voice. "They are not *your* people. They belong to Rome and you are one man representing Rome, and then only indirectly since you aren't even a senator now."

This is not going well. Either he has something against me, or he only wants sycophants around him. He apparently wanted people to agree with him, whether or not he was right. "My apologies Gemellus… They are most definitely Rome's people and not mine. I am here to serve Rome and Caesar." He added the latter to try to appease Gemellus specifically.

His answer seemed to confirm this. "Well… Alright Proculus, what is it you think I should know about the Jews?"

"That the Jewish people have a long and distinguished past. They are spread around much of the Mediterranean and have great influence on Romans. They are a subjugated people, but they have their own religious practices that are very different than Rome's and they will die before changing."

Gemellus stared at a statue of a half-naked woman to his left. "I believe as Tiberius does and as Augustus did as well. We let subjugated people believe as they wish as long as they live by the Roman laws and they pay their taxes. I have no wish to alienate the Jewish people just as I have no wish to alienate any of the nations we have conquered. Rome is becoming too large to manage and we have to find a way to live happily as a people without the continuous warfare and expansion."

"Pardon me Gemellus, but there is one issue with the Jews that crosses both religion and taxes. Their religion says they cannot plant the fields nor do any other work one year out of every seven. Augustus and Tiberius both allowed them to forego paying taxes that year since they did not produce anything with which to pay the taxes. Would you continue that policy?"

Gemellus' face flared red as his neck muscles tightened. "Do not pretend to interview me like you have any say in who will become Caesar. Tiberius has already said he would appoint me as Caesar, possibly with Caligula as well."

Proculus withdrew in supplication. "Again my apologies Gemellus, I did not mean to offend you or imply anything. I only want to know in order to help prepare the provinces around Syria and Palestina for what is to come once you are Caesar."

Gemellus seemed to ignore Proculus' response and continued. "To answer your question, I don't see any reason to change that policy or to push the Jewish people into paying more taxes than they are capable of paying."

"A wise position Gemellus."

"Of course, why would you expect anything else?"

Proculus was seeing why Maximus and others were so concerned about the man. His confidence was so obviously fake that he came across as incapable and ineffectual. He also seemed to assume the Empire could continue on its current course. The military had to be kept active or it would turn on itself and overthrow the government. *The last thing we need is a stratocracy.*

This relaxed attitude about the Jews also ran counter to propositum. They needed someone to stir things up in Jerusalem and Gemellus' stance would not accomplish that.

Proculus would ponder the question for weeks to come, but unless something unusual came to mind, it was clear who had to become the next Caesar of Rome. It was also clear that spending a couple of days at Gemellus' residence would be difficult and distasteful. After some insincere discussion with Gemellus, to be sure he was not offended, Proculus took his leave. The trip back to Rome was uneventful but gave Proculus time to contemplate the next steps. Now that the decision had been made, a number of courses of action became apparent. He would have to discuss the details with Maximus.

* * *

Spring was approaching quickly with the last winter storm passing through. It was late February and Proculus was starting to ponder returning to Antioch. It looked like June had successfully found Curia a potential husband in Quintus and Tiberius could not last much longer. It was time for a planning session. The question on Proculus' mind was whether to have Curia attend the meeting. She had the potential to be a stalwart supporter of the plan and a member of the inner circle. They would need someone to carry on with the plan after Proculus and Maximus were gone. Propositum could take decades, even centuries, to play out and it would need help along the way. The problem was that during this meeting, Proculus might have to ask Maximus to use a heavy hand. *That is not something a daughter should ever have to hear about her father*, he thought paternally. It was quite a dilemma for him and he suffered a number of restless nights. Of course, he could not tell June and it was obvious that she knew something was troubling him. He had to make a decision.

In the end, he decided the future of the plan was more important than a daughter's perception of her father. He invited her.

Proculus had originally arranged to have the meeting with Maximus at some private baths, but that would not work with Curia coming, especially after the scene in the bath with Caligula. He therefore changed the location to a private estate Maximus located. The owners were away on vacation and Maximus had arranged to dismiss the staff for the evening, instead obtaining a single deaf attendant.

They met at the house and had a pleasant dinner with fine wine that Proculus had found in the market. As they sat down in the modest reading room, Proculus began. "Tiberius is very sick and cannot last much longer. It is time we consider what happens next."

"Excuse me Proculus," Maximus interrupted, "I just received word that Tiberius seems to be recovering."

"Vah! How long can an old man like that last? The people no longer tolerate him and Caligula and Gemellus are in abeyance. One of them should just kill the man."

Maximus disagreed, "You have to remember that Gemellus is his grandson and he adopted Gaius at a young age. Both of them are very close to Tiberius and they wouldn't easily take his life. Also, even though killing one person to become emperor isn't risky, killing two is. They won't want to kill Tiberius and also the other successor."

Curia was looking back and forth between the two men, eyes large, and hardly breathing. The men all but ignored her while she kept her silence.

Proculus said, "You know," a pause with a quick glance at Curia, "we may need to help this along. The timing is right for a new emperor. If we orchestrate Tiberius' ousting, perhaps Caligula will be comfortable dealing with Gemellus."

"So you've decided on Caligula."

"Yes, of course. Do you disagree?"

"Not at all, we just hadn't discussed it."

"I met with Gemellus and he is exactly as you described. He will try to be reasonable with Jerusalem, and everyone else. Moreover, he lacks the confidence to do anything bold. He thinks Augustus' dying wish of wanting the Empire to maintain its borders and not expand is still the best policy. He will negotiate with subjugated people and will try to maintain reasonable relations. He will not further this plan and his actions will not help Rome. Assassination would be likely within a few years, but there is no telling who would take over."

They both leaned back in their chairs, deep in thought.

"Tell me Maximus, do you have some contacts you can trust in Tiberius' retinue?"

"Yes, two. One will do whatever I ask without question. The other will for payment." Proculus smiled at the obfuscated answer, remembering how Maximus always kept names to himself.

"Then I would suggest that you take a trip to Misenum and work out how to help Tiberius make his way to the plains of Elysium."

Curia finally spoke up, "I still have a hard time believing that you two are sitting here and casually talking about murdering the ruler of the Roman Empire. Do you know how staggering that is?"

They both stared at her for an uncomfortable number of seconds. Proculus sometimes forgot just how enormous this all sounded to someone who had not been involved from the beginning. "You have to understand Curia, your father and I have been planning this and slowly working on it for years. We have known for much of that time that it might come down to critical moments like this where we would have to take decisive, and sometimes unpleasant, action.

"Additionally, we have been around the Senate and other politicians enough that we do not regard them as highly as you do. There was probably a time when this type of action would have bothered us, but no more. If we are going to accomplish all that we have set out to do, it will not be easy." He added after a second, "On any of us.

"But you are right, we do take it for granted sometimes and we have never talked of this to anyone else. You are freshly exposed to these ideas and to the concept of a plan that could take centuries and might include covert acts like this. Please do not take our nonchalance for a lack of empathy or respect for what we are trying to accomplish."

He waited to see if Curia had any other questions. When she did not, he continued with his ideas. "Whatever happens, it needs to be discrete and preferably appear completely natural. I would rather you pay someone to do this. You also want to make sure more money does not lead to exposure."

To make sure Curia was aware of certain information, Proculus continued with points Maximus already knew. He looked directly at Curia. "The people will be happy with Tiberius' passing. He has not been much of a ruler and they know it. They want someone who will actively lead and who will try to regain some of the glory of Rome.

"While you are in Misenum," he turned to Maximus, "I will start working with Caligula to ensure that he becomes the sole emperor. I think he already knows what has to be done; I am just not sure he is willing to do it immediately. If he waits, Gemellus may surprise him."

Turning back to Curia, Proculus asked, "You seem pensive. Do you have any questions that your father or I could answer?"

"No, it is just a lot to absorb."

"Understood." Curia was young and this was all very new to her. It had to be confusing and on a scale like nothing she had ever dealt with. He was still convinced she was the right choice; it would just take time.

* * *

Maximus left for Misenum the next morning. He was appalled that Curia had the audacity to ask to go with him. His answer was an immediate and emphatic "No." While he made his way out of town on horseback, he recalled the conversation because it had been so shocking that she had asked and he wasn't sure he handled it well. He had explained that while he was willing to let her be his eyes and ears in Rome, she wasn't a soldier and he wasn't going to let her get involved with this kind of subterfuge. If anything clandestine had to happen, he would take care of it or he would find a contact he could trust to work with Curia. Under no circumstances was she to try to develop a similar network.

He continued going over the conversation until he reached the edge of the great city and then decided to let it go. There was something about it that bothered him; maybe just that he wasn't sure Curia was convinced. In any case, there was no point belaboring the topic.

He arrived in Misenum in the middle of March. A celebration was underway where Tiberius planned to announce his successors formally. Tiberius had laid out the co-successors of Caligula and Gemellus previously in a will, but never publicly. He also wanted to show everyone that he was still healthy.

Tiberius began the celebration with a short accolade for the house he was staying at and how Lucius Lucullus originally owned it. He also apologized for Caligula's absence and welcomed Gemellus.

Maximus stayed in the background, speaking quietly with Macro, his trusted member of Tiberius' retinue. Macro was slightly taller and thinner than Maximus with wide set eyes and short curly hair that had a hint of red. He was young and strong and had a deep calmness about him. Tiberius' physician, Charicles, was there as well and was explaining the real situation with Tiberius. "He is faking. It's shocking he can stand this long, let alone give a speech. Mentally he is fine, at least for a 77-year-old, but his body is failing. His lungs can no longer sustain him. It will be two to three days at most before he passes. Isn't it astonishing that he can remain standing?"

Maximus and Macro looked at each other. "Yes, it is," Maximus said quietly. He was wondering if this doctor knew what he was talking about. *How can Tiberius be standing there giving even a short speech if he is two or three days from death?* Suddenly, Tiberius sat down on some pillows and, rather abruptly, ended his speech. He was obviously tired and stayed only a few minutes longer before retiring.

Maximus and Macro spent the next day contingency planning. They were hopeful that, given the deteriorating health of Tiberius, they wouldn't have to act. In tactical planning, chance was not a factor, so they tried to predict various scenarios and their response.

During lunch three days later, they received word that Tiberius had passed. Maximus and Macro smiled and toasted their good fortune. There would have been risk in any operation they might have undertaken, so this natural conclusion was for the best.

They went into the streets to hear crowds of people rejoicing at the news. Tiberius was not a well-liked Caesar. He had abused his title, his position, and his people for too long for them to appreciate him. He was also an immoral man and mistreated many of those around him. The only exceptions were Gemellus, Caligula and a few of the trusted guards.

Maximus and Macro heard many people yelling for Tiberius to be thrown into the Tiber River, which would deprive him of his noble burial and prohibit him from becoming a God like the Caesars before him. Macro commented that that was a rather harsh reaction and then they heard worse chants. Chants to Mother Earth and the Manes to "allow the dead man no abode except among the damned." And others threatened his body with the "Hook and the Stairs of Mourning."

Maximus reflected. *Maybe it would have been better to have Curia here where she could see what these people really thought of the man.*

The rejoicing went on for hours. There were multitudes drinking and dancing. Overtaken by the emotion and drink, they began stripping and enjoying acts of passion in the streets.

The two soldiers sat at a café, watching the merrymaking, but drinking in moderation. They both knew the risks; if Gemellus saw them celebrating, he may very well seek retribution on them and their families in the coming weeks.

After watching the cavorting for hours, one of Charicles' assistants came running through the plaza yelling that Tiberius lived and that he was recovering. Maximus and Macro looked at each other and couldn't stop laughing. This was just like Tiberius; he loved to illicit shear emotional turmoil in people and this kind of resurrection was the type of trick he would play. Of course, it may not have been on purpose, but it was incredibly appropriate for Tiberius.

After several minutes of the laughter subsiding and then erupting again, the two finally settled down and began to discuss things to come. "The time is now, Macro. The doctors say he is close and the people want this to happen. It won't be a surprise to anyone if he really does pass in the next day or two."

"Geganius is on staff tomorrow late-morning with me supervising. That would be the perfect time. Tiberius naps during this period, even in good health. I can make sure that nobody else is in the room and have Geganius suffocate him. We will call the physicians to come tend to him after his regular napping time ends and they will find him dead. We can settle with Geganius in a night or two."

"We should probably handle Geganius tomorrow night, immediately following. It's possible he would go out directly and celebrate his new-found wealth and end up telling someone how he made the money."

"Very well."

* * *

The following morning, Macro arrived with Geganius at Tiberius' room and found him asleep in bed with two beautiful women. It wasn't unheard of, but Macro knew it was all a bluff. Tiberius was seventy-seven years old and hadn't actually been with a woman in years. But he still liked to think he was capable and he liked others to believe he wasn't completely impotent. Macro went to the bed and quietly ushered the two naked women out of the room. They were nonplussed, but weren't about to object to Macro and they wouldn't dare wake up Tiberius. Macro teased them and gently slapped one on the rear to put them at ease. The last thing he wanted was for them to notice this day was special.

Macro then went and checked the three entrances to make sure there weren't any eavesdroppers and positioned himself at the main one. Geganius walked slowly over to Tiberius' bed and looked around for something to use. Macro saw him hesitate. He patted the back of his head to show Geganius to use the pillow. The guard gently took the pillow from behind Tiberius' head, but then stood staring at the sleeping Caesar. *This imbecile will be the end of us.* He threw his hands to the side, palms out, and grimaced at Geganius. Finally, Geganius quickly climbed onto the bed and covered Tiberius' face with the pillow. He moved to straddle Tiberius and pressed the pillow down over each side of his head. Tiberius moved slowly at first and then when he was running out of what little air his lungs could contain he struggled in earnest. It had little effect; he was an old man and very weak from his prolonged illness. He was no match for Geganius, who had the advantage of youth, size, and training. It took barely a minute for Tiberius to stop breathing.

Geganius climbed off the bed and Macro came over and quickly checked for a pulse. When he found none, he replaced the pillow under Tiberius' head and smoothed out the blankets so that they looked natural. Geganius stood the entire time by the edge of the bed looking at the face of the dead emperor of the known world. *He's not handling this well.* Macro was worried about how he would get him out of there without anyone noticing his behavior. Thankfully, they had another twenty minutes before the physicians would be there. Maybe he could get Geganius acting somewhat normally by then.

Macro pulled the guard away from the bed and close to his assigned entrance. He grabbed him by the shoulders and shook him lightly. "What is wrong with you?" Geganius' eyes were glassy and unfocused. He didn't answer. This was more serious even than what Macro feared. He slapped him on the face lightly. "Get a hold of yourself." Geganius looked up at Macro, but still didn't answer. Macro glanced around concernedly and decided that he had to get the man out before the physicians found him. He took him to the seldom-used east entrance and told him to leave quietly and to go to the tavern where they had talked the night before. Macro would meet him there later. He opened the door for Geganius, let him out, and stood watching as the man made his way down the hall. He was relieved to see that his gate barely faltered.

Macro made up a story for the physicians about Geganius being sick so that they wouldn't be suspicious of his absence. When they arrived, they asked after Tiberius and Macro answered, "He's been asleep the entire time. I started to check him, but I didn't want to disturb his sleep given who he was with when I came in." The corner of his mouth turned up impishly.

The physicians caught his hint and chuckled. Charicles went over to Tiberius and kept looking around the room on the way. His pace quickened and, upon reaching the bed, he tried to wake Tiberius with a gentle rocking of his shoulder. When Tiberius didn't move, he felt for his pulse and found none. Charicles called over the other physicians and asked them to verify that Tiberius had no pulse.

"Is something wrong?" Macro asked from the door. The physicians talked among themselves. Charicles had one of his minions inform Macro of Tiberius' apparent passing and that they would wait for some time to make sure. He agreed, "That makes sense; we don't want to go through the confusion we went through yesterday. I'll wait here."

The physicians kept murmuring among themselves. Periodically one of them would go over and feel for a pulse and then would return to the group. After this went on a while, the group went to Macro and told them they were sure he was dead this time. "I'll inform the staff," Macro said and left the room.

He did as he said and then stood quietly, presumably there in case the staff needed anything from him. In truth, he wanted to see if anyone noticed that Geganius had left prematurely or that he was acting strangely. He was comforted to find that everyone was relieved to have Tiberius finally gone and unconcerned about the details. He lingered long enough to be positive there were no suspicions and then disappeared.

They met behind the agreed-upon tavern and then walked a short distance into the woods. Macro gave Geganius his money, thereby fulfilling Maximus' promise, and told him he should leave the area. He agreed, but not until the next morning – he mumbled something about celebrating tonight. As he led the way back to the road, Macro quietly pulled out his gladius, reached around his neck to choke him and silence any yells, and thrust the sword through the center of his back. With a fast twist of the blade, it was a quick and silent death. Macro retrieved the bag of coin, wiped the gladius on Geganius' sagum, threw some foliage over the body and went to meet Maximus at the tavern.

Macro reached across to Maximus with the bag, but Maximus said, "Keep it; I know this isn't about money for you and that you would have done this for me regardless. But I also know you have a sick child and that you could use that money for your family. I want you to have it."

Macro stared at Maximus, tossing the bag up and down in his hands for a few seconds. "Thank you, Maximus."

The two enjoyed a quiet drink together, at one point lifting their glasses in a silent toast to a job well done.

* * *

The news arrived in Rome and at the Duccius residence two days later. Proculus was not surprised, "Now the question is, who will be emperor? Tiberius named both Caligula and Gemellus. That cannot last long."

June offered, "Given the reputation Caligula has for cruelty and debauchery, I certainly hope its Gemellus. However, given that very nature, it seems likely that Caligula will strike first."

"I agree." After a thoughtful few seconds, he added, "and Caligula has the advantage in that he is here in Rome. He can gain the voice of the Senate before Gemellus reacts, if he moves quickly.

"On the other hand, it is not an easy thing to murder a person, and those two have been close to each other for years. It may take many months before one of them decides to act. We will have to wait and see."

* * *

The next week was one of the most frustrating of Proculus' life. He tried multiple times to gain an audience with Caligula, only to be thwarted by minions. Supposedly, they were preparing Caligula for the coronation, which usually occurred within a couple of weeks of the appointment and only after the Senate's confirmation. Proculus was not used to having people reject him, or worse ignore him. He spent hours trying to come up with some way to get

Caligula to accept an audience without alienating the new co-Caesar. In the end, he had to be patient.

Just when he was about to give up on the possibility of manipulating the situation, Caligula sent word that he would accept an audience. It was only two days until the coronation.

They met in private chambers, but there was a small retinue in attendance. So many attendees in fact, that Proculus could not possibly talk to Caligula about the succession. He would have to be circumspect until Caligula figured out what he was talking about and dismissed them.

"Congratulations! And thank you for seeing me Caligula, I know you are busy."

"Yes."

That's terse, but he will realize soon enough how important this is. "I am not sure what to call you at this point, are you Caesar?"

Caligula cocked his head oddly at Proculus. After a second, he answered the question as if it had no other meaning. "Yes, you can call me Caesar or Caligula. We will just have two Caesars."

Conveniently, right then, there was a lull in the presence of immediate attendants. "That is what I wanted to talk to you about." He lowered his voice just enough to appear secretive, "You know we cannot have two Caesars?"

Caligula stared at Proculus intently. His eyes narrowed and his jaw muscles were tightening and loosening in turn. He glanced around at others in the room. "Now is not the time Proculus, you should know that." Caligula said it with enough authority that it stopped Proculus. *I hope that was on purpose.* If there was going to be any conspiracy, nobody here could know about it. "You should come to the baths tonight so we can talk quietly." Proculus closed his eyes and shivered. Caligula laughed. "Don't worry Proculus, we won't have any special entertainers present. Please come by after the evening meal."

"I thank you for your time and consideration Caligula Caesar. I shall see you tonight." He gracefully left the room.

* * *

Caligula was in the same private baths they had used previously. As he had promised, the alcoves were empty and it appeared there were no attendants this evening. Proculus made his way into the bath and over to where Caligula was luxuriating.

"How are the preparations coming along?" Proculus asked.

"Well enough. It is mostly for the people. They want to see their new princeps taking office and they do love celebrations."

However, small talk was not Proculus' purpose. "The idea of having two princeps is what I want to talk with you about." He waited, expecting Caligula to say something, but when nothing seemed forthcoming, he continued, "You know that cannot last?"

"It occurred to me," Caligula responded, but his eyes narrowed and his forehead crinkled in a pained expression. "I always figured Tiberius would pick one of the two of us and not put us in this situation. But he did and we need to live with it."

"Not necessarily. I submit to you that Tiberius may have been testing you. He had to know that one of you would eventually emerge as the Caesar of Rome. Every time we have attempted to appoint multiple leaders, one has ascended. Perhaps Tiberius postulated that the one who figured out how to eliminate the other would be the rightful emperor."

Proculus' eyes tightened as he waited for that to sink in. "Caligula, we have an opportunity to do this legally and within the bounds of the Republican system. That way, the people would still have their precious republic, as well as their respect for you, and we would have the single leader that we need."

Caligula blinked a few times and the corners of his mouth turned up in a deviant smile. "How, exactly?"

"You know Macro, the head of the Praetorian Guard in Misenum?"

"Yes, I've met him. He's competent and well respected."

"Yes he is. He also spent a considerable amount of time with Tiberius and was present at the succession announcement." Proculus paused for effect, "More importantly, he is willing to make certain statements in front of the Senate to support you. He knows you are the better Caesar and he thinks that Tiberius knew that as well." This last was a stretch, but it might help Caligula if he knew Tiberius felt this way. "He's willing to say that Tiberius' mind had faltered at the end and that he had intended to name just you. The Senate does not want another civil war. With a little evidence, they will be willing to void Tiberius' appointment of Gemellus and grant the position to you and you alone.

"That way, we have followed the Republican way and the Senate has specifically chosen you to lead. Once that is done, you can handle Gemellus any way you want." *He may not like this.* "However, I would strongly recommend that you have Gemellus and his family executed. If you do not, you risk dissension from those who know that Tiberius left the Empire to both of you and who do not understand the consequences of divided leadership."

Caligula surprised him, "Of course, Proculus. If the Senate can confirm me, then the next logical step would be to have Gemellus executed. I'm not convinced that his entire family needs to be killed, but Gemellus... certainly."

"Then I would suggest that you convene a special session of the Senate before Gemellus arrives from Misenum. Then, you will be able to arrest him prior to his entering Rome. We do not want to make a scene out of the arrest, so it would be better in the outskirts. If you can get the Senate together, I can make sure Macro will be there.

"If you do not want to be the one to introduce this, I can talk to the Senate and tell them that Tiberius had confided in me that if there were to be a single Caesar, then it would have to be you. Then I can bring in Macro for support. That way, you are not directly involved at all."

"It is a good plan Proculus. If we do this, how many people will know?"

"Only you, me, and Macro. Macro is very loyal." He intentionally failed to mention Maximus.

"Yes, but to who or to what? Macro will need to be kept close from now on. I can't have him becoming disgruntled to the point that he uses this knowledge against me. I'll make him head of my Praetorian Guard."

Caligula continued, "You, though..." He reflected long enough that Proculus became nervous. "You will need to return to Antioch and concentrate your affairs there. I don't ever want to hear about any of this. If I have a hint that you aren't keeping this confidential, I won't hesitate to have you and your family, as well as Maximus and his talented daughter Curia killed."

Proculus' froze, his face ashen. *He knows about Curia!* Caligula smiled. "Good, you understand me."

"Yes," he said breathlessly.

"Then we are agreed?" Caligula asked.

Proculus swallowed in fear, but knew it was too late to change course. "Agreed," he said hesitantly.

"I'll let you know when the Senate will convene. I'll try to make it prior to Gemellus' arrival, but no guarantees... and, yes, I know it will be much more difficult if Gemellus is there to counter our arguments."

"Then I will let you relax. I have a short speech to prepare for the Senate. Hopefully I have a day, but it will be ready in any case."

"Good night Proculus."

* * *

The next afternoon Proculus received word from two messengers within minutes of each other. The first was that Gemellus was on his way to Rome and would arrive early that evening. As the messenger was leaving another arrived bearing word that the Senate would be meeting in late afternoon and that Proculus was invited to present. "This is going to be close," Proculus muttered aloud.

June was walking through the entrance. "What's that dear?"

He had to respond quickly, "Oh, I need to speak to the Senate again, this time at the confirmation of Caligula and Gemellus. Caligula is making his move, but Gemellus is on his way and if he can get here in time, then he can counter whatever Caligula is doing." It was better to stay close to the truth.

"Why would the Senate want you to speak at their confirmation?"

"I knew Tiberius and was with him when he wrote the original will. Also, Macro – you remember him? – was with Tiberius when he died and he wants my support with the Senate since he is not used to the politics."

"Hmm..." she muttered as she left the room.

As the hour approached, Proculus gathered his notes and made his way to the co-viria building. He took a circuitous route in order to find Maximus. He explained the situation and emphasized that Gemellus could not be allowed to reach the Senate. He also had him send a messenger to retrieve Macro who had arrived the night before. Macro would see Proculus' participation in this, but that could not be avoided.

Macro was on the steps of the Senate building when they arrived. *That messenger was fast.* Proculus walked right past him and into the building. Maximus stopped to explain the situation.

Proculus spent the next half hour talking to the Senate, explaining his relationship with Tiberius, and why he was there at the signing of the will. He also explained Tiberius' dilemma and that he really did not want to appoint two successors, but he also could not disappoint either of his grandchildren.

He knew Caligula was in the audience but he would stay silent through this because it had to be a Senate concern, not something he dictated. At the end, Proculus introduced Macro who was standing in the back with Maximus. Macro came forward. His steps were hesitant and he was perspiring as his eyes darted around the imposing structure. He began sheepishly, but warmed up after only a few sentences and his natural confidence as a leader in the Praetorian Guard emerged.

He glanced at Proculus a number of times during his speech and appeared to mimic the approach Proculus had taken with a background, his positions, and his daily interactions with Tiberius. He ended with a summary of why he was privy to information unavailable to others.

Proculus was impressed with how quickly Macro adapted to the Senate. It was a rare individual indeed who could overcome his fright of being in front of the rulers of the known world. *Macro is definitely too valuable to lose. I am glad Caligula will be keeping him close.*

Proculus saw Maximus motioning near the side entrance and went to him. "Gemellus is near," Maximus whispered.

"We cannot let him get into the Senate," Proculus said and immediately turned and left the building. Maximus continued to watch Macro, hoping that Proculus would return before he was finished.

Proculus "borrowed" one of the senator's carriages, explaining that it was an emergency and he would return it. He was able to reach Gemellus while he was still quite a ways from the Senate building. He stopped Gemellus' asking, "Were you aware the Senate is meeting?" Gemellus responded casually, "What are those pundits in the Senate doing now, arguing about the noise from all these horses and carriages in the streets of Rome."

"Actually, they seem to be reviewing Tiberius' death and his will."

Gemellus' hand went flat on his chest and he took a sharp intake of breath before freezing. He raised his voice. "Why would they be talking about that now, the confirmation hearing isn't for two days?"

He heard the sounds of the two boys stuffing boards between the carriage's back spokes.

"For… some reason, they are meeting early."

Gemellus exclaimed disdainfully, "Caligula!"

"Caligula is there. And there is something else Gemellus. Do you know a man named Macro?" *Anything to keep him busy.* As long as the Senate agreed to void the appointment of Gemellus as co-Princep, it did not matter if he found out that Proculus had anything to do with it.

Gemellus thought for a moment, still perplexed at the situation. "One of Tiberius' guards was named Macro."

"I think that is him. He is also at the Senate hearing, talking about Tiberius death."

"Then it is best I get there immediately!" The carriage leaped forward, almost knocking Proculus down. Then the board in the wheel caught the back of the carriage and tore through the spokes. The carriage listed to one side about twenty feet in front of Proculus and ground to a halt.

Proculus did not want to allow Gemellus to use his borrowed carriage to get to the Senate, so he disappeared around the corner, threw a few denarii to the boys, and climbed aboard for the ride back. His only hope was that he had delayed Gemellus enough.

* * *

Maximus heard Macro conclude his speech, but the praetorian looked around, apparently not knowing what to do next. Maximus had expected that Proculus would be here for final remarks, but he was nowhere to be seen. Maximus stepped forward. He motioned for Macro to step back and began recalling for the Senate the two civil wars Rome had suffered when they chose to appoint a triumvirate to lead the country. There had never been a successful appointment of multiple leaders of the Roman Empire. He purposefully used "Empire" even though it was frowned upon in public to make the point that it couldn't support multiple emperors.

He was even able to quote Augustus Caesar: 'A country divided by multiple rulers is a country at war with itself.'

He knew he had limited time, considering the approach of Gemellus. "This proposal does not come from Caligula, but from representatives of the Senate, the military, and the praetorian guard. We must, and I do mean must, void Tiberius' will with respect to Gemellus and appoint Caligula to be the one princep. He was the preferred appointee of Tiberius' and dividing this appointment is dangerous beyond measure. None of us wants to have another civil war. I leave it to this August body to debate quickly and take immediate action."

Maximus walked to the side of the room with Macro following behind. He stayed to listen for the senate's decision.

"What say you Caligula?" one of the senators asked, though Maximus couldn't make out which one.

Caligula stood and bowed his head in apparent supplication. "I did not expect this, but I'm glad of it. It was my understanding from Tiberius that he was going to appoint me instead of both of us, so I was as surprised as anyone when I heard that he had confirmed his will." Caligula took a deep breath. Maximus thought, *he had better be careful. The Senate has power over this appointment.*

"I do agree with what Proculus, Maximus, and, what was his name… Macro said. However, even though Maximus referred to us as an empire, it is still this body of senators, representing the people of Rome, who have control right now, as is appropriate. You should decide what you think is best for Rome. Is it best to have co-princeps reside over the Senate or a single princep to be Caesar, and if so, which one." He knew that they would not appoint Gemellus. He sat down.

A pause by the Senate and then, 'here here' by someone, quickly followed by applause. It appeared they had made their decision. Someone called for an immediate vote. It wasn't unanimous, but it was overwhelming and, Maximus knew, the few dissenters would be dealt with.

Gemellus entered the building with impeccable timing. The guards didn't hesitate when Caligula ordered him arrested. They had heard the exchange. Gemellus was dragged away screaming, "Caligula, you fiend, you know this is not what Tiberius wanted!"

Caligula's cheek twitched and there was humor in the creases of his eyes.

* * *

Caligula left Rome that evening to prepare for the grand entrance. It was traditional for the new Caesar to enter Rome after the Senate conferred the appointment. The people were ecstatic. They had disliked Tiberius and were frightened of the dual appointment because of the potential for civil war.

Proculus went home that evening exhausted.

June asked, "What happened dear?"

"Gemellus was too late. Caligula was appointed Caesar and Tiberius' will was voided with respect to Gemellus. He has been imprisoned. It seems likely that Caligula will have him executed.

"I am tired of Rome and want to return to Antioch. Let us leave this place; it only reminds me of why I resigned from the Senate." This seemed like good cover for his exhaustion and was mostly true. The tension had worn Proculus down and their success was anticlimactic. Mostly, he was in a surreal fog. It was one thing to have a grandiose, far-reaching plan like propositum, but another thing altogether to experience it.

What they were trying to do bordered on the impossible and sometimes it was all too much for him to handle. He could not let the others see that, especially Curia, but now he was alone with June and she did not know all of the plan's details. June brought him wine as he sat in the house's most comfortable chair. She smoothed a lock of hair out of his face and ran the back of her hand down his cheek, but said nothing.

When he felt recovered enough, he wrote a long letter to Saul explaining what had happened and asking him to return to Antioch. It was time for them to start the next phase.

* * *

The next day, at the end of March, Caligula entered Rome as if he was a conquering hero. The crowds loved him and cried "Our Baby" and "Our Star" and a few people even proclaimed "Our Lord" and "Our Savior." Caligula's head was high and he stood tall and erect as he rode the quadriga down the brick road to accept the vast powers of the Principate of the Roman Empire.

VII. Paul of Tarsus (37 AD – 39 AD)

"Go. Look, I send you out as lambs among wolves."

- The Book of Q

Saul arrived at the Antonius residence in time for the colloquium. June led him to the courtyard. He was hoping to avoid conversation, but she casually commented, "I am so glad you are here Saul. Proculus has been anxious about this get together for weeks." Saul remained silent, looking only towards the entrance of the courtyard.

It was early summer, the flowers were blooming, and there was a gentle breeze. Saul found Proculus and Maximus sitting at a small round table in the middle of the blooming foliage.

Proculus stood up and shook Saul's hand. "Welcome, Saul. You look well."

Saul bent to shake Maximus' hand and answered, "I've been in town long enough to rest."

He then turned and cocked his head at June, wondering why she was still there. Rebekah arrived with drinks and cheese bites for the group. June helped distribute them before they both departed.

Proculus said, "Let us begin." Saul sat down. "Saul, would you please give us a summary of what you have learned? I know we have exchanged letters, however you may have come to new conclusions in your recent travels and it would help to refresh all of us on the pertinent information."

"Sure," Saul began and then decided to compose himself and took a bite to eat and a drink. The others were equally introspective. Then Saul began, "The first half of my trip was exceptionally useful. I learned a great deal about the Essenes and about what hinders the spread of Judaism among the Gentiles. I have some very specific ideas about what we might change in order to make this work, but that can wait."

He looked directly at Proculus and continued, "I must say, Proculus, that the extent of your influence is impressive. Your name helped me multiple times, including in Jerusalem with the pillars - but you know about that from the letters - and also in Alexandria." Proculus smiled at this but said nothing.

Saul took another drink, looked down at the edge of the table and a grimace spread across his face. He recalled the difficult experience he had with John the Baptist.

When he and Daniel were traveling by the Dead Sea, they heard that John the Baptist was near. Saul had first heard of the man from the Thomasites who taught in aphorisms. One of their clipped sayings mentioned John the Baptist and the speaker later explained that John represented a modern shift into the earthly presence of the Kingdom of God.

When Saul heard that John was near, he changed directions to visit the man. He was practicing on the shore of the Dead Sea near a tanning camp called Qumran. Saul and Daniel joined roughly a hundred people who were there waiting for the baptizer. It was a quiet, solemn group of people. Within a half hour, a man came from the east wearing an outfit that appeared to be made of camel's hair. He had long grayish-black hair and a full beard of the same color. He seemed to be remote, almost aloof. The others didn't approach him as he walked quietly through the crowd. Instead, they moved aside to let him pass in a direct line towards the sea.

As John removed his Camel's hair coverings and entered the sea wearing a short undergarment and no shirt, the crowd seemed to arrange themselves into a rough line. There was little talking and no arguing about the order; it was as if everyone knew there place and they took it without debate. Saul wondered how they could be so organized without direction.

John took the first person into the water and quietly asked him a couple of questions. Saul couldn't hear what was asked or answered, but it must have been acceptable because John dunked the man under water and looked to the sky while praying. The man in the water didn't struggle at first, but John kept him there for a long time. When he started to move, John lifted him up and Saul could hear him say "Arise and enter the Kingdom of God."

Saul began to move towards the shoreline. He must not have understood the etiquette because the people looked at him oddly and murmured misgivings. Then John spoke in a loud voice, "Be gone the two of you. You are not of us. You are not ready for the Kingdom of God." Saul and Daniel looked up at the baptizer and saw him looking at them and pointing a finger back to the road that led away from Qumran. They were bewildered and Saul wondered how it could be that John knew anything about them from such a distance and without speaking with them at all.

John stepped towards them aggressively and spoke even louder, "Be gone I said. You are not of us and are not ready for the Kingdom of God. Leave us, at once." There wasn't much the two could do, so they slowly backed away, still facing John. When he turned to take the next man, they turned around and walked away.

Saul recovered from his reverie to find the two older men staring at him. He explained the experience with John the Baptist, ending with, "I want to visit him again on my next trip."

Proculus' head tilted and his eyes narrowed at Saul. "Saul, excuse me for interrupting, but have you not heard?"

"Heard what?"

"John the Baptist was put to death."

Saul stammered, "What, a… how, when?" He gave up trying to ask coherently.

"Herod Antipas had him executed. We are not exactly sure why, but it is Herod's right as the appointed king of Judea." Proculus examined Saul with sympathetic eyes. "All we know is that John was becoming increasingly popular with his preaching and baptisms. Herod came to believe that John was so popular that Jews would follow whatever he said and he saw troubles coming with Rome and wanted to make sure there was no chance of rebellion. Then John spoke out against Herod's marriage to Herodias because they were related. It was rumored that Herod had danced with Herodias and vowed to steal her from her husband, then went about doing so.

"I heard that John was imprisoned at Machaerus for a time and then was beheaded." Saul slumped into his chair. "I am sorry Saul; I did not know he meant so much to you."

"It isn't that I knew him, just that he was the only one to doubt me on my travels, so I wanted to prove myself. And now I'll never have that chance." Saul looked into the distance with his lips tight and downturned. "However, this practice of baptizing is something we ought to explore. He was the only one practicing it among the Jews and, for him, it symbolized entrance into the Kingdom of God, even though the people he baptized were supposed to already be righteous."

Proculus asked, "Do you mean to say that it was symbolic beyond the simple ceremony and was being recognized as something momentous?"

"Yes, exactly. Maybe we can use baptism with the Gentiles as a symbol of entering the church. We may also be able to use his death as a martyr to help spread the practice. That would give him recognition too."

* * *

Proculus liked Saul's quick recovery, and appreciated how he was able to turn it into something positive for the plan. "That is a good idea, Saul. We also have to consider the ramifications of Herod thinking we are close to a rebellion. It means we are nearer than we thought to our goal. We do not want actual rebellion, of course, but we want to have enough strife that we can convince the leaders in Jerusalem to let us openly proselytize."

There was a lull in the conversation. Proculus glanced at Maximus with a single raised eyebrow. Maximus said, "Well then, let me give a quick update."

Proculus interrupted, "Before you begin Maximus, I have one question for Saul." He turned and looked at Saul whose eyebrows raised in anticipation. "You mentioned the Judas followers in one letter and Daniel indicated you spent quite a while interacting with them, but I did not see any suggestions of helpful information from them. Did I miss something?"

Saul replied hesitantly, "No, not really. They have some fascinating and complex ideologies and I was hoping they would have something useful, but that didn't turn out to be the case. They are a fringe group and both Jew and Gentile have a difficult time accepting their beliefs. They also have this notion that only some people are capable of understanding their beliefs sufficiently to enter the Kingdom of God." He paused. Proculus could see doubt float across his face. "It just can't work for the majority of people, including most Gentiles."

"Very well," was all Proculus replied and then turned his attention back to Maximus.

Maximus began, "The situation in Rome is also progressing, roughly according to plan. We have successfully transitioned to a new emperor." Saul quickly looked at Maximus with narrowed eyes, but said nothing. "Caligula is now Caesar, and the Senate is concerned about Iudae but not enough to act. And finally, we have someone positioned in Rome to keep us informed of the situation and to provide aid if needed."

Saul's eyes tightened and his lips formed a straight line. "May I ask who this person is and how we know we can trust him?"

Proculus spoke up, looking intently at Saul. "You have not met her, but Curia is Maximus' daughter and is an incredibly capable young woman."

Saul's eyebrows went up as his head jerked back in surprise. "You mean to tell me that you put our future in the hands of a woman, and a young one at that? I'm, well, shocked that you would be willing to risk it." Proculus and Maximus stared at Saul with open disdain. "It's just that I've found women to be, umm, less than trustworthy, especially when it comes to making difficult decisions."

Proculus knew that many men felt this way, but it was not going to serve the plan for Saul to have a problem with Curia. They could not address his views of women here, but they could, at least, alleviate his fears. Proculus said, "Our future is not in her hands and she will not need to make any hard decisions. She is there as our eyes and ears in Rome and will inform us of events so that we can take steps if needed. And as far as trustworthiness, I would trust her with my life as I am sure Maximus would, so you need not worry." He tried to say it with a finality to put the issue to rest and hoped that Saul's attitude would not cause them problems in the future. At a minimum, he realized, they might have to figure out how to handle congregations with female leaders.

They took a break from talking and ate some of the delicious food the staff had provided. "We are now positioned well and are getting close to our goal. We each have much we must do, but most of it falls on you, Saul." Saul looked up and stopped chewing, but did not say anything. "You will need to take one more trip around some of the more obscure communities in the Eastern Empire. Specifically, you should go to smaller towns and cities that do not have an appreciable Jewish presence to practice preaching. That way if it does not go well, it does not have significant impact on the plan and you get a chance to find out what works and what does not.

"However, before you can do that, there is some planning that must happen. You need to come up with a list of talking points; ideas that you have for converting Gentiles to Judaism and for spreading the Essene way of life to other Jews."

Saul furrowed at that last statement. "Why would we care about spreading Essene ideas to other Jews?"

"Because the more that they believe in these new tenets the quicker it will spread and the easier it will be to convert Gentiles. Also, it will be good practice to deal with other Jews as that will happen when you formally start to proselytize."

Proculus continued with the original discussion. "You should also consider where you want to travel. That will help Maximus prepare the way for you. He should accompany you, at least initially. Some of your talking points may cause distress and we do not want you in any danger.

"Finally, Saul, I would like you to contemplate a mild change in identity. You still have a reputation as a Sadducee enforcer, which could hinder your ability to be allowed to speak. I think it is detrimental that you are from the Roman peninsula and I would not want to put your family in any kind of danger. You should not appear more Roman than Jewish. So perhaps you should name a home town that is closer to Judea; somewhere here in the eastern empire."

Saul objected, "How dangerous do you expect this to be? Is it really necessary to change my identity?"

"Necessary might be too strong of a word, but I would certainly advise it. Think about it and about what you would preach and we will get back together to discuss it. How long do you need?"

Saul's eyes flitted as he looked down. Proculus wanted to assume he was considering the question, but it seemed apparent he was distressed about the possible dangers. He decided to let Saul absorb that without more intervention. After a few moments, Saul looked up at Proculus and answered, "I'll need a few days."

* * *

It was over a week before the three of them could get together again. It was a dreary day, overcast and threatening rain. It was also early evening, so they took drinks in the reading room where they could all sit comfortably. Saul noticed that June sat with them this time, but he ignored her.

After they settled, Saul started the conversation. He leaned forward to speak and saw Proculus smile at him. "I've spent a great deal of time thinking about this. There are a number of minor points to make, but it comes down to three main ideas. There may be a fourth, but I don't know how to accomplish that one, at least not yet.

"The first is that there is a Kingdom of God and it is attainable, today. It isn't some incorporeal idea for the distant future, but is something people can experience in their lifetime. They just need to believe in the One True God and practice a righteous life."

He looked around to see how they were reacting and felt he had their attention. Nobody was asking questions so he continued. "The second is that Gentiles can become Jewish and that it doesn't require outlandish steps. I'll have to make the strict Judaic laws around this look archaic and unwarranted.

That won't be difficult because they are absurd to any Gentile who hears about them.

"Those two are obvious enough. The third is less so and will take some explaining. During my travels, there were two things the Romans specifically missed when it came to practicing Judaism. If we can bring these two things into Judaism, it will make it that much easier to accept for Gentiles. The first is that Judaism doesn't really have heroes, at least not in the way Romans think of heroes. We have Abraham, Moses, and other prophets, but they were average, everyday people who believed in God and were extraordinarily faithful. Some of the Essenes do see The Teacher as a hero; I even heard stories of him doing miracles, so it appears that Jews may need a hero as well. I propose that we elevate The Teacher to something more akin to a Roman hero. To do this, we need to give him a name; we can't continue to call him The Teacher."

He was expecting some kind of comment here, so he stopped. Proculus obliged, "Please continue Saul. What you have said so far is insightful, but I would like to hear the potential fourth point before commenting."

"This last one is more esoteric. It has to do with the fact that Romans tend to view the world, primarily, through imagery and for hundreds of years now the Jews have been restricted regarding images. For Jews, it is sacrilegious to worship imagery and some of them even refuse to have any in their households. To attempt to introduce imagery might alienate us from the majority of Jews. However, the Romans I spoke with had a difficult time recognizing a God they couldn't picture. Their belief system centers on images of Gods. It's a core difference between the two, and one that we may need to resolve. To get a majority of Romans to convert, we will have to introduce imagery to Judaism and that is very clearly against the Judaic laws and against what almost every Jew believes. It's also so abstruse that it will be difficult for Jews to accept a need for it." Then he added, as a comparison, "Unlike the Judaic restrictions on conversion, marriage, and eating, which everyone understands."

Saul leaned back in his chair. He had been so engaged and animated during his little talk that he found himself sitting on its edge, so he consciously tried to relax by reclining.

Proculus and June were both smiling at Saul appreciatively and Maximus was shaking his head. None of them spoke for a few seconds, so Saul finally asked, "What?"

June was the first to speak, "Saul, this is just so wonderful. You've done an outstanding job of analyzing what needs to happen and you were bold enough to come up with things that are counterintuitive, but nevertheless required. For me, that was remarkable."

Proculus added, "Yes Saul, exceptional and I agree with every point you made and I have to tell you that none of us had ever thought of this split around imagery, we will need to ponder that."

All three looked at Maximus to see what he would say. He stared intently as Saul for a moment, and then finally spoke, "Saul, I have to say: I've had doubts about you being able to do this. You seemed too hesitant to me and I wondered if you could break away from your strict religious beginnings. But what you have done here is no less than The Teacher's miracles you spoke of. It shows a true transformation and a very impressive one."

They fell into an awkward silence. Saul wasn't used to such compliments, especially from people like Proculus and Maximus.

Proculus finally spoke up, "You know, we had already talked about the possibility of giving a name to The Teacher. It was not to make him a hero exactly, but it was because we knew it would resonate with Gentiles more; they need a familiar figure. I did some research and found one that we might be able to use. It is a common enough name that it could have been his and yet is not common at all among Romans." He paused waiting to see how Saul reacted.

Saul replied tersely, "Well?"

He smiled. "The name is Jesus, and it means salvation or 'one who saves,' I think that describes what we are expecting out of the myth; saving the Jews… and Rome…"

Saul closed his eyes and leaned his head back. Proculus must have seen him because he stopped talking. Saul was trying out the name to see how it sounded. His lips kept forming *Jesus*. The others continued to wait silently.

After less than a minute, Saul opened his eyes. "I like it. It's a simple name with the kind of dignity we need and there was a Jesus mentioned in the Torah who was to be a successor to Moses. It fits well."

There was an uncomfortable silence until Saul realized Proculus was waiting for him to continue. "I also considered your suggestion that I change where I was from and my identity.

"First for a home town, I didn't want it to be too different than Tarus because I might mistakenly say it sometime and you had said you wanted it nearer to Jerusalem. But it can't be too close or the inhabitants would know me. So how about Tarsus? Its north of here and is a large enough place that I could have come from there and not be known by some of the townsfolk."

Maximus was the one who responded, which surprised Saul. "That's a good choice; the closer to the truth the better and that will be easy to remember. I also know a few people there who could corroborate any story we come up with."

Saul looked at Maximus strangely until Maximus nodded his head questioningly.

"It's just that you seem to know people everywhere."

Maximus smiled, "That's what I do," and he left it at that, leaving Saul contemplative until he finally shook his head and continued. "As far as a name change, it should also be similar to Saul and have an appropriate meaning. I like Paul. It means humble or small-one and I want to appear humble to people even as I am trying to change some core elements of their religion."

This time June spoke. "Are you sure it isn't too demeaning? Might you want a strong name, one that gets people's attention?"

Saul coughed as if trying to clear something distasteful from his mouth. "I thought about that, but we have to make The Teacher," he paused. "I mean Jesus, the strong one and not me." I should be meek and humble and just be spreading his word."

Proculus spoke up with finality the way only he could, "Saul, you should use whatever name you want. You are the one who will need to live with it. If Paul is the name you want, then so be it. We should all start calling you Paul now so that you can get used to it and we all need to try to use the name Jesus frequently as well."

After a pause in the conversation, Proculus continued, "Now that we are settled on names and places, there is one more thing you brought up in your letters, Paul," he smiled, "that we should discuss. You mentioned a few times about sayings and stories of Jesus that his followers all know, but nobody is writing them down."

Paul interrupted, "It wasn't 'nobody,' and there were a few writing some things down. But, predominantly, that's true."

Proculus continued, "In any case, it might be time we help them out by documenting some of this. We do not need to go into detail or come up with long, involved stories. However, getting Jesus' sayings into a written form could help us promote the idea and could eventually be a source for gospels if we need them.

"Paul, you should keep a notebook with you on this trip and write down the sayings and stories you hear. You probably should not do this in front of anyone; first because we do not want them knowing that it comes from you; and second, they may get upset with their aversion to the written word. Then, the next time we are together, we can form it into a small book, possibly even one that looks more like a diary, and you can then present it as coming from Nazarene communities."

Maximus and Paul both started and Paul's nose wrinkled at the mention of Nazarenes. Proculus continued, "It is a term I have heard people use when referring to the Essenes and can mean holy or separated, both apply. We could begin using it to differentiate the followers of... Jesus. Of course it is all one group, however, as we have already seen, a new identity can make a big difference."

Paul thought about that for a moment and then answered, "I don't really see what good it does to try to change their label without some fundamental shift." After a short pause, he added, "But we can use it on our travels to see how people react to it. It might make more sense to come up with a name after we have formal permission to proselytize. That might be enough of a shift to warrant such an change. Even if it is, I wonder about Nazarene as a name. It doesn't signify the difference with the Essenes enough." He looked around the group and saw them thinking about what he was saying.

They spent time together over the next couple of weeks discussing the possible routes Paul could take and decided that he and Maximus should head southwest to Libya for the winter. It would be warm enough there for them to continue traveling around the towns. Then they could head north to Macedonia. They would have to be more careful up there because there were some Jewish communities, but they decided going to both places would give Paul exposure to different cultures within the Roman Empire while he experimented with the new ideas.

* * *

It was two months before Maximus and Paul arrived in Libya, just in time for a fall storm. They landed in the port of Apollonia after a turbulent trip on a dilapidated ship. It was near the lush city of Cyrene that some called the Athens of Africa. The Greek city had become rich under Roman rule through the sale of silphium, an herb that induced abortion. It even had a small Jewish quarter that Maximus and Paul would avoid.

After a couple of days recovering, they went about obtaining supplies and two pack animals. During one of Maximus' scouting trips, he was fortunate enough to find a shop that sold him a map of the area. After examining it, they decided to initially head to a nearby town called Shahat. From there they would go south through a number of small towns to Meroe on the Nile river and then west along the Nile. Finally, they would return on a northern route, hopefully arriving in Carthage around springtime when they could obtain passage on a ship leaving for the European continent.

On the way to Shahat, Maximus asked, "Paul, have you decided what you will preach about?" Paul hesitated in answering and lowered his head in contemplation. Maximus scowled and added, "You know that Shahat might be a good place to start. It's small enough that a wandering preacher might go unnoticed and it's close enough to Cyrene that they might at least know about Judaism, so they might be more receptive."

Paul finally answered, "I've thought about it a great deal and I have some notes prepared, but I'll need some time to finalize them. I'm just so nervous, I don't know if I can do this."

Maximus shook his head. "That's the idea behind starting with these small, distant towns. If you have problems, it won't really change things much and you can learn and get better. Just treat it as practice and you'll do fine."

"I suppose," Paul replied, but he was still unsure. *Can I become this evangelical speaker Proculus needs? Who am I to think I could convince people to change their beliefs?*

* * *

When they entered the woody hill town of Shahat, they found that IT was so small that it didn't have public lodging. Maximus noted two roads into the town and realized it would be a substantial route if it weren't for the prominence of Cyrene. The locals were friendly enough that one of them offered to let the two stay at their house. They settled in and Maximus went to explore the town while Paul tried to work on what he would say.

Maximus and Proculus had previously talked about not helping Paul out on the first few speeches. They wanted him to see improvement over time and to build his confidence. If needed, they would find local people and pay them to applaud and encourage Paul when appropriate. Maximus was nervous not having local contacts, so he tried to befriend some residents. Unfortunately, the size of the town hindered his progress. *Maybe it is a good thing we don't need any paid supporters yet.*

He arrived back at the local's house to a modest meal, but found that Paul was still in the room they had prepared, working on his script. Maximus decided to take the meal to Paul and went to sit with him.

Upon entering the room, he saw Paul was sitting hunched over the table tapping a quill. As Maximus watched, Paul ran his hand through his hair, which explained the disheveled look. He hadn't wanted to listen to Paul practicing but maybe that was what he needed to get comfortable with this.

"What's wrong? Do you want me to listen to what you are going to say to see how it sounds?"

"That's just the problem, I can't settle on what to say. I want to reach people, but there's so much to choose from and I don't know what will work and what won't."

"Paul, settle down." Maximus added, with a slightly raised voice and tightened jaw, "You don't have to worry about that. Just try something here and we'll see if it works. Then try something else in the next town and we'll see how that works. Over time, you'll find what resonates with people, you'll see. You're trying too hard to get this perfect the first time and this is an exploratory trip, a time to learn. You don't have to be successful... yet."

Paul turned back to his notes, apparently without any more to say. Maximus left Paul's dinner on the table and walked out to eat with their hosts. If Paul didn't work through this, Maximus was going to have to get rough with him, or at least a lot sterner. Somehow, this had to work whether Paul had the courage for it or not.

* * *

Maximus ended up falling asleep in the common area of the house and awoke to first light. He looked in on Paul to find him bent over the table he had been working at the previous night, asleep. He decided to go out and stretch his legs while Paul slumbered. While exercising, it occurred to him that he could make this happen by arranging an audience. If Paul had a deadline, he would do what he had to. He had previously shown the kind of nerve and temperament they needed.

On the way back, he stopped every villager he found and told them a friend of his was giving a talk that they would all find interesting. They asked what it was about, but Maximus thought it would be better leaving it a surprise; it would be more mysterious that way and possibly would draw more people, not that there were that many to draw from.

When he arrived at the home where Paul was, he told him what he had done and that the talk was to be early that afternoon, just after the mid-day meal. Paul stood with his mouth hanging open for a time and stared at Maximus. Then he began pacing back and forth and mumbling his displeasure. Maximus left the room to Paul and his troubles.

* * *

They arrived in the central part of town, near the main well in early afternoon to find a couple dozen people there talking quietly. The residents were curious enough, it seemed, to see the unknown speaker that they had waited for him to arrive.

Paul began with what he determined was a clear and definitive statement, "I'm here to talk to you about the One True God." He immediately saw a few people turn to each other, speak a few words, and then smile or even laugh quietly. Their doubt made him even less confident, though he continued. "A God who has protected my nation for a thousand years. All these other Gods are just icons, symbols. They aren't true Gods and have no power. There is but one God and he is the God of Abraham and Isaac." People started walking away, shaking their heads and, in some cases, snickering. Paul continued for a short time, and then fell to mumbling and left.

* * *

Maximus shook his head, not because of Paul's ineptness, but because he had taken the wrong tact with these people.

He went into Paul's room later with an evening meal for both of them and ready to talk about what had happened. Paul looked distraught, but that wasn't a surprise. "Paul, it isn't as bad as you think. This is why we went to a small town, far from Iudea. All it means is that you found one method that won't work, at least not here."

Paul looked up at Maximus with swollen red eyes. Maximus realized this wasn't the time or place to make any suggestions. "Well, when you are ready to talk about what could be done differently, let me know." Then after a pause, he added, "We leave tomorrow, there's no point in staying here any longer."

"How can you expect me to go on after what happened here today?"

Maximus raised his voice and answered vehemently, "Oh, we will go on. We have a couple of years, at least, to improve on your ability to speak in public and to preach about your 'One True God,' One failure at the start of that means nothing. You may end up failing the first fifty times as long as you eventually learn how to make it work." Then he terminated the discussion with a commanding voice, "Eat your meal and get packed, we leave at first light," and he went to do the same.

* * *

The performance in the next town was equally disappointing. However in the third town, Paul tried something different, "Let me tell you a parable that our master, the son of man, told to his disciples." He saw that, this time, he seemed to have their attention. "Jesus said, 'look around you at all the trees and, in particular, at the fig tree. As they begin to leaf in the spring, you know that summer is near. There were signs of my coming to those who were observant. You should know that the reign of God is near. The heavens and the earth will pass away, but my words shall not. You must be on guard, for the great day will come suddenly and close in on you like a trap, if you are not prepared. So you must be on watch, and stand secure before the son of man.'

"You see, the son of man has been here on earth and has told us what we must do to enter the kingdom of heaven. We can all attain glorious entrance." Then Paul noticed someone trying to get his attention and he motioned for the woman to speak. She hesitantly asked, "What does it take?"

Paul was thrilled. This was the first time anyone had even spoken, let alone asked a question. He looked up to see Maximus near the back of the crowed, smiling. Maximus turned to a local, said a few words Paul couldn't hear and the local walked away.

Paul ignored the exchange and returned his attention to the woman. He attempted to explain righteous behavior, but it was more complex than she wanted and she lost interest. Paul shifted course and told another parable. After which, he went into the crowd answering questions and talking animatedly among the people. He was ecstatic the entire afternoon.

The next day Maximus sat him down and told him not to expect that response every time and that he would have to gauge and measure the audience and choose what to say based on their makeup. More importantly, he would have to observe, as his first parable suggested, and figure out what worked and what didn't with different types of people.

* * *

After almost thirty towns with varying degrees of success, they approached Meroe on the southern side of the great Nile River. Maximus decided they should stay there for a while, rest and send word to Proculus on how things were going. They would also plan their summer trip enough to allow them to inform Proculus of where they would be by autumn so that he could send word back. It wasn't the right town for practice, so Maximus asked Paul not to try any preaching there.

* * *

Paul didn't listen. He had had enough success that he wanted to try a more pluralistic crowd. One day after they had been in Meroe for just under two weeks, he went out to preach. He spoke to a few people quietly telling them to gather friends and family because he had something important to tell them.

After a crowd of almost fifty people gathered, he began by telling one of the parables from his collection. Before he could complete it, someone from the gathering yelled, "We've heard that before from some traveling Jew and he was much better at story telling. You said you had something important to say." The group around the antagonizing man laughed at Paul's discomfiture. The aggressiveness of the crowd made Paul uncomfortable, frightened even. He tried to continue, but now he had lost his composure and whatever he said lacked conviction.

Just then a man in the back of the crowd picked up a rock and was going to throw it at Paul when Maximus walked up behind him, placed a hand gently on the man's shoulder. "You don't want to do that." The man took one look at Maximus and dropped the clump. Maximus then walked to the front of the gathering and motioned for Paul to follow him. They both headed back to their rooms, thankful nothing more serious had happened.

* * *

Over the next few months, they made their way north back to the coast and to the sea port of Carthage. There they found word from Proculus waiting for them, but the news that was most important came from Curia. She was asking Maximus to return to Rome. Apparently, there had been several attempts on the emperor's life. Caligula's reign was in trouble.

VIII. The Living God (39 AD – 40 AD)

"A good man produces good things from his store of goods and treasures; And the evil man evil things."

- The Book of Q

"So Curia, why did I have to abandon Paul and come back to Rome?" Maximus asked before even greeting his only child. It had been a long and tiring trip and he wasn't at all sure he should have made it.

The edges of Curia's mouth turned down in a lingering grimace as her head shook slowly. "Well father, how much do you know about what has been happening with Caligula's reign?"

Maximus' eyes narrowed as he looked into her eyes, trying to see if she was being facetious. Curia's letter had been concerning, but it was hard to imagine what could have gone so wrong that he had to return and leave Paul practically alone and nearly helpless. He was happy to see her and she looked wonderful, but he was in no mood for antics.

"What you've told me in your letters and information I have gathered from my contacts. Obviously things aren't going well."

"Aren't going well? Aren't going well! His reign is an atrocity and we have to do something about it."

Maximus considered her emotions and realized he needed to understand her viewpoint better. "Why don't you start at the beginning, assume I don't know what has been happening and tell me everything."

After a sigh, she began, "I can't tell you everything, but let me give you some history so you see the difference." She composed her thoughts. "You know that the people hated Tiberius and were glad to have him gone. I mean, everyone knew, or thought they knew, that Caligula had Tiberius killed and then Gemellus as well, but they didn't care because of their hatred of Tiberius and all the profligacy.

"And Caligula proved to be insightful and reversed many of Tiberius' policies. For instance, he got rid of the treason trials that were gruesome at best. He brought back some of the games and seemed to be taking care of the people; taxing them less and providing bonuses to those who deserved it. He even seemed to be more moral than I expected when he banished the undesirables."

At that, Maximus raised both eyebrows in surprise. "What undesirables?"

Curia turned a slight pale pink. Her hesitation and the blushing tone of her cheeks was enough to tell Maximus what she meant by undesirables. He thought it odd that Caligula would try to appear so moral when he was clearly predisposed to the same behavior. With a slight chuckle, he shook his head dismissing the idea. "Never mind Curia, go ahead with your story."

"Anyway, this behavior went on for many months. The gladiator competitions advanced to some of their former glory and the people really loved Caligula, even as many of us wondered how he was paying for all of it.

"Then in October of that year, he had an attack that looked like parliamentary disease. He was bed-ridden for some time and I couldn't find anyone who would tell me how he was doing. I started to worry that he might not recover. The people were devastated about his illness. Thankfully, he did finally recover, after a number of months, and we saw him in public again. He was thinner and moved slower and he had a crazed look to him that wasn't there before.

"Then the changes began. He became paranoid of everyone around him except his sisters. Maximus, he had Macro put to death, can you believe it, Macro? Macro would have done anything for him, and did if the rumors are right."

Maximus tried to control his reaction to this. He hadn't heard from Macro for a long time. *Could he really be dead? Why haven't I heard?* Then a more frightening possibility occurred to him. *Does Caligula know of Macro's true allegiances?* If that were the case, then Maximus would have been arrested already.

Curia paused during Maximus' ponderings, but when he didn't say anything, she continued. "Then we heard all kinds of rumors about Caligula and his drinking and lavishness. He had his favorite horse brought into the palace and put into an indoor stable made of ivory and gold. There are rumors of sexual exploits even worse than Tiberius,' You know that he has three sisters, right? Well, people are saying that he prefers having sex with them instead of his wife or the consorts.

"He has ruined the country financially. His extravagant spending and bribes to keep people happy has drained what funds Rome had. He has started falsely accusing people of crimes in order to seize their property. He reinstituted taxes again, and heavily, even worse than Tiberius,' Taxing things like marriages that were never taxed before and auctioning gladiator's lives after a match. The people are sick of him and see Tiberius' reflection, only worse, and now there are plots in the Senate to have him killed."

Curia exhaled and seemed to deflate.

Maximus looked at her and smiled at the obvious relief on her face. He briefly wondered if she would be able to handle the stress of the responsibility he and Proculus were placing on her, but then he remembered just how young she was and how she had always taken on what was needed. He placed his hand gently on her shoulder. She would be fine and he was more proud of her than he thought possible.

"First things first, have you evaluated what we can do about the situation?"

Curia looked at him aghast for a number of seconds before finally replying. "What could we possibly do?"

You brought me back, so you must have thought I could do something. Maximus smiled gently. "Curia, you have to understand that we can do whatever we need to do to advance the plan. Rome, as it is, is dying. We are trying to bring about a more lasting government and society, kind of like the Phoenix; something reborn out of the ashes. There isn't a limit to what we can do if we have to. For instance, if Caligula has a strong right-hand-man, we can slip Caligula some poison that makes him sick and doesn't kill him. It would be best if we have an antidote, that way if the replacement doesn't work out, we can *cure* Caligula. We could also try to work with his sisters; they probably have a lot of influence over him. We could organize a minor rebellion or at least a large rally of people objecting to what he is doing. We could have some of the military leaders threaten him to get him to act more reasonably. We could start by having someone he trusts talk to him honestly, even bluntly.

"Of course there are challenges with each of these, so we must consider each carefully. We also have to gather more information. Now, I'm tired and need to get some rest. Tomorrow I'll contact my network, see what happened with Macro, and try to figure out what options we have."

* * *

The next day Maximus met with some people who had known Macro. It turned out that Caligula had caught Macro talking about how disgusting Caligula's acts were and Caligula had him executed for it. Macro's death was disturbing, but he should have known better.

He then went to talk to praetorians who could tell him about the situation. After Macro's death, it was difficult to get any of them to open up, but when he got four of them together drinking over a game of dice, their tongues loosened and he finally heard the story from the inside.

It turned out that Curia wasn't far off. After five hours of bantering and drinking, Aulus, the quietest of the group, spoke up. "You know Maximus; there will be an attempt on Caligula's life tonight." The group looked at him in surprise. Maximus wondered why he hadn't spoken up before.

"How do you know this Aulus, and when and how will it take place?"

"I heard some senators talking about it. I'm not sure if they knew I was within range. They are becoming less prudent, so they might not have cared. Anyway, it's supposed to be tonight after dinner. Caligula usually uses the bathes then and he frequently doesn't take guards in with him. They plan to use a short sword hidden under some towels. That was all I heard."

Caligula can't die, not yet. "Thank you for the information. If you'll excuse me, I need to leave. I have an appointment that I mustn't miss." He looked around the group, "and none of you should worry about what we have talked about. Nobody will hear a word from me. Understood?"

He received nods and quietly left the establishment. Once outside he picked up his pace. He headed straight towards the palace and told the guards to introduce him to Caligula and to indicate that he was a good friend of Proculus', Maximus knew that Caligula had taken to Proculus and, more importantly, had trusted him. Maybe that would be enough to get an audience. Just in case, his hand slowly found his sword and tightened around the grip.

Surprisingly, the guard came back and said that Caligula would see him. However, he did relieve Maximus of his gladius.

When he was brought to Caligula's chambers, there were half-a-dozen attendants within range. Audience or not, Maximus would have to proceed.

Caligula saw Maximus looking at the attendants. "Don't worry about them, their tongues were cut out many years ago and we never allowed them to learn how to write, so they won't be able to tell about anything that happens here."

Maximus looked up at Caligula. *Where is the crazed look Curia mentioned?* In fact, it was Maximus who felt somewhat crazed. "What's on your mind

Maximus? You know I knew of your father when I was a boy. I respected him and Proculus has proven his worth. Hopefully you are of the same ilk."

"Proculus and I are good friends and trust each other with our very lives, Caesar." When Caligula didn't say anything, he continued, "The reason I'm here is that I heard some disturbing news today and felt you should be told immediately." Caligula still sat there not saying anything, so Maximus went on. "There will be an attempt on your life tonight after your last meal when you take your bath."

Maximus stared at Caligula waiting for him to say something to this revelation. Caligula languidly looked up at Maximus with constricted pupils, "There have been attempts on my life already. You don't get into my position by being nice or by letting people plot against you." *He's on opium. That's why he isn't crazed!* Caligula continued, "You see those guards at the door and in the alcove behind me? They have their bows trained on you right now and are ready to loose their arrows at the slightest indication of a threat or if I just want to see you die."

Maximus felt a shiver, but kept his composure. "I understand that, but my information indicated that you only maintain one or two of these guards during your bath and the people attempting this are well supported and know what they are doing." He saw blurred agreement in Caligula's nod. "Caesar, I would like to be in attendance and stop this assassination attempt before it happens. We should cut off the head, or heads, of whoever attempts it and post them on spears outside the entrance where everyone can see what happens to traitors."

Caligula laughed, "That's good Maximus, however, you should be aware that I will have one extra guard with an arrow aimed directly at you."

"That is expected, Caesar. Just keep that guard out of site. The last thing we want to do is scare these quislings away. We need to make an example out of them."

Caligula's eyes closed slowly, a clear sign he was fading. "Guard, call my sister Drusilla, I want to see her. Maximus, I'm tired and am going to lie down, come back at sunset and we will execute your plan. All will be arranged."

Maximus nodded. "Yes Caesar, I will be ready," and then he backed out of the chamber with his eyes downcast. He was marveling at Caligula being so obvious about lying down with his sister. *How long will he live if he is so blatant about this?* Maybe they would have to accelerate their plans.

* * *

The sun set and Maximus arrived at the personal baths of Caligula Caesar and was immediately made to enter and to keep his gladius.

When he entered the baths, he briefly looked at Caligula, but neither one said anything. After a short pause, he looked around the room to evaluate his tactical position. He chose a location near the emperor to protect him, but hidden by some curtains. After he was happy with the positioning, he nodded to Caligula and then took a deep breath to relax and wait for the would-be assailant. He noticed that the one guard, normally at the door, was gone. It made things easier for the traitors, but any change in routine might alert them. He stood quietly and prepared himself by tightening various muscles to get the blood flowing and ready for action.

It was almost half-an-hour later when Maximus heard a quiet thud outside the baths. Caligula didn't seem to notice or was concealing the fact well with eyes closed and head resting on a folded towel.

The assassin made his way around the side of the bath quietly, taking the expected route. He passed the pillar next to a soundless Maximus. As he continued beyond the curtain, Maximus stepped out, reached around the man with his gladius in his right hand and quickly brought the sword across the man's throat while pushing his back forward with his left hand. He cut the throat cleanly and quietly laid the man out on the floor just as he saw a flicker of movement at the door. He ran, wanting to catch anyone else involved in the conspiracy and saw another man sprinting away. He quickly threw his gladius. It traveled swiftly between the two and sank deep into the man's right lung. He went down with a cry of pain. When Maximus was able to reach him, he took the sword and stabbed him through the heart to finish the job. *We don't need him naming others and Caligula on a killing spree*, he justified.

When he turned the body over, he saw that it was none other than Caligula's brother in law, Marcus Aemilius Lepidus.

A number of guards came out of hiding along with Caligula in a robe. They hadn't been taking any chances, but for some reason they left the killing to Maximus. *Maybe it was a test.*

This time when Maximus looked at Caligula, he could see the wild-looking eyes that Curia had mentioned. He seemed to be fighting to be in command of himself. Caligula looked away from the sight of his brother-in-law dead on the floor, barely in control, and spoke with an unneeded intensity. "Well done Maximus, I praise you for your devotion and your decisiveness. Now, take these two lumps of merda and do as you said. Maybe that will send the right message to my enemies."

Maximus found some guards to help post the decapitated heads. Then he left to clean up and get home to his daughter. He couldn't tell her what he had done, but he could report that there was another attempt to assassinate Caligula. They needed to move quickly if they were going to get Caligula to incite the Jews. He would have to write a serious letter to Proculus telling him of the situation and asking him to come to Rome. It was time for the next phase of their project.

* * *

Proculus and June had been enjoying their time together while waiting to hear from Paul or Maximus. There wasn't much Proculus could accomplish in terms of the plan other than to start instilling some of the ideas into the local Jewish community in preparation for Paul's return. The news so far from Maximus about Paul's progress was not good, but they were hopeful that he could still become the proselytizer they needed and the fact that he was continuing was encouraging. Practice would improve his skills.

They were invited to a *covenant of circumcision*, the Jewish ritual called *brit milah* for a boy who was now eight days old. The family was a progressive one and had invited Proculus as well even though he wasn't Jewish. He and June would have to stay at the back of the small building, but receiving an invitation at all was an honor. The community had a lot of respect for Shimon and Dara, the boy's parents, and Proculus was hoping they would be active in the church based on The Teacher, Jesus. If so, then this boy may be one of the first born into the new church, even if it did not exist quite yet.

They arrived early enough to watch the gathering of family and friends. The women were off in a side room and one of the attendants invited June to go there as well. Apparently, they were not to be present for the actual ceremony. Proculus was conveniently positioned to be able to see into the side chamber where Dara was holding the child and waiting for everyone to settle. Once she was happy with the attendance, she began passing the baby among the relatives, starting with the women. Once the women were complete, the last of them passed the curious boy through the open door and to one of his uncles who continued the process with other relatives in the room.

The one man who did not receive him was the godfather or guardian. Instead, the Rabbi took the boy and placed him in a special chair. "It is in sitting in the chair of Elijah that this boy is allowed redemption through Abraham and God." Then the rabbi picked up the boy and handed him to the godfather. Proculus recognized this man, but could not recall his name. As the man laid the boy on a soft blanket and prepared to hold him for the ceremony, the Rabbi spoke again, "The brit milah is an ancient tradition of our people. This is where we recognize and confirm that this boy is a Jew and abides by the covenant of Abraham. No longer will he be a child of Adam, alone and wondering, lost and drifting. He will recognize the One True God and will live in the community and may one day obtain the kingdom of heaven.

"Shimon, do you wish the boy to be governed by the covenant and do you entrust the ceremony to the mohel?"

"Yes Rabbi, I do."

"And what name is it that you wish the boy to be called?"

"I wish him to be called Theophorus."

Looking now at Theophorus, the Rabbi continued, "You shall be called Theophorus bar Shimon."

The mohel then began his operation of removing the foreskin. While the baby wailed, the crowd and the Rabbi remained silent, probably not wanting to startle the man. Afterwards the godfather picked up Theophorus and turned to Shimon. "Whom would you honor as the first guest to hold the newest member of our community?"

Shimon turned and looked directly at Proculus. "Proculus Antonius, would you please come forward?"

He gasped in shock. To allow him here at all was an honor, but to break with tradition and permit a non-Jew to be the first person to hold his son after the naming was, well, inconceivable. Nevertheless, Proculus strode up to the front of the crowd as if he had expected just this honor and gently took Theophorus in his hands. During the entire time, the Rabbi was muttering prayers and blessings on the boy. Once he completed the blessings, the crowd said in unison, "Just as he has entered the covenant, so may he enter Torah, the wedding canopy, and good deeds."

It was interesting to Proculus that they should tie a lifetime of ceremonies into such a simple statement and should consider it so critical that it was the first community-spoken words that a child hears. It did set the tone for what was expected of parents and of members of the community.

The crowd then began to break up and talk in small groups. Shimon came to Proculus and accepted Theophorus from him. "Thank you Shimon, you have bestowed a great honor on me."

"One you deserve Senator. Remember that it was you and June who introduced Dara and me and who helped us through difficult times." He then quieted his voice conspiratorially, "I would have had June in here as well, but the Rabbi would not allow it. He was reluctant to have you here, but then he didn't know I was going to name you or he might have refused." Proculus wondered at the subtle influences he had on people at times. *I would not have thought my minor assistance would have meant so much to them.*

He and June were still talking animatedly about the naming and circumcision ceremony when they arrived home an hour later. They both agreed that Shimon and Dara were just the kind of couple they needed in the new church of Jesus.

When they arrived home, there was a parchment waiting there from Maximus. In it, he outlined the situation in Rome and the assassination attempts on Caligula. It appeared that Caligula might not last much longer and they still needed certain things from him. Proculus quickly made the decision to return to Rome. June wasn't happy and mentioned accompanying him, but before Proculus could object, she decided against it. Proculus was relieved because he needed to focus on Caligula during this trip.

* * *

When Proculus made it to Rome he found Maximus in control of the situation, but he wanted to hear the details from Curia, both to give her the impression she was the true eyes-on-Rome and to get her to take ownership. The three of them met in private, but Proculus had warned Maximus to stay quiet and let Curia talk.

"Curia, tell me what has been happening."

Curia quickly glanced at her father who sat straight-faced. She turned back to Proculus and described what had happened in the past. However, she provided more detail and included specific examples.

"Well done." His brows furrowed as he leaned forward slightly. He knew this next question might be sensitive, depending on how much Curia knew. "And what do you think of this last attempt on Caligula's life?"

Curia looked immediately at her father and then she looked down as her face flushed.

"They came close to succeeding and Caligula's response was barbaric. However, I have to admit that it appears to have quelled the dissenters, at least for the time being."

Proculus leaned forward and garnered the rapt attention of his co-conspirators. "The time has come for us to take the next step. We have to get Caligula to offend the Jewish state in some way without launching an outright war with them. Any suggestions?" Proculus had his own opinions on the matter.

They sat for a couple of minutes. Proculus knew Maximus was so inclined towards war and violence that it was difficult for him to propose solutions that did not involve open fighting. Curia, on the other hand, was more of a politician. She was the one to speak up. "There seems to be two obvious ways you could do this." She paused, "The first would be to repeal some of the special liberties the Jews have. The most significant one might be the seventh-year tax relief that they enjoy. The second would be to do something that violates their religion." Her eyes floated to something in the distance as her brows furrowed. "And I don't mean something Caligula does, but something that he requires Jews to do. They do not care what Caligula or the Romans do."

Proculus smiled at how close she was. "Your second idea is something I have been pondering. It is hard to see how requiring the tax would upset Jerusalem enough, especially when I am referring to the high council. However, requiring them to worship a Roman God or even to worship an idol might work. Saul, I mean Paul, said something about the Jews disallowing images in their religion. How that sets them apart from other religions.

"Let me meet with Caligula and see what his temperament is like. Maybe something more specific will present itself."

* * *

It took Proculus three days to obtain an audience with Caligula. He had assumed it would take much longer, but his support during the transition to Caesar and Maximus' recent actions probably aided in the expedited approval and in the invitation to share dinner.

His first impression when entering the dining room was of tension. There were multiple guards and all appeared to be ready to strike instantly. There were also bowmen on the balcony with arrows strung. The attendant sat Proculus at the opposite end of the table from Caligula. He noticed that Caligula had started eating without him. *Rude, but that is his prerogative.* He spent his time waiting for Caligula to speak first by observing a clearly deteriorating man. Caligula's eyes were darting around the room in apparent suspicion of someone or everyone, his hands shaking mildly, his face drawn and haggard, and he had drooping skin under his eyes.

As he was scrutinizing the condition of this leader-of-men, a servant came in and placed some food and a glass of wine at Proculus' place, but still Caligula said nothing. Proculus began to eat in silence.

Then Caligula's sister, Agrippina, came in and walked straight to the side of Caesar. She was wearing a thin palla, with her right shoulder exposed, that did little to hide her sublime figure. Instantly, Caligula appeared to waken as he became animated and talked quietly with his sister. She then looked up at Proculus and smiled a smile that Proculus could not interpret until he saw Caligula's face. He then realized that the Princep was seeking approval from his sister to trust this ex-senator from Antioch. Proculus made a concerted effort to look senatorial and, more importantly, trustworthy. Then Agrippina's palla fell a hands-width, exposing her right breast. She did nothing to cover it as both men's eyes fell immediately to her full bosom. Proculus stirred awkwardly and Caligula's right hand made its way slowly up Agrippina's legs and under her palla. The hint of Caligula's hand pleasuring her under the palla brought enticing and disturbing images to mind. Proculus felt his loins react as he stared at the outline of Caligula's hand. Her eyes closed softly and her lips parted as a soft moan escaped. Then she opened her eyes ever so slightly and spoke to Caligula, "Little boots, you are making our guest uncomfortable." She stood more erect and discreetly replaced the palla across her breast. Caligula withdrew his hand and began licking his fingers.

Agrippina sashayed amiably to Proculus and held out her hand to be kissed. *Apparently, I passed.*

After a perfunctory greeting she excused herself and Caligula began the conversation, "My dear Proculus, how is the situation in Iudea?" Oddly, Caligula seemed more like his normal self now. Proculus wondered at the quick and reasonless switch.

"The province does well Caesar. They are flourishing under the peace that Rome brings to all vassal states." He hesitated for effect and Caligula looked up expectantly. "However, they still do not seem to accept that they are Roman. I know we allow a people's culture and religion to continue when we absorb their nation. However, the Jews take it too far and expect us to bend to their wills. Sometimes it frustrates the governors you have in place."

"Maybe it is time we teach them a lesson."

"How do you mean, Caesar?" Proculus asked, hoping Caligula did not mean war.

"I could send a legion of men there to put them in their place."

"You know better than I, Caesar." Proculus' eyes squinted in concentration, and then he added, "but it seems to me that the legions are better served on our frontiers or expanding the Empire."

"Well Proculus, what would you suggest?"

"I do not know yet Caesar, but that is one of the reasons I am here in Rome. I would like to explore possible ideas with some of the senators."

"That vappa! They couldn't solve a problem if the Gods demanded it. They aren't like the senators of the old Republic who took responsibility for their posts and tried to better Rome."

The mention of Gods gave Proculus an opening. "You know Caesar, the problem is that the Jews do not seem to recognize your greatness. You are descended from Gods. The people now recognize Julius Caesar as divine and you yourself had Tiberius Caesar proclaimed a deity. The Jews just do not understand this because they do not recognize any God but their own and they will not worship idols." He hoped Caligula would take the hint, as it would be better if the actual idea were his.

Caligula stared at his food and then finally spoke. "It might be an interesting lesson, or experiment if you will, to require each temple in the Empire to place a bust of Julius or Tiberius in their temple and worship it as they pass."

Proculus tried to look thoughtful as if he was evaluating the idea for the first time. "Yes, that might get the idea across Caesar and if they refused, you would have justification for punishment."

"Perhaps, but it still doesn't seem sufficient. They need to recognize me, not my dead ancestors. I could require a bust of me instead, but they wouldn't worship it because I'm not a God." This time Caligula was the one to pause. "But why not? I've done miraculous things for Rome, much more than Tiberius did and he was made a God."

What miraculous things? He said nothing and kept a straight face. This was the time to let Caligula speculate.

"It's time I am declared a God, by the people and the Senate." He smiled at the notion and his shoulders became more erect as his chin rose. He slapped the table and chuckled.

"But Caesar, nobody has ever declared a living person a God."

"So! I am Caesar of Rome. I can do whatever I like. Nobody ever declared a leader of Rome a God until the Senate declared Julius Caesar to be one. What's the difference if I'm alive or dead? The fact that I'm Caesar means I am a God."

Proculus thought it was going too far and that it might infuriate Rome as well as Jerusalem. However, it would certainly do the latter, especially if he required worship of his bust.

Over the next pair of months, Proculus saw Caligula appear in public dressed as various Gods, with Jupiter his favorite. The living God also ordered temples built to worship him and some busts in existing temples replaced with his own.

Then the proclamation came. Caligula had declared that his bust must be placed in every temple in the Republic and worshipped by each entering person. It was time to return to Antioch to see how the eastern empire would take the news.

* * *

When he told Maximus and Curia he needed to leave, they were both exceedingly disturbed. His eyebrows came together questioning their reaction. They both looked at each other and back at Proculus. Maximus finally spoke up. "We were about to tell you that Curia and Quintus are going to be married and we were hoping you would be here for the ceremony."

Proculus looked back and forth between the two as a smile slowly spread across his face. He finally said "Congratulations!" and embraced Curia. "When are you planning to have the ceremony?"

Curia looked at her father. When he did not reply, she answered, "Not until the fall sometime. We haven't chosen a specific date yet and you know how important the date is."

"Oh," he said sadly, "there is no way I can stay that long. The situation is developing too quickly. Maybe I could come back by then, but I cannot be sure." He hesitated, thinking of an alternative. "What if you take a trip to Antioch in the spring as husband and wife and June and I will entertain you and show you the splendor of Antioch and Iudea?"

Curia looked again at her father, who nodded slightly. "I'd love to, but let me speak with Quintus before I say for sure. When will you be leaving Rome?"

"Within a couple of weeks, I want to renew some old acquaintances and see the reaction here in Rome to Caesar's proclamation." He turned to Maximus, "By next spring it will likely be time for Paul to return to Antioch. We can all get together for planning. Could you accompany Curia and Quintus?"

"Of course, assuming he agrees to go. If not, Curia and I may need to make the trip anyway." Maximus hesitated and looked directly into Proculus' eyes. "I think she should be there."

Proculus squinted at Curia. *Are you mature enough to become critical to this team?* Curia did not waiver from Proculus' stare or offer any opinion on her father's suggestion. *He is probably right.* "I agree," he said and was rewarded with dancing eyes and raised cheekbones from Curia.

* * *

Proculus arrived back in Antioch to mayhem. The church there was outraged at Caligula's proclamation and rebellion was on everyone's lips. He was hoping Jerusalem was experiencing an equally negative reaction, though rebellion could be a problem.

Two weeks after his arrival in Antioch, he found out that Caligula was not going to wait for Jerusalem to act. The Living God had sent Legate Petronius with three legions of soldiers to quell any resistance in Iudea and force the Jews to raise the statue of Caligula in their temple. Proculus knew enough about Petronius. He was an honorable and decisive general who would not favor such action but would follow orders. Consequently, he dispatched a messenger with instructions to find Petronius' army and deliver a message to the Legate. It pleaded for him to delay any action against the Jews with the promise that Proculus would attempt to resolve the situation peacefully.

The messenger returned seven days later with Petronius' reply. He had said that no ex-senator was going to influence his actions. However, he wanted Proculus to know that he had already decided to combine his forces at Ptolemais and remain there through the winter. That gave Proculus seven to eight months.

* * *

The next spring, Curia and Quinn were the last to arrive for the meeting they had planned in Antioch. Paul had been at Proculus' residence for two weeks when the newlyweds arrived. They relaxed and enjoyed each other's company and the sights of Antioch for a few days before Proculus had June take Quinn out for a tour of some more interesting buildings in the area. The intent was to get enough time for the other four to talk and work out plans without him interrupting or suspecting them. Proculus had quietly explained to Curia the limitations of what Paul knew and why and how sensitive he was to his mission parameters.

Proculus noticed that Paul sat away from Curia and seemed to be uncomfortable with her. He decided to ignore it for the time being.

"First, let us each provide an update of the situation. Maximus, will you start with a report on the strategic situation between Rome and Judea?"

"Of course," he began and after a moment's hesitation, continued, "The situation is precarious, at best. Petronius is still camped at Ptolemais and is ready to move on Jerusalem. He's hesitating because he's a good man and believes this action is wrong. Something will have to change to avert war. The Jews, in my opinion, can ignore Caligula's claim of Godhood, but they will not accept an idol in their temple.

"There are also thousands of Jews going to Ptolemais to try to plead with Petronius to not use force against the Jewish people. I heard that he told them he had to do what Caligula ordered even if that meant force and then asked if they would go to war over a simple statue. They apparently told him that the statue was a violation of their beliefs and they would lie down and let Petronius cut their throats before allowing the statue into the temple. I don't yet know what Petronius will do."

He glanced at the branches behind Proculus. "There's still a lot of unrest and we are at immediate risk of isolated incidents of violence. Rome has a considerable number of troops in the area already, but they aren't on alert and aren't planning any immediate action. If the requirement to worship Caesar's statue is rescinded, then they will be pulled out of the area as they are needed elsewhere."

Proculus waited a moment to see if Maximus was done. He smiled at the terse summary. "Curia, what's the situation in Rome?"

Her eyes darted around the three men before she replied. "People are growing restless again. The last assassination attempt and the display of heads made people stop for a while, but I think the attempts will start again soon. Caligula has had a number of senators put to death and, if they are threatened with death anyway, they might as well try to have him killed. My guess is that we have six months, maybe a year, before there is a successful assassination."

Proculus noticed Curia's succinctness. It was not like her to be so concise. *Is she nervous or just trying to follow her father's lead?*

Proculus summarized, "So we have successfully upset Jerusalem without causing open conflict. It seems we are poised to approach the council for permission to aggressively convert Gentiles." He then turned to look directly at Paul who was staring at Curia. "Paul?" When he did not answer, Proculus raised his voice, "Paul?"

With obvious effort, he pulled his questioning attention away from the girl. "Yes, um, Proculus?"

"Do you think you are ready to approach the council?"

"Maybe…" He looked at Proculus keenly. "It seems to me that we should go to Jerusalem with a success and with something, well tangible, to offer. Maybe if we work with the church here a while and then can take examples of successful conversions to Jerusalem it would help. If possible, we might even try to take an offering to them."

Proculus said, "You know, Barnabas has talked about coming here to Antioch and working with us for a while. Maybe we should take him up on his offer and make use of his knowledge and contacts. He could help us figure out what kind of offering would work and could be a witness to our successes."

"Yes, that could help a great deal."

"Then I shall write to him with an invitation to come and stay. We should try to accomplish all of this within the next year at most while Caligula is still alive. If we get some other emperor, then the attitude in Jerusalem may shift and we will have lost our opportunity. Curia, your job is to keep Caligula alive for one more year. We will need Maximus here to help prepare people in Jerusalem and to aid Paul when he is there asking for the council's blessing."

Paul looked at Maximus with an open grimace, "Why would he need to be there?"

Proculus ignored the question and changed the subject, "Paul, we should also talk about what you found on your trip and what ideas worked well. Maybe we have time to adjust some of the message before going to Jerusalem."

Paul leaned back in his chair and took a couple of minutes. "I struggled with that on the way here and could use help. At first, it was very difficult, but that was my style and nervousness as much as the message." He glanced at Maximus to see him smile. "After a while, I overcame that and was able to present the message in various ways to try to figure out what worked and what didn't. The problem I'm having is that there wasn't any consistency. The same message would work in one community and fail in the next. I couldn't see any specific pattern that would allow me to adjust the message to the audience.

"The other thing of note, and one that I did notice that was consistent, was that it was clear very early in the talk whether I would be successful. I could tell you within seconds of starting the speech if it would go well. And I don't think it was the speech or the delivery; it was something in the audience."

Proculus said, "Some questions come to mind. What was the makeup of the audience in the towns? How many were women versus men? What were the age variations? How pluralistic was the town? What was the split between Jew and Gentile? If you can remember whether there was any pattern in any of these groups, it might help."

Paul considered the questions. "I don't remember any patterns around age and almost none of these towns were ethnically mixed. There were variations in men versus women, but I can't tell you if one or the other predominating was where I was successful. The split between Jew and Gentile might be interesting to explore. It's difficult to remember if this was true everywhere, but the places

I was the most successful definitely had Jewish and even Essene presence and the ones that were outright failures were specifically non-Jewish communities."

"Well, we may have to ponder this for a while. I am not sure we can have Jewish presence everywhere you will need to preach. What about your comment that you could tell early whether it would be successful. What did you observe that told you that?"

He reflected, "Nods, smiles, little gestures that they understood, even friendly faces."

Proculus stared into the distance. After a few moments, he was surprised to hear Curia speak up and then he immediately looked at Paul for his reaction.

"We could plant a few people in the crowd for some of these, to elicit a positive response. We wouldn't have to do it forever, just until you built up a positive reputation so that people would know what to..."

Paul was shaking his head before Curia's idea was completed. He interrupted, "I don't like the idea of manipulating people like this. The message and what it means to them should be enough."

Proculus wanted to agree with Curia, but he could see that Paul was objecting just to object and decided to table the idea. He did not want Paul thinking the other three were taking sides against him. "We can all contemplate the problem and Curia's suggestion. We have time since we will not be going to Jerusalem for a number of months, at least."

The meeting started to breakup when Paul interrupted them, "Um, there's one more thing to discuss. At your suggestion, Proculus, I took notes on the various sayings and parables that I heard from the Essenes during my travels and have compiled them into a journal." He handed the journal to Proculus. "I'm calling it *The Book of Q*. I guess the idea is that it might one day be the source for a more comprehensive document on Jesus. It isn't much yet and it will probably improve over time, but it's a start."

Proculus asked, "Why Q?"

"For *Quod*, since it is used to indicate the main point."

"I see."

Paul asked, "One question I had was whether or not we want to make copies of it?"

"I do not think we should yet. Feel free to show it to people who will not be adverse to the written form, but keeping one copy makes it mysterious, even if it does increase the risk of losing it. Just be careful with it. It could prove to be quite valuable." He browsed a few pages and then looked up, "Can I ask why you wrote it in Aramaic? Don't you use Greek in your travels?"

"Yes, normally it's Greek. I've found that most of the larger towns use Greek as their language of business and, even in the smaller towns, I was able to find translators for the local language. However, Aramaic is the language The Teacher would have used for a journal and is the language these sayings were developed in. Also, we wanted to keep it somewhat private and having it in a foreign tongue would facilitate that." He added, "And, as you say, it makes it more mysterious."

* * *

The spring and early summer were unusually hot and tempers rose. The situation with Caligula, Petronius, and the Jews became even more dire. Proculus decided to write to King Agrippa, who was the ostensible king of Iudea, and who was friends with Caligula.

> *Salutations my Dear Herod:*
> *I hope you and Cypros are well and that Marcus is maturing. I know he will one day make a great king, just as his father has.*
> *As you are aware, the situation between the Roman Republic, with Caligula Caesar's recent proclamation, and the Iudean people is precarious. Though Iudea is officially a member state of Rome and must abide by her laws, they constitute a proud people with a long history of religious devotion. They have ignored the religious beliefs of Rome and in particular the god-like proclivities of the Caesars.*
> *However, they will not abide images of a foreign god in their temples and you, of all people, know this. We must convince Caligula Caesar to rescind the proclamation or to offer Iudea an alternative method of adherence that will not violate their beliefs. The only alternative is war and these people will not survive a conflict with Rome.*
> *I implore you to speak to Caligula on behalf of the Iudean people and to convince him that the province is loyal to the Republic, but would serve the Republic better if they were left to their own religious beliefs.*
> *Sincerely, your friend, Proculus Laronius Antonius.*

The results of the letter and of Proculus' own efforts were convoluted. As Proculus heard, Agrippa held an extravagant banquet for Caligula to gain favor. It was so beyond his means that it impressed Caligula immensely. He told Agrippa he could have anything he wanted, assuming he would ask for land or some title. Agrippa obsequiously told Caligula there was nothing he needed. Caligula insisted and so he said that he did not need anything but that the people of Iudea needed to be able to worship their own way and that included not having statues in their temple and he humbly asked that Caligula call back Petronius.

Caligula was openly upset, but with so many people present and with his insistence that Agrippa get something in return for the overgenerous party, he had little choice. He wrote to Petronius telling him to discontinue the campaign. It seemed as if all was settled.

Meanwhile, Petronius had written to Caligula explaining how obdurate the Jewish people were and asking for confirmation of his orders to install the statue by any means necessary. The two tabellae crossed in transit.

Caligula received the message from Petronius and was overwrought that the Jews were trying to tell him, a God, what he could and couldn't do. He wrote again to Petronius rescinding his previous orders and telling him to deal with the Jews any way he had to, but to get that statue erected in the temple.

However, before Petronius received the second letter, he received others from people close to Caligula and from members of the Senate telling him not to proceed and that the situation in Rome was volatile. Proculus received a final message from Petronius indicating that he would continue negotiations with the Jews long enough to require him to stay camped for the next winter. If the situation in Rome was not resolved by spring, then he would have to march on Jerusalem.

IX. Permission (41 AD)

"If you enter a town and they receive you, eat what is set before you. Pay attention to the sick and say to them. 'God's kingdom has come near to you.'"

- The Book of Q

"You know Proculus, I heard something the other day that gave me an idea," Paul began. He had been working with the church in Antioch for almost five months and had become a leader and frequent speaker. He was becoming quite adept at presenting the word of God. "A man, who is new to the church, referred to Agrippa as the anointed one. I've heard it before, but it hadn't struck me how wrong it is. Agrippa is a false king, placed there by Rome. He wasn't the king referred to in the old documents. The last rightful leader of the Jewish people was The Teacher. He was of the line of Zadok, which is required to be the High Priest. Those in place since then have all been imposters. I wonder if we shouldn't be applying the 'anointed one' moniker to The Teacher. "We could call him Jesus the Christ."

"I like the sound of that Paul, but have the Jews not named other leaders Christ in the past without it having substantial import? It never lasted, if I recall correctly."

"Yes, that's true, but I have another idea that might make this one resonate with people." He considered how to introduce the idea. "If you recall a while back, you said that we should come up with a new name as we diverge from strictly Essene teachings. I didn't agree with it then, but I've come to recognize the potential. We've experimented with a number of names like "Jesusites", but none of them sounded right. Then, when I had this idea the other day about calling The Teacher Jesus the Christ, what followed was using the name Christians.

"It marks us as true believers of the Jewish anointed one and links us irrevocably with them while separating us from any particular sect." When Proculus didn't immediately say anything, he added, "What do you think?"

"Hmm, I do like the idea, but it is a significant change and an important one. Let me mention it to June and a few other people who would need to support it."

"Thanks Proculus." After a pause he added, "You should know that Barnabas and I have already talked about this and we both support the idea."

Proculus looked at him oddly, "You and Barnabas have become quite close?"

"He is a good man, a man of God, and a supporter of what we are trying to do."

"Just how much have you told him about what we are doing?"

Paul stammered, "He doesn't know everything. Just that we want to convert the Gentiles to Judaism and to an Essene brand of it. He believes the more people who become Jewish the better and he doesn't seem to care about the formal restrictions."

"Yes, let us keep it that way. We do not need any more people knowing details of the plan."

Paul wondered why the secrecy they felt was so important. *What we are doing is a good thing, why don't they share the idea with everyone?* But he kept quiet; it was something those two were adamant about and Paul wasn't going to change their minds.

* * *

That winter two events precipitated the intended trip to Jerusalem. The first was that Curia finally lost the battle to keep Caligula alive. In January he was assassinated by Cassius Chaerea and two other praetorian guards. As Curia told Proculus in a letter, Caligula had taken to making fun of Cassius because he was somewhat effeminate. Members of the Senate made use of this and convinced him, along with the other guards, to murder Caesar. Some guards had tried to rescue Caligula, but were too late and were themselves slain by the assassins. Cassius went on to murder the emperor's wife, daughter, and his one living sister. It was apparent that Cassius was trying to wipe out the entire imperial family.

Curia went on to explain that only Claudius, Caligula's uncle, remained alive and the Senate had immediately appointed him as the new Caesar. She would have suspected Claudius of instigating the assassination, but Claudius had fled the scene and gone into hiding until Cassius and his small band had finally been caught and killed. She added, almost as an afterward, that some thought Herod Agrippa had something to do with orchestrating Caligula's death. Proculus decided it might possibly be true since Caligula had become so dangerous to Iudea. However, Caligula had appointed Agrippa King of Iudea and Agrippa felt allegiance.

This could only mean that Petronius would abandon his mission and they might lose their leverage with Jerusalem. They did not know a lot about Claudius, but Curia indicated he was a reasonable person without any of the insanity displayed by the last two Caesars. However, he was uxorious and had displayed some affliction that caused his head and hands to shake and him to drool at times.

The second event was in early spring. There was a mystic in Antioch named Agabus. He had what he called powerful visions. Everyone knew he used mushrooms, that only he seemed to be able to obtain, to induce them. Quite a few members of the community respected Agabus and believed his dreams had meaning.

Agabus came into the congregation one day in an obvious prophetic state after having eaten some of the psilocybin fungus. He was ranting unintelligible words, though they seemed vaguely familiar to the brethren. Then he looked up and proclaimed loudly and clearly, "There shall be a grave famine among our people, many shall suffer, all must prepare." Then he went back to the unintelligible rants and ran out of the church.

Paul was present and told Proculus of the prediction. They agreed it wasn't a hard prediction to make given the combination of the recent lack of planting when the Jews were trying to convince Petronius not to force Jerusalem to worship Caligula, and the fact that next year was a sabbatical year.

Even though Proculus doubted the supernatural origin of Agabus' dreams, they recognized in it the opportunity to take something tangible to the council. They gathered the church and implored everyone to help raise funds in relief of Jerusalem, even though Jerusalem was not yet suffering. Proculus spoke at the event and offered to contribute some funds to help. So convinced were the Christians of Agabus' predictions that the church was able to raise a sizable sum.

It was time to return to Jerusalem. They had a momentous vision to tell of, examples of conversions to proclaim, and funds to provide in relief. They also had the recent dangers of Caligula Caesar and of Petronius' mission to use as argument that something had to be done to better position Jerusalem within the Roman Empire.

* * *

Maximus went with Paul and took two other men with military background. Barnabas went as well to help support Paul in his efforts with the council. Paul complained that the military escort was excessive, but relented when Maximus told him he had wanted many more men, but would have to obtain them in Jerusalem instead. Maximus had one man travel ahead to make sure the road was clear and then he and the other soldier traveled behind Paul and Barnabas along the road to Jerusalem.

They arrived at Ptolemais to stay the night and Paul went to the local Essene group. He had been working with them for some time as they agreed with his stance that Judaism should be spread to the Gentiles. Philip, one of their leaders and an evangelist, took them in, as Paul knew he would. He showed them the new building they used for gatherings. Above the front door was a sign reading:

The Church of Jesus
Enter the Kingdom of God

Paul was elated to see the word spreading, though if he had known they were doing this he might have suggested "The Church of Jesus the Christ" or "The Christian Church of Ptolemais", but he didn't want to complain about such a notable achievement.

That evening when Maximus and his cohorts were away in the city somewhere, Paul asked Philip, "We are traveling to Jerusalem to talk to Cephas and the council to try and get formal permission to proselytize the Gentiles. Would you be willing to come and support us in this endeavor?"

"Of course Paul, I would consider it my honor. In fact, Noam is here as well, you remember him, he believes as we do and I'm sure he'll want to accompany us."

"The more support we show the better."

As easy as that the party became seven. Seven men would enter Jerusalem seeking a change in the council's position, a change that might alter the direction of Judaism and of the Roman Empire, which was the extent of the known world to these men.

Maximus came back later that evening and told Paul and Philip that the three soldiers had found accommodations. Paul pulled Maximus aside. "It's good that you are lodging elsewhere. These men make Philip nervous."

Maximus looked at Paul and simply replied, "Good night."

"Wait, Maximus. You should know that Philip and Noam will be traveling with us to Jerusalem. Also, they cannot be ready until the morning of the day after tomorrow."

Maximus' eyes narrowed at the news, but his only reply was a terse, "Understood," and he left.

* * *

When they got close to the revered city, the three military men broke off and entered the city separately. Paul was thankful for that; the last thing he wanted was to look like he was entering Jerusalem by force. They settled into an inn late at night planning to approach the council in the temple the next day. Maximus and his men were nowhere to be seen, but Paul knew one of them was probably watching them regardless.

Paul got up early the next morning and went to the temple. He wanted to see it before the confrontation and to confirm that the leaders would be there later in the day. On the way, he met the Roman Trophimus, the Ephesian who had converted to Judaism and was a supporter of Paul's efforts. Paul asked, "I'm on my way to the temple, would you walk with me?"

"Of course, Paul."

They spoke of the coming plans and Trophimus was ecstatic that the day was here.

They went through the Court of Gentiles, past which no Gentile was ever allowed. As they approached the temple grounds Trophimus stopped. There was a sign in Latin and Greek warning them that entering was risking execution. Paul decided this would be a clear statement that these practices were archaic and unwarranted and asked Trophimus to follow him into the temple grounds. Trophimus hesitated, but followed another dozen steps and then became too afraid and withdrew.

Paul smiled, "Don't be troubled, Trophimus, we'll get these rules changed and then you'll be able to enter the Temple."

* * *

That afternoon, Paul, Barnabas, and the other brethren went to see the council. Cephas and James were both present. They had been informed of Paul's arrival.

"Cephas, James, it has been many years."

Cephas answered with a welcoming smile, "Yes Paul, it has. My friends call me Peter and so should you." Some of the council looked at Peter oddly, almost grimacing. Paul sighed in relief at the positive start and smiled along with the rest of his companions. He nodded his head towards Peter in appreciation and began.

"As you know, it has been thirteen years since my vision on the road to Damascus and my forsaking the Sadducees. In all that time, I have been traveling among both Jews and Gentiles and working with communities to bring people to the Kingdom of God. We stand before you with gifts from the churches in Antioch and Ptolemais. There has been a prediction by Agabus that there will be a great famine and these gifts are meant to relieve the future suffering."

The council said nothing to this, so Paul continued with the real intent of his visit. He summarized his thirteen years of work with the Gentiles, emphasizing the work God had accomplished through him.

At the end of this monologue, James finally spoke up. "God is truly glorious and his works wonderful." He looked down, frowning. "There are many Jews, both here and spread out among the gentiles, who are zealous about the laws of our people and they've heard about you forsaking Moses, saying that men don't need to be circumcised, women don't need to walk or dress properly, and that our eating requirements are not important.

"Before we will consider what you have to say, you must show us that you still believe in Judaism and our laws. There are four men who have taken a vow of consecration. Perform the ceremony with these four men and pay their expenses and you will have proven to us that you are not against us."

Paul squinted as he looked at the panel of men. There was no reason he couldn't do this since it wasn't the vow that was wrong or even the laws themselves. It was just that people shouldn't have to follow some of the more archaic laws to become Jewish. He bowed to the council. "I will do as you ask and will return to this council in seven days when the consecration is complete."

* * *

The seven days were almost done and Paul was walking with the four vow-takers when a small group of men approached. The apparent leader walked up to Paul. "You are Paul of Tarsus." Paul could see the anger in the man's rigid stance and narrowed eyes. "Yes," he said hesitantly.

The man grabbed Paul's shirt, but turned toward the onlookers. "Men of Judea, this is the man who teaches the blasphemers everywhere that our ways are wrong. He besmirches the Law of Moses and he's brought Greeks into the temple grounds defiling the holy place."

The four men tried to help Paul, but others pushed them back. One of the attackers cried, "Remove him from the temple. We cannot do as we must on sacred ground. Paul was then dragged out of the temple, where Maximus and seven other Romans in full military regalia stood. "What is going on here?" Maximus bellowed. "What has this man done that he should be beaten by you?" He received confusing and conflicting answers by those in the crowd. "Let me speak with him," and he pulled Paul away from his assailants.

When they were separated sufficiently, Paul said, "Let me speak to them, I want them to understand that I'm not against Judaism."

Maximus hesitated and then said, "If you must, but be careful to not antagonize them and we aren't leaving until we know you're safe." One of the soldiers found a crate that was nearby and set it down for Paul to stand on.

He spoke to them in Hebrew. "Listen to me faithful Jews. I am a Jew from Tarsus and I have studied at the Pharisaic school. You think what I preach is against Judaism, but it is not. I was just as zealous as you are about the laws. The laws of our people aren't destructive. They are just antiquated and are preventing the spread of Judaism to other people. We have a chance to bring many thousands into the Kingdom of God. You must see that righteousness is not defined by ceremony, but by a person's beliefs and actions. These gentiles are not evil simply because they aren't circumcised or because they eat improperly prepared foods."

He looked around the crowd and saw some accepting looks. The original attackers were still scowling, but they were also glancing at the soldiers standing there. He went on to tell of his vision.

At that point the original group had dispersed and the crowd was welcoming Paul's word. He was content; it would appear that he had stopped the crowd with words and not with force.

* * *

The next day the council invited Paul back to the temple. He was worried about another encounter with the anti-Christians until Trophimus informed him that the council had ordered them to disband.

When Paul and his compatriots entered the council chambers, Peter spoke, "Paul, you have proven that you still believe in our laws and you have brought us this great gift. What is it you ask of us?"

"For thirteen years I have been traveling, listening and learning. I believe that Jerusalem is in great danger from Rome and that our people may be destroyed by tyrannical rulers who call themselves Gods. I fear for our race and our religion. So far, we've been fortunate, but this monster called Caligula came close to causing open war. We don't know Claudius, but he is related to Tiberius and Caligula, so he can't be much better."

"And what is it you would have us do about that?"

"If we were to convert many more Romans to Judaism, they would be more accepting of our beliefs and less likely to demand that we do something against those beliefs. It is righteous to convert people to Judaism and save them from their pagan ways. Nothing bad can come of converting the Gentiles to Judaism and there is every possibility that it could save us.

"I ask you for formal permission to proselytize the Gentiles."

James spoke up, "Why do you need our permission for this? You have been doing it for some time now and anyone can attempt to convert the Gentiles, they don't need our permission."

"Yes, but we won't be successful unless we stop requiring them to follow the old laws. Those laws are not wrong or destructive, but they are no longer needed. Having your permission would lend credence to my endeavors and more communities would be willing to listen to what I have to say. I could also work in Judea and the surrounding areas.

"I'm only asking that you consider removing the requirement that Gentiles be circumcised and you allow them to continue to eat their traditional foods and for them to share meals with Jews. I know this feels like it violates what you believe, but is there any reason, any good reason, to disallow this? Does it hurt you in any way? Just possibly, this may bring many thousands of people to God. I implore you; consider what Judaism could gain by this."

After a short pause while the council stared at Paul, Peter answered, "We will consider what you have said and will have an answer for you within the week. You have to understand, Paul, this is not an easy thing you ask of us. It goes against what we have been taught and what we believe, but we have seen the benefits of your teachings, so we understand the value as well. We will consider this carefully."

* * *

The next five days were the longest in Paul's life. He paced and fumed, slept little and ate less. His heart seemed to be racing all the time and he couldn't settle down. It all came down to this one decision by a group of men with only a superficial understanding of what could be accomplished. Paul had no idea what he would do if they said no. Barnabas was an empathetic man and tried to comfort Paul, but it had little effect. Finally, a courier came from the council with a parchment for Paul. Since they were being impersonal by not inviting him back to the temple, he assumed it was bad news and was immediately dejected. He couldn't even bring himself to read it and instead handed it to Barnabas. Then he went and sat down on a wooden chair and put his head in his hands. Barnabas began to read it in silence and a smile spread across his wide face. He read the letter aloud to Paul; it was a letter of introduction for Paul and gave him authorization to spread the word to Gentiles, with the council's blessings. It was implied that they wouldn't object to Gentiles who weren't circumcised and who continued to eat their own foods.

After thirteen years, he had succeeded. He started to rise, but with the release of the tension of the last week and the elation at having succeeded, he dropped back into his seat and openly wept.

* * *

Four days later word reached Proculus of the success of the mission. He was overwhelmed with relief, immense satisfaction, and a total sense of accomplishment. June was standing next to him and watched the emotions play across his face. He placed his hands lightly on the sides of her face and, with watery eyes and a single tear tracing a path down his cheek he bent and kissed her forehead gently.

PART TWO

Proselytizing

X. Paul's First Mission (42 AD – 46 AD)

"Jesus said to his disciples…
How fortunate are the poor; they have God's kingdom.
How fortunate are the hungry; they will be fed.
How fortunate are those who are crying; they will laugh."
  - The Book of Q (Revised)

"Proculus, we must make some changes to The Book of Q," Paul said thoughtfully. He had been working in Antioch, and the surrounding area, for six months since the council gave them permission to proselytize the Gentiles. The community of followers of The Teacher had grown tremendously with hundreds of new members and many of the surrounding towns expanding their membership. Some were even using the name of Jesus the Christ or calling themselves Christian.

Proculus raised a single eyebrow. "Why do you say that?"

"Because these are old sayings of The Teacher and don't reflect some of the new philosophies and they don't even mention the name Jesus. We need to insert Jesus' name some places and add some new ideas."

"Just be careful not to change too much too fast or your constituents may dissent."

Paul began to walk away when Proculus stopped him. "Paul, there is something else we need to discuss."

"Yes?"

"I received a letter today from Cephas. He is very impressed with what you have accomplished in such a short time and has asked for permission to come and work with the brethren here in Antioch for an extended period."

A cross between a sigh and grunt escaped Paul's lips before he closed them in a tight frown. He glanced at the ground near his feet for a few seconds before replying. "Why wouldn't he write to me with such a request?"

"I agree it is unusual. Possibly he does not want to threaten you or your position here and probably thought the request might have more success coming from me."

"Still, it's very inappropriate." Then he squared his shoulders and added, "He should know he can't threaten my position here."

"Of course," Proculus replied. *He may do just that.*

"Well, let him come if he wants. We can use all the help we can get and he was one of the pillars of the Essenes in Jerusalem, even if many didn't know it." Paul hesitated as if he wanted to say something else and then turned and walked out the door. On the other side of the entrance, he glanced back. "You know he's going by Peter now, right?" and then he left.

Sometimes Proculus wondered if Paul understood how big of a shift they were causing. Antioch, and not Jerusalem, might end up being the center for Christianity. *If Peter realizes that, it may be part of the reason he is coming.* Proculus watched Paul walking away. *Peter taking over the church here would free Paul for traveling.* It was something Proculus would have to consider, carefully.

* * *

Proculus was not surprised when Peter arrived and informed him that he had found a Jewish patron with a room to share. He immediately began working with the local Christian communities and showed every sign of unwavering support for Paul.

After almost three months working with the local church, Peter went to Proculus and Paul and said he had some ideas to discuss. Proculus invited them into the reading room and asked June to join them. She understood Jewish thinking much better than he did and he valued her opinion, especially when dealing with these men.

"Well Peter, you brought us together, what is on your mind?"

Peter looked at Paul, "First, I'd like to say that you have accomplished extraordinary things here in Judea. Your name has become both respected and feared. There are many that think what you are doing is violating basic Jewish tenets. However, my feeling is that what you are doing is giving Judaism a way to grow. To break free of its beginnings and embrace the world."

"Uh, thank you."

Peter's mouth tightened and his forehead crinkled in concentration. "However, it seems to me that it's still too tied to Jerusalem and won't thrive beyond the borders of Judea." He stopped and looked at the three others in turn expecting comment, but received none. "You see, with Jerusalem at the center, and with it being the location of the Second Temple, the religion just can't sustain itself far away. It takes too long to travel and too many wouldn't be able to worship." He looked around again.

June obliged, "What do you propose Peter?"

"We should establish temples in every town." Then after another pause, "I mean every reasonably-sized town." He became more animated and excited, leaning forward and gesticulating, "Picture a place to actually worship and possibly a rabbi, or priest, to lead them, in every community. They would all be self-supporting and self-propagating, kind of like the spread of the Greek city-state. We could eventually organize it like a government where the local priest would report to a regional presbyter who could report to some head of the church back in Jerusalem, or maybe even here in Antioch." He wound down at that point, looking at the others expectantly.

Proculus was barely breathing as the others sat silent. *Astounding. His concept of merging Roman or Greek hierarchical government with Judaism is almost identical to the plan.*

Paul broke the silence. "Peter, you know that there would be an enormous outcry in Jerusalem if we were to do this. One of their most sacred tenets is the sanctity of the Temple. It's the one symbol the Jewish people accept and even revere. Also, synagogues already exist, how do you plan to turn these into temples?"

"It's true that there would be an outcry, which is why we would have to start away from Judea. Paul, you could do it on your travels and it would take a long time for the news to reach Jerusalem. By then, it would be too late, especially if it were successful." Peter then lowered his head.

Proculus stepped in, "Peter, you have obviously considered this carefully. I personally think it is an excellent idea if we can make it happen without completely alienating the leaders in Jerusalem and the orthodox Jewish population."

"It's quite possible, as long as we don't flaunt it to them or even tell them directly. They won't believe it's happening at first and by the time they decide what to do about it, the temples will be too prevalent."

June interjected, "I too think it's a very good idea. However, the key to the power in Jerusalem isn't the building, but the symbol it represents. It's the one symbol, the one image allowed in all of Judaism. For this to work, you will have to come up with a symbol equally as powerful; something that will draw people to it and bring them to worship at these new remote temples." After a few moments of additional pondering, she added, "Maybe that's how you turn the synagogues into temples; by providing an image or symbol for them to worship there."

Proculus looked at his wife with the corner of his lips turned up in an appreciative smile. *She always gets right to the critical point.*

The two Christians looked at her while she was speaking. Then they hunched over, apparently considering her proposal.

Paul spoke up, "The other possibility is to introduce baptisms by the local," he looked at Peter, "priest. If they performed the ceremony in the synagogue, it would be like it was becoming something sacred. It doesn't replace the need for a symbol, but it could help with the transition."

The silence grew. After an uncomfortable few minutes, Proculus decided to change the subject. "While you are all here, we should discuss Paul's trip." Looking at Paul, he asked, "Have you thought about where you are going to go?"

"Yes. Barnabas wants to go with me and he has contacts and friends on Cyprus, so we should start there. It being an island, they haven't experienced the changes we have seen here and there are enough Gentiles, so it would be a good representative community. We would probably work on Cyprus for a while and then take a ship north to the Galatian mainland. There are a number of communities there that are primarily Gentile with a small Jewish presence."

"That sounds fine. Do you know when you would start?"

"I need to wait for the spring winds, so six weeks, maybe two months at the most."

"Excellent. Then I will write to Maximus in Rome and ask him to meet you in Salamis. He should be able to get there in time."

Paul's eyes narrowed, but he said nothing.

* * *

Just under two months later Paul and Barnabas found themselves in Seleucia, coincidentally at the same dock where Proculus, Maximus, and June had departed for Rome years ago. They obtained passage for Salamis on a small trade ship, but had to wait two days for the departure.

There wasn't anyone at the dock to meet them in Salamis, but then no one knew exactly when they were to arrive, so it wasn't a surprise. Barnabas led Paul to the house of his uncle, Reuben. Reuben's wife had passed away years ago and his children had families of their own, so he had plenty of room and enjoyed the company.

With Reuben's help as a local leader of the church, they arranged to speak in the synagogue in Salamis on the next Sabbath. In the meantime, Reuben introduced them to a number of families who were knowledgeable of The Teacher, which enabled the two travelers to gain some support for their ideas prior to a full gathering of the congregation.

On Sabbath, they entered the synagogue to a crowd of people. Paul observed mixed feelings from the group. Some were smiling and showing acceptance of the two Christians even before they spoke, but others appeared ambivalent and a few looked almost hostile. Paul went to the front of the room. *This might become interesting.* He spoke quietly with the elders and then mounted a small platform.

"My name is Paul ben Aharon of Tarsus." Barnabas had stayed at the back of the room with Reuben, so Paul didn't bother to introduce him. "I come to you today as a follower of Jesus the Christ; you may know him as The Teacher of Righteousness. His word is spreading through the Roman Empire and Jerusalem has granted us permission to extend his teachings to the Gentiles." He hoped that was a bold start, especially the use of 'Jesus the Christ' so early. He saw that some in the crowd appeared receptive, so he continued with more confidence.

"Jesus, the Son of Man, understood and taught us that the Kingdom of God is available to us all, Jew and Gentile alike, and it is ours for the taking. Why would God limit it to Jews when all of Mankind is his children?

"To show you the magnificence of Jesus' teachings, I have a story to tell you."

> *One time a Jewish lawyer decided to test Jesus. "Teacher," he asked, "what must I do to enter the Kingdom of God?" "How do you read what is written?" asked Jesus. The man answered: "Love the One True God with your heart, your soul, all your strength, and your entire mind; and, love your neighbor as yourself." "You are correct," Jesus replied. "Do this and you will live." But the lawyer wanted to justify himself, so he asked Jesus, "And who is my neighbor?" In reply, Jesus said, "A man was traveling from Jerusalem to Jericho, when robbers found him. They stripped him of his clothes, beat him, took all his belongings and money and left, leaving him half dead with no clothes. A church leader happened to pass by, and when he saw the man, he passed by on the other side. Also, a Levite, when he came to the place on the road and saw him, passed by on the other side. But a Samaritan*

came to where the man was; and when he saw him, he took pity.
He walked straight to him, bandaged his wounds, and clothed
him with his own clothes. Then he put the man on his own
donkey, took him to the nearest inn, and took care of him. The
next day he gave money to the innkeeper to take charge of the
man. So which of these travelers was a neighbor to the robbed
man?" "The answer is obvious," the lawyer replied, "The one who
had mercy on him." And Jesus told him, "Go and do likewise."

After a short pause, to let them all consider the story, he went on to tell them a couple of the Thomasite parables, but he avoided the one about circumcision believing it to be too soon to introduce it. During the short sermon, Paul held the Book of Q, and glanced at it periodically. He knew the stories without need for the book, but he felt using it furthered a reputation that he was simply a messenger.

After Paul was done and the gathering had asked their questions, he stepped down from the dais and went to Barnabas to confer. "What did you think?"

"Well, this is a friendly group who had already heard some of this. I did see a few people who looked surprised at the mention of Jesus the Christ, but I didn't notice any hostility. May I ask why you used your little book?"

At that point, Paul noticed a man standing off to the side listening to the conversation. "Let's discuss that later," he said as he turned to the eavesdropper. "May I help you?" he asked with a smile.

The man was small, a good head shorter than Paul, and wiry. He had trim, cropped hair and ears that stuck out too far. *He seems quite enthusiastic.*

"My name is John and I've been a student of The Teacher, I mean Jesus, for some time now. Would you mind dining with me tonight so we can discuss his teachings? Unfortunately, I'm not married, but my sister can prepare an acceptable meal."

Paul looked at Barnabas to see if he had an opinion only to see him shrug indifferently. "Yes, that sounds wonderful. What time would you like us and where can we find your home?"

John explained how to get to his house and asked that they come at sunset.

* * *

Paul thought the meal more than acceptable and halfheartedly thanked John's sister Shayna. Unfortunately, the house was too small for a sitting room, a reading room, or any other room where they could comfortably talk. So they stayed at the dining table and enjoyed some wine.

John started the conversation, "You should know that I've been an Essene for many years and I've been following what you've been doing in Antioch. It's not easy being here on an island, but we get enough travelers that I've been able to glean some of what you're accomplishing." He looked back and forth between Paul and Barnabas. "I can be of help to you here on Cyprus. I know the towns and the roads and, more importantly, the communities. I can introduce you to the right people."

Paul cocked his head in confusion. "I'm sorry, what exactly is it you are asking of us?"

"Not of you, for you. I want to travel with you on your journey through Cyprus. I assume you will be going to Paphos, and on foot, so you must know there a number of important towns along the way. You could use a companion who knows the local communities." He looked back and forth at the two travelers. "So may I accompany you?"

Barnabas was the first to recover. "You have to excuse us. We've been traveling and talking to communities and synagogues for a long time and we've never had anyone want to accompany us before." After a hesitation, he added, "And we don't really know you."

John smiled. "True, you don't know me, but you will find I'm an honorable and devout man and you are welcome to ask anyone in town about me, especially within the Jewish community. It's just Cyprus; we can decide in Paphos if I should return or if we should continue together. Is there really any harm?"

Shayna spoke up for the first time since their arrival. "He doesn't want to tell you, but he's been obsessed with The Teacher and wants to learn everything he can about the man. Going with you can help you, but it will help him more."

John scowled at his sister, but didn't disagree.

Paul spoke up without having looked at the girl, "No, there's no reason not to have you travel with us and we could use the company. We'll talk to some of your brethren, but I'm sure they will confirm what you've told us. Given that, we welcome your company."

* * *

After one more meeting with the local church, they set out on the road to the west side of the island. John turned out to be an able assistant, arranging for their needs along their route.

Roughly sixty miles later, just past the third town they had visited, they came across a traveler from Paphos. John saw him while he was still a ways away and warned his two companions, "I'm sorry for intruding, but you may want to be aware of the man traveling toward us. He goes by the name of Bariesous, possibly because it could be interpreted as son-of-Jesus and he claims to be a prophet like Jesus. The local governor in Paphos, Sergius Paulus, admires him, but any true believer knows him to be a charlatan."

At that moment, Bariesous stopped walking towards them and cocked his head to the side. He stood there for a few seconds and then turned and walked away from them, toward the direction he had come from.

"Apparently," Paul said, "he isn't ready to meet us yet." He smiled at the reaction they had caused, "Maybe we'll come across him in Paphos."

"Oh, you most definitely will," John said. "He'll be trying to turn Sergius against you even before you arrive. He isn't the brightest person, but he is very passionate and Sergius likes him. But Sergius is an intelligent person, so he may listen to you."

* * *

After five more stops, mostly successful, Paul, Barnabas and John found themselves entering Paphos. They went immediately to the local Synagogue where the brethren received them. After introductions, one of them handed Paul a letter. "I've been invited to an audience with Sergius," Paul announced.

John spoke up, "You realize it isn't an invitation? Bariesous will be there and Sergius will expect a debate between the two of you. He won't like it if anyone else joins in, but he does enjoy a good argument and especially likes passionate displays."

"Then we will have to comply and we'll see how this Bariesous does." He recalled the event on the road and added, "If he is as you say, then it isn't logic that will win the argument, but a force of will." He walked quietly away.

Since it was still early, they rested and ate a light meal. They also sent word to Sergius' court that they were ready for an audience and asked for an appropriate time. The word came back that he would see them immediately at the administrative center of Paphos, the Roman capital of Cyprus.

* * *

They entered the grand building called The House of Theseus and found four wings that surrounded a central courtyard. They were escorted to the east wing where there was a reception area with Sergius Paulus sitting on an elegant bejeweled chair on a dais. There were five of them including Paul, Barnabas, John, and two local brethren. Paul walked toward Sergius as the others fell behind. They hadn't been invited to the audience, so it wasn't their place to participate directly in the conversation unless asked to by Sergius.

Paul bowed slightly to the Roman leader of Cyprus. He was a thin man, almost emaciated, with wiry muscles stretched tight around his skeleton. He was young with thick wavy hair down to his shoulders and deep, wide set eyes. As Paul was observing the Proconsul, a man walked out from the left side of the room. In a loud and forceful voice he said, "Do not listen to this person Sergius, for he is a blasphemer and a liar." It was Bariesous. Paul turned to apprise the man who would confront him in front of Sergius even though he ran away on the road. Bariesous was slight with a disheveled look about him; he was probably trying to gain favor by appearing to look more mystical. *He seems somewhat pathetic.*

Paul smiled at Bariesous. In a quiet, inquisitive voice he said, "Why do you attack me Elymas, without having even heard what I might say. Is my presence here such a threat to your income?" Sergius leaned forward to hear Paul better, which was the intent. The Proconsul smiled, encouraging Paul. He had used Elymas, a reference to Bariesous being a magician or charlatan, on purpose and it seemed to have stung the man.

Paul turned towards the dais. "I see the rumors we heard that you are a sagacious man were correct." Since he had gained Sergius respect with his more subtle introduction, he decided it was time for a more direct assault. He returned his attention to Bariesous and raised himself up to be the most imposing he could. "You are full of lies and deceit and you know this. You are spawn of the devil and an enemy to righteousness. Will you not stop your perversion and corruption of the ways of the One True God? Will you not follow the teachings of your namesake, Jesus, the son of man?" As Paul spoke, he elevated his voice and began walking toward Bariesous with a determined gate.

Bariesous withdrew at Paul's continued onslaught. He tried to reply, "How dare you…," but Paul overrode him with a commanding voice.

"Yes, I dare. There is nothing to you." Bariesous shriveled and became silent in response. Paul took the opportunity to end this without much of a fight. He walked straight to Bariesous and raised his hand. Bariesous knelt down in supplication as Paul placed his hand on the man's forehead. "The hand of God is upon you. The teachings of Jesus the Christ are with you if you would but accept the One True God." Bariesous began to weep.

Paul walked back to the center of the room and turned to Sergius. "The way of Jesus the Christ is one of love and understanding. It is accepting our place in the Kingdom of God and worshiping the One True God." He glanced at Bariesous and added, "This servant had lost his way and only needed reminded of the power of Jesus the Christ."

Sergius, mouth hanging slightly open and eyes wide, asked for Paul and his travelers to stay in Paphos for a time to teach him the Christian way. Paul agreed that they could stay for a short time, but then they would have to continue their travels.

Elymas, as he now called himself in an attempt to be humble, became a frequent attendant of Paul and his retinue. *At least*, Paul thought wearily, *he has given up the bar-Jesus name, which was an abomination.*

They had stayed in Paphos for three weeks, working with the community there and converting the entire Paulus family, when Paul announced that it was time to move on. He wanted to get to the Galatian mainland during the summer months to spend the autumn traveling around the communities prior to settling for the winter. Paul obtained passage on a boat to Perga in Pamphylia.

* * *

They arrived on a bright summer day, much too hot according to Barnabas, with the air so still it was stifling. When they debarked and strode down the dock, hundreds of people were heading east along the shore towards some hills, where a crowd gathered in the distance. John asked a stranger what was happening and was told that three criminals were being crucified. Paul noticed the large eyes and gaping mouth of his two companions. *They have never witnessed a crucifixion before*, he realized. John was openly intrigued and wanted to attend. Paul and Barnabas considered it barbaric, at best. However, in the end, John's enthusiasm and interest in the spectacle won them over and they agreed to follow the crowd to the hills.

They had an attendant from the ship take their meager belongings to the nearest synagogue and strode off at a brisk pace keeping with the other spectators.

As they arrived at the foot of the hill where the crucifixion was to take place, they saw five large posts permanently implanted in the ground and the three criminals there with crossbeams across their shoulders and tied to their hands. They had apparently carried the cross beams that would be used for their crucifixion from the center of town to the hills.

Two soldiers removed the crossbeams and laid them on the ground. They then arranged the three men across them, in turn. A third soldier came with a hammer and nails. As the crowd looked on with squinted eyes and scrunched faces as if the air carried a foul smell, the soldier nailed each of the criminal's wrists to the ends of the crossbeams. Two of the crucified men cried out in pain as the nails pierced their wrists, but the third held his tongue with a slight whimper. Paul was openly appalled at the sight and felt only compassion for the men, but John stood wide-eyed at the spectacle.

The three men were lifted up to the three center posts. Paul noticed a notch that was in each of the posts and a corresponding one in the crossbeams. There was a small seat placed half way down the post that the men sat on temporarily. The seat was angled, so they wouldn't be able to sit on it for long. The notches of the crossbeams and the posts fitted together and a rope was tied around them diagonally to hold them in place. Then the soldier with the hammer and nails approached. The crowd moaned and cried in disgust as the soldier began to nail each man's ankle to the side of the post. This time all three cried out from the pain and the onlookers could clearly see the blood dripping down the sides of the posts. Some looked away at the gruesome sight.

The spectacle transfixed the three travelers. They had equal responses of disgust, revulsion, and captivation. John whispered, "Fascinating," in a hushed voice. Both Paul and Barnabas turned to him with a scowl. When nothing more was said, Paul returned his focus to the scene. *It's clearly meant to deter others from committing crimes*, he thought and wondered how effective it was.

When everything seemed to be in place, all but one of the soldiers left for the town. Most of the crowd stayed silently watching the three crucified men. Paul wanted to leave, but it seemed disrespectful since everyone else was staying and John wanted to stay as well. They waited, with all the others, in silence.

After almost two hours, one of the men slipped off the small seat. This seemed to accelerate the process as the man quickly fell unconscious.

A few minutes later the soldier must have grown tired of waiting, or possibly he decided the exhibition had accomplished all it could, because he picked up an iron rod and approached the crucified men. He took the rod and swung it hard at the legs of the two men who remained conscious. The sound of breaking bone was sickening and made Paul want to vomit. All four legs were quickly shattered. The intent seemed to be to get the crucifixion completed quickly. The effect on the crowd was immediate; they shrank away from the brutality, some left, and some appeared to be sick. "It will be over soon," John said. Paul and Barnabas turned to leave, but John asked if he could stay for a while and then meet them at the synagogue. They agreed, though Paul shook his head at John's apparent interest in such a gruesome display.

* * *

That night, Paul's sleep was restless. In his dream he saw a foggy desolate hill with The Teacher crucified the way those three had been. It was disturbing because it could have happened that way. Nobody knew how The Teacher had died. He woke before dawn, perspiring and drained, trying to understand. He decided to go for an early morning walk. Not paying any attention to where he went, he found himself approaching the same hill where the three men had suffered and died. He looked at them from the west of the hill and saw the sun rising over a treeless expanse of smooth mounds. A slight breeze tickled the stalks and shrubs and they swayed gently. The crosses stood resolute and alone. A soundless reminder of the horrors they represented. A rallying cry against cruelty wrought upon subjugated people. Finally, he understood his dreams.

Later that morning Paul pulled John aside. "I have a mission for you." John grew visibly excited. "I need you to take this letter to a man named Proculus in Antioch. This and a small package as well. You must not open either one and you have to give it only to Proculus and none other. Peter will be there and Proculus' wife June. Either of them may ask for the package. Do you understand?"

John scowled, but he answered, "Of course, I understand."

"You should travel by ship, it will be much faster. Once there, you should spend some time with the church in Antioch to see firsthand what true Christians are like. Then spend some time in Jerusalem before returning to Cyprus.

"I expect once you have done all of this, you will have the knowledge to help lead the Christian churches there. Are you ready for this?"

John was rising and falling on the balls of his feet. After only a slight hesitation, he said, "I will humbly do what I can to further the teachings of Jesus the Christ in Cyprus."

* * *

Three days after John left, Maximus arrived by boat. The two of them met at the synagogue in a private meeting room. Maximus didn't bother with small talk, "I heard things went well in Cyprus."

Paul wondered how Maximus could have possibly heard that already, but he put his curiosity aside. "Very well. The communities there seemed eager to receive the word and we were able to convert Sergius Paulus and his family, which will help advance the cause appreciably."

"And how about here on Galatia?"

"So far, not as good. The brethren are receptive, but not at all eager." His shoulders drooped in humility for a moment and he added, "It's probably more me than them. When we arrived, we witnessed a crucifixion and it disturbed me greatly. I'm finding it hard to concentrate and very difficult to preach or debate with any aplomb."

Maximus considered the situation. "Well, maybe you should move on. One town isn't critical and getting away from this one and traveling for a while might release the tension."

"Yes, I've been thinking the same thing. It's just difficult to give up on a community, especially when it's potentially my fault."

"You can always return here on the way back home or on another trip sometime." Paul didn't say anything more and looked distracted. "Where are you planning to go next?"

"To Antioch, the one here in Galatia, and then to Lystra and Derbe. We'll probably stay the winter in one of those two cities and then in the spring reverse our route and sail for home."

Maximus said, "You know Galatia is much more dangerous than Cyprus. I've hired a man to accompany you. His name is Aulus." Paul's lips turned down in a grimace. "He is very discrete. I will travel ahead to Lystra since there is a small garrison there."

Paul' eyes narrowed as he said, "As you wish." He walked away thinking concernedly, *he's not telling me everything.*

* * *

Five weeks later Paul and Barnabas arrived in Lystra without the guard Maximus had hired. Maximus met them at the edge of town. "Where is Aulus?"

Paul smiled, "There was nothing unusual in Antioch, so I sent him back to Perga."

"Eho! Paul, you damn fool, just because it seems safe doesn't mean it is and the road is a great deal more dangerous than the city. You should have at least let him accompany you here," Maximus replied shaking his head.

Paul became sheepish, but said nothing. *He's overreacting.*

"Well, that won't happen again," Maximus said slowly.

Paul and Barnabas made their way to the synagogue and met a Jewish family, with knowledge of the Christians, who were gracious enough to invite them to stay at their home, which was near the synagogue.

With the help of the family, they met at the homes of prospective converts over the next week. Paul noticed Maximus lurking as they traveled the town and twice he saw him talking to another man Paul didn't know. However, he kept a discrete distance, so Paul said nothing.

The ninth day after they arrived was a Sabbath and Paul was invited to preach, and possibly debate, at the synagogue. He was talking about the Kingdom of God and the new stance on welcoming Gentiles into the community when a man started to make his way to the podium. It was disrupting because the man was a cripple and was sitting on a splintered wheeled platform pulling himself towards the podium by his hands. His bent legs were at an odd angle, apparently to keep them on the platform, and he was frail with thinning gray hair, an extended stomach, and a gaunt look.

As he neared the podium, Paul stopped talking and the man looked up at him. "Will you bless and pray for me that God might see fit to heal my disfigured legs?"

Paul was stunned. He wasn't a healer or a prophet with some mystical connection to God. He was just a messenger trying to spread the word of God and of The Teacher. He went slightly white with a loud intake of breath, but he had to do something.

He looked at the man. "I can... of course." He then closed the distance between them, laid his right hand on the man's forehead. "Jesus, this man is a servant of the One True God, as you are, and as I and the rest of this congregation are. We implore you, hear our words, intervene on his behalf, and ask the Lord Almighty to heal this poor man. We know all is possible through you. In your grace and your love, we pray to you. Amen."

The congregation answered in unison, "Amen."

The crippled man had closed his eyes when Paul placed his hand on his forehead. Now he opened them slowly. "Thank you." And he headed back to his original place in the audience.

Paul didn't know what to make of the scene and was still astounded enough that it was difficult to continue his preaching. After a few moments, however, he regained his composure, shook off the disturbance and continued. He was almost done with a concluding parable about Jesus when there was yet another disruption in the crowd. It emanated from the same area as where the cripple had been. The people around him seemed to be backing away and the man was moaning. Paul made his way to the growing circle of space around the man and stood watching the cripple with the rest of the congregation. The moaning became louder as his eyes rolled up into his head. As the brethren stared in stupefaction, the man's crippled legs straightened out from under him, his body shook in convulsions, and then he lay still.

After a few moments of silence, Paul approached the man. His eyes opened and he smiled, though his eyes were crossed and unfocused. He slowly got to his knees and then, to everyone's astonishment, stood up. He immediately, though slowly, walked the few steps to Paul, grabbed his hand and kissed it over and over. "You cured me. You cured me."

The crowd broke into cries of "Miracle! It's a Miracle" and "Praise Paul, the miracle worker" and "Praise be to God." Some of the people began to get on their knees to Paul as if he had done it and not God.

After watching this, dumfounded, Paul said, "Please, please stand up. I'm no God. It is He you should worship and not I. If I did anything it was to ask Jesus to help this man."

But the crowd refused to listen and gave Paul the credit for the miracle. After many minutes of having his hands and feet kissed by members of the congregation, Paul made his way out of the synagogue. He wanted peace and quiet to meditate on what had happened.

While Paul had been receiving praise, the healed man had furtively left. As Paul left the building, he saw the man rounding a corner and followed. When he came around the bend, he saw the man speaking with Maximus. Paul couldn't hear the discussion, but Maximus appeared very intense and was waving a finger in the ex-cripple's face. Then the man suddenly left and strode toward the docks.

* * *

Paul struggled with his newfound fame. He couldn't quite believe that God had healed this man and wondered why he had disappeared. *Did Maximus have something to do with it? Does it matter? If it helps spread Christianity, then isn't it good?*

He spent more and more of his time alone over the winter as he struggled with the meaning of the miracle and as there was less he could find to accomplish with the brethren in Lystra. As weather permitted, he was able to take some side trips to the nearby towns of Derbe and Iconium. They had all heard about the miracle, but the brethren in the other towns were skeptical. In early spring, a group arrived from Iconium that tried to dispute the event and when locals refuted their claims, they vociferously doubted Paul's participation in it. They were successful enough that the townsfolk felt challenged to find the cripple-who-was-healed. His disappearance made Paul look more like a charlatan than a man of God.

After eleven days of arguing and complaining, they had convinced enough of the local Christians to be suspicious that violence ensued. It began by the group arguing more openly with Paul and Barnabas in the street. Paul was trying to defend himself when one of the Iconiums threw a stone. It missed but incited the others to do the same and soon the stoning began. Barnabas ran and was able to escape because he was not the target. After a few well-thrown stones, one of which opened a wound in the side of his head, Paul staggered and fell to the ground.

He could see Maximus approaching from the tree line. The stoning stopped at Maximus' presence, so he was able to bend down and examine Paul. He whispered, "If you want to live then act dead." Paul hesitated. Maximus exclaimed in an urgent murmur, "Now!"

Paul immediately closed his eyes and collapsed. Maximus spoke up, "It looks like you may have killed this man; at least he is well on his way. I suggest you drag him over to the woods there and leave him to his fate."

The Iconium Jews hesitated, but looked at Maximus in trepidation. A few of them ran away. The others went to drag Paul away with cautious glances at Maximus.

When the Iconiums were out of sight heading for the synagogue, Maximus went to Paul only to find Barnabas by his side weeping. He said, "They're gone, you can get up." Barnabas' weeping stopped suddenly as he looked at Paul. "I suggest you quickly clean yourself off and go straight to the synagogue. Your showing up there after them believing they killed you will be such a shock that they won't dare try anything against you again."

That's fast thinking. Paul stared as Maximus. *Could he have known this would happen?* He shook his head to shake the feeling. *He just saved my life.* With Barnabas' help, he did as Maximus asked.

When he arrived at the synagogue, the blood and most of the dirt was gone and Paul was able to ignore, temporarily, the pain coming from wounds on his head and right shoulder. To the Iconiums, he looked like a man who had returned from the dead. They staggered away.

He took his time looking at each of them in turn and then spoke to the group. "I understand why you did this and I forgive you. It's difficult to believe in Jesus without witnessing what I have seen. When you witness miracles, it is easy to believe in God and in Jesus the Christ. Do you see now that he is the Christ and we all must heed his word?"

The group was too stunned to speak. They glanced at each other shiftily and some bowed their head in supplication. He left the synagogue and went to find Maximus and Barnabas to get some help with his injuries. He quickly gave them an update, "That went as you said Maximus, they are unlikely to bother me again and the word will spread."

Maximus smiled. "Spring is coming soon; you may want to consider moving on."

"Actually, it's time to head back. We'll leave for Attalia in a few weeks. There are some tent-makers there I'd like to spend some time with. I did some tent making on one of my other trips and can help them while talking about Jesus. Maybe we can start another community there. After that, we can sail for home."

"Good," Maximus replied. "You should be safe here now; I'm going to Rome instead. I need to see how Claudius is doing."

* * *

A little over two months later, Paul and Barnabas arrived in Seleucia and then made their way to Syrian Antioch and home. Barnabas disappeared to spend time with his family and friends. Proculus and June welcomed Paul back, but they deferred any serious discussion until he had settled in and acclimated himself.

Three days later, Proculus, Paul, Peter, and June met at Proculus' house for dinner. It was spring and the rains made an outdoor gathering infeasible. Paul was happy to see Peter eating with them; prior to his departure, he had still declined to eat with gentiles.

After completing most of the meal and exchanging pleasantries, Proculus began, "Paul, tell us about your trip."

He described the trip through Cyprus and up into Galatia, including the miracle cure and the stoning. Despite the stoning, the trip had been extremely successful and they all voiced their appreciation.

Peter spoke up, "I'm sorry, but it's difficult to believe that God performed this miracle at your request."

Proculus responded, a little too quickly, "I wonder. There have been numerous miracles in the Jewish histories and we know Jesus is with God. So could he not intervene and provide a miracle for Paul to help gain credibility and convert the Galatians?"

Paul and June both looked at Proculus askance.

After a pause in the conversation, Proculus changed the subject. "Paul, what is the meaning of this cross you sent me? The letter had hints about what you had in mind, but it begged clarification."

Paul was expecting this question and had spent a great deal of time considering how to answer it. He composed himself and began, "You remember that one thing missing from Judaism was images. It's strictly forbidden to worship idols, so we can't make images of Jesus or any other patron. We need some symbol that represents Christianity and that can be used as a kind of image without it being an idol. Also, we need some symbol at the synagogues that brethren can use to worship and make it more like a temple."

He had been speaking quickly without taking much of a breath, so he stopped, inhaled, and continued, "When I was in Perga, I saw a crucifixion. It was... horrific... but it brought all kinds of feelings to the surface. Feelings of disgust and anger, of compassion and suffering, and others made me want to fight against the perpetrators and maybe unite others to do the same.

"Then, the next morning, I went back to the sight and saw just the empty crosses standing on the hill. The sun was rising behind them, and in them, I saw the image we were looking for. The cross isn't an image of a God or a person, but it represents death and solitude and suffering. An image that can unite a people. I saw it in my head for weeks and dreamt of it nightly. I imagined Jesus suffering and dying on the cross and I experienced all the emotions we want to bring out in people. We can even place it in the synagogues to provide a representation of Jesus or God without using an idol."

All three of Paul's audience were listening intently. There was a void left when he stopped talking. June recovered first, "Paul, What does this crucifixion have to do with what we are doing here?"

Paul looked around the room and wondered why they hadn't made the connection.

Then Proculus appeared to, "He means to intimate that Jesus was crucified. I assume by the Romans since they are the only ones who do crucifixions."

June stammered, "But... but Jesus wasn't crucified. I know we never heard how he died, but saying that he was crucified, seems... preposterous."

"Even duplicitous," Proculus added.

Paul answered, "Yes, I agree, we would be taking a chance. But the gain in having a symbol that binds us all and that we can use in the synagogues outweighs the difficulties in creating a story about The Teacher's demise."

Peter finally gained enough composure to speak. "We can't do this! It's bad enough that we're stretching Jewish laws beyond what is acceptable. And in our quest to recruit Gentiles, that we've given him a name when we don't know one, but to make up stories about him just to give ourselves an image to use is..., " Peter glanced around with a pained expression and then ended, "blasphemy."

Proculus espoused, "Well, it is not really that far from creating a name and I can see Paul's point. It would make a perfect image. However, we have to consider the impact to the relationship between the Romans and the Jews. It would have to be the Romans who crucified him."

Paul saw a slight smile and interested eyes on Proculus. *What is he thinking?*

XI. The Council of Jerusalem (48 AD)

"Some said to Jesus, 'Teacher, we wish to see a sign from you.' He answered them, 'a wicked generation looks for a sign, but no sign will be shown to it.'"

The Book of Q (Revised)

"James, I think you know Proculus, and this is his wife June. They've both been a tremendous help to the church in Antioch and have supported my travels as well. Proculus, June, this is James ben Zebedee from Jerusalem. He was one of the supporters of converting Gentiles when we first asked for permission."

James looked a little sheepish and kept glancing back towards the temple. "Yes, it's very nice to meet you. Unfortunately, that's exactly what we are here to discuss. The Pharisees are upset about us loosening the restrictions, especially around circumcision and want to rescind your permission to convert the Gentiles. More importantly, they want to send their own missionaries out to counter yours and to tell people that you have no authority.

"Be prepared Paul, the two men traveling with me are against this Christian movement of yours. The discussion may become contentious. But you should be aware that you still have supporters in Jerusalem."

Paul's eyes narrowed, but Peter was the one who spoke. "Why do you target Paul? You and I both supported this movement."

"I believe the Pharisees assume Paul is easier to attack because of his past."

At that point, a man came from the temple at a fast walk. He approached the five of them and looked at James. "They are ready for you."

James nodded and the man walked away, "We shouldn't keep them waiting." Then he looked at Proculus and June and said, "It was very nice to meet you. I hope we can spend some time together while I'm here in Antioch, though I fear that shall not be for long."

Proculus answered, "Thank you James, we hope so as well." After a pause, he turned to Paul and added, "And good luck in there Paul." Peter, Paul, and James turned and left for the temple.

* * *

Proculus and June waited patiently at their residence. A few hours later, Paul pounded on the door. Upon entering, he stormed up to the couple flushed with anger. Proculus and June looked at each other with deep concern.

Paul was trying to catch his breath when June said, "Daniel, please get Paul some water." Then she turned back, "Paul, what is it, are you all right?"

"Yes, yes. I'm… furious with Peter. I can't believe how much of a fraud he is and I don't understand how people can respect a man like that." Paul was pacing back and forth and looking everywhere except at the couple. He finally settled down some, but still stood there shaking his head.

Proculus said, "Maybe you should tell us what happened."

Paul looked up at Proculus. "I was with Peter and James and a couple others from Jerusalem. I invited them to dine with us tonight and Peter looked embarrassed as if he didn't know how to respond. I stared at him, wondering what was wrong. He finally said, 'Oh, I couldn't.' I replied, 'What are you saying Peter, of course you can, you have many times before.' He said, 'No, no, that wouldn't be appropriate.' I stood there aghast with Peter looking at me as if I had suggested something sacrilegious. The others, including James said nothing.

"How can Peter act like a member of our Christian community and then turn on us so easily when one of his Pharisaic brethren are around? How can we trust him to run the church here if he isn't committed to living what we teach?" Paul shook his head again and his shoulders slumped in defeat. He walked a few feet to a nearby chair, sat down and bent over putting his head in his hands.

Proculus looked at June for help. This was mostly a Jewish concern and had more to do with emotions than reason, so she was the better person to handle it. June walked over to Paul, knelt down in front of him, put one hand on his knee, and lifted his chin with the other. She said, "Paul, it's all right. Peter is one man, he's immersed in the Jewish ways, and he's a politician. He cares what people think of him, much more than you do. Maybe he isn't as strong in his faith or as accepting of Jesus as you are. But he didn't have the vision you had and even with his faults, he's a good leader and has helped to further the community. You know he has. Maybe that's all the more reason he

147

should be here in Antioch instead of Jerusalem where the others might influence him."

Paul was still shaking his head, but his face returned to a normal color and his hands stilled. Then he started to get excited again, "I just don't understand how he could change his ways just because of who he is around."

June became sterner, "Paul, we have to concentrate on what is important. Right now, that's the fact that Jerusalem sent men here to tell us they are concerned about the path we are taking. What was decided about that?"

Proculus watched the exchange and was impressed with how June had handled it. He certainly would not have been as effective.

Paul looked up at June as if just realizing she was the one speaking to him. He stood and looked at Proculus. "They came mostly to complain about the lifting of the requirements around circumcision. But the congregation here knows how important that is to our efforts so they handled most of the discussion." He looked up at the ceiling and shivered in reflection before continuing. "I figured it would be better if they heard it from the locals.

"We'll need to go to Jerusalem and defend our position in front of a *min'yan*." Then he clarified, "A group of ten religious leaders. We will stay here through the Sabbath and then leave for Jerusalem. Peter, Barnabas and I should go and maybe two or three others."

* * *

Ten days later Paul led the group into Jerusalem. Most of the local men headed for their homes. As they left, James stopped Peter and Paul to speak with them for a moment. "It's obvious that there's some kind of contention between you two. That happens, but you will both have to put that aside if you are going to be successful with the council. We all have to have a united stance when we speak to them or they'll use our disagreements against us."

Paul and Peter looked at each other and, begrudgingly, agreed.

They were asked to meet with the council the very next day. The fact that the council agreed to see them so quickly was evidence enough that they considered the topic urgent.

The council greeted the Christians warmly. Some of the men had been present when they originally gave Paul permission to proselytize. Interestingly, Peter and James sat with the council, presenting the Antioch Christians as a separate group. Paul was offended at first and then realized that it might be an advantage to have pro-Christians with the council.

Paul stood up to address the group. "You know why we are here. There seems to be some concern about us proselytizing the Gentiles. We want to tell you about what has been happening so that you might better understand how important these efforts are."

He paused, partly for effect, and then continued, "You have seen how the churches in Antioch and other cities have swelled with new brethren. The Gentiles long for the One True God and those who have converted have proven to be just as pious as traditional Jews." A few of the council scoffed at that. Paul ignored them and continued, "There have also been many examples of Jesus helping us with the Gentiles and even some miracles. You have heard about these, I am sure."

One of the council, a man by the name of Uriel, cleared his throat. Paul stopped speaking and looked in his direction. It was somewhat rude of the man to interrupt Paul's oratory, but he didn't want to alienate the council by saying so. The man stood up. "We know of your exploits Paul and have heard of some of these miracles. Are you trying to say that the Teacher was responsible for them, as if he is God?"

Paul smiled at the notion, "No, of course not. However, Jesus may have intervened on our behalf and requested the miracle from God. We know that Jesus is with God and that he hears our prayers. It has seemed to us that asking Jesus for help has been more successful than asking God for help directly. But nobody is suggesting that Jesus is performing the miracles."

Uriel sat back down with a grunt and a grimace. Then Reuben stood up. Paul remembered him well because he had been on Paul's side previously. "Thank you for coming to see the council Paul, and you Barnabas, we appreciate your willingness to travel." Then he cast his eyes downward solemnly. When he raised them, he said, "We also appreciate the new converts and all the work you have done to further spread Judaism. However, we have talked about this at great length and we all feel it is absolutely necessary that these male converts go through the ritual of circumcision. It represents the covenant between God and Man and they can't be Jewish otherwise."

Many of the council were nodding their heads in agreement while Peter and James looked at them with narrowed eyes and crinkled foreheads. Most of them supported Christianity. Peter stood up. Reuben yielded with a nod and sat down. Peter looked around the group and began, "It is true that Jews are the chosen people and Jerusalem the chosen city. God laid down the covenant to Moses and we have lived by it ever since, and circumcision has been an important part of that covenant."

Paul wondered where Peter was going with this, but trusted him enough, despite the recent disagreement, to support him by nodding and smiling.

"However, God has made it clear to any who would listen that things have changed." He lowered his head in doubt. The council waited patiently. Peter looked up with eyes brightened and continued. "Let me tell you a story. You know that I went up to Caesarea some time back and visited the church there. They were devout God-fearing brethren and I was pleased to speak with them. Then they introduced me to a Gentile named Cornelius. He had been learning about the One True God and about Jesus from the church members there and he wanted to believe, but the restrictions seemed harsh to him and he couldn't bring himself to be circumcised. I told him of the Kingdom of God and how it was available to all, Gentile and Jew alike. I explained the teachings of Jesus to him and why they were so important.

"He became truly excited as we talked about God. Then, I told him he didn't have to be circumcised or follow all of the old requirements. He asked how this could be and I explained that we could baptize him in a symbolic representation of throwing away his old life and beliefs in exchange for Jesus and the Kingdom of God. We went through what was involved in the baptism and he said he wanted to do it right then.

"So we went to the temple where they had a half-barrel. He stripped his clothes and entered the barrel that we filled with water. We performed the rite and gave him a new robe to put on in place of his clothes.

"Then, his head rolled back, he looked towards heaven, and began speaking in tongues." Peter stopped at that point and looked around the room, one by one.

Paul looked also and saw they were surprised by Peter's revelation of a Gentile glossolalist.

"Yes, we were astonished as well. The Holy Spirit had entered Cornelius as soon as the baptism was complete.

"It should be clear to you all, as it is clear to us, that God is doing something new here. There is a new covenant, one around baptism and not circumcision. Who are you, in this council, to counter God's wishes?" At that, he sat down and let the council contemplate what they had heard.

After a few moments, James spoke up, "Paul, Barnabas, could you continue and tell us about some of what you saw on your travels. Maybe that would help us to understand God's new path for us."

Paul went through some of the more interesting events in his travels, though he left out the crucifixion, and he let Barnabas tell about the miracle healing.

It was an hour and a half later when they finally left to let the council deliberate. Paul was exhausted, but convinced that they would again agree to support their efforts. After Peter's speech, it was hard to imagine them openly going against God.

* * *

They all returned to the council chambers two days later to hear the results. Paul and Barnabas sat in front of the council and Uriel stood up to address them. "Thank you again for coming here to discuss these important matters. Given the events that you and Peter have spoken of so eloquently, it is clear that God wishes the conversion of Gentiles to continue.

"You should be warned, however, that many of the prominent Pharisees are still adamantly against this movement. You would therefore do well to pursue your efforts far from Jerusalem, at least for the time being.

"Finally, the council, and those here you might call Christians, have asked that Silas and Barsabbas accompany you on your next trip. They can learn from you and help us to understand God's new covenant. We will draft a letter of introduction that will confirm your authority and our backing."

Paul nodded, thanked the council, and left. The following day, he received the letter of introduction:

> *The council of elders, who are your Jewish brothers in Jesus and the One True God, sends their greetings to the Gentile brothers in lands near and far. Since we have heard that you are distressed and concerned about the disagreements in Jerusalem around conversions of Gentiles, we have penned this epistula to be carried by our beloved Barnabas and Paul. We have also sent you Silas and Barsabbas to give you the same message, personally. For it appears right and true that the Holy Spirit has entered Gentiles and has shown us that God's plan for us includes the conversion of Gentiles to Judaism. You must continue to avoid worshiping idols, eating what has been sacrificed to idols, tasting blood, and sexual immorality. Keep yourselves clean and righteous and you may enter the Kingdom of Heaven.*

Paul felt the letter was a little vague and it failed to proclaim his authority, as the council said it would. *It should suffice for now.*

* * *

Proculus grew impatient waiting for Paul to report what had happened in Jerusalem. The proselytizer had been back in town for three days when Proculus sent word strongly requesting an audience.

Paul arrived a few hours later. After they exchanged some brief niceties, he began. "The council seemed reticent until Peter stood up and told them a story of a man in Caesarea who had been converted and, when baptized, spoke in tongues. I don't know if the story is true or not for I've never heard it from Peter or anyone else, but it convinced the council that God's plan has changed and that baptism is the new covenant with man, especially for Gentiles.

"You should know, though, that they warned us there are still Pharisees against us. They indicated to Peter privately that the Pharisees might send some of their own preachers to the Jewish communities telling them that we do not represent Judaism and Gentiles cannot enter the Kingdom of Heaven without circumcision."

June raised her voice, "The Pharisees are idiots. They don't understand that this can only be good for Judaism and their obstinacy will hurt us all."

Proculus smiled and added, "Yes, there seems to be a growing split between the Christians and the Pharisees. We will have to watch this carefully and will probably have to take steps to make sure the Jewish communities recognize Paul's authority. We may even have to discredit the Pharisees somehow."

Paul examined the ground and was so still that Proculus decided to wait to see how he answered. Finally, he spoke up, "It seems to me that we have to provide something concrete to show Jew and Gentile alike that Christianity is real. We need Jesus to be a martyr and we need the symbol we've been discussing. Also, I agree that we need to disgrace the Pharisees. What if Jesus was indeed crucified as I have suggested and the Pharisees were the instigators?"

Both Proculus' and June's head snapped back in astonishment. June stared at Paul with her mouth agape and her round eyes opened wide. Proculus was the first to recover as he put aside the emotional response to such subterfuge and considered the true ramifications. It was bold and risky, but it could accomplish what they needed. "Paul, I must admit that it's difficult to imagine introducing a falsified story like this, but I do see that it could accomplish exactly what we are after. Personally, I think you should try it in a few towns, far from here. You were talking about going back through Galatia; maybe if you kept going over to the eastern side of Europe, you could bring Judaism to the people there and introduce this story to see what impact it has."

June looked askance at her husband. She exclaimed, "Proculus, you can't be serious. Fabricating this story could ruin everything and it's highly unethical, to say the least. How can you be contemplating such a thing?"

Proculus turned to her and realized that he needed to end this discussion gracefully. The last thing they needed was for Paul to see June and him disagreeing about the course of action they needed to take. "I understand that it is risky, but we do need to discredit the Pharisees and this story could do exactly that. However, it is an enormous step and we should be extremely careful deciding to do anything like this.

"Paul, you will be here in Antioch for a while, I assume. You have been traveling a long time and could use some recuperation and the church here could use your leadership." *That was a stretch.*

XII. Paul's Second Mission (49 AD – 50 AD)

"Jesus said, 'The Kingdom of God is like a grain of mustard which a man took and sowed in his garden. It grew and became a tree, and the birds of the air made nests in its branches."

- The Book of Q (Revised)

It had been a harsh winter in Antioch, but church activities had gone well with Paul's leadership. Peter decided to stay in Jerusalem and promote Christian interests there since Paul would be in Antioch for the time being. In the sickly months at the height of summer, when they were just starting to examine plans for Paul's next trip, he contracted malaria. Usually the disease wasn't lethal for otherwise healthy people, but this was a particularly strong case and Paul suffered.

At first Proculus wasn't too concerned. When it carried on for many weeks, he and June began to wonder if Paul would recover. He certainly could not travel in that condition and might have to stay in Antioch for another winter. As the sickness progressed, Proculus worried about what would happen to their plans if Paul did not recuperate.

Curia came for a visit in early fall. Proculus, June, and her sat down to discuss the ramifications of Paul's illness. Proculus began, "First of all, I know this conversation may seem harsh and unsympathetic, but we have to separate ourselves from our feelings for Paul and consider what his illness, incapacitation, or death, might mean to our plans and any mitigation steps we should take."

He looked at June and then Curia to see them both with their heads inclined. After they didn't answer or even look up for a few moments, he continued. "We have made great progress in establishing Judaism among the Gentiles in the form of a nascent Christianity. However, discontinuing the proselytizing at this point would slow the efforts at best and at worst break up

154

the cohesion the communities feel and cause them to all become independent splinter groups. Even without Paul getting sick, I have been wondering if we need to recruit others who can travel and spread the word."

He glanced between the two in anticipation. Curia said, "Yes, it seems prudent to get more Christians out there spreading the word and to not rely quite so completely on Paul. We do have to be careful that they spread the same message to keep the consistency, and cohesion, as you put it."

Curia added, "We also need to start work in Rome. It's the largest city in the Empire with a diverse population, including a Jewish quarter. We need to establish a Christian group there to start it growing."

Proculus thought that somewhat aggressive, and tangential to the topic. "I agree, as long as we can spare the people."

June asked, "Could Peter take over Paul's role?"

Proculus considered the idea and then answered, "Partially. Peter's a little old for extensive travel, but he could lead the church from here and write letters to try to keep the communities coordinated. Then with other proselytizers traveling, we should be able to maintain the momentum. The difficulty in using Peter has been the need to keep Jerusalem content when Peter is here. They are a capricious group." After a moment's consideration, he added, "Maybe we could convince James to take that role."

They all went quiet, trying to find answers. June finally spoke up, "How do we find more proselytizers, especially if Paul doesn't recover enough to travel to find them?"

All three shook their heads. Proculus offered, "I suppose we would have to find someone here in Antioch to do the initial traveling with the goal being to find others. Maybe Barnabas could do it, but he seems to be losing interest in the endeavor. There is Silas from the council in Jerusalem, but I cannot tell if he is truly on our side or a spy.

"June, can you start to ask around, quietly? My prodding would not be well received."

"Yes, certainly."

"Curia, you and Maximus should try to find someone in Rome who could start a group there. The challenge will be that you are not Jewish, so you might have to find a Jewish person you can hire initially. If you can find the right person, or persons, you could send them here for guidance."

* * *

It was some time before Paul showed signs of true recovery. It was obvious that it would be many months before he could possibly resume travels. He was still very weak and had visibly lost a significant amount of body weight.

They ended up sending Barnabas out on a couple of short excursions while Paul recovered. Paul stayed through the next winter in Antioch gaining strength and leading the Christian Church.

Then, in early spring, Maximus arrived from Rome. He, Proculus, and Paul met to plan the second mission. Proculus began, as usual, by asking Maximus for an update of how things were going in Rome.

"Well, Claudius has turned out to be a much better Caesar than anyone imagined. It's humorous; he was the only living adult male in Augustus' family when Caligula was murdered and he was only alive because Caligula didn't see him as a threat. Growing up, he stuttered, so nobody took notice of him. Until Caligula made him a consul and that was out of pity.

"His rule has been tenuous the entire time, but he turned out to be decisive and one who could make harsh decisions when needed. He's had quite a few senators killed when he suspected they were plotting against him; some just to make an example out of them. It's kept him alive and in control; that and the fact that he hasn't upset too many people."

Paul asked, "And the families of those he killed?"

Maximus looked deeply at Paul and answered, "He had the family killed too, exiled them to a distant land, or rewarded them sufficiently to keep them quiet.

"In any case, he's used public money well, repairing and building in Rome, extending aqueducts, expanding temples, and holding a judicious number of games. He's also expanded the road network in much of the Empire. Most importantly, he has expanded its boundaries with key victories in Mauretania and Britannia. And he made a trip to Britannia to oversee the final battles. He reportedly granted the supreme British general, Caractacus, clemency."

While Maximus took a drink, Paul asked, "What about his religious views?"

"He isn't Christian if that is what you're asking," Maximus answered with a smile on his face. Paul stared back at him. "Let's see, he has refused to be recognized as a God, so he's quite different from Caligula in that respect. In fact, some Greeks wanted to build a temple to his divinity and he declined, saying that only the Gods could make someone a God. He seems to think that Rome should return to old Roman Deities and has tried to stop the spread of alternative religions in Rome proper. He has exiled or killed a number of druidic leaders because they were trying to spread their views of reincarnation."

He looked back and forth between the two and added, "In fact, that's the main reason the Christian group we created there hasn't spread more. They are afraid of actively proselytizing because of the harsh stance Claudius has taken towards them.

"But his time will come and then we'll be able to accomplish more. Personally, I don't see him lasting past a few more years. His health is not good and word is that he fights constantly with his wife Agrippina."

Proculus finally spoke, "Thank you Maximus, that is sufficient. You and Curia should do what you can to help the Christian group expand. Soon it may be time to get more aggressive about a significant community in Rome.

"Paul, have you thought about where you would like to go on your next trip? It appears that your health has returned sufficiently enough that you could make another one."

Paul leaned forward and began gesticulating as he spoke.

He is quite enthusiastic, Proculus thought.

"Yes, I want to go back through Galatia again, but this time by land. The communities in Cyprus are doing well, so they don't need a visit, but those in Galatia are struggling. I also want to try some of the ideas we have discussed and that should probably be done far from Jerusalem, so I was considering continuing to Macedonia and Greece."

He paused, a little out of breath, and Maximus interrupted him, "I have contacts in Philippi since it holds the garrison for that area. The one town I can think of that you might want to avoid is Corinth. It's a free-spirited place with most of the population being recently freed slaves. There's a lot of debauchery there; you can get anything you want in that town."

Paul responded, "That sounds like the very place I do need to visit. It's people like that who are most in need of firm religion. I would speculate that it might prove one of our most dedicated communities."

Proculus and Maximus both looked at Paul askance. Proculus decided there wasn't enough information to argue the point. Paul continued, "The other town of note there is Thessalonica. They are renowned for their glossolalia skills. I've become quite adept at speaking in tongues, so I want to see how they respond to my abilities."

Proculus asked, "When might you leave?"

"In a few weeks, when the roads are dry. I'll take Silas with me. He has proven to be an able assistant."

"Paul, there is one other topic I would like to discuss." Proculus hesitated until Paul raised questioning eyebrows, "The communities are growing, just as we all hoped they would. It seems to me time to bring in others that can follow in your footsteps and help expand Christianity. You can't be everywhere and this would allow the communities to keep in contact with each other and would help us to expand even faster." *He needs to agree with this.* "What do you think?"

Paul bowed his head for a few minutes. He stammered a response, "It sounds reasonable. Um, what do you want me to do?"

"Be looking for people who could proselytize like you do," he said, relieved at Paul's acceptance. "Maybe they won't be as good as you and they certainly would never become the leader you are, but they could help." *That was mostly true.*

"Yes, I can do that," Paul answered hesitantly.

* * *

Almost four weeks later, Paul was ready to leave on his trip. Maximus had left for Rome a few days prior. Proculus had asked him to keep track of where Paul was and to be in Philippi and then Corinth when Paul arrived just in case there was trouble.

Paul and Silas made their way north and then west towards Galatia. Unfortunately for Paul, they would have to travel through Tarsus where he purportedly grew up. Since that wasn't exactly the truth, he did not want to linger. He broached the subject, "Silas, I'd like to just resupply in Tarsus and move on as quickly as possible."

Silas' brows furrowed as his lips stiffened. He asked, "Why is that, may I ask?"

Paul had prepared his excuse, which wasn't far from the truth, "My parents are orthodox Pharisees and don't agree with the new Christian ideas. We haven't spoken in many years now and I don't want to embarrass them by showing up unannounced." Silas' eyes tightened, so Paul added, "Also, this isn't really a town we need to concentrate on. Derbe and Lystra are much more important. If we can establish strong Christian communities there, the other towns in this area will follow."

Silas cocked his head in doubt. "If you say so, Paul."

They resupplied, stayed one night, and then left on the road west towards Derbe.

In Derbe, they made their way to the synagogue, hoping someone there could provide accommodations. The congregation had heard of Paul and his teachings of Jesus from the community in Lystra. So Paul and Silas were pulled into an impromptu discussion of some of Jesus' sayings with a handful of Jewish men who were at the synagogue.

Paul thought the conversation was lively enough and the men were interested in learning, but at the same time, they seemed hesitant. Then one of the men finally provided a hint, "Paul, you must be frustrated with our lack of knowledge and ability to discuss these matters. You really must meet with Timothy. He is away in Lystra right now."

"Tell me about him."

"Timothy has devoted his life to Jesus and his teachings and has begun to spread the word to other communities. We all have a great deal of respect for him."

"Then I should certainly meet with him. Do you know when he will be back in Derbe?"

"It should be within the week."

"Well, we wouldn't want to miss him, is there a house here in Derbe that could accommodate us until his return?"

"Timothy would take you in himself, but with him gone, it would be inappropriate for you to stay with his wife. We'll try to find another family. Will you be attending services on the Sabbath?"

"Yes, of course. If your elders are willing, I would like to speak of Jesus and his teachings to the congregation."

"I'm sure they would appreciate that."

* * *

Two days after the Sabbath, Timothy arrived. He was early and Paul could only surmise that he had returned when hearing the two were in Derbe waiting for him.

Paul, Silas, Timothy, and another Derbe resident named Reuben met at the synagogue. Paul and Timothy were smiling freely. "It's a pleasure to meet you Timothy. The people here speak very highly of you."

"The pleasure is mine Paul. I was sad that I didn't meet you on your first trip through Lystra. I've wanted to speak with you ever since, but haven't had the time to travel to Antioch or Jerusalem. I'm... actually, we are so happy that you are here. We've been hoping and praying for this for a long time."

The next two weeks went faster than Paul could have imagined. Timothy held events and discussions in towns all around the area. Paul, he, and sometimes Silas, enjoyed many hours of discussions of the meaning of Jesus' sayings and specifically how to present the ideas.

It wasn't until the two weeks were almost up and Silas mentioned that they should continue their voyage, that Paul finally remembered Proculus' request to find more proselytizers. Paul sought out Timothy as soon as the idea occurred to him. "Timothy, I want you to know that our time here has been invaluable and you have done an outstanding job of organizing the Christian communities. But it's time for Silas and me to continue our mission."

"Oh no, not so soon! There's plenty of time," Timothy responded quickly.

"We have a long way to go and want to reach Eastern Europe before winter."

Timothy's shoulders slumped, "I understand Paul, it's just that I'll miss our talks."

"I will too. I wonder, might you consider coming with us? There's plenty of work to do throughout the Republic," Paul caught himself just in time and didn't say 'Empire,' "The communities here are doing well and we could use your help."

Timothy replied hesitantly, "I... I don't know. I would love to, but I've lived in this area my entire life and my wife and all my friends are here."

"I hope that you have come to consider me a friend too," Paul said with a smile. "Think of the good you could do bringing the word of God and the teachings of Jesus to new communities. You have a calling Timothy, do not ignore that."

Timothy's face flushed and he looked away trying to hide it. "I need to ponder this and I'd like to speak with my wife and some of the elders. May I give you an answer tomorrow?"

"Of course; it will take us a day to resupply and prepare for the departure." In actuality, he and Silas could be ready to leave the next morning, but he wanted Timothy to have time to consider his offer.

The next morning, Timothy told Paul he had spoken with his wife and a number of constitutes and decided he couldn't shirk his responsibilities to further Christianity. He would travel with Paul and Silas.

* * *

They traveled through Lystra and other towns Timothy was familiar with, but Paul only allowed them to stay for a short time, in many cases less than a day. He knew that the area was doing well and he wanted to get to places that didn't have such a strong Christian influence.

When they arrived in Phyrgia, west of Lystra by roughly a hundred miles, they met a contingent of Jews. The Jews appeared hostile and told Paul that he wasn't welcome there. When he asked why, a man came forward. "I am Eli, from Jerusalem, and I've told these people about your blasphemous ways. They want nothing to do with your false teachings."

Paul looked around at the group of men and saw the determination on their faces. "You must be a Pharisee to speak of the teachings of Jesus the Christ as false." He started to pull out the letter from the council in Jerusalem and then looked again at the number of men present and their resolve and decided it would be better to move on. Perhaps he could come back through this area at a time when the people were more receptive.

He said, "If that is your wish, then we will continue on our way. Do you mind if we resupply and sleep the night here before we leave?"

Eli appeared confused at Paul's acquiescence. He sputtered, "Yes, that will be… acceptable." Then, he stood more erect and squared his shoulders. "Just don't attempt to preach your falsehoods while you are here."

"We understand," was all Paul answered.

They met with the same welcome at other towns in the area including Galatia, where Paul had been before, and Bithynia. Paul came to two realizations during these rebuffs. First was that something had to be done soon about the Pharisee's and second was that they had to move faster and farther away in order to leave the Pharisaic influence behind. They therefore traveled as quickly as possible to Traos and hired a boat to take them to Samothrace and then immediately to Neapolis and, finally, Philippi.

* * *

Maximus received word three weeks later that Paul and company had skipped ahead and gone immediately to Phillipi. He left the next morning to try to reach them. Proculus would be disappointed that he hadn't met them there, but Phillipi wasn't the big concern since the garrison was present. He just didn't want Paul going to Corinth without him.

* * *

As Paul and his retinue disembarked at Phillipi, he found his spirits lifted and he commented jovially, "This is really the first city we've entered that could be called part of Europe. Maximus told me it's a garrison-town, but it's also the most important city in this area with extensive trade routes and a diverse population. We should be able to find receptive people here."

Timothy said, "Do you think any of them would have heard of Jesus?"

"Oh, some might have, though I would think only vague stories. It'll be our job to bring the true word of the Christ to these people and to establish a community that can thrive and grow."

With an appreciative smile, Timothy replied, "We have a lot of work to do here." Silas' face remained passive during the exchange. Paul wondered why he wasn't enthusiastic.

It was obvious enough that it was a garrison town with the number of Roman soldiers within sight of the docks. Paul went up to one and asked where the Jewish quarter was. The Roman laughed. "It isn't exactly a quarter, but there's a small section on the northwest side of town. If you follow the road heading that way," and the guard pointed roughly northwest towards a dirt road, "then you'll come across it."

"Thank you," Paul replied and they headed in that direction.

When the group approached the Jewish section, some men greeted them. Paul made introductions and the apparent leader, a man named Tobiah, introduced his people. Paul told the locals that he and his group were from Jerusalem and that they had important information to share and asked when a gathering would occur where he could talk. As it turned out, they were planning a dinner that evening. Paul and his entourage could attend and speak after the meal.

Paul sent Timothy and Silas off to try to find accommodations and he spent the day with Tobiah learning about Judaism in Europe.

The meal was a jovial event with roughly thirty people who all knew each other well. It was more like an extended family than a Jewish community, but maybe that wasn't unreasonable considering their limited numbers and distance from Jerusalem.

When they were finished, Tobiah stood. "You've all met Paul and his fellow travelers. They would like to say a few words about events in Jerusalem."

Paul stood and spoke calmly and eloquently about how the Christ, the savior, had already been here, and about the Kingdom of God. The group listened attentively, but when Paul was finished, they turned to Tobiah expectantly.

Tobiah stared into the distance for a moment and then looked back. "Are you really suggesting that the prophesy came true and we didn't even know? What kind of anointed one was it that couldn't convince the elders he was the Christ?"

A woman, Paul remembered her name as Lydia, turned to Tobiah. "That seems perfectly reasonable to me. The elders would not have wanted to lose their power and this man, being the Christ, would change everything. When I was very young, my father was excited about a new star in the sky and he wondered if it hailed the coming."

Paul looked oddly at Lydia. *Why would she assume it was recent*, he wondered. However, he wanted to address her first comment more, so he left the temporal inaccuracies alone. He sat down. "In fact, the leaders in Jerusalem did fight about Jesus the Christ and there are still some who don't believe he is the messiah."

They continued talking for a little over an hour more when Tobiah said it was time to be retiring for the evening. Lydia spoke up vehemently. "I want to be baptized." The other locals looked at her and when nobody said anything, she added, "Tonight, and my family wants to be baptized with me." Paul knew she could not have consulted with her family, but she seemed adamant.

Paul explained what they would need and Tobiah had some men find a tub they could fill with water. The baptisms went well and Paul looked at Lydia and proclaimed, "You are the first Christian convert in Europe."

Lydia smiled. "You must all stay with me and my family while you are here in Philippi. We have plenty of room and I want to learn all I can about Jesus the Christ."

"Timothy and Silas already arranged a place for us to stay."

Lydia replied, "We'll take care of that. I won't hear of you staying anywhere else."

Paul was reticent about staying with a widowed woman, but it was their entire group, not just him, and Lydia had older children. The local men didn't seem to be objecting, so he reluctantly agreed.

They stayed in Philippi for three weeks and enjoyed great success convincing the local population that Jesus was the Christ foretold in the prophesies and that the Kingdom of God was in each of them.

Then one day a teenage girl came running out of a store and looked at Paul and Silas, who were walking along the marketplace. She cried, "These men are servants of the One True God!" She kept saying the same thing over and over until the owner came out of the store. He said, "Excuse her; she has the power of divination."

Silas' eyes grew, but Paul looked at the owner with a grimace. *Why would God be working through this dispossessed girl?* He began a conversation with the man and quickly came to the opinion that the power was fake and that this storeowner was using the slave girl to make money. He turned to the girl. "With the power of Jesus the Christ, I command the evil spirit in you to depart. Leave this girl, never to return. I command you in the name of Jesus the Christ."

The girl collapsed in a pile, apparently unconscious. Paul bent down to her and she winked at him. He smiled and stood up, but straightened his face before turning to face the owner.

The owner's mouth was hanging open in shock and he was looking back and forth between Paul and the girl. He finally looked at Paul and yelled, "What have you done to her? How could you do this?" Then he spotted a magistrate across the street and ran to him saying, "These men have ruined me." The magistrate stared at him without saying anything. He added, "They are Jews and have caused nothing but trouble here in Philippi. They want us to worship some dead king. I'm a Roman, you must do something."

The magistrate looked at the two Jews. "Come with me."

Paul said, "Why, we have done nothing wrong."

"We'll see about that, just come with me."

Paul and Silas saw nothing they could do right then, so they went with the magistrate. He put them in a jail cell and disappeared.

The next day, Timothy was relieved to find the two in jail. The magistrate was there as well. He explained that there were some who didn't believe as these men do, but many who did and that they weren't preaching against Rome. The magistrate indicated he didn't want trouble with the Jewish community and hadn't actually seen Paul and Silas doing anything wrong. He let them go.

A jail-keeper was unlocking the gate when Timothy said to the Magistrate, "You know that Paul is a Roman citizen. I'm surprised he would be arrested for this." The magistrate turned and apologized to Paul, but also said, "The shop owner you fought with is very influential here. You should consider leaving town as soon as possible."

Paul, Timothy, and Silas discussed it and agreed that they had accomplished what they could in Philippi and they wanted to move on so they could get to Corinth before winter. They spent the day in preparation and left the following morning through Amphipolis and Appollonia and then to Thessalonica.

* * *

Thessalonica turned out to be a complex situation. Paul and Timothy were able to convert many Jews and Romans to Christianity, but there was also a strong Pharisaic contingent that became upset at the proselytizing. As they grew vociferous, Paul and Timothy met with the brethren and decided they would move on to Beroea. They left Silas in Thessalonica to continue trying to establish a Christian community there, but without the disruptive proselytizing that Paul and Timothy had been doing.

Unfortunately, some of the local Pharisees found out and sent a contingent to follow them to Beroea. The community in Beroea was receptive, but when the Pharisaic Jews showed up to disrupt them, the brethren ushered Paul and Timothy to move on, this time to Athens, where they were sure the Pharisees wouldn't follow.

* * *

Of course, Paul had heard a great deal about Athens and its philosophers. The city was known for its progressive freethinking. He was duly intimidated. However, he decided he had to deal with this directly by confronting them in a dialog. He had Timothy meet with the local synagogue to try to find accommodation and to speak with them about Christianity. Timothy asked what Paul was going to do, but he just shrugged and indicated that he wanted to get a feel for the city.

Paul asked a passer-by and was told how to find his way to the local forum, where he was likely to meet the philosophers. It wasn't hard to locate given its importance to the city.

When he arrived there, he saw a group of three men by a fountain and walked up to them. "May I join you for discussion?"

"Of course," one of them answered with a smile, "we always enjoy lively discussion. You aren't from around here; may we ask where you are from?"

"You would call it Iudea."

"Ah, a fellow subjugated province of the Roman Imperators." After a pause, he added, "What would you like to discuss?"

Paul hesitated because he wasn't at all sure how to approach this or what the result might be. He decided to start by discussing their religion. "Well, I want to try to understand your religion. You believe in many diverse gods, correct?"

Two of the men seemed to shrug slightly, but didn't say anything. The third just stared at Paul. Finally, one of the two who had shrugged spoke up, "It depends on what you mean by 'believe.' The gods have their uses, but do we believe there are really beings sitting around in Olympus, actively interfering with our lives?" After an obvious pause, he added, "Of course not."

"And what of the One True God of the Jews, do you think this God might be real?"

"Ah, I thought you might be Jewish. The answer to that is also a resounding 'of course not.' He is just another manifestation of Man wanting to explain the natural workings of the world through supernatural explanations and possibly a vain hope of life after death."

"What if I told you that I know God resurrected a man named Jesus for all to bear witness to his divineness and to show us the Kingdom of God."

The man who had previously just stared at Paul answered. "Then we would ask if you personally saw him dead and then arise, and even then we would have many other questions that might illuminate some other way this could have happened without there being divine intervention."

It seems like any one of these Greek philosophers can answer these questions, as if they are interchangeable. Paul decided to take a different tact, "In Judaism, there have been many prophecies through the ages and we can show how many of them came true, including the appearance of the messiah we call Jesus the Christ."

"Prophesies are easy to alter with hindsight and later readers wouldn't be able to tell the difference."

"I have personally seen miracles occur and glossolalists speaking the word of God."

The three smiled and the one who originally spoke up answered, "All things easy to fake." Then after a pause, he became adamant, "You have to understand that we believe the world is explainable without resorting to supernatural explanations. Relying on Gods is childish; man must work to understand the natural world, learn to respect it, and live within it. Even more importantly is to appreciate it in all of its complexity and beauty.

"Reliance on Gods is causing people to not appreciate what is all around them. It doesn't even really matter whether Gods, or in your case God, exists. What is important is that we base our lives, our laws, and our politics on what we can see and understand around us, and that we practice compassion.

"Now, if you'll excuse us, we'd like to continue the conversation we were having previously."

Paul looked at them with no idea how to address what they were saying. They seemed to be dismissing him as inconsequential. He stared, mouth slightly agape, at them for a moment trying to figure out what he might say and then gave up and left to find Timothy.

He caught up with Timothy and some of the elders at the Jewish synagogue. They confirmed that it was very difficult to talk religion with the Greek philosophers with their reliance on reason and logic. Paul decided to spend only a few days in Athens with the Jewish brethren before moving on to Corinth.

* * *

With winter fast approaching, Paul and Timothy were glad to make it to Corinth. They knew that the city was a key seaport and major trading post between Greece and the rest of the Empire. It included a sizable mixed population that might be willing to listen to the teachings of Jesus the Christ. It was also a town of debauchery and sexual immorality. Paul realized that, properly converted, it could be one of the most important Christian outposts and he intended to stay there for an extended period in order to build a thriving community.

They had received word from Silas that he was still in Thessalonica and was planning to stay there for the winter. His intention was to travel to Corinth in the spring to meet up with the other two.

After finding a place to live and introducing themselves to the local Jewish brothers, both Paul and Timothy found work; Paul as a sail-maker and Timothy as a carpenter. The work would help them get to know the locals and would provide some needed money for their extended stay.

There was a Jewish quarter in Corinth, but it was disorganized and apparently in conflict since there were multiple synagogues that weren't cooperating. In some cases, it would seem, they weren't even speaking with each other.

At Paul's second visit to one of the Synagogues, he met a man named Aquila who had recently come from Rome. Paul was interested to hear news of Rome, especially since he hadn't heard from Maximus and was worried. He was ingratiatory enough that Aquila finally invited him and Timothy to dinner at his house.

Paul and Timothy arrived that evening at a humble abode that Aquila and his wife Priscilla had found only days before. "You'll have to excuse the house,"

Priscilla said after being introduced, "we are still settling in. I wouldn't have expected Aquila to invite guests over so soon."

She was gracious enough, though she obviously did not want company. *I don't need to be here, especially if we aren't wanted,* he thought haughtily. "Well, we didn't mean to intrude," he said and turned to leave.

Priscilla's face softened. "No, of course not, you are welcome here."

The men settled in while Priscilla went to attend to dinner. After some pleasantries, Paul began in earnest, "What news do you have of the communities in Rome? I've heard that there are now Christian groups and I'm interested in how they are faring."

Aquila answered, "That's one of the reasons we are here. There are Christian groups in Rome and throughout the peninsula and they are successful enough that their proselytizing, along with that of the Druids, has irritated Claudius. He doesn't like anyone proselytizing, so he decreed that the Jews – he doesn't separate Jews from Christians – and the Druids had to leave the city."

Timothy asked, "Is there contention between the Christian-Jews and non-Christian Jews?"

Aquila looked at him askance, and answered, "It is true that they are both sects of Judaism, but in Rome, they tend to keep apart from each other. They worship separately and only occasionally get together and argue theology. Clearly the Romans see them as the same church since their decree was for Jews and not Christians, but the Christians seem to be trying to separate themselves."

That got Paul's attention, "And which are you if I may ask?"

"Oh, Priscilla and I are both Christians. In fact, when we were told to leave and discussed where to go, we heard that you and Silas would probably be going to Corinth, so we decided to come here. Is Silas with you?"

"No, he is still in Thessalonica, though he should be arriving next spring." Then, somewhat as an afterthought when he realized that Aquila hadn't mentioned Timothy, he added, "But we are lucky enough to have Timothy as well. You will find him very knowledgeable about Jesus the Christ."

"Excellent, I look forward to spending many evenings speaking with both of you and I want you to know that Priscilla and I will do what we can to aid in the development of Christianity here in Corinth."

Priscilla came in at that point with the food. The three men continued their conversation throughout the meal and then Paul and Timothy left, encouraged by the progress in Rome but dismayed that Claudius would oust the Jews. After all, Claudius had seemed a reasonable emperor, especially with respect to the Jewish population. *Where is Maximus?* Paul wondered.

Nine days later, he was standing with a group of men discoursing fervently when he noticed a sizable man standing in the shadows watching them. The man smiled and nodded slightly. Paul rubbed his chin for a second and then realized it was Maximus.

Paul recalled the time with Maximus in North Africa preaching and realized just how far they had come. He was so much more confident and even eloquent than he had been. And Maximus had been so serious and dedicated with a smile rarely seen. They had come a long way and so had Proculus' propositum.

The group finished their discussion and broke up. As Paul made his way down the street, Maximus emerged from the shadows and fell in-step beside him.

Paul said, "I wondered when you would show up." Then after a pause where Maximus didn't reply, Paul added, "You had me worried, I thought you would already be here when we arrived."

"Yes, I was delayed."

That's Maximus, terse and mysterious. Paul glanced at him and decided that pleasantries weren't needed or appropriate. "We have things to discuss. I've heard that the Jews were expelled from Rome and that Claudius appears to be turning against us."

"Some of that is true. He isn't exactly against the Jews. He's more against any religion trying to spread. He wants everyone to let everyone be. Although, he does seem to be trying to reinstitute the Eleusinian Mysteries, but that's probably because he associates them with the old Republic and wants us to return to the 'good days.' In any case, it isn't specifically Jews, or Christians, for that matter. He's expelled the Druids and some others as well and, even then, he let many of them stay if they promised not to spread their religion. He also expelled many astrologers and is supporting the Haruspices instead, so who knows exactly what he's thinking."

Paul laughed at the mention of Haruspices, "Those old entrails-reading soothsayers are a bunch of charlatans."

Maximus cocked his head. "I'm surprised you know of them." After a moment, he added, "Yes, I agree, but Claudius is doing anything he can to bring back a semblance of the Republic and he associates some of these practices with it."

"How are the Christian groups there? Are any of them still active?"

"Yes, certainly. Curia, with her subtle influence, convinced many of them to suspend active recruiting for now and to keep to themselves. Some left at Claudius' orders, but most stayed. When Claudius is distracted with other matters or when we have a new emperor, they will renew their efforts." He turned his head in thought and then prompted, "You should consider coming to Rome sometime to meet and encourage them."

Paul looked doubtful, but just mumbled, "Hmm."

Maximus added, "They are definitely Christian, but they don't have access to any of the apostles. You, Peter, or maybe James, really should go there to teach, if nothing else."

Paul perked up. "Yes, maybe you're right. But I won't be able to for a few years. Maybe I can send word to Peter to see if someone from Jerusalem could go."

The conversation seemed to dissipate, so Paul changed topics. "How long will you be staying in Corinth?"

"At least for the winter, I'm assuming you will be staying here as well. I want to renew contacts and establish a network of people who could aid you and the church here if needed. I've also seen some evidence that there are military personnel interested in Christianity and I want to see if that's the case with any stationed here. Maybe we can start attracting Roman soldiers."

That seems unlikely. But Paul couldn't think of a reason not to try.

When he didn't answer, Maximus added, "I'll be around," and then he turned towards a path between two buildings and disappeared.

Paul smiled at the infrequent and yet evocative meetings he seemed to have with Maximus. Even though he didn't particularly enjoy his company and he seldom saw the man, he felt safer in a town when Maximus was there.

* * *

The winter was an extraordinary time for Paul and Timothy. Many of the Jews were receptive to their teachings, as were more than a few Romans. They were also successful in amalgamating the splinter groups into a more cohesive Christian-like community.

In the spring, Maximus departed for Antioch and Silas arrived from Thessalonica. The following days were exciting as the three men exchanged details of the happenings in the communities.

Shortly thereafter, a pharisaic contingent arrived and began disrupting the brethren with attacks on Paul and the Christians. After a number of days of contentious debates, Paul was beginning to get irritated. He found himself in front of a synagogue with a group of brethren arguing with the Pharisees. They were attacking Jesus and arguing that he wasn't the Christ and Paul had no business stating so.

As other men were arguing with the Pharisees, Paul was contemplating the fact that the men weren't arguing whether or not Jesus existed or about his teachings, just about whether or not Jesus was the Christ. With that thought, he realized it was time to go on the offensive and he knew the perfect weapon.

He spoke up with a loud enough voice to interrupt the other arguments. "You know, I'm becoming quite irritated by arguments from the likes of you Pharisees when you were the cause of Jesus' death."

Both groups immediately stopped talking and stared at Paul.

"I haven't spoken of this before because I don't like needlessly attacking other Jews, but your attacks on me have gone far enough and people should understand just how undermining you can be." Both groups continued to stare at him. He straightened and raised his voice to the crowd. "There's something you should know that few people are aware of." He slowly perused the men. "Jesus was crucified. We don't talk about it because of how horrible it was."

One of the Christian men looked at him with a serious expression. "You don't mean to imply that the Pharisees crucified Jesus, do you?"

"Of course not, that's a Roman practice. However, the Pharisees turned on Jesus and told the Romans he was pretending to be the King of all the Jews. The Romans consider that traitorous. Jesus didn't deny it since he was in fact the true High Priest and leader of the Jews, and was of the line of Zadok. The Romans crucified him."

Paul became more forceful, "But they never would have cared or even noticed him if the Pharisees hadn't gone to them with proclamations of his kinghood. They had the Christ crucified, which is why they work so hard to convince us he wasn't the anointed one. They can't accept that they were the cause of his death."

The groups were silent at this revelation. The Pharisees stood with eyes opened wide and mouths agape. They were stunned to silence. Some of the Christian men then turned and looked at the Pharisees with disdain. The Pharisees glanced around at the hostility as Paul looked on curiously. *That ought to keep them busy*, he thought smugly. There were harsh exclamations from the crowd and more of the Christians began staring at the Pharisees and mumbling invectives. The Pharisees backed away and left the synagogue.

As the story circulated through the community, many brethren became anti-Pharisaic. Paul stayed away from the conversation and appeared sheepish and defensive when asked about it. He wanted people to believe he hated that he had mentioned such an atrocity and that he was embarrassed for revealing the truth.

Within a week, the Pharisees left the area.

XIII. Nero the Boy Caesar (51 AD – 54 AD)

"Whoever is not with me is against me, and the one who does not gather with me scatters."

- The Book of Q (Revised)

Late that fall, Paul and his retinue arrived back in Antioch. After a short rest, Silas headed for Jerusalem and Timothy for his home town of Derbe. Proculus insisted Maximus and Curia arrive before they did a full review, even though Paul wanted to meet immediately.

While waiting for the rest of the group to arrive, Proculus began to ponder his advancing years. He knew from the beginning that this plan was multi-generational. Curia might be able to be the strategist in Rome, but she needed a Jewish advocate and he didn't have any reasonable prospects. Unfortunately, these thoughts were not something he could share openly. He would just have to find the right sort of person on his own.

It was just over three weeks later when Maximus and Curia arrived. As June and Proculus greeted them at the door, all eyes immediately fell to Curia's extended belly and smiles spread across June's face just as subtle lines of concern crossed Proculus'.

June didn't say anything. She simply walked up to Curia and gave her a gentle hug.

Proculus thought, *how will this impact the plan*? But he held himself in check. "Congratulations are in order." Maximus beamed like Proculus had never seen.

Proculus waited three days to let Paul know that the two had arrived and to arrange a meeting between the four of them. He felt it best to let June and Curia spend time together and he enjoyed Maximus' company without the intensity of dealing with the situation and the future.

It was a pleasant spring day and they met in the courtyard surrounded by new blooms exuding fragrances of hope and rejuvenation. Proculus wondered if Curia might catch the subtle link. Paul arrived last to find the three sitting at the table. He looked directly at Proculus and without preamble said, "What is she doing here?"

Proculus eyes grew wide and his head tilted at an angle, taken aback. Maximus stood up, knocking his chair over, and exclaimed, "You have a lot of…"

Proculus interrupted and overrode Maximus with the intensity and depth of his voice, "Paul, what is the meaning of this? You know that Curia is a member of this group and she has been instrumental in starting the Christian church in Rome. She is vital to our plans. I thought this attitude of yours was behind us."

Maximus stayed standing, glaring intently at Paul. Curia seemed to have a quirky smile at the corner of her mouth as she too stared, waiting for an answer.

Paul tried to form a response while he looked back and forth at the three antagonistic expressions. Finally, he sat down and bowed his head, silent.

Proculus and Maximus were still fuming and staring at Paul, though Maximus begrudgingly straightened his chair and sat down. Curia broke the impasse, "Shall we begin?"

Proculus looked dubiously at Curia while he admired her nonchalant attitude towards someone who was blatantly misogynistic. He shook himself to clear his annoyance with Paul and began. "Paul, let us begin with you telling us about your travels."

Paul furtively glanced at Curia and took a moment to compose himself. "The trip had mixed results. Early, we were plagued with places the Pharisees had been and later Pharisaic groups would show up to try to discredit us. They seem to be actively attacking us and it was difficult to counter them since the people see them as the official representatives of Judaic doctrine.

"Near the western end of Galatia, we traveled by boat into Europe and found welcoming cities without their influence and became more successful. In particular, there are now thriving communities in Thessalonica and Corinth and a number of surrounding towns.

"There were two events that stood out and should be discussed." Paul mostly looked at Proculus and it appeared as if he was avoiding Curia altogether. "The first is that Silas stayed in Thessalonica while Timothy and I traveled to Corinth. Silas helped the Christians there, but didn't seem to work to make it an independent, thriving community. When he left, it diverged from the teachings of Jesus. Timothy had the notion to write a letter that put down in words what kind of behavior was acceptable and how the community should act. I wrote the letter and Timothy reviewed it.

"It was so well received by the Thessalonians that we wrote a second one to them before leaving Corinth. This one Timothy penned and I reviewed.

"I have copies of each of the letters. I have to tell you that they were so influential in binding the community together that we should consider writing more to other communities of brethren and we should make many copies." He looked around the group, and even glanced at Curia.

The three were nodding, though Maximus still appeared on edge. After a long pause, Proculus spoke up, "Please continue, Paul."

His lips tightened, but he relented. "The other event was in Corinth. Timothy and I had spent the winter there establishing a working community, one that could survive and even grow without us. In the spring, a group of Pharisees arrived and attacked our views. At first, Timothy and I defended the views of Jesus and we did well enough since the European towns, so far from Jerusalem, didn't have inflated opinions of the Pharisees. But there were nine of them and they could talk to many more people than we could. Opinions slowly turned.

"Then one day, there were five of them arguing with Timothy and me and a group of about fifteen local brethren were listening." Paul leaned forward and looked into the distance clearly picturing the events in his mind. "I was getting more and more irritated at their antagonistic slurs towards everything we were trying to accomplish. Finally, I couldn't stand still anymore and I let them all know that Jesus had been crucified and that it was the Pharisees who had caused it by telling the Romans that Jesus believed he was the King of the Jews. I made it look like I was embarrassed to divulge something like that.

"It caused exactly the kind of reaction we were hoping for. The brethren turned on the Pharisees. Later I wouldn't talk about what had happened; I wanted the local community to be the ones driving out the Pharisees and not us. Partly because I didn't want them coming back to Jerusalem and saying I drove them out with lies, but also because it made the locals concentrate on the Pharisaic crimes and not the legitimacy of what I had said."

Paul leaned back in his chair, spent. Curia's mouth was slightly open while Maximus was smiling. Proculus pondered where it might take them. He said, "That is quite a story. We will talk about the ramifications shortly, however we should review what has been happening in Rome."

Paul sighed and his body relaxed into the chair.

Maximus leaned forward to talk about Rome, but Proculus motioned for attention. "If you do not mind Maximus, I would like Curia to report on Rome and then you can add whatever else you think is important." Curia raised a single eyebrow and glanced quickly at her father, but leaned forward to speak.

"Well," she began slowly, "Claudius has been more successful than any of us would have predicted. He was such an ineffectual leader up until he became Caesar. However, he has shown some prowess at organizing and he has catered to the military. If you remember," she glanced surreptitiously at Paul, "he became Caesar through the Praetorian Guard and not by a senatorial appointment; the first one to have done so. There are a number of senators who are still irked. He has kept control, mostly through outright bribes to the military, which also annoys some of the senators. Additionally, he expanded the Empire, both by conquest and by negotiated settlements. In fact, he did another census since there hadn't been one since Augustus and because he wanted to impress everyone with his gains. Since he gave many of the new colonies citizenship, he now boasts that there are almost six million Roman citizens.

"Now, about him personally," Her eyes concentrated on the table, and then she continued "He seems to be an odd mix of true emperor, meaning that he doesn't even pretend that we are in a Republic, and someone who believes in the old ways. By that I mean he has been restoring old temples, expelling astrologers, and bringing back some of the old religious practices, including the Eleusinian Mysteries and the use of old languages in rituals.

"He also thinks of himself as knowledgeable about religious practices within the Roman empire. If you remember, he was the author of Augustus' reforms on religion. Unlike his predecessors, he hasn't allowed people to deify him or even to build temples in his name, which seems very reasonable. On the other hand, he doesn't like competition between religions or anyone actively trying to convert others, especially if they are foreign. So he drove out most of the druids, many Jews, and some Christians. And, by the way, he doesn't see the difference between Jews and Christians, which is why both were officially expelled. The only reason it didn't really work with the Christian groups is that we asked them to stop proselytizing for a time and to stay indoors as much as possible and not talk about religion when they were in public. That stance seems to be working, at least for now."

Curia leaned back in her chair, apparently finished. Proculus quietly turned and looked at Maximus.

Maximus returned the look for a second and then said, "The only point I might add is that Claudius has shown a strong inclination to use the military. He's the first to conquer lands again since Augustus asked that expansion cease. He also has no qualms about displacing populations or upsetting entire groups of people. He has had more than one person killed for his own reasons. Rebellion under Claudius would be dealt with swiftly and harshly."

Proculus started to speak and Curia interrupted him, "Sorry, there is one more thing you should be aware of. Last year, Claudius married Agrippina and then adopted her son, his great nephew, Lucius Domitius Ahenobarbus. Lucius is now Claudius' oldest male 'son,' so the assumption is that Claudius is planning to make Lucius his successor. There is also a rumor that Claudius is going to have Lucius declared an adult so that he can become the next Caesar at any time."

Proculus asked, "How old is Lucius now?"

"Fourteen."

"It seems unusual to me that Claudius would take these steps. It is as if he is expecting to die sometime soon. Do you know if anything is wrong with him?"

"Not that I am aware of. There are some senators who would like to get rid of him, but none dare with the military support he enjoys."

"Then I suspect it has more to do with Agrippina than with Lucius."

"That may be," Curia replied.

"Do we know much about Lucius?"

"We know that he wasn't raised by Agrippina. Caligula had her exiled for joining a plot to assassinate him and Lucius was sent to live with his Aunt. After Claudius became emperor, he allowed Agrippina to return to Rome and was reunited with her son. I don't know much after that until Claudius had his third wife, Messalina, executed so that he could marry Agrippina. If the boy is proclaimed an adult, I've heard some senators say they want him to address the Senate in person. If that happens, we might get some hints at what kind of a leader, or at least speaker, he is."

Proculus looked away. He had almost said too much in front of Paul. *It's easy to forget that he does not know the entire propositum.* "Unless we have some hint that Claudius is going to die, then it does not seem like there is anything we need to do."

Curia opened her mouth to respond, but then closed it and relaxed back into her chair.

Proculus continued, "Let us return to Paul's discussion." Paul lifted himself to more of an upright position.

"I would like to see these letters you and Timothy wrote. My inclination is to keep and even disseminate them for everyone to see and for potential use as roots of the Christian sect. These could be one of the main differences between us and other groups. Having documents that define and defend what you are preaching could solidify the movement.

"Paul, what are your plans for the foreseeable future?"

"Hmm, I'm a little tired of traveling right now and Peter has been in Jerusalem, so I'd like to stay here in Antioch and work with the local communities. I'm hoping to have at least one more, long trip in me. Maybe I'll stay here for a year or so."

"While you are here, it might make sense for you to write a few more letters, maybe to the community you established in Corinth."

"Yes, that's appropriate. I may also write to the Galatians and try to counter some of the Pharisee influence there."

Proculus changed subjects, "We should also discuss the crucifixion story. June is quite adamant that we should not pursue that avenue. In any case, we should probably wait to see what happens with Silas in Jerusalem. He will undoubtedly tell the council about the incident and there may be adverse, possibly severe, reactions."

Proculus turned to look at Maximus and Curia, "When are you two planning on returning to Rome?"

Curia answered, "I need to return in a few weeks before the pregnancy is too far advanced." She added with a smile, "Quinn would be furious if I was forced to stay here."

Proculus turned to Maximus who answered reluctantly, "I was planning to return with Curia, but I could stay here for a while to make sure there isn't any overt reaction from Jerusalem."

Proculus deliberated the situation. *He could be needed in Jerusalem, but Curia needs him more right now.* "That will not be necessary. Paul is among friends and supporters here. The council would not do anything blatant. You should return with your daughter."

Both Curia and Maximus visibly relaxed.

"Paul, what about our notion of sending out other proselytizers?"

"As you know, we found Timothy early in this last trip. He stayed with me the entire time and is now headed home to Derbe. He will make an excellent representative if we can get him to travel, though he was reluctant to leave his home and wife the last time. However, he should at least be able to travel around Galatia and Macedonia."

Then he added, "Believe it or not, Silas is another choice. I know he has ties back to the council in Jerusalem, but he did seem to be an avid Christian supporter, he knows the teachings of Jesus, and he's a fair advocate and speaker. He may not be willing to present the crucifixion, but that's not necessarily a bad thing. That story will spread of its own accord and our not talking about it will just increase its mystery. At least that's my opinion.

"The other person we should consider is Peter, and maybe even James. I had one person from Rome suggest that Peter or I visit there to aid the fledgling Christian community. I'm not yet ready to go, but possibly Peter is."

Proculus wondered, *why is he reluctant?* "Peter and James may be getting a little frail for any extended trips, especially on foot. However, they might be willing to work with the church in Rome for a while. Let us try to make that happen." *He may need to follow them later.*

"Curia, you should find out more about Lucius and his teachers. They are likely to take the role of advisors if he becomes emperor anytime soon." Proculus looked around expectantly only to find blank stares. Paul still seemed morose, but Proculus did not want to address that here. "That appears to be all."

They stood up to leave when Paul stopped them, "You know, something occurred to me the other day. I met a boy named Theophorus who is one of the oldest children from any of the truly Christian families. It was interesting to hear him speak because he could be one of the very first people raised Christian and his manner and approach to religion is different from anything I've heard out of anyone before. He's totally accepting of the teachings of Jesus in a way that an adult who has come into Christianity isn't."

Proculus wasn't sure what point Paul was trying to make. Paul turned and left. Maximus and Curia shook their heads at his back while Proculus stood still in contemplation. *Could one of these children be the Jewish partner Curia needs? Do I have enough time left to wait for one of them to mature?* He realized he would have to start watching Theophorus and some of the other children more carefully and maybe try to determine how open-minded they were in addition to their religious convictions. *Maybe one of them will reach maturity in time.*

* * *

Exactly one week later, near mid-day Proculus, Maximus, and Curia met at the Rock Rest. He chose an isolated table and asked Josephus to keep other patrons away. The mood was solemn and made more so by the dim lighting and the emptiness of the tavern.

They ordered drinks and sat quietly waiting. Once they were alone, Proculus began. "We are nearing the last phase of the plan. In many ways, this will be the most difficult because many people may be put in harm's way, including some whom we love. We must persevere, however, for the plan's success."

Maximus' face was impassive, but Curia leaned on the table with avid attention on Proculus.

"Christianity is doing well, but it is still a sect of Judaism. The intent of the changes we have put in place is to make it appealing to the Roman citizenry. Eventually it needs to become a favored religion in order to influence the government. However, that is many years away.

"For now, we need to work at getting Judaism and Christianity separated in the minds of the Senate and Caesar. Then, we need to encourage discord against the Jewish leadership."

Proculus continued, but was interrupted by Curia, "What? Are you saying there might be war? That can't be something we want, Rome would destroy Jerusalem and many Jews would die."

Proculus looked sheepish, but Maximus face was emotionless. During Proculus' hesitation, Curia's eyes crinkled. Proculus continued carefully, "Of course we do not want open war, but we do need Judaism to diminish in terms of importance to the Empire. That is the only way for Christianity to become the dominate religion. The obvious way to do that is to foster discord between Rome and Jerusalem while demonstrating compatibility with Christianity."

Curia stared at Proculus while he waited to see if she had any more questions. She said, "With Paul discrediting the Pharisees, they would be the obvious target." Her eyes flitted around and then she added, "Paul won't like this; not at all. In fact, he may end up fighting against us if he realizes that we are encouraging strife between Rome and Jerusalem."

Proculus was glad to see Curia using 'us' since it meant she considered herself an integral part of the plan. "True. We will have to consider how best to handle that."

Then Maximus spoke up and it had been long enough since he had said anything that both Proculus and Curia started slightly. "A movement like this needs a martyr at some point. As much as I've grown fond of Paul and have been impressed with what he's accomplished, he might make an ideal one. Somehow, though, the Pharisees would have to be at fault and not the Romans for our plans to work."

All three were silent while contemplating the possibility. Curia was shaking her head slightly. Proculus spoke up, "It is difficult to envisage, almost traitorous. However, it does make some sense. It would help to solidify the movement and Paul's place within it, and it would be a way to stop him from causing damage to the movement if he finds out we had anything to do with hurting the Jews." As he struggled with his emotions, he added hastily, "On the other hand, it might be a little early for a martyr and it could be difficult to prove Pharisaic involvement."

After an uncomfortable silence, he changed the subject, "We can spend time considering it. Paul has at least one more long trip in him and we are not at the point yet of causing anything serious.

"On another topic, Curia, you should continue pushing the growth of the church in Rome. Hopefully, it will eventually become the headquarters for Christianity. In addition, if the crucifixion story does not appear in Rome on its own, you should disclose it, surreptitiously. That could be the start of us placing a wedge between the Jews, in this case the Pharisees in Jerusalem, and Rome."

* * *

For three years, the plan progressed apace with Paul traveling and Curia helping to build the church in Rome. With a letter from Curia that Claudius' reign was in trouble, Proculus decided he needed to take a trip to Rome. He also wanted to meet Lucius who was now going by Nero Claudius Germanicus, having been granted 'adulthood' by Claudius.

Proculus, Maximus, and Curia met at the Scaevola house on a day when Quinn was away on business. Curia took them into a well-furnished library where they could close doors and enjoy some measure of privacy from the staff and from her precocious two-year-old son.

Maximus offered a hand to help her into a chair since she was well into her second pregnancy.

Their moods were cheerful and Proculus jumped to the point of the meeting, his smile and energy contagious. "You both know of the superb growth of Christianity we have seen over the last few years. With Timothy in Galatia and Macedonia, Silas in Syria and Asia, and Paul around Antioch, the communities have grown tremendously. Even the one here in Rome and those in Europe are expanding at a steady pace. Moreover, I have heard recently that a group has formed in Alexandria, Egypt, and without us specifically sending someone.

"The other news is that Paul left last year on his third trip. Word finally reached Jerusalem about the crucifixion story and they were, as expected, furious. Paul had already decided it was time for another trip and getting him out of the area seemed prudent. So he is heading up through Galatia again and then over to Europe, similar to his last trip."

Curia interjected, "Did he ever write more letters like the ones to the Thessalonians? It seems to me that they could become quite important."

"He did write one more, to the Corinthians, when he heard they were using some of the relaxed rules to justify abhorrent behavior, but just the one. I have encouraged him to write more while he is on this trip. It was upon hearing of the distasteful behavior in Corinth that he was convinced another trip was needed. He will try to find someone there as strong as Timothy to lead the church in Europe.

"The other good news is that we were finally able to convince Peter to come to Rome. He should be here within the month. That will aid in the growth of the church here and will solidify this area as an important one to the Christian movement.

"How are we doing with separating Jews from Christians in the eyes of Caesar and the Senate?"

Curia answered, "Almost nowhere. We've been very successful at separating them from each other in their own eyes, especially because of the crucifixion story, but the Romans in power just don't seem to care and they are both considered foreign religions. The politicians are apathetic, at best, towards the religious practices of others."

"Ei!" *What can be done?* "What about the letter you wrote suggesting that Claudius might be in trouble?"

"It isn't political as much as personal. He certainly has his enemies in the Senate and elsewhere, but he hasn't hesitated to eliminate people if he feels a threat, so I don't think anyone in the Senate is prepared to challenge him.

"However, he has been having a great deal of trouble with Agrippina and there are rumors that he is going to disown Nero. Do not forget that he had his last wife executed. Agrippina is very nervous. She has also shown her willingness to kill for her son and some of us believe she will act first. Or Claudius may execute her and disown Nero and then we have no idea who Claudius' successor would be, though Britannicus is the next oldest male heir, from a previous marriage."

Maximus added, "I've spoken with Britannicus before. He's a mild-mannered boy who is unlikely to be able to lead for long and there is little chance he will be aggressive."

Proculus said, "It would seem I need to meet Nero. Maybe we can help Agrippina's decision along or possibly protect her, though if Caesar wants her executed, and he is willing to follow standard practices and not do it covertly, there will be little we can do."

Curia added, "Nero married his stepsister Claudia last month and there's a reception being held next week by the Senate for them. You being an ex-senator, I could get you into the reception. You would go mostly unnoticed, but you also wouldn't be able to get any time alone with him."

"I just want to observe him. An affair like this with other senators present should suffice."

"You know, he did appear to the Senate just after being proclaimed an adult. He did fairly well given his age; he certainly wasn't timid."

"Yes, I had heard that."

* * *

Proculus and Curia ended up attending the wedding reception together. They were both dressed formally with Proculus' purple sash showing his senatorial rank. They entered down a small staircase into a large entertainment room the Senate frequently utilized. As they strode in, a mischievous smile played across Proculus' face. "People will assume you are my wife," he whispered. Curia laughed.

However, after entering the room, the two spent little time together. The idea was to get an impression of what kind of Caesar people imagined Nero might make, and talking to others was the way to find out.

After almost an hour of mingling with the political elite of Rome, Nero and his wife Claudia were announced, the room quieted, and all eyes turned to the elaborate curved staircase the married couple were descending.

Proculus' first impression of Nero was that he was pretentious. He walked with an air of superiority, but not of regality. He also was not a handsome man with a large nose, thick dull lips, and a deep vertical line in his forehead. Claudia, however, was clearly aristocratic with the kind of dignity Proculus expected of such a role. Her hair was long and curled into elegant waves and she flowed with grace and dignity. *They seem ill-matched.*

After a suitable amount of time passed, where Nero and Claudia circulated among the senators with casual conversation, Proculus positioned himself within hearing distance of the sixteen-year-old boy. *A boy slated to become the leader of the most powerful nation in history.*

Proculus saw Curia within earshot as well. There was a hesitance about the boy. He seemed to be trying to hide the fact that some of the senators intimidated him, especially if they showed any kind of intelligence. His boisterous overriding of those around him and apparent disregard for what they said made that all too clear.

The two observed, as best they could, for another hour before departing. When they reached the Scaevola house, Maximus and Quinn were waiting for them. The four had drinks in the library and discussed the young heir. Unfortunately, with Quinn there, they had to speak superficially, but they knew each other well enough to converse through ambiguity.

As the conversation progressed, Quinn became agitated, looking furtively between the other three. Finally, he said goodbye to the three, ostensibly to wish his son a good night.

Proculus became serious, "Curia, what did you find out about Nero's teachers or anyone who might become an advisor?"

"The obvious one is a man named Lucius Annaeus Seneca, he's a philosopher…"

Proculus interrupted her, "Yes, I have heard of him. Claudius exiled him at Messalina's request. I was told he was back."

"Apparently Agrippina brought him back specifically to tutor Nero, but rumors indicate it may have been to aggravate Messalina. In any case, Seneca has been tutoring Nero for four years now and they've reportedly become very close. Many expect Seneca to have a lot of influence on the boy for many years.

"The other possibility is a prefect named Sextus Afranius Burrus. He seems to be very close to Agrippina and, some say, hired by her to protect her son and to ensure his ascension.

"The last one I know of is Alexander of Aegae, but he tutors Nero mostly on math even though he is also a philosopher."

Proculus thought aloud, "So he has at least one philosopher and a prefect for teachers and advisors; that should make an interesting combination. I would like your opinions, but mine is that we would be better off with Nero than anyone else likely to become emperor. Claudius is never going to care enough about the Jewish situation to accomplish what we need done. That implies that we should take steps to help Nero become emperor."

Maximus interjected, "Do you think we are ready for that?"

Curia's eyebrows furrowed. "We should not take active steps to end Claudius' reign. It's too risky and there isn't enough obvious gain from such a move."

Her eyes grew large as she continued, "We could wait for an attempt on her or Nero and then stop it from happening. That would cause her to blame Claudius and we would immediately be on Nero's side." Her posture relaxed as she added, "I can have my network try to warn us if anything is planned."

Maximus offered, "That does keep us from being the perpetrators."

Proculus admired the approach. *Subtle and cunning.* "I am in agreement." Proculus concluded, "We will try to protect Agrippina and her son and watch for action by Claudius."

* * *

Proculus had resigned himself to staying through the winter. However, the more he heard the more he believed there was enough contention that action was imminent. One sunny afternoon Curia came, out of breath, to where Proculus and Maximus were having lunch at an outdoor cafe. When she recovered enough to speak, she said, "Sometimes I hate being pregnant, I can't even walk at a fast pace without becoming out of breath." She sat down and continued, "There are two men planning to kill Nero tonight at the games he is attending. From what I heard, Claudius can get the Senate to approve executing Agrippina, but not Nero, so he is going to assassinate him instead and then proceed with Agrippina."

Proculus quietly turned and looked at Maximus. The soldier stood up, offered a slight nod, and left. Within a few strides, however, Curia stopped him. "If this goes as planned, we need to inform Agrippina. I should go to her during the games to tell her we heard about the assassination plan and that Proculus has dispatched you to take care of it. That will make her worry so vehemently that she will react more fervently towards Claudius. It will also make it clear who exactly was responsible for saving her son."

Admirable manipulation, Proculus thought with pride. "It is somewhat risky," he interposed, "if Maximus should fail, Agrippina may blame us."

Curia looked to her left. "That is not likely. I can make it obvious that we do not know if we'll succeed because we only just found out."

"I agree. It is an acceptable risk. You two know what to do." At that Curia stood up as well and both her and her father left in silence.

* * *

Maximus brought three other men with him. It took them a while to spot the two assassins at the games who were intensely watching Nero. Maximus had two men follow one and he and the other soldier took the second. He wanted to wait for them to make their move before proceeding. That way Nero would know what was happening.

After the third gladiator competition, the crowd stood to cheer. The two men approached Nero, one from each side. Maximus signaled for the other two to take the man on the far side. They stealthily approached from behind. One of them grabbed the would-be assassin around the neck and the other shoved a sword through his back and up into his left lung. They dragged him away quickly as if nothing had happened.

Just as the other assassin was getting close to Nero, he noticed his compatriot being dragged away and looked around alarmingly. He started to swing his sword around, but the soldier with Maximus caught his arm as Maximus drove his gladius into the man's side. The soldier carried him away as Maximus looked up at Nero. "That was close. You should leave in case there are others."

Nero hesitated and then walked away. He stopped just after passing Maximus and turned. "Who are you?"

"My name is Maximus, I'm a friend. Proculus Antonius and I heard this might happen tonight, so I gathered some men and came here to help. You should talk with your mother." Maximus then quickly walked by Nero and left the coliseum.

* * *

Curia stood by Agrippina, who was sitting in a chair crying, when Nero arrived. Her hand was gently resting on Agrippina's shoulder. When she saw Nero approaching, she whispered into his mother's ear and the woman looked up to see her son alive and apparently unhurt. She stood, ran to him and held him, openly weeping, "You are safe! Are you hurt? Oh my Lucius, what has that evil man done?"

"I'm fine mother. A man named Maximus and some soldiers saved me. I don't know who ordered the attack, but we will find out."

"I know! It was Claudius. Who else would have done such a thing?" She wiped tears away from her reddened and swollen face. "The coward couldn't come after me, so he attacked you." Then Agrippina stopped and looked at Curia uncomfortably.

Curia caught Agrippina's suspecting glance and realized it was time for her to go. "If you will excuse me, I am sure you two want to be alone. If you need me, send a messenger to Proculus or to Quintus Scaevola. Goodbye." Then she quietly and quickly left the residence and went to find her co-conspirators.

Claudius died by poisoning seventeen days later leaving Nero to be the youngest emperor ever to rule the Roman Empire. The assassin was never found.

XIV. Paul Imprisoned (54 AD – 60 AD)

"The law of Moses and the prophets were authorities until John. Since then the kingdom of God has been overpowered by violent men."

- The Book of Q (Revised)

For three years, Curia and Maximus watched the young emperor attempt to run his vast domain while the elders in his life vied for the most influence over him. There was serious contention between his mother, Agrippina, and his two closest advisors, Seneca and Burrus.

Curia wrote to Proculus, trying to keep him informed.

Salutations my dear Proculus. I trust everything is well with you and June. Servius and Marcia are both doing well and Quinn's business is thriving, as always. His mother passed away two months ago and he misses her, but is otherwise well.

For being the youngest Caesar ever, Nero has performed acceptably. Unfortunately, the adults around him have not done as well. Nero tries to take advice from each of them, but he has grown tired of the contradictions and petty bickering.

At one point, his mother tried to sit down next to him when he was meeting with an Armenian envoy. Many of the senators present audibly groaned and Burrus stepped forward to stop her. It is just one example of her assuming too much and going too far in the presence of others. A few months later she tried to stop Nero's relationship with the slave Claudia Acte, but Seneca defended Nero. Finally, it was rumored that Agrippina started suggesting Britannicus should be emperor. The day before Britannicus was to be proclaimed an adult, Nero had him poisoned and then Agrippina ejected from the imperial residence. He also removed many of Agrippina's supporters, so I believe she is no longer influential.

Unfortunately, that wasn't the end of the in-fighting. Later, each of Nero's advisors were caught in embarrassing predicaments including embezzlement, conspiracy, and affairs. For Nero it meant an opportunity to consolidate his power and gain an independence from the elders in his life and he didn't hesitate to take it. Burrus was assassinated with poison. Though Seneca is still in the high court, his advice is now just that.

My father suggested Nero might have invented some of the claims in order to justify the purge. It is possible, but not particularly important. I believe this to be a positive step as it solidifies a clear individual in power instead of the array of people we previously had to watch.

The terse reply from Proculus indicated Paul was returning from his third mission and he wanted Maximus and Curia to join them in Antioch.

* * *

Curia elected to take her two children, Servius and Marcia, with them. When they arrived, they found that Paul was still weeks away, so Curia spent the time with her children and June exploring Antioch. June was becoming something of a surrogate grandmother to the two children and relished being with them. Maximus enjoyed time with Proculus, but then took off for Caesarea to renew old relationships in the area.

Paul arrived almost three weeks later, but was exhausted from his trip. Curia took one look at him and suggested quietly to Proculus that they wait a couple of days for him to recover before meeting. *That was probably his last trip,* she thought resignedly.

It was a dark and dreary day with low clouds and likely rain, so the four of them met in the library. June was invited, but she chose to spend the time with Servius and Marcia instead.

After everyone got comfortable, Proculus began, "Paul, please tell us about your trip."

Paul was slow to start. Curia wondered if he had something difficult to say or whether he was just tired. As the others were becoming impatient, he began, "There really isn't much to tell that you haven't heard before. The communities are growing steadily, some more than others, but overall we have had many converts. There have been problems with some groups not understanding the teachings and behaving as if the cessation of some of the old Abrahamic laws meant they didn't have to follow any of them. They became," he hesitated, looking at his feet, "well… immoral.

"The best news is that we've added a number of new proselytizers, including Apollos in Ephesus and Erastus in Thessalonica. They'll mostly concentrate in and around their own communities.

"I also wrote a couple more letters, one to the Corinthians, and one to the church in Rome. I have copies for you to keep."

He grimaced and looked at the table with sad, downturned eyes. He finally continued, though sheepishly, "Lastly, I'm getting older and I find all of the travel difficult." He looked around at the group. Curia did as well and saw looks of compassion and concern. Paul looked down at his lap, "I also think it's time I visited Jerusalem again. I haven't been there in a long time and I want to proclaim our progress to anyone who will listen."

At the mention of going to Jerusalem, Proculus' eyebrows went up in surprise, Maximus looked worried, and Curia was bewildered. Maximus was the first to speak, "You do understand that Jerusalem could still be dangerous?" When Paul did not answer, he continued, "There are a lot of Jews there who don't believe in what we are doing and could easily influence enough people that you could be jailed or even killed."

Paul replied, "Yes, I understand that. I believe it's a risk worth taking. I've collected money from a number of communities to help the church in Jerusalem. That should make them more accepting of my being there and reluctant to do anything harmful."

Curia casually mentioned, "They know about the crucifixion story and can't be pleased with it."

Proculus added, "You should also know that Peter is in Rome working with the church there. James is still in Jerusalem and is likely to support you, but he has limited power with the elders, especially if they call a Sanhedrin."

As Proculus was speaking, Curia contemplated the martyr idea. She felt mildly ashamed at how cold the idea was and then irritated with herself for feeling ashamed. She knew this plan would have casualties.

Proculus gently asked, "When will you be going?"

Paul looked up quickly, apparent surprise on his face. "I'd like to rest here for a number of weeks and possibly write another letter or two and then go. I don't want to take anyone with me, in case there is trouble."

Maximus interjected, "I'll have someone there to help protect you if it really comes to that. There are some Jews I know that I can hire, so they'll be able to go most places you would be without attracting attention."

Paul opened his mouth, obviously ready to object and then relented, saying simply, "Thank you." He started to leave, but Proculus stopped him, asking, "With you, Peter, Barnabas, and James elsewhere, who should run the church here in Antioch?"

"Evodius has proven a reasonable leader and can take over," Paul answered and then walked from the room.

Curia had spoken very little during the entire meeting, but once Paul left she said, "I know you two have considered whether Paul might make a good martyr, and maybe he will, but in my opinion, it isn't the right time. Without cohesion among the communities, they may splinter and go their own route. Paul holds them together with his travels and his letters. Even if he can't go far any longer, he can still write and help the communities." Then she looked directly at her father, "If something does go awry in Jerusalem, you may want to consider that prison time would lend itself to Paul writing letters, but martyrdom wouldn't. He can always be a martyr later."

Proculus looked up at Maximus. "I agree."

* * *

Paul looked up from his discussion with Philip, in the Gentile Court in Jerusalem, to see James running towards him. When he approached, he was breathing heavily. "I'm sorry Paul. I mentioned the crucifixion story and some Pharisees became upset. They are on their way here to confront you."

"Do not worry yourself, James. This is something we expected."

A few minutes later the group approached. They yelled at Paul and accused him of breaking the covenant, which to them was the equivalent to breaking the law. One of them picked up a stone and Paul saw the man Maximus had hired leave. *So much for protection*, he thought stoically. The man with the stone kept throwing it a few inches into the air and catching it as he stared at Paul. The others continued to berate him. A few minutes later Maximus' man returned with a Prefect who approached and proclaimed Paul to be a Roman citizen and that this was a Roman matter. He arrested Paul.

Unfortunately, the procurator wanted nothing to do with the volatile situation. He had Paul moved to the jail in Caesarea where he was quickly forgotten.

* * *

The first few months in jail were some of the longest in Paul's life. He vacillated between a sense of deep satisfaction with his life and overwhelming ennui. He had visitors, including Proculus and June, Peter, and Barnabas along with his cousin Mark. After days of talking with Mark, Paul convinced him to become another proselytizer and to depart on a mission to northern Africa, an area Paul had not been able to reach.

The months dragged on as Paul settled into a routine of prayer, meditation, and contemplation of Jesus the Christ and the One True God. As time passed, he wrote letters to the communities and received a few responses from brethren.

After almost two years, a newly appointed procurator announced that he wanted to lower jail occupancy to lower the cost of housing prisoners. However, Paul was a notable person, so he ordered him moved to Rome where someone there could make the decision on what to do with him.

Paul received Proculus at the jail in Caesarea during the final relocation preparations. Proculus informed him that his influence in Rome would allow for a negotiation of Paul's release. He also pointed out that Paul had wanted to travel to Rome to work with the Christians there and could do so after his release. Paul was quiet and felt trepidations about the move even with Proculus' reassurances. To make sure they were not lost, he gave the letters he had been writing to Proculus.

Just over a week after Proculus' visit, Paul and twelve others, five of them Christians, set out for Rome. It was the wrong time of year to be trying to get to Rome by boat. The group had to turn back multiple times to wait for favorable winds and ended up wrecking the small ship on the shores of Malta where they had to winter. Three months later, they finally obtained passage on an Alexandrian ship to Rome.

During the voyage, at Paul's bidding, the five Christians worked hard and ingratiated themselves with the guards. Over time, the guard in charge, a Roman by the name of Opiter, befriended Paul and listened to his teachings of Jesus the Christ. When they arrived in Rome, he requested permission for Paul to stay with him instead of in jail. Approval was granted as long as Paul agreed to stay in Rome, with him, until a final judgment was rendered.

Five days after they settled in, Curia and Peter appeared at Opiter's house to find Paul recovering from the long and harrowing journey.

Opiter welcomed them in, "Paul has told me about you, Peter," and then, almost as an afterthought, "and you as well Curia. Please, both of you come in." Curia, standing slightly behind Peter, nodded gently.

Paul stood and welcomed them. "It is good to see you," he said, looking at Peter.

"And you," Peter said. "We were so worried about you when we heard that your ship had wrecked. We praise God you are safe and that you have been freed from the grasp of the Roman authorities."

"Not completely freed. I have to stay near Opiter until they decide on my disposition."

"But you are available to work with the church here, are you not?"

Paul looked at Opiter who nodded and then Paul answered, "Apparently."

Opiter offered, "Please, sit down and I will bring drinks."

"Is the church thriving?" Paul asked.

Peter smiled and crooked his head. "Two years in jail, almost dying in a shipwreck, and you are worried about the community here!" He shook his head and answered the original question. "Yes, it is thriving, though it's a difficult situation with the Roman antagonism. They are so accepting of conquered peoples continuing to practice their religions, but not here at the heart of the Empire. Here they think of foreign religions as barbaric."

Curia added obsequiously, "It is more like they find any culture or ideas from conquered peoples backward."

Paul grimaced at her, but Peter responded amicably, "That may be, but it's still something we have to counter." Then he turned back to Paul. "Your help here will be most appreciated. In fact, I have wanted to return to Jerusalem, but we didn't have anyone who could take my place. That is until you arrived. Once you settle in, you could take over the church leadership here and I can return to Jerusalem to work with James and the council."

Paul pondered that and realized he would prefer to lead the church here without Peter around, though he wasn't about to say so. Instead, he answered, "Yes, that's a good idea. James could use your help. Hopefully you can stay here for a few months while I get acquainted with the community."

"Of course; the winds won't be favorable for a southward-bound journey until then anyway."

The conversation died down, so Peter excused them, "Well we should let you rest. We would love to have you come to temple on Saturday. We can send someone by to show you where it's at if you like."

"Yes, I would enjoy that. Thank you for coming by."

* * *

Paul was overwhelmed for the next few months as he tried to get the churches organized and working together. Peter was a highly devout and spiritual leader, but he wasn't an organizer and didn't work to get the churches consistent and cooperative.

As Peter was preparing to leave, Maximus arrived and asked for a meeting with Paul and Curia. Paul reluctantly accepted. He saw no reason to meet with those two since they had almost nothing to do with the Christian church and the communities around Rome.

They met at a small outdoor café on a sunny afternoon with a light wind blowing from the west. They exchanged niceties for a few minutes until their drinks arrived. Maximus began. "I have to say that I'm concerned. You two need to be working together and you've had almost no interaction since Paul arrived here in Rome."

He began to say more, but Paul interrupted him. "I see no reason why we have to see each other much, if at all. Curia has nothing to do with the Christian church here and I have no interest in Roman politics."

Curia smiled mischievously, but Maximus' jaws tightened. He raised his voice. "Well you should. Rome could make life very difficult for Jews and Christians alike and being aware of what the Roman politicians are doing can only help you." He grunted and then added, "And you should know that Curia is responsible for getting the Roman Christian churches going. If it wasn't for her, you wouldn't have any communities here to lead."

Paul looked at Curia, aghast at the idea. The lines of discomfort grew on his face and his mouth was agape. He shook his head dismissively. "We both know that the church would have begun here regardless. And whatever happened in the past, the church has been established and is growing. As for Roman politicians, they will do what they do, and I leave it to God to make sure it isn't detrimental to Jews."

Now Maximus leaned forward menacingly and his fists were tightening along with his jaw. "That is just ignorant. The Jews have been conquered and beaten multiple times in the past and your God did nothing to stop that. You may think you are the chosen people, but you've still been subjugated by Rome and your God sits idle. If you alienate the Senate or, worse, Caesar himself, you may find Jews and Christians alike ousted from Rome, mistreated, or even enslaved."

"You misunderstand me Maximus. I'm aware that Rome is capable of all of those things. However, I am also aware of what has been happening with

Caesar to know that he's distracted with his and his family's wickedness and misconduct. Between his affairs with slaves and him executing his mother just because she didn't support him, and there being rumors of his advisors stealing from the imperial funds, he's too busy with his own intrigues to worry about the Christians who are causing him no harm.

"Now, if you'll excuse me, I have work to do." Paul quickly stood and left.

PART THREE

Christianity

XV. The Burning of Rome (62 AD – 65 AD)

"Whoever welcomes you welcomes me, and whoever welcomes me welcomes the one who sent me."

- The Book of Q (Revised)

Curia was trepidatious walking up to the forbidding house. For two years, she had kept her distance from Paul while he took over leadership of the local churches. He was required to stay within the Seven Hills of Rome and to live with Opiter until the authorities decided on a resolution. Curia had kept track of what he was doing, but had made very little contact. However, this news was too exciting not to deliver in person.

Opiter opened the door and frowned. *It's nice to see you too*, she thought dryly. "Is Paul at home?" she enquired pleasantly. He looked into the house and then back at Curia with his mouth opened slightly, but said nothing. "I have urgent news for him; you must let me in." Opiter slowly moved aside.

Paul came from his room at Opiter's call and stopped when he saw Curia. He was both surprised and irritated to see her. The edges of his eyes narrowed, but he continued approaching. Before he could say something negative, she exclaimed, "Paul, I have great news. We have been able to get the charges against you dropped." She handed him a scroll and added, "This document shows that all charges have been vacated. You are free to travel where you wish. It also restates your citizenship."

Paul reached out hesitantly to take the scroll and he started to say something, but then stopped. Curia could see the conflicting emotions playing across his face. *He hates that I am the one delivering this.* He finally stammered, "How were you able to do this?"

"Well, I've been working at it, as time would allow, for the last two years. I finally became irritated with the inability of anyone to make a decision and I went to a friend of my husband's, a senator by the name of Gurges. I heard that he had a lot of respect for Proculus, having read a number of his senatorial papers, and I figured the combination might make him amenable to helping." She took a breath, smiled, and began gesticulating. "And it worked. He took only a few seconds to gauge what I was asking of him and then reached for the paper and signed it."

Paul looked at the scroll with glistening eyes as the tight muscles in his body relaxed. Opiter offered, "Any senator's signature is valid for a release like this, so it's true Paul, you're a free man."

Paul gained his composure. "This will help a great deal. Now I can travel around to other areas on the peninsula to preach the word of God." Graciously, he added, "Thank you Curia, I do appreciate your efforts on my behalf."

Curia's smile spread across her face. *That must have been difficult*, she thought impishly. They discussed Paul's specific plans for a few minutes and then Curia left to write to Proculus and Maximus that she had finally succeeded.

* * *

Paul spent much of the next two years aiding small Christian groups around the peninsula. Some already existed and some he helped to create. He was so successful at setting these up and differentiating them from the Jews that conflicts arose between the Christian brethren and the Jewish population.

A side effect Paul hadn't anticipated was that the conflicts annoyed Nero further. He began to have both Jews and Christians arrested and, in some cases, tortured. He also exiled a number of them, though he couldn't outright ban all of them from Rome, as their numbers had grown too high.

* * *

Curia and Maximus were talking amiably near the shops of the great hippodrome, Circus Maximus, when they smelled a fire. They both stopped, looked towards the Scaevola house, and saw rising smoke in that general direction. Curia looked at her father with huge eyes and exclaimed, "Servius, Marcia," and ran towards her home with Maximus not far behind.

The shops in the hippodrome used flammable materials and were known for having to deal with fires daily. But Curia felt in her heart that this one was different. She could now see smoke from multiple areas, all low lying around the Palatine Hills. *Why are there so many?* She wanted to stop and investigate, but images of her children drove her on. The fires grew in intensity and then merged. They created a strong updraft that caused them to spread up two of the great hills. Curia thought distractedly, *they are going to destroy the senatorial residences.*

She arrived at her house and found the blaze engulfing the southeast side. She was able to get through the front door, ran in and up the curved stairs to find two of Quintus' maids and Servius crouched in a northern bedroom, scared to death and doing nothing to escape. She was furious with them, screamed at their ineptitude, grabbed Servius and ran for the stairs and safety. The maids followed, but as Curia reached the top of the stairs, she found flames swallowing the bottom half of it blocking her only reasonable escape.

She turned back and ran for a bedroom with a window. When she looked outside, she saw her father running up to the house. He sprinted to the side just below her and shouted, "Drop him, it's the only way." When she hesitated, he ordered in a demanding voice, "Drop him!" She hesitated for a second more and then dropped Servius to his grandfather. Maximus caught the child gracefully and set him on the ground. "Now you," he said to Curia. She coughed several times before replying. "No, I have to find Marcia." Maximus opened his mouth to object, but Curia turned and sprinted into the house.

Curia saw the two maids headed for the window while she ran towards the fire. She looked everywhere she could, but fire and heavy smoke kept stopping her. It was getting difficult to breath and the coughing was slowing her down. As the smoke thickened, she could no longer see more than a few feet in front of her. She fell to her hands and knees and crawled trying to find her daughter. She made her way to the east side of the house and saw an open window. Her lungs were on fire and her muscles ached to rest. She leaned out the window to try to breathe better air and slumped on the window sill.

Her father ran up and yelled, "You have to jump."

"I can't," she breathed hoarsely, "I haven't found Marcia."

"Curia, if you don't jump, you'll die from the smoke or the flames will overtake you," Maximus pleaded.

Curia turned inward to see where else she could look for Marcia and found the only door out of the room ablaze and the room filling with more smoke and yet she still couldn't bring herself to jump. Instead, as she backed away from the flames, she tripped and fell through the window. Maximus rushed next to the house even though there were flames coming from it and was able to catch Curia and get her away from the doomed house, but not before the side of his arm and Curia's face were singed.

They ran from the house, coughing, into an open area and watched as the remaining portions burned and then finally collapsed.

Nobody spoke while watching the house, but when it collapsed, one of the maids quietly said, "Maybe she got out before the fire took her."

Curia was in shock. As her mind clouded, she stared at her home and tried hard to avoid picturing Marcia burning in the remains. Some part of her registered what the maid had just said and she was livid. All she could say, between clenched teeth was, "You better hope so."

* * *

The fire continued for six days and five nights. It completely destroyed three of Rome's fourteen districts and seriously damaged seven others. Only four remained unaffected. Those destroyed included Palatine Hill that housed many of the senator's estates as well as Caesar's estate, and most of the Esquiline Hill, which was where Nero chose to build his new villa.

Maximus found he had no words to console his distraught daughter. Her husband, who had been away during the fire, occupied himself with rebuilding the house. Maximus watched as Curia first denied that Marcia was in the house and then was inconsolable when it became obvious her daughter would never be found. As the weeks passed, she became less morose, but found comfort only in spending time with Servius.

* * *

Almost two months after the fires raged, Proculus and June arrived to offer what aid they could. On the trip there, they found they were on the same boat as Peter, so the three went first to see Paul to determine what they could do to help the Christian church after the calamity.

Paul informed them that fires had severely damaged two of the three main houses where Christian groups met. Proculus offered funds and supplies to help rebuild. Paul was appreciative and said that the brethren would supply the manpower. Proculus and June excused themselves because they wanted to find Maximus and Curia as quickly as possible.

As they traveled the streets towards the Scaevola estate, they observed the massive amount of damage that was done to Rome, especially the Palatine and Aventine hills. It was overwhelming. When they reached Curia's home, they found Quintus there supervising the work to rebuild. They had already cleared the debris and the beginnings of a foundation were apparent. They walked up to Quintus and stood near him while they surveyed the area. Quintus spoke first, "Hello Proculus, June."

Quintus was being terse, which told Proculus he didn't really want to talk. He said, "You are obviously very busy Quintus, so we will not keep you. We just wanted to say how sorry we are about all of this." When he did not get any comment in reply, he continued, "Do you know where Curia and Maximus are?"

Quintus turned to look at Proculus for the first time. His eyes were distant and he appeared deflated. He answered, "Curia will be at my brother's house with Servius. His house was only mildly damaged. Do you know where it is?"

At least his voice is steady. "Yes, we can find it. And Maximus?"

"I don't know where he's at, though he visits with Curia and Servius frequently, so you should be able to find him through her." Quintus then yelled, "Hey, stop there," at a worker and walked away. Proculus and June left to make their way to Curia.

They found her playing a game of latrunculi with Servius. She swiftly glanced at the couple and then returned her attention to her son.

Proculus saw her look of disinterest and turned to June. He whispered, "Maybe you should spend some time with her, she does not look like she wants to see me."

June looked at her husband oddly, but answered, "If you say so."

"I will try to find Maximus," and he turned and left the room.

* * *

Maximus heard that Proculus and June had arrived so he made his way to where Curia was staying. He arrived a few minutes behind them to find Proculus leaving through the front door. They saw each other and Maximus turned around so the two could walk together.

They headed down a street away from the house. After they were far enough away, Proculus finally spoke, "How are you and Curia doing?"

It took Maximus a minute to respond because his feelings were too complex to explain easily. Proculus waited patiently, and Maximus finally answered. "Quinn is shaken up, but is dealing with it by immersing himself in work and in rebuilding his home. Curia... is struggling." He paused, trying to figure out what to say. "She seems to have lost interest in anything or anyone, except for Servius. She spends most of her time playing with him and hasn't been eating or sleeping well. I'm very worried."

After a delay, Proculus asked, "And you, how are you doing?"

Maximus looked at him with poise. "I've seen a lot of death in my life. It's always harder when you know the person and especially difficult when it is family. But I'll cope with it as I always have." He quickly changed the subject, "You should know, though, that we have bigger problems right now."

"Yes?"

"Since the fire, Nero has announced plans to build a new palace on Esquiline Hill. A number of senators recalled that he had told them he wanted to do this. Rumors are spreading that Nero had the fire started in order to clear room for this Golden Palace of his.

"People also noticed that the fire seemed to go up both hills at once, which makes it look like it began in more than one place, and many think that means it was arson.

"They are threatening to rebel. Nero is in serious trouble and he has no viable heir, though there are half-a-dozen people who could possibly ascend. There could be civil war."

Proculus folded his hands behind him and looked around at the dark and damaged street they were traversing. "We can't afford this right now. Nero has been the perfect emperor for what we want and having a civil war or even minor conflict trying to replace him would just distract Rome from the situation with the Christians. Somehow, we have to find a way to convince people that Nero was not the cause of this fire." After a moment's hesitation, he added, "Even if he was."

* * *

Four days later, as Proculus was speaking quietly with June about Curia's situation, a messenger arrived with an invitation for Proculus to have an audience with Nero. It surprised Proculus because he hadn't realized Nero even knew who he was, let alone might be interested enough to invite him to an audience.

The next day, Proculus arrived, on time, at Nero's temporary palace for the audience. His first impression was that the thirty-year-old emperor looked weak. He had discolorations on his face, a rather large belly, thin blond hair, and unremarkable eyes, which gave him a frail look. He caught himself. *I must be careful not to underestimate this man.*

Proculus bowed appropriately in front of Nero and then waited for the emperor to speak first. Nero cocked his head and the corner of his mouth turned up slightly.

He spoke in a definitive tone, "Proculus, I know we haven't met, but I've had positive reports about you and you seem to know these Christians that have caused me so much trouble."

At the mention of the Christians, Proculus hesitated, thinking there was something important there, but he could not quite figure out what it was. A delay in answering would be rude, so he hurried a reply, "I know something of the Jews, my lord, I assume you mean them and not the Christians; the Christians are different and much more favorable towards us."

"It matters not, they are all the same to me, but I think of them as Christians." Proculus found it interesting that the Christian name had gained acceptance somehow with this emperor since there were still far more Jews than Christians. The troubling idea attempted to surface again and he looked down trying to bring it to the surface.

"Before this calamitous fire, that everyone says I caused," Nero said with a smirk, "the Christians were becoming the most interesting sport in the city. What do you make of them?"

Proculus thought the question was so general as to be almost unanswerable, but he had to try. "The Jews are an independent and proud people," he offered, "and they struggle with Roman leadership."

"Aren't they the ones who kept saying 'Rome must burn'?"

"Many people have said that my lord," he began. *Vaha! That is it.* "However, you might be able to use that to divert this concern about who caused the fire."

Nero looked down with furrowed eyebrows and then his eyes went up in realization. "Are you suggesting that the Christians started the fire?"

"Oh, I would have no knowledge of that my lord. I am sure your investigators and spies will determine that. If, however, it turned out to be the Jews, then few would be surprised and the attention would turn away from you." Then he added, "I would suggest though that if it was them, it was the Jews and not the Christians."

Nero said, "You seem keen on separating these two. I don't see the point." Proculus started to reply, but Nero continued, "However, if it is found that they did start the fire, then I shall make sure it is the Jews who are blamed."

Proculus felt this magnanimous of Nero since he had no reason to care about separation of the groups. "Thank you my lord. Is there anything else I can do for you?"

"Yes, I would like you to send reports about the situation in Iudea, at least twice a year, to me, so that I can gain a better understanding of what is happening there."

"As you wish."

When Nero didn't say anything more and then turned to speak to someone at his side, Proculus backed out of the room.

On the way out, his mind roamed. *Did I just advance the plan or destroy it?*

* * *

The next month, Paul said goodbye to Proculus and June. If they had stayed any longer, then they would have had to winter in Rome. Peter remained in order to help with reconstruction and to work with the Roman Christian Church.

It was shortly after Proculus and June left that Paul began to hear rumors that the Jews had caused the fire. After all, everyone cried, the Jews always said Rome needed to burn and figured someone had finally done it. Over the months of late fall, the rumors spread and changed into blaming both the Jews and the Christians, but that wasn't unexpected because the Romans viewed them as sister beliefs of the same foreign God. At first, it was just malicious looks and a Roman bumping into one of them when it was avoidable. Then it escalated to snide remarks and to fights that broke out between the Jews and Christians on one side and the Romans on the other. They tried to tell the Romans they had nothing to do with the fires and asked what happened to them thinking it was Nero. The one thing everyone agreed on, because the fires went up two separate hills at the same time, was that it must have been arson.

Paul suggested they redirect the blame back to Nero, but the emperor was inaccessible and the Jews and Christians weren't. Over time, the difficulties spiraled into violence and people on both sides were hurt.

Then one day, Paul was walking with Peter when some Romans started jeering at them. They tried to ignore the men and walk around, but the men wouldn't allow it. One Roman picked up a stone and threw it. It missed, but that ignited the others to do the same. Most of the stones were small and did only minor damage. The two Christians backed up, trying to get away from the onslaught. But one large rock hit Peter on the left temple. He cried out in pain, his eyes rolled up, and he fell straight to the ground. His eyes stared vacantly at the sky as blood began to pool under his head. Paul screamed, "No, No! What have you done?" He turned on the men to scream his hatred, but they were already running away. He turned back, sat down, and lifted Peter's head into his lap. He cried "No," repeatedly as the tears fell into Peter's still face.

* * *

Paul was horrified. After the burial, he went and found Iram, a trusted member of the Christian church in Rome. "Iram, I know it's winter, but I need you to find a way to get to Jerusalem and tell them what has happened. You need to explain the situation with us being blamed for the fire and about what happened to Peter."

"They may react strongly to this news," Iram replied.

"I know, but they need to hear it."

"I will do as you ask, Paul."

"God be with you and be safe."

Iram started to leave and then turned around. "You know, I'm not saying there is any connection, but it seems an odd coincidence to me that your patron Proculus met with Nero shortly before the rumors about the Jews and Christians starting this fire broke out."

Paul looked at him and shook his head slowly. "There's no way... Proculus could have had anything to do with that." The corner of Iram's mouth turned downward, but he said nothing and then left quietly.

Is there?

XVI. Rebellion (66 AD – 69 AD)

"Don't be afraid of those who can kill the body, but can't kill the soul."

- The Book of Q (Revised)

When Proculus heard about Peter's death at the hand of Romans, he asked Barnabas, who had become one of the leaders of the church in Antioch, to join him and June. They gathered in Proculus' reading room since it was late winter and the weather was predictably inclement.

Barnabas was noticeably agitated when he entered. He began without preamble and with only Proculus present. "I assume this is because of what happened with Peter." He began pacing back and forth. "This is horrible. I can't believe what those barbarians have done. Peter was," he stopped his pacing, "our icon."

Proculus eyes went up at that. *Where does that leave Paul?*

Barnabas continued, "And I don't just mean for Christianity. Every sect, Christians, Pharisees, even the old Essenes, admired him. Maybe not the Sadducees, but that doesn't matter."

June came in, walked directly to Barnabas and gave him an extended hug, which calmed him down. They sat and Proculus finally spoke. "I know how difficult this is; we all loved Peter, but we have to be rational right now so we can determine implications."

He looked directly at Barnabas, "What will the reaction from Jerusalem be?"

Barnabas was still upset. He took a deep breath and brushed a strand of hair out of his eyes. "First, it won't be just Jerusalem. This will upset Jews of every kind, everywhere. The worst will be here in Judea because there are many more Jews than Romans. Elsewhere, there will be problems, but probably nothing major."

He took a breath and then became agitated again. June interjected, "There has always been contention between the two here in Judea. The Jews believe themselves to be the chosen people of God and that they shouldn't be ruled. The Romans were right when they said the Jews have said many times that Rome must burn."

As she wound down Barnabas continued, "There will probably be reprisals against Romans. What's worse is that the Romans, thinking that we caused that fire, will fight back. This really could turn into war."

Proculus interrupted, "You know we cannot win that."

June asked rhetorically, "Does that ever stop people from going to war?"

The three looked at each other with solemn faces.

Proculus said, "Barnabas, can you go to Jerusalem for a while and report on what is happening? We need direct, impartial information from someone we trust."

"Yes, of course. I want to be there in any case. I can send you my observations."

* * *

The first message, though short, arrived less than a month later.

As expected, there have been isolated incidents of contention between Jews and Romans. Casual collisions of people in passing, mumbled name-calling, and a few brawls. There have been some arrests, but the offenders have all been released.

My feeling is that the conflicts are slowly escalating and it is only a question of when the first serious offense will occur.

Two weeks later, a more troubling dispatch arrived.

It has begun. A few days ago, in Caesarea, a group of Greek and Roman men performed a bloody ritual in front of the synagogue. They acted out some kind of mock ceremony, cut off some birds' heads, and let them flop around bleeding on the steps.

As you know, this is highly offensive and it will not go unanswered. Word of the odious act has spread quickly and everyone is anxious. Another group of men tried a similar act here in Jerusalem, but were beaten for their foolishness.

Proculus did not hear from Barnabas after these short notes for almost two months. He was beginning to wonder if the situation would calm down. Then he was told that Nero had dispatched Cestius Gallus and the XII Fulminata legion to put the Jews in their place. He sent a messenger to Barnabas asking for an update. Barnabas replied with a parchment.

> *My apologies Proculus, the situation is dire. Shortly after the last message I sent you, arsonists burned down the Jewish synagogue in Caesarea Maritima. In retaliation, Kohen Gadol, the son of the high priest of the temple in Jerusalem, ordered prayers for the Roman emperor at the Temple to cease.*

Proculus recalled that the Jews had been regularly praying for the emperor since the time of Tiberius.

> *Unfortunately, Nero has taken this as an insult to him personally. Between that and hints that the Jewish High Council has discussed refusing to pay taxes, I suppose Nero had no choice. He dispatched a small army of approximately three thousand soldiers.*
>
> *However, the commander made a fatal mistake in believing the Great Sanhedrin was the seat of power. He marched his force, lined up in straight imposing columns, directly towards the Bezetha, where the Sanhedrin sits in session. I suspect he believed the show of strength would quell the resistance.*
>
> *Bezetha fell easily, but then he moved on to the temple and the Jewish fighters became true warriors in its defense. Thousands joined in defending the Great Temple. After a short fight where the Romans made no progress, they withdrew.*
>
> *I thought that might be the end of the fighting, at least for now. But we Jews are a proud people and would not let the army leave unmarred. Small parties of archers followed the army to harass them and deny them any rest.*
>
> *That was when the general made his second mistake. He withdrew through the pass of Beth Horon. The Jewish military council recognized the opportunity. They sent archers to the cliffs and a party of men to cause an avalanche at the far end of the canyon. Others continued to harass the army from behind to force them forward without rest.*
>
> *As they neared the far end of the canyon, the advance party collapsed the narrow pass as best they could and the archers began*

to rain arrows onto the army from both sides. The Romans were slaughtered and had no way to escape with the way forward mostly blocked by rock and every able man ready to fight behind them.

The general and a small number of men did escape through the rocks and was reportedly heading to the coast to meet reinforcements.

The victory has caused the ranks of volunteers to swell.

I fear a true war is upon us.

* * *

The next dispatch Proculus received was from Maximus. He was trying to track the situation in Rome.

Proculus:

As you would expect, few Romans even knew there were serious problems in Iudea. They are still furious with the fire and simply figured the Jews deserved whatever happened to them. There have been a few incidents, and one death, between Romans and Jews here, but the level of intensity is only slightly elevated.

However, general Cestius' defeat woke the people, not to mention the senate and Caesar. Nero's response was immediate and impressive. He sent Titus Flavius Vespasianus, a very honored and successful general, along with two legions to Iudea. Vespasian will not make the mistakes of Cestius and will not have any qualms about destroying Jerusalem to satisfy his orders.

I also heard that Cestius' legion is being rebuilt and will join Vespasian's two legions. They will join with the XV Apollinaris legion, commanded by Vespasian's son Titus, and armies from three local allies. The combined force will total more than sixty thousand men and should be positioned near Ptolemais this coming spring.

I know Vespasian. He will be methodical in his quelling of the rebellion, as it is being called in Rome. He will subjugate towns in the surrounding provinces first and will secure them with local recruits. Then he will march on Jerusalem with an unstoppable force.

* * *

Barnabas returned to Antioch for the winter assuming there would be little progress with the rebellion during the cold months. Once he returned to Jerusalem the next spring, the short messages regarding the conflict continued.

> *Vespasian has wasted no time in making use of his enormous army. He has already retaken much of Galilee. From my understanding, the Jewish war council agreed they could not fight a continuous war for each small town throughout Judea. Instead, they are concentrating on the defense of three cities. Jerusalem is, of course, one. The other two are a closely held secret. I will send more as events occur.*

Two months later, Barnabas disclosed the first of the actual battles.

> *The loose Jewish army finally made their first stand. They chose Yotvah, a town on a hill with three sides protected by steep ravines. Men from the surrounding towns gathered there, built barricades, and prepared to defend the town.*
>
> *Vespasian tried a frontal assault with infantry, but was unable to break through the barricades with sufficient force to attack the archers. What men could break through were quickly dispatched by the waiting Jewish infantry. Vespasian pulled his forces back and prepared for a siege.*
>
> *The siege lasted six weeks with our men showing no sign of relenting. They were even able to injure Vespasian – I believe it was an arrow in the thigh. However, two days after Vespasian was wounded, a group of Romans, posing as Jews entered the city and that night destroyed the barricades. The Romans advanced with their full force and overwhelmed the Jewish defenses.*
>
> *They razed Yotvah to the ground.*
>
> *The only other town in Galilee to resist was Gamla. The resistance there was headed by Josephus Flavius, but the town was not as fortified and Josephus was unable to build sufficient barricades in time. Vespasian was able to attack with a siege ramp and overpowered the defenses. Thousands of the defenders and the town's occupants were slaughtered and many of the others were sold into slavery. Vespasian kept Josephus as a prisoner and, reportedly, as his personal historian.*

The last message from Barnabas before the next winter was a short one indicating that Vespasian had completed conquering Galilee and was hunkering down in Caesarea Maritima until spring.

* * *

Early the next spring Barnabas again wrote to Proculus.

> *The winter has been both quiet and troubling. Vespasian's army has done little other than to pillage the area around Caesarea Maritime. However, the remnants of the rebellion from other areas have come to Jerusalem to help defend the city. They've joined with Sicarri, a group of Jewish zealots who use subterfuge and obfuscation as weapons of assassination. They are adamant that we fight on and have murdered anyone notable who was sympathetic to ending the war. Consequently, the remaining Jewish leadership is steadfast in their determination to fight the Roman tyrants.*
>
> *However, Vespasian has not advanced. We seem to be at an impasse.*

* * *

Maximus was standing outside of the imperial residences. He had just heard that the Praetorian Guard had abandoned their post and were throwing their support to Galba, an aspiring emperor. Nero was in serious trouble. *I may be able to help.*

As he stood waiting, he pondered what he would need to include in a message to Proculus. Nero's popularity had been declining for some time with odd behavior like joining the chariot competitions in the hippodrome and singing songs in public that he had written himself. Most concerning, however, was the number of rebellions around the empire. Iudea was just one of three that had recently rebelled and were in the process of being put down. The loss of the legion in Iudea meant Nero lost respect of the military.

In early spring, the same year Vespasian set out to crush the southern Jewish rebellion, Gaius Julius Vindex rebelled. Gaius was an inconsequential governor of a province in Europe. When Nero dispatched Lucius Rufus to crush the rebellion, Gaius called on Servius Sulpicius Galba, a neighboring governor, to come to his aid. In return, Gaius would support Galba in proclaiming him emperor. Lucius easily defeated Vindex, but Galba's popularity in Europe, especially in Germania and Hispania, rose. Lucius refused to move against Galba, thereby undermining Nero further.

The Praetorian Guard's actions were just the latest in a string of incidents. *Nero is failing*, he thought conclusively. Maximus spotted the emperor leaving the palace and nodded to him. When Nero approached, he said, "Have I neither friend nor foe?"

Maximus didn't answer the apparently rhetorical question, and instead said, "Come with me."

Nero followed him to the villa of a friend who would support the emperor, at least temporarily. Maximus stayed at the door, watching for followers.

A few minutes later a messenger arrived and told the group that Nero had been declared an enemy of the state. Maximus let him through and continued to watch for trouble. A short time later, he wondered how Nero would handle the news. He went inside to see Nero sitting in a shallow grave holding a knife at his own throat. Maximus strode towards him and exclaimed, "Wait!"

Nero's hand was shaking and he quoted Homer's Iliad, "Hark, now strikes on my ear the trampling of swift-footed coursers!" Epaphroditos, his secretary, said disappointingly, "Whatever that means." They heard approaching horsemen as Maximus continued trying to make his way to Nero. Epaphroditos grabbed Nero's wrist and helped him shove the knife into his neck. Nero fell backward into the grave, bleeding profusely.

As the horsemen entered, Maximus and the other men who had tried to help Nero stood and watched him bleed to death. Maximus cursed himself for allowing this to happen. Without Nero, the plan was in jeopardy.

Nero had no heir and his death ended the dynasty begun by Julius Caesar. More importantly, for the first time since becoming an Empire, Rome was without an emperor.

XVII. The Year of Four Emperors (69 AD – 70 AD)

"Jesus said to them, 'Every kingdom divided against itself is destroyed, and every house divided against itself will not stand.'"
— The Book of Q (Revised)

Proculus received a letter from Maximus telling him what had happened with Nero and detailing how he had tried to spirit the emperor away only to find the man dead by suicide. Proculus was enraged and began pacing back and forth in front of June who was supervising some mending. He exclaimed, almost frantically, "Nero's been assassinated and Servius Galba has been proclaimed the new Caesar." June looked up questioningly at the name. He added, "A popular general in Europe."

Thinking aloud he continued, "This may ruin everything and we were so close! I cannot understand how Maximus could have let this happen."

June interjected, "It should help the war. Maybe Galba will be more reasonable. As far as Maximus is concerned, I'm sure he did his best, he can't control everything."

Proculus realized that he had said too much. He stopped pacing, took a deep breath, and tried to calm his anxiety. "I must travel to Rome, immediately," and he turned towards their bedroom to pack.

June's head snapped back in surprise and her nose crinkled. She followed Proculus into the bedroom. "Proculus dear, I don't understand. Why isn't Nero's death a good thing? He was waging a war against the Jews and this might halt that war. Most of it was caused by misunderstanding about the fire, that he probably instigated, and this general Galba won't care about that."

"I can't go into it right now, but it upsets our plans." *How do I get out of this?* He added hurriedly, "And Galba is notoriously anti-Jewish. He may make it much worse for the Jews and may use the war as an excuse for genocide." *I hate lying to her.*

June's eyes narrowed in doubt, but Proculus kept his face impassive. "Why do you have to go to Rome? You know it's a long trip and you aren't as young as you used to be. It could be dangerous."

Proculus stopped packing and looked at June with more compassion. "I have to do what I can for the Jewish people and my presence in Rome early in Galba's reign could help tremendously." *At least that was the truth.*

"Shall I come with you?"

Proculus reached his hands up and placed them on June's shoulders gently. "Not this time. I am hoping to make this a short trip and you have things to attend to here." Then he dropped his hands, turned, and continued packing.

* * *

Almost a month later, Maximus met Proculus on the road into Rome. It was uncanny how often Maximus knew Proculus was coming even if he had not sent word ahead. They looked at each other for a moment; long enough to know that both were upset about the situation and that there was no benefit in examining how it had happened.

Maximus asked, "Would you like to get settled in first?"

"No, we are already behind with Galba marching into Rome like some conquering hero. I heard some soldiers met him on the road into Rome and he killed them for making demands."

"Yes, that seems to be true," Maximus replied hesitantly.

Proculus saw he wanted to say more, "What is it?"

"I'd like us to have this discussion with Curia. I know she's been distant and uncooperative lately, but this crisis might just be the thing to draw her in. Also, we're still rebuilding from the fire. There aren't many places to stay, so do you mind staying with us at Quintus' brother's villa?"

"That will be fine. At a time like this, I am not about to be demanding. Is there a place at the villa where we can meet privately?"

"Yes, they have a small study."

"Then let us proceed."

* * *

Proculus was surprised at how pale Curia was and how her vacant eyes made her look disconnected from the world. He hugged her as he would a daughter, but did not say anything. The three took seats prepared to discuss the situation, though Proculus wondered if Curia would participate at all.

He began, "Maximus, tell me about Galba. I know of him, but only indirectly."

"I've only met him a couple of times, but I can tell you my impression and what I understand from others who are close to him."

He cocked his head and then straightened and began. "First of all, he's old; close to 72 now. That alone will make him a target because people will see it as a weakness. He was a good general in Germania and Gaul and more recently in Hispania. He had actually retired for a time during Claudius' reign and then Nero brought him back by giving him Hispania Tarraconensis to govern.

"His men are highly loyal to him, some of the most loyal of all, and I've been told he is a fair and impartial leader, if somewhat strict. That popularity eventually turned Nero against him. Of course, Nero was turning against anyone he saw as a threat by then.

"He also prefers men to women. He was married and had two children, both of which died, but he prefers adult men who are fit and strong."

Proculus smiled at that. "So he might like you?"

Curia looked up. She appeared to notice the smiles and then looked back down. The movement wasn't lost on Proculus, but he knew not to push.

Proculus asked, "That covers what kind of man, but what kind of an emperor will he be?"

"He's frail and doesn't seem to trust himself. He's relegating most decisions to Titus Vinius and Cornelius Laco. Cornelius is the commander of the Praetorian Guard and the one who backed him and caused Nero to commit suicide. Titus was the commander of one of Galba's legions in Spain.

"Unfortunately, Galba's first acts were all about saving money and he's now refusing to pay the Praetorian Guards the money he promised them to back him for emperor. I can understand his reluctance to bribe officers to behave honorably, but he needed to consolidate his power before he made a move like that.

"He also abhors the normal pomp and ceremony that goes with being emperor. That's like shunning the aristocracy, so he seems to be slowly alienating everyone."

As Maximus wound down, Proculus looked up contemplatively at some window decorations. "It sounds like he will not last long, which I suspect is appropriate. I cannot imagine he cares enough about Iudea to concern himself with their affairs or this war. We need someone who will." Then an interesting notion occurred to him, "You know, since he has no heirs, and we no longer have a clear lineage from Julius Caesar, and the Senate seems unwilling to step in, the only potential Caesars are military leaders. I wonder if Vespasian would consider it. He seems bent on totally subjugating Iudea and it seems unlikely he would veer from that course if he became emperor."

Curia looked up as if she wanted to say something, hesitated, then shook her head slightly and looked back down. *She almost joined the conversation,* Proculus thought sadly.

The two men were silent for a few moments, hoping she would speak. When she didn't, Maximus asked, "We can do something about Galba, but how do we get Vespasian in a position to take control?"

"That is what we need to work out. I will get in touch with a number of senators and you can find out what the military is thinking. I also need to meet with Paul to see what kind of an effect this is having on the church here.

"It has already been almost three months since Nero's death and winter storms are approaching, so I expect to stay here for the winter. June will not be happy with my absence, but there is nothing I can do about that."

* * *

Paul had been traveling around towns either setting up or working with fledgling Christian communities when Proculus finally found him in a place called Alusium.

He was both pleased and concerned to see his benefactor. Ever since he discovered Proculus' possible involvement in Rome's persecution of the Jews, he had been conflicted. Seeing Proculus brought out his old familial feelings as well as a strong sense of doubt.

Proculus tilted his head as he watched the emotions play across Paul's face, but he said nothing.

The two found a quiet place to speak and Proculus began, "How are things, Paul?"

"The church is doing well, though I feel like I have to continuously fight heretical ideas that keep emerging. I'm also a lot slower than I used to be and that's making it difficult to accomplish everything."

"That is understandable. Have the persecutions slowed down with Nero's death?"

"Yes, people seem to be distracted by this new emperor and often complain about him. The Jews and Christians don't seem to be the target any longer."

"Well, the war in Judea appears to have stopped as well. Everyone is waiting to see what Galba will do."

Paul sensed a disappointment from Proculus, so with furrowed brows, he asked, "That is a good thing, isn't it?"

With only a slight hesitation Proculus said, "Of course."

He grew serious. "Paul, with Peter's death, I've been wondering. Is there anything else we can do to spread the word of Jesus and maybe the teachings of some of his followers? People outside of Judea and Rome should know about Peter and his fine works."

Paul stared into Proculus' eyes. "I've also been thinking there is more we could do. The thing that people seem to want now is stories that demonstrate Jesus' teachings." Then, after more thought, he added, "Maybe even stories of Jesus' life. I know we don't really have those, but from the sayings and the oral traditions, we have some of it and we could use the Christ prophesies to fill in some of the blanks. These life-stories would be allegorical, but they could connect with the brethren in ways that the sayings we have can't."

"That makes sense. Do you know of anyone who could write such a story?"

"Not that comes to mind, but let me consider that more."

"It might help if they were in Judea or maybe even Antioch so the church there can work with them and I can organize copying the document once it is produced."

Paul mumbled, "You do like your control." Then he spoke normally, "If you'll excuse me now, I have some things I must attend to. If you're going to be in town for a while, I should see you again," and he got up and left.

* * *

Maximus was following Galba and a small force of men. As he sat upon his stead, he considered how Galba had come to this point.

It hadn't taken long for his reckless financial measures to cause problems, especially those relating to not paying the legions. Late in the year some of the legions in Germania refused to swear loyalty to Galba and then they had the gall to demand that a new emperor be instated. Next, the people of Germania Inferior rebelled, saying that Galba was invalid and they proclaimed their own governor, Aulus Vitellius, as emperor.

To try to protect his dictatorship, Galba Caesar named Lucius Piso as his successor. However, the appointment backfired as the populace saw the appointment as a sign of weakness. It also irritated Marcus Otho, the governor of Lusitania, who had supported Galba, along with the Praetorian Guard in Galba's push to become emperor.

Otho was a consummate manipulator and politician. He used bribes to negotiate with the Praetorian Guard and local legions to be named emperor. He also brought his army into the outskirts of Rome, which was a risky move considering the Roman rule that armies were not allowed in the great city.

Galba, resting in a litter, was being taken to meet Otho. He was too old and feeble to ride on his own. Maximus watched from a nearby hill as Otho's men slaughtered the small force and took the head of Galba to Otho. It was unclear who had actually killed the emperor, but Otho wasted no time in ordering Piso's death as well.

Piso was dead two hours later.

* * *

Three weeks later Proculus, Maximus, and Curia had to meet again to discuss a new emperor. Proculus was in a foul mood, frustrated at the change to yet another militaristic emperor that he was not familiar with and who probably would not support the war against the Jews. He was also irritated that he and Maximus could not seem to get control of the situation.

Proculus closed his eyes in meditation for a moment to calm his nerves and began. "I have spoken with a number of senators and can provide an update on Otho. To start with, he has added 'Nero Caesar Augustus' to his name, probably in an attempt to associate himself with Nero who everybody seems to remember fondly now. He has also been wiser in his treatment of the Praetorian Guard, paying them what Galba had promised and reinstating some that Galba had unjustly dismissed.

"However, he has shown little interest in the Eastern Empire, and he has a serious problem with Aulus Vitellius."

Maximus interrupted, "You mean the commander of the army of the lower Rhine? Why would there be a problem with him?"

"Yes, him. As it turns out, two of the legions in Germania had proclaimed their support for Vitellius as emperor even before Otho marched to Rome and claimed it himself. Some of the military wants Vitellius to be emperor. There is a fair chance that we are heading for civil war. In fact, Vitellius' army is on the way to Rome as we speak."

"We can't have a civil war, we would never regain the momentum we've developed," Maximus said rhetorically.

"Agreed; we have to find a way to stop this," Proculus offered. "As little as I like Otho, we have to stabilize the leadership and then we can work towards a specific conclusion.

"Maximus, we may need to help Vitellius lose this confrontation."

Curia looked up then and spoke quietly, "You're being too rash."

Both men leaned back slightly and looked at Curia. Maximus had a hint of a smile at the corner of his mouth while Proculus' smile was more obvious. "What do you mean?"

Curia shook her head and frowned. It was clear she was not going to continue, so Proculus looked back to Maximus to continue the conversation.

Maximus responded to Proculus' previous statement, "I'll need to find out what resources we have near Vitellius, if any."

"Yes," Proculus replied, "and I will try to determine Otho's plans."

* * *

It was seven weeks before Vitellius' force neared Rome. Maximus was finding it difficult to penetrate Vitellius inner circle with anyone he could trust, though he had been able to get contacts close enough that he knew what was happening in his camp and Proculus had men reporting what happened with Otho's forces.

What contacts they did have reported that Otho had ridden out to meet Vitellius with a strong force and with more legions on the way. He should have waited for the rest to arrive, but poor advice and overconfidence had made him impetuous and he sent the main portion of his available units to meet Vitellius' army.

Unfortunately, Vitellius had the advantage of having camped at a tactically sound location and Otho's force was unable to overwhelm their defenses. When they retreated, Vitellius' force pursued them all the way to Otho's base camp, but withdrew at the sight of the additional men Otho had kept in reserve.

When Maximus heard this was happening, he rode to the outskirts of Otho's camp. He maneuvered to a position near Caesar's tent when he heard a commotion. Otho, apparently troubled about the potential of a Roman civil war and about the shame he felt at his rash attack, had come out of his tent and exclaimed, "It is far more just to perish one for all, than many for one." He then drank a glass of poisoned wine and fell dead.

When Vitellius organized an attack, they found Otho's force welcoming them into the camp and proclaiming Vitellius emperor.

* * *

Proculus tried to arrange yet another meeting with Maximus and Curia, but Curia had left town for a couple of days with Servius, and Maximus was unwilling to meet without her. He reiterated that getting her involved in the politics of the situation was the best way to cure her malaise.

Before Curia returned, however, Paul sent word that he wanted to meet with Proculus, alone. The note felt ominous, particularly since Paul had never asked to see him alone before.

Paul had chosen a secluded park at daybreak for the meeting. When Proculus arrived, Paul was admiring a clear glistening stream cascading over smooth boulders with birds bathing in the shallow waters. Proculus walked up next to him. "Beautiful, is it not?"

"Yes, quite. And tranquil as well," Paul replied.

They both stood quietly admiring their surroundings for a couple of minutes when Proculus finally broke the silence, "You look well Paul, if a little distracted, what is on your mind?"

Paul's eyes were drooping sadly and his furrowed eyebrows indicated deep thought. He shook his head slightly and then seemed to steady himself. He leaned on the railing in front of him and without looking at Proculus said, "This is difficult to say and in some ways I can't believe I have to." He faltered again and then continued, "A while back, I was told of some coincidences that disturbed me. The first one didn't bother me a great deal, because I believed it was just that, a coincidence. But when I heard of more, I began to wonder."

When Paul did not continue right away, Proculus asked, "Paul, what is this regarding? What coincidences?"

Paul looked up at Proculus with distaste and then back at the stream. He said, "Over the past few years, it appears that when Rome does something aggressive towards the Jews, or Christians, you've been involved somehow. At least, you had liaisons with key people involved in the decisions."

How could he have figured that out? He looked at Paul intently, trying to determine just how much he knew.

Paul continued, "Because of these suspicions, I worked to get people placed into positions to be able to observe you."

Futuere! The cunnus spied on us! Proculus was shocked at Paul's temerity and somewhat irritated at the violation of his privacy. He started to speak up, but Paul interrupted him, "Please, let me finish." He sighed and looked down at his feet for a moment before continuing. "They have confirmed my fears." Paul now stood up straight, turned, and looked at Proculus directly, "You are encouraging this war between the Romans and the Jews and you had a hand in starting the persecution of the Jews and Christians after the Great Fire."

It was a bold statement, but without any question, Proculus was not sure how to answer. However, before Paul could continue, he said, "Paul, you know that isn't true. I've been dedicated to helping the Jews and the Jewish people half my life, why would I want or encourage a war with Rome?"

"I don't know. That is why I'm here. So you... tell... me..."

Proculus shook his head in mock annoyance at the implication. "I cannot tell you why because it simply is not true. I may have been in contact with some of the people that made those decisions, but if I was, it was to talk them out of it, to try to reason with them, or to try to minimize the damage."

"I hear what you are saying Proculus, but the evidence suggesting otherwise is overwhelming. I'll obtain proof at some point and then we'll see how much real influence you have," and Paul walked away leaving Proculus deeply concerned.

* * *

Proculus was not able to find Maximus that evening, but he did early the next morning and got straight to the point, without preamble, "We have a situation with Paul."

"What's that?"

"Somehow he has figured out that we are influencing the war with the Jews. He has apparently placed spies in our midst and has confirmation from them that we are involved. He is now looking for proof and it looks like he will try to publish it in some form to discredit us."

Maximus turned his head away looking into the distance. Smiling, he said, "I have to give him credit, he's got more nerve than I would have thought possible. Are you suggesting we have him killed?"

Proculus looked down from the distasteful question and answered, "No, there would be too many people suspicious of that, especially since he just spoke to me about this." His mind raced as Maximus waited. He added, "We seem to have two options; we can try to have him discredited first, or we can have him jailed again and keep him in isolation. Discrediting him would severely hurt the Christian movement, but having him jailed would agitate the right people and might make him more of a martyr, especially here in Rome."

"That's easy enough; one conversation and I can have him arrested and put in jail for an indeterminate amount of time."

Proculus pondered that before answering, "Give me one day to consider this; it is too important to make the move hastily. Let us meet here tomorrow morning at sunrise."

At sunrise, Proculus found Maximus right where they had met the previous day. All he said was, "Make it happen."

Paul was incarcerated two days later.

* * *

The morning after Curia returned, the three met once again about a new emperor. Both Proculus and Maximus noticed that Curia seemed more alert and refreshed than they had seen her since the fire. She had been on a short vacation with Quintus and Servius. *Maybe the vacation helped,* Proculus thought.

Maximus began straight away, "It's been only a week since Vitellius was made emperor by the military and he's already made some bold moves. For instance, he saw the praetorian guard as the cause of instability in the government, so he dismissed them at sword point, and installed men he trusts from his legions as the guard."

Proculus offered, in a perturbed tone, "But he still is not the emperor we want. He is yet another general from the western empire who cares nothing about what happens with the Jews. He also has little support here in Rome and he became Caesar through proclamation of the military. There is no reason to think he will last any longer than the others."

They both sat in contemplation for a minute. Curia spoke up, "You are both going about this all wrong." The two older men looked at her. Proculus kept his response terse, hoping Curia would take the lead. "How so?"

Curia sighed, sat forward in her chair and placed her hands together. "You need to quit worrying about these temporary proclamations for emperor and concentrate on building full support for Vespasian, assuming you still want him. Ignore what is happening here in Rome and get out in the Empire and convince governors and generals to back him. Proculus, you should travel through Galatia and Macedonia, meeting with your contacts. Father, you should meet with leaders from the legions in Africa and on through the Eastern Empire. Then, when you have true support for the new emperor instead of a legion or two, you can get him instated and keep him there.

"Quintus and I can work here in Rome with the senators and equestrians. Together we can form the new government by consensus instead of military coup."

Proculus and Maximus looked at each other for a few seconds and then they both started laughing. Curia looked back and forth between them with a firm face. When their laughter slowed and they looked at Curia and saw her staring at them, they began laughing all over again. Curia said sternly, "What are you two laughing about?"

Maximus calmed sufficiently to reply, "It's just so obvious that we don't know why we didn't come up with it and we're laughing at ourselves," and then he added after some hesitation, "and we're glad you're with us again, we obviously need your help."

Proculus offered, "Clearly, we are not as capable as we once were."

* * *

Within a week, Curia had Quinn convinced to help with a propaganda campaign in Rome, though she realized she would have to do most of the work. Proculus and Maximus prepared for an extended trip and wrote letters to some of the commanders in the Eastern Empire, letting them know what they were planning and asking for their support.

Over the next few months, while Curia, Proculus, and Maximus were executing their plans, Vitellius did his best to run the Empire and consolidate his power. He had gained a reputation in Germania through prodigality. However, that tactic was insufficient for establishing a reputation beyond local legions, and consequently the Eastern Empire had no reason to recognize Vitellius as emperor. Even Africa, Vitellius' previous station, was apathetic about the new leader of the Roman Empire and never officially recognized him. However, the Senate did, and gave him the titles expected of Caesar, but that was partially because of the licentious army that he had marched into Rome.

Between Vitellius' invasive army and his extravagant and self-indulgent behavior, the people of Rome, and the Senate, became frustrated. The latter gave Curia and Quintus the opening they needed. They began a campaign to convince key members of the Senate that Vitellius wouldn't last as Caesar and they needed someone chosen for the position rather than someone appointed by the army. As they began to gain support for that concept, they surreptitiously suggested that Vespasian was that person. He was both a politician, being of the senatorial rank, and a true leader of men. He also had a viable hereditary tract with three capable and successful sons.

In late winter, Curia wrote to her father and Proculus telling them to complete their missions and to have dispatches from supporters sent no later than July. She made plans to travel to Caesarea Maritima.

She arrived to find the port city built by Herod in ruins. It had been a beautiful area with a quiet harbor and lush surroundings, but a year of thousands of Roman soldiers trampling and pillaging the area had devastated the terrain.

She told an officer at the entrance to Vespasian's camp her name and was surprised when he led her directly to the command tent. She entered to find Vespasian and some senior officers standing at a table with maps and the remnants of a meal spread across it. There were other guards around, but she ignored them and strode confidently to the table. Vespasian was a broad-shouldered man with a receding hairline and narrow eyes. However, he appeared confident and at ease with his men and the stance of those around him showed their deference.

"My name is…," she began.

"I know who you are. Your father is a very respected soldier and a number of senators have quietly mentioned your influence."

He knows me? The Senate thinks I have influence? Curia's mouth was open slightly. She recovered and stood straighter. "I have a dispatch from the senate that could not be trusted in other hands." She glanced around furtively at the other men in the room.

Vespasian caught the hint and dismissed them, leaving a single guard at the entrance. Curia handed him the parchment. He stared into her eyes for a moment, opened it, and quietly read the contents.

Curia noticed his eyes narrow slightly while he read, but his face was otherwise inexpressive. He looked up at her, again staring deeply into her. *He's wondering if we are serious.* She opened her mouth to reinforce the message, but Vespasian preempted her, "When?"

Astonishing how decisive he is. "Dispatches from half the legions in the empire are already on their way to Rome and the Senate has proclaimed their intent. The time is now."

Within weeks, the legions of Iudea, Syria, North Africa, and portions of Macedonia, Galatia, and Gaul sent notices to Rome indicating support for Vespasian. Some of them saw a way to stop the cycle of short-lived emperors they had seen and to stabilize the Empire. Others, after being convinced, saw Vespasian as a true emperor and one who would stop a civil war from tearing the country apart.

Vespasian sent six legions marching towards Rome.

When Vitellius heard, he consulted his advisors and, more importantly, a number of senators. He found that Vespasian had the support of the Senate and more than half of the Empire. Resignedly, he told his legions to retreat to their assigned territories in Europe and awaited Vespasian on the steps of the palace.

Instead, he received Vespasian's son, Domitianus, at the head of the army. When Domitianus approached Vitellius on the steps, he drew his gladius. Vitellius raised an eyebrow. "Yet I was once your emperor." Domitianus swung the sword and beheaded Vitellius.

Vespasian Caesar arrived five weeks later with vast quantities of food and supplies from Northern Africa. Curia watched the parade of supplies and thought, *this is an emperor who knows how to win the hearts of the people.*

XVIII. The Battle for Jerusalem (70 AD)

"Do you think that I have come to bring peace on earth? No, not peace, but a sword."

- The Book of Q (Revised)

Curia spent the winter with her son while watching Vespasian complete the consolidation of his power and repair the damage done by the quick succession of inept Caesars.

The following spring, however, she and Maximus made a trip to Antioch to evaluate the situation with the war in Iudea. They had received word that Vespasian had ordered his son Titus to take control of the legions and put an end to the Jewish rebellion. The rest of Iudea had already fallen and only Jerusalem stood, with its series of three walls and ample food supplies to withstand a siege.

The two septuagenarians were sitting in the reading room when Curia entered. She felt their eyes upon her as she walked briskly to the third chair and sat down. As soon as Maximus shut the door, she blurted, "I had to, politely, ask June not to join us."

Proculus leaned forward on his desk and was visibly concerned, "She was supposed to be with some friends who had lost a child, what is she doing here?"

"I do not know, but clearly her plans changed. Regardless, she will not be joining us, but she is going to be suspicious."

Proculus leaned back. "That could prove to be a problem."

Curia answered, "Possibly, but what can she do at this point?"

"Nothing, I just had not intended her to know."

The three sat in silence for a moment and then Proculus shivered and looked at Curia. "Well Curia, your plan worked magnificently. Vespasian is emperor and he seems to have achieved control in Rome. He even appointed Titus to complete his work in Iudea."

"Yes, it does appear that it all worked out the way we intended," she said modestly. The two men sat staring at her with admiration until she looked away in slight embarrassment. "Let us proceed."

They both smiled and Proculus folded his hands in front of him. "We are at the final stage of the plan, at least as far as Maximus and I had envisioned it. Only one task remains, and it will be up to you Maximus."

He replied solemnly, "Yes."

When nobody spoke for a moment, Curia asked, "What task?"

Proculus looked at her ominously. "We must make sure that Jerusalem is destroyed and along with it, the temple."

Merde! Is he serious? "Wha…" was all she could mutter.

Proculus continued, "It is the seat of the Jewish religion and the symbol and heart of their power. It represents the only remaining control they have over Christians. For Christianity to bloom and become a full and independent religion, the center of Judaism must fall."

Fall? He means die! All those people. There has to be another way. What if they found out? Her eyes grew and she exclaimed, "Does Paul know?"

Maximus answered, "Of course not. Only the three of us. It was the plan all along, that is if we made it this far, but Paul would never have done what we asked if he knew this was coming."

After some silence, Maximus added, "Paul is another loose end. If this works as we are expecting, he will assume we had something to do with it. We've been able to prevent him from writing letters so far, but he will find a way at some point and discredit us, and possibly Christianity as well."

"Yes, I agree," Proculus replied, "One of us will have to go to Rome and deal with that."

Curia trembled at the notion, but she decided to let the two men deal with it.

Proculus looked at Maximus, "The siege of Jerusalem has already begun, so I assume you will be leaving shortly?"

"Yes, within a few days."

Proculus turned to Curia and leaned forward in his chair. With an emphatic tone he said, "There is one more topic we must discuss. I am sure you are aware that Maximus and I have been extremely lucky to live long enough to see this plan to fruition." Then he added with a smile and a glance at Maximus, "Especially your father, given his adventures."

Curia's eyebrows went up and she glanced at her father, but said nothing.

"We have done what we can to set things in motion for a Christian Republic, but there are decades to go. We need someone to monitor its progress and to nudge it along in the right direction."

Curia looked down. *Me? I can't take Proculus' place! Alone?*

Proculus continued, "You might have to take direct action sometimes, but more likely it will need your ability to manipulate the situation discretely."

She realized she didn't have to take Proculus' place. His role was as a visionary and her father's was tactical. The vision was set and her job would be to ensure it stayed on the right path. She finally looked up at Proculus. "I need to consider this carefully. It is an enormous commitment and I am not sure I can do it."

Maximus answered, "We are both absolutely sure that you can, and in fact, you are the only person that can."

Proculus glanced at Maximus with a slight grimace and added, "You certainly have the right to spend some time thinking about this, but you cannot take long because we do need someone to carry on and we will not have long to find someone else."

"I understand."

"There is one more thing. There is a man here in Antioch who might be able to help you. His name is Theophorus and some consider him the first real Christian because he is the oldest of the children to grow up with Jesus' teachings. He is also intelligent enough and, more importantly, wise enough to understand that difficult decisions will be required. We cannot tell him everything, but like Paul, we can probably divulge most of it."

He leaned back in his chair saying with finality, "You will need a Jew here in Iudea, and preferably Antioch, which is ostensibly the headquarters for Christianity, to be your eyes and ears to Judaism and to the eastern empire."

After some contemplative silence, the three stood to leave. As Curia reached the door, Proculus said, "Oh, you should also know that I found someone to write the first story of Jesus' life. He is Jewish and a relatively unknown writer of plays, but I agreed to pay him to pen it. He is doing some research in the local synagogues about prophecies around the Christ figure and then he will begin. We should have it within the year."

Curia mumbled, "Good," distractedly and continued through the door with her father.

* * *

Maximus arrived at the Roman encampment outside of Jerusalem six days later. Titus had already received a letter from Proculus introducing him and intimating his contribution in the legions backing Vespasian as emperor. Upon entering the encampment, Maximus received instructions to take a tent near the Roman commanders. At the tent was an invitation to meet with Titus. Maximus smiled at Proculus' orchestrations and nodded to the messenger who took it as dismissal and left.

It was late evening and Maximus was tired. He would have preferred to wait until morning to meet with the commander, but he didn't want to offend the general and thus he put his horse in the stable, dropped off what supplies he had brought at his tent, and went quickly to the command center.

His first observation was that the Romans expected to be here for a while since they had taken the time to build a permanent structure for Titus and his subalterns. When he entered the building, he saw the general and several other men looking over a map of Jerusalem. He recognized a couple of the men as ones he had served with before.

Titus looked up, cocked his head for a second and then straightened. "You must be Maximus Octavius."

He knows me? No, he must have deduced it.

Titus confirmed Maximus' thoughts, "You're the only person I'm expecting that might have enough presence to just walk in here. Welcome."

Maximus continued into the room with aplomb. He strode confidently to the table where the men were examining the map. "It's well fortified, isn't it," he said rhetorically.

"Yes and well stocked also. We've had them under siege for over a month now and have been disrupting their supplies for most of the winter and they've shown no signs of being worried about provisions."

"I've heard they have large stockpiles, but they can't last forever." Maximus looked at the map and considered Jerusalem's tactical situation. There were a series of three walls with gates as well as towers at strategic positions. The last wall would be the most difficult, but they would have to deal with that later. He offered, "Their supplies are located mostly inside the third wall, so you will cut off most of them if you can take that."

"That is the immediate goal, but these towers have proven troublesome."

"Might I suggest you move further north and attempt to breach it near the Women's Gate? I know the terrain is more difficult there, especially for a ram, but your legion on the Mount of Olives can protect your men while they build a siege tower or a ram and there are no Jewish towers near that gate."

Titus looked up in admiration. "You've been here for ten minutes and you've suggested what it took these men a month to figure out."

The men around Titus were looking chagrined. *Don't alienate me from your men.* Maximus replied, "I've been studying this area for a long time and know it well." *Hopefully, that will ameliorate them somewhat.*

A soldier came through the door and stood at its entrance. Titus looked up immediately. "Yes?"

"There are thousands of people asking to be let into Jerusalem for Passover."

"Turn them… wait. Let them enter, but let nobody leave. If any attempt to, have them arrested and then crucify them facing the wall. That ought to make their supply situation worse."

That's harsh, but probably effective.

After the man left, Maximus asked, "Sir, I'm quite tired, do you mind if I retire to the generous tent you assigned? Of course, I'm available anytime you need me."

"Certainly. Thank you for joining us, Maximus."

"Thank you, sir. Tomorrow I'll scout the area to see if I can make any other suggestions."

* * *

Maximus heard nothing from Titus for a few days. He occupied himself exploring the area and making contact with soldiers that might aide him. On the fifth day, Titus sent word for him to report.

When he arrived at command, Titus and a retinue of men were preparing to leave and Titus asked Maximus to join them. They mounted chariots and horses for the ride around the third wall towards the Women's Gate. Maximus could see that they had been busy setting up a defensible camp and preparing the makings of a siege ram that they would assemble nearer the gate where there was traversable terrain.

As they approached the makeshift camp, they slowed and dismounted. Just as the last man was on the ground, they heard a commotion coming from the gate and looked to see a squad of Jewish zealots attacking. A volley of arrows was loosed and fell among them. Maximus heard cries of pain and knew that some had found their mark. His first worry was for Titus. He looked towards the general to see an arrow through his left shoulder and his men trying desperately to scurry him away.

Maximus drew his gladius and headed for the attackers. *I'm too old for this.* At sight of him advancing on the attackers, other soldiers joined and they formed a line between the attackers and Titus.

The Jews saw the organized advance and hesitated. It was enough to spur the Romans forward and to encourage others to join the counterattack. As the Roman force grew in size and confidence, the Jews withdrew to the protection of archers from the wall and on through the gate.

Maximus made his way back to Titus to see the arrow being extracted and a bandage put in place. Titus looked up, clearly furious at what had happened. He said, "Thank you Maximus; that was very brave of you, especially at your age."

My age won't stop me. "I'm honored to help, sir."

Titus looked up at another man, one Maximus didn't know. "Fetch me that wretched Jew, Josephus." The man turned and left. The group of officers remained somber while they watched Titus fuming.

When the man returned with Josephus, Titus looked up and exclaimed, "Josephus, I'm tired of this siege and we both know how it will end. I want you to go to the Jews and try to negotiate surrender."

"Yes my lord, but you know they won't listen to me. They believe I was in collusion with your father at Gamla."

"I've heard that, from you, but I want you to try anyway. Now leave."

Without another word, Josephus left. Maximus turned to Titus. "May I accompany him?"

Titus gestured with a flip of his hand. Maximus took that as agreement and left. When he was outside he found Josephus standing there deliberating with himself. He said, "You better not hesitate or it will be much worse for you."

"But they may kill me."

"Possibly, but if you don't go, Titus will execute you for sure."

Josephus looked up at Maximus, pleading with his eyes. Maximus stared back.

Finally, he walked toward the Women's Gate. Maximus went with him until he was just outside of arrow range and then stopped. Josephus looked up at the old soldier one more time with the same hopeful eyes and then straightened and walked on.

When he was about half way to the gate, Maximus saw two arrows loosed. He watched as they silently closed the distance to Josephus. One missed by a couple of feet, but the other found his left leg just above the knee. He crumpled to the ground instantly while laughter emanated from the walls. Maximus turned to one of the soldiers working nearby. "Go fetch him."

The man started to object and Maximus turned more fully toward him with a stern look. The man ran to Josephus and hurriedly dragged him back to safety.

* * *

Maximus waited patiently while Titus' recovery delayed the attack on the Women's Gate. Three weeks later, the general was strong enough to command the legions again and ordered the attack. It began with a phalanx of foot soldiers with large shields protecting a battery of archers as they made their way towards the gate. They were able to get close enough to fire volleys of arrows at the wall to harass the Jewish archers.

Maximus sat with the Roman commanders on their steads as the attack played out on the field before them. Men, somewhat protected by planks positioned over their heads, pushed a siege ram up to the gate and began to batter it. As the Jewish archers took to aiming at the ram, the Roman archers began an aggressive onslaught. The Jewish archers loosed fire-arrows to try to burn the siege ram and were getting more successful with hitting the soldiers pushing it. However, just as it looked like they might repel the attack, more soldiers rushed up to help. The burning of the ram now aided the Romans as it crushed partially through the gate catching it on fire.

They left it in place and fled. It was over an hour before the blaze had done enough damage that Titus ordered the attack. Two legions, the V'th and the XV'th, poured through the Women's Gate to take the third wall and the area the Jews called *Bezetha*.

Maximus heard Titus order an immediate attack on the second wall. The Jews wouldn't yet be prepared to repel an attack there. The V'th, the first legion to break through the third wall, was held in reserve and to defend their hold on the Woman's Gate. The XV'th and the XII'th advanced quickly to attack the second wall. There was only one gate, so it was clear where they needed to go.

The Jews tried to organize a defense around the wall and some continued to fight hand-to-hand in Bezetha, but it was no use. Seeing that they had lost the second wall as well, the Jews retreated to the protection of the first wall and the temple.

Titus knew that wall would be difficult to take and ordered his men to regroup and to move their encampment into Bezetha while keeping enough men within the second wall to defend the area.

* * *

It took weeks to fully secure the areas. Maximus was astonished at the amount of death and destruction. The Romans razed much of the town within Bezetha as they pillaged their way through the streets. They seemed to kill indiscriminately at times, but then Rome was never kind to a rebelling province. What surprised Maximus most was the level of starvation. He had shown the Romans where most of the provisions would be, but they were all but gone and the people were clearly emaciated.

As the situation seemed to be coming under control, Maximus went to speak with Titus. He was admitted into the command tent without challenge and entered to see Titus addressing a young soldier who looked overly nervous.

Titus was completing a sentence, "... and how are they getting out?"

"We don't know sir."

"Well, find out." When the man didn't leave, he added, "Dismissed."

"Yes sir," and the man left.

Titus looked up and saw Maximus. "Come in Maximus."

Maximus walked forward to the command table where Titus was standing, but didn't say anything.

Titus stared at the map. "It seems the Jews are sending small raiding parties from behind the final wall to get supplies and to harass us. If they can get out, then we can get in."

Maximus replied, "I've heard of a secret tunnel that comes from the south side of the temple area and comes out in the lower city somewhere, but I don't know exactly where it is."

Titus turned to another man and told him to find the messenger and have him concentrate on the south side.

Maximus looked at Titus' wound. "Your shoulder seems to be healing well."

Titus looked up questioningly. "I'm sure you're not here for idle talk about my injury."

Admirable. "I can probably help find out how to get into the temple area or get some men in there to open the gate at night," he stated. Then he hesitantly added, "However, I came here to suggest that you might want to consider utterly destroying the temple instead of just taking control of it."

Propositum – A Novel

Titus's eyebrows went up at that, "And why should I consider that?"

"It and some of the treasures in it are the only real symbols in Judaism. They don't allow the worship of icons, but they have this temple. It represents the heart of their religion and their faith. Without it, they'll spread out and won't have a center from which to rebel, ever again."

Titus stared back at Maximus with creased eyes and then replied, "I'll consider what you are saying Maximus, but I don't usually believe it's best to destroy prized cultural structures when conquering a people. It causes discontent and makes it harder to assimilate them. Also, much of the temple was recently built by Herod, a Roman. It would be a shame to destroy such an accomplishment."

Maximus wanted to argue and stood there a moment trying to find something he could say.

Titus looked back up. "Is there something else?"

Maximus recognized that as a dismissal and realized any further argument would just irritate the general. He said, "No sir," and left.

* * *

The following week Maximus found the messenger. He was disgusted to find he had made no real progress. His attempts to find the tunnel were restricted to trying to beat it out of random civilians.

Accordingly, he took matters into his own hands. He organized a set of the men who he had been enticing to help in the final assault on the temple, and placed them at locations around the lower city where they could observe a good portion of the streets. They took turns waiting until another raid happened, which turned out to be in a little over two days. They weren't able to get the exact location of the exit of the tunnel, but they did determine the area.

Maximus repositioned them to observe that specific area in more detail and they waited. They still could not discover the exact exit, but they narrowed the location further. Maximus then pulled most of the men back as he didn't want to alarm the Jews. He had two men join him in taking turns watching from a single vantage point.

One evening Maximus was leaning against a wall near an intersection of paths, watching all four directions as best he could when he saw a door in a small house open slightly, someone look around cautiously, and then a series of men leave stealthily.

The process of finding the secret entrance to the temple mount took a week and a half. Maximus then found the messenger and showed him where it was. "Now, report to the general with this information. Also, tell him that I respectfully suggest the raid should be in the middle of the night for low resistance and the only goal for the raid should be to get the gates opened." Maximus gestured with a flip of his hand toward the command tent and the messenger left.

He later returned with a handwritten papyrus for Maximus. It indicated the attack would be in six days with the new moon.

At the arranged time, Maximus gathered the men he had inveigled and explained what had to be done. They weren't all members of the same squads or even legions, but once the fighting began, they could form up into an independent group with Maximus leading them.

A squad of brave men broke into the unassuming small house that hid the entrance. They quickly dispatched the residents and chased one man into the tunnel to make sure no alarm sounded.

Forty minutes later, as two full legions were standing ready for the assault on the Temple Mount, the gate began to open. It only opened a few inches, but it was enough. The Roman soldiers pushed their way through to see roughly half of the original tunnel-assault squad dead on the ground. *Only half made it to the gate*, Maximus thought sadly.

The legions poured into the Temple Mount against fierce fighting by the Jewish Zealots. The defenders threw themselves at the Romans with little regard for their own life. *What a waste.* He, Titus, and the Roman commanders held back on horseback while waiting for the entrance to be secured. Once Maximus saw Titus moving forward, he galloped his horse through the gate and to the southeastern corner where he had told his men to meet. Fourteen of the seventeen men who had agreed to help him were there.

They waited, defending themselves when needed, until they were sure the rest of the legions had cleared most of the open area and were nearing the temple proper. Then they ran forward with burning torches into the temple itself and began setting fire to anything they could find that would easily burn.

A group of Jewish zealots saw them, ignored the rest of the Romans and their own safety, and rushed forward to attack the heathens burning the temple. Maximus, being older and slower than the others, found himself in the rear of the group and turned to see the crazed men attacking from behind. Two other men joined him to fight with their torch in one hand and a sword in the other.

They were able to kill the first few of the attackers, but there were too many. Maximus was the first struck. A sword found his right shoulder and cut deep into his flesh causing him to drop his gladius. Two near-simultaneous arrows in the chest felled the second man. The third began to run further into the temple, but a zealot stabbed him in the back. Maximus was still swinging his torch, trying to keep the attackers at bay, when one of them struck the handle with a sword and cut it in two. The flames fell to the ground and left Maximus holding a useless wooden stick. As one, the zealots rushed forward and impaled him with two stabs into the chest and one in the back. Maximus fell to his knees silently bleeding. The attackers withdrew their swords and rushed towards the other defilers.

Curia, I shall see you in Elysium. Maximus fell face-forward, dead.

XIX. The Funeral (70 AD – 71 AD)

"Whoever tries to protect his life will lose it; but whoever loses his life on account of me will preserve it."

- The Book of Q (Revised)

Proculus received word of Maximus, both the success of his mission and his death, while sitting on his bench staring at the resplendent Lake Yosef. He struggled to maintain serenity; his face flushed in anger as his stomach knotted with pain. The messenger stood watching silently. Proculus took a breath to loosen his jaw muscles and bowed his head in reverence to his lifelong best friend. After a minute of silence, he opened his eyes and dismissed the messenger with a flick of his hand. *I can't believe it.* He clasped his hands together to stop them from shaking. Maximus had been in so many battles and dangerous situations, that it was impossible to accept that he did not come through this one.

Proculus found it more and more difficult to support himself and fell forward to his knees. As his hands met the dry ground, he sobbed at the profound loss. He felt rudderless without Maximus. *How do I go on?* After what seemed like hours, the sobbing subsided. Proculus felt spent but gathered himself up, and without looking back at the lake, slowly made his way to Curia and June.

He walked into the house to find that June had left to speak with some people at the synagogue, but Curia was still there in the reading room. Most likely, she was thinking about her decision to lead propositum. Proculus considered not interrupting her, but she deserved to know about her father and to hear it from the man who was at fault.

When he walked into the reading room, Curia looked up from the couch and her eyes narrowed at seeing the look on Proculus' face. His eyes were still somewhat red and glassy and his body sagged in defeat. Proculus could see her reaction to the sight of him. He watched as she considered the possible reasons.

When her eyes grew large, he said quietly and deferentially, "He's gone." Curia turned away.

"How?" was all she could say.

"Apparently in the final battle for the Temple he was attacked from behind by a group of zealots and was overwhelmed."

Curia lowered her head and Proculus could see the sharp intakes of breath, but he could see no tears. After a couple of minutes, she straightened. "That is the best possible way he could have gone. He was a true soldier and to die any other way would have belittled him." Then she patted the cushion next to her and said, "Come, sit next to me and let us talk about my father."

Proculus hesitated and then sat. They spent the next hour reminiscing about Maximus. They laughed at his foibles and were proud of his many accomplishments. They were happy that he had lived a grand and honorable life and would be welcomed into the underworld.

Then Curia turned the subject away from her father and to the plan, "What of the temple, was it destroyed?"

Proculus turned at a sound just outside the reading room, but then returned his attention to Curia. "Yes, Maximus took a group of men in to destroy it and they succeeded even though he and two of the others were killed. Almost as important was that Titus, upon seeing the destruction, decided to plunder the treasures and return them to Rome. Between that and the razing of most of Jerusalem, the Christian movement has little to stand in its way. We have accomplished all that we envisioned."

* * *

Unbeknownst to the two conspirators, June had been listening to the conversation from the other side of the door. At first, she hadn't wanted to disturb them as they spoke of Maximus' glories, realizing that he must be dead and that they were commiserating. She silently cried for Maximus and for the two in the room knowing how close both of them were to the old warrior.

Then the conversation turned to the destruction and the Temple and she had a hard time comprehending what they were saying. She put her ear closer to the door. *They couldn't have been part of this!* She shook her head. *I must not be hearing them correctly.* She stepped away from the door, reviewing their words repeatedly. She left to find some quiet place to try to understand.

* * *

When the conversation died away in the reading room, Proculus left to find June. She was sitting on their bed bawling. *What could be wrong? Maybe she heard about Maximus.* He didn't want to presume. "What is it June?"

She held up a hand for him to stay away and shook her head. He waited a minute trying to let her regain her composure and when the bawling turned to sobs he walked slowly to her, knelt before her and put his hands on her knees. He tried to look into her eyes, but she kept turning her head and refused to look at him. It was then that Proculus realized that her emotions were about him and not Maximus. *What could this be?*

He asked again, more earnestly, "What is it?"

June finally looked into Proculus' eyes with fury. Behind gritted teeth she said, "How could you have destroyed Jerusalem?"

Futuere! She knows! After all these years. Proculus inhaled in absolute shock. His eyes grew wide and he leaned back as if slapped across his face by her question. "How?" he murmured.

"I overheard you and Curia talking about Maximus and it was so touching that I didn't want to interrupt and just kept listening." She trembled. "And then I heard you talking about the destruction of Jerusalem as if it was some toy." *The noise…*

The trembling grew as the fury burst out of her. "How could you? You're a murderer and you destroyed my people, my religion. Some are saying a million Jews died during this war and you're at fault."

"Let me try to explain, June."

"No," she bellowed, "it would just be more lies. How can I ever trust you? How can I even look you in the face after what you've done?"

"Please June, let me explain. There are good reasons for what we've done."

"We? We? You mean you and Maximus and Curia? You aren't even human. You're repugnant. I thought I knew you, but this, this is so unimaginable, from anyone, but especially from you. I thought you loved the Jewish people."

Proculus started to reply, but June cut him off, "No, I don't want to hear any more from you. I want to be alone. Just leave!" She knocked his hands from her knees and buried her face in her hands. Proculus lingered for a couple of minutes and then decided that she would have to settle down before he would be able to talk to her, so he left the room.

* * *

That night when Proculus went to bed, June was nowhere to be found. He figured she needed time alone and would return when she was ready. Four days later Theophorus arrived at the door with a message from June that she wouldn't be returning for the time being. Proculus tried to find out how she was and where he could find her, but Theophorus was reluctant to answer any questions.

After absorbing this, Proculus changed the subject and invited Theophorus in. It was time that he met Curia. It might also be time to inform him of the goals of the plan. He asked Theophorus to wait in the greeting area while he found Curia. After some searching, he discovered her in the garden. "Good morning, Curia. Theophorus is here and it seems an opportune time for the two of you to meet. Have you made a decision about being the caretaker of our plan?"

"Yes, I've decided to. Assuring the success of the plan makes my father's death meaningful and is his legacy to me," she answered with composure.

That brought a smile to Proculus' face, "Excellent. Then let us introduce you to Theophorus." Proculus turned and headed back into the house. Curia sighed, straightened her shoulders, and followed.

They entered to find Theophorus admiring a painting of Lake Yosef with Proculus' bench in the foreground. Proculus said, "Perhaps we can meet in the reading room where it is more comfortable," and the three made their way into Proculus' favorite room.

"Theophorus, this is Curia Octavius, Maximus' daughter. Curia, this is Theophorus ben Solomon; he will be the leader of the church here in Antioch."

Theophorus was immediately empathetic, "I'm very sorry to hear about your father, he was a great man and we shall all miss him."

Proculus felt it overly dramatic since he did not know Maximus well, but it was also gracious. Curia nodded and answered, "Thank you."

"Shall we sit?" Proculus asked, and they all sat down.

Proculus was not quite sure how to begin since this was impromptu. Curia spoke confidently, "I have heard said, Theophorus, that you are the first true Christian."

Theophorus smiled and laughed a little. "Yes, I've heard that as well. It's just because I was raised as a Christian."

"Did you know that Proculus here is one of the main reasons Christianity exists?"

Theophorus eyes narrowed. "I know he supported Paul and others in their travels and proselytizing and that he continues to support the church here in Antioch."

"Oh it is much more than that. He might be too humble to say, but he orchestrated many of the events that helped Christianity form." Curia saw Theophorus shaking his head slowly. She added, "It is quite true Theophorus, and my father had a lot to do with it as well."

Proculus was concerned that Curia would go too far, but he recalled asking her to take control of the plan and she had accepted. If she wanted Theophorus to know, then it was up to her. She would be the one to have to live with the consequences and with Theophorus if telling him ended up being a mistake.

Theophorus answered, "The main force behind Christianity is Jesus the Christ and they had nothing to do with him or his teachings."

"True, but they had a lot to do with spreading the word about those teachings and making use of his teachings around universal acceptance bending the Jewish restrictions on Gentiles."

Finally, Theophorus looked directly at Proculus who stared back, straight-faced. Theophorus asked, "Is this true?"

"True enough," Proculus answered.

"But why, what was your motivation?"

Proculus' eyes narrowed. *He needs to know enough to help the plan, but I can't tell him anything that might implicate us in the destruction of Jerusalem or the Temple.* "You have to remember that Jesus was a great man with teachings that are universal and that can save people from an otherwise wretched life."

Curia leaned back in her chair as Theophorus' attention centered fully on Proculus.

Proculus continued, "Those teachings are reason enough to want to spread the word and encourage the move to Christianity." He paused for effect and then leaned forward. "However, there is more." Another pause, "Rome is dying. At least the heart of Rome, what it once was. Ever since we became an Empire, we have been on a downward spiral that will end in destruction. What I saw in Christianity, or rather in the Essenes, is an opportunity to make something better. To merge your religion with the Roman Republic in order to make a stronger government that appreciates its people.

"So the main goal was to spread Judaism among the Gentiles sufficiently to eventually cause the Roman government to formally adopt it as its religion. That goal turned into promoting Christianity." There was more to say, of course, but Proculus stopped there to see how Theophorus was reacting.

"Are you really suggesting that Christianity wouldn't have come about without your ministrations?"

Yes. "Of course not. But it might not have spread as fast or as far."

"Frankly, this is a lot to absorb. I have to wonder, though, why you're telling me this."

"There are two reasons, but before we get to that, there's still more you need to hear." Proculus knew he had to get Theophorus to accept what they had done; at least enough to determine if he would be willing to join them.

"You see, we have also changed a few minor things about Christianity in order to get Gentiles to accept it. We have made Paul's and Jesus' actions more supernatural in order to show that Christianity is the new covenant with God and not, necessarily, Judaism."

Theophorus mouth tightened in concern. "Like what?" he asked reservedly.

Proculus sighed. "Like some of the miracles Paul performed and some of the stories about Jesus." He looked deeply into Theophorus' eyes and continued, "You have to believe me when I say that these were not unreasonable; the events could have happened that way. We just embellished them and made them more attractive to Gentiles in order to promote the proselytizing."

Theophorus sat back in his chair openmouthed. He muttered, "How can I believe any of this?"

At least he has not rushed from the room. Maybe he will accept this.

Curia leaned forward and offered, "Theophorus, what you have to consider is how important Christianity is. We know the Teacher was real and we have the ideas he passed down through his followers. Those ideas have already begun to transform our society. Having his teachings spread to the Gentiles can only be good. If Proculus and my father took liberties with some of the actual events, it was only to aid the spread of Christianity to allow it to help more people. What could be the harm?"

Proculus was impressed with how Curia had phrased that; it was a hard argument to counter and was at the root of his justification.

"I understand that," Theophorus replied looking at Curia, "However, it throws into doubt much of what I've been taught."

"No it does not," Curia countered. "What you have been taught is an ideology that brings people to the Kingdom of God and… that… has not changed. Believe in that and we can accomplish what my father died for."

Theophorus' eyes grew large. "Maximus died for this?"

"Yes," Curia said with her head held up proudly.

A servant walked in and told Theophorus that an elder from the church was looking for him. Theophorus said, "Oh my, I was supposed to be at service by now. We have a baptism today. I must leave at once." He started to leave, but turned when he reached the door. "I understand what you have told me this day and I don't disagree with it, but it will take some getting used to. And I still want to hear why you've told me all of this, though I think I'm beginning to guess. Goodbye."

Curia and Proculus looked at each other and recognized that they had done what they could. They would now have to wait to see how Theophorus absorbed the information. Curia said, "I need to get back to Rome. My father's body is on its way there and I need to prepare for the funeral."

Proculus lowered his head in renewed pain. "I'll go with you. It will give June time to think and I want to attend the funeral. However, there is one more person I would like you to meet. I will arrange a meeting for early tomorrow morning and then we can depart immediately afterwards."

* * *

The next morning found both Curia and Proculus ready to leave for Rome. Tobiah, the author Proculus wanted Curia to meet, was almost an hour late and Curia was agitated. *Why is this so important? I need to get to Rome!* When he finally arrived, she was in a perfunctory mood.

Proculus' introductions were terse, suggesting he felt the same way. "Tobiah, this is Curia. Curia, please meet Tobiah. He is going to be the author of the story of Jesus' life." The two shook hands and sat down. The man was dressed well, but he was balding with age and plump with too much food. He was also holding a set of documents and a piece of rounded glass that he seemed to use to magnify the text when reading.

Proculus said, "I am sorry Tobiah, but we do not have much time since we have to depart for Rome. I wanted the two of you to meet and you to know that Curia speaks for me in all matters. If anything should happen to me, she will be your contact and will retain my authority as well as funds."

Curia looked quickly at Proculus. *His funds? I had not considered that, but it does make sense.* She knew she would need resources to continue and Proculus would want his wealth to help.

"Very well," Tobiah replied as he turned towards Curia, "I have been gathering stories of Jesus, Saul's letters, and his *Book of Q*. Also any Jewish prophesies about the Christ that might apply. There are some things I'd like you to ask Paul if you are going to see him."

Curia and Proculus glanced at each other. Curia answered, "Yes, we will be seeing him. Leave us your list of questions and we will see what we can do."

Proculus interjected, "You remember that I do not want the Book of Q to leave this house. You can use it as much as you like and can take verbiage from it for your story, but there should be no copy and no one else should ever see it."

"Yes, I understand. We spoke of that previously. Will I have access to this house and to your library?"

"Yes, either June or one of the servants will be here and I will inform them that you should be let into the library whenever you wish. You know where I keep the book?"

"Yes."

Curia asked, "How do you plan to justify merging the stories with the prophesies about the Christ?"

"There is a tradition in Judaism called *Midrash* where we take the written word and apply *Homiletics* to it, which is the art of applying rhetoric and current events to existing text or an old story. It isn't unheard of to merge disparate information and stories into a single, consistent narrative. The more difficult aspect is to get people to believe that it is true and to get it distributed widely."

Curia offered, "If you write well enough that it is believable, we will take care of reproduction and distribution."

Proculus concluded, "Now, if there is nothing else, we really must be on our way."

"Very well, thank you for seeing me and I am honored to meet you, Curia."

"As am I, Tobiah. We will see each other again, I am sure. Please let us know as you progress. I do not know how long we will be in Rome."

"I shall write you at least once a month until I hear you are returning."

"Excellent, goodbye," Curia answered with finality.

Tobiah picked up his papers and eyepiece and left.

* * *

Curia and Proculus made their way to Rome as quickly as possible. It was bad enough that the conflagration at the Temple had burnt part of Maximus' body, but having it decompose on the trip to Rome would make the viewing difficult. *The longer we delay, the worse it will be*, Curia thought.

They arrived in Rome late in the evening and agreed to begin the funeral process the very next morning. They spread the word that the start of the ceremony and the viewing would take place in front of the old Scaevola residence, which had been rebuilt and was almost ready for occupancy. *It is a fitting location. The fire precipitated the war that killed him. He would appreciate that.*

The next morning, just after sunrise, they began the ceremony. Only Maximus' family and closest friends, mostly wearing dark colors in mourning, attended the preparation of the body. Maximus' body had been wrapped in a cloth saturated with saltwater to preserve it as much as possible. Three hired men placed the body on the viewing table, still wrapped, and then backed away. The remainder of the ceremony was Curia's responsibility as his only living child.

At twenty paces, Curia could smell death and decay emanating from her father and was struggling with what she had to do. The stench was repulsive and she could not imagine having to move any closer, let alone having to touch him.

Proculus glanced at her, turned to one of the hired caretakers, spoke to him quietly, and gave him some silver coins. The man hurried away and Proculus turned back to Curia and whispered, "Wait here a few minutes and we will try to do something about the smell. Your father was too great of a man for people to remember him this way."

After many drawn-out minutes, the man returned and went up to Maximus' body and poured two flasks of perfumed oils on him. The smell did not go away, but other scents emerged. *That is… tolerable.*

Curia gathered what will power she could muster and walked to the table, though her jaw was tight and her muscles stiff. She first cut away the wrapping and exposed his bare body, which was now covered only by a loincloth. The smell threatened to overwhelm her and she felt a gag approaching. She swallowed hard to control the reaction and continued, taking rags from a pail of clean water to wipe the body clean. Proculus and the others watched in silence.

When she was done, she pulled a Roman coin from a pocket and looked at it. The coin had the likeness of the general of the armies, Cincinnatus, a man Maximus had admired greatly, on the face. She placed it in his mouth as an offering to Charon to ferry Maximus to the underworld. In a voice she wanted to be strong but that sounded weak, she said, "Maximus Servius Octavius." She did all this prior to closing his eyes so that he could see the coin he would need for the crossing. She reached up and repeated, "Maximus Servius Octavius," as she closed the left eye. Again, "Maximus Servius Octavius," as she closed the right eye.

With the help of a couple of the men, she then lifted her father's body enough to dress him in military garb. The clothes had been sliced down the back to make it easier. She put his gladius, with the hilt on his chest, facing downwards and she wrapped his hands around the hilt. When she was done, she stepped back to view the results and then returned to adjust the coat. Finally, it was complete and she walked back to stand next to Proculus. The friends of Maximus Servius Octavius viewed the prepared body in silence.

His body would stay like that for three days while the public was allowed to mourn his passing. Curia sat in a special chair, as much as she could bear, near the site for anyone to offer condolences. Proculus spent much of his time standing behind and to her left with his hand laid gently on her shoulder. Each morning, at his request, perfumed oils were spread on Maximus' body.

On the morning of the fourth day, at daybreak, a crowd of people began to gather around the viewing area. This time they were dressed in bright colors to celebrate the life of their departed friend and to encourage him in his travels through the underworld. An hour after sunset, Curia nodded to the group of Maximus' six closest friends, including Proculus and Quinn. They walked to the platform and picked up the wood plank Maximus had been laid on. They began to march through the city to the outskirts where funeral burnings were held, since none were allowed in the city.

As they walked through the streets of Rome, additional friends, acquaintances, and mourners joined the march. Some knew Maximus and wanted to pay their respects for the man by joining the throng. Some were impressed enough with the number of people that they joined the march even though they didn't know the deceased. By the time they reached the vacant hill and placed the body on the platform where the funeral pyre would occur, there were over a thousand people observing the proceedings.

Curia was drained so much by the previous three days that she asked Proculus to offer the eulogy. He waited for the number of stragglers to diminish and then walked up to the platform where Maximus was laid, turned, and addressed the crowd. "If you would come a little closer then those in the back will be able to hear." He waited until everyone seemed to be within hearing distance.

> *As many of you know, Maximus was not the most effusive of people.*
> *In respect for him, I'll keep this brief.*

As I look around at all of you, I see not just a significant number of people, which speaks for itself, but an incredible variety of people. There are soldiers, politicians, senators, equestrians, tradesmen, philosophers, lawyers, physicians, sailors, craftsmen, lenders, and even some slaves. There are also people here from a wide range of religions and locals. Look around you and you will see people from Gaul, Egypt, Iudea, Spain, Mesopotamia, Asia, and many other places.

All of this diversity speaks to the breadth and the versatility of Maximus Servius Octavius.

Maximus was an Old Roman, with allegiance to the Republic, and he had a stronger drive to defend it than anyone else I have ever known. He was a soldier from the time he could walk, from a soldier's family, with a long tradition of serving their country. However, they had troubled times when Maximus was young and had to live with the experience of being ostracized by the people they fought with. That did not deter Maximus who worked harder, became stronger, and proved his honor and dedication to all.

Maximus demanded and received respect from everyone he came into contact with. I saw soldiers, generals, politicians, criminals, and scoundrels, each bow to his "suggestions" as they recognized the power and the wisdom that those suggestions offered.

There were few who did not stop and listen when Maximus spoke.

There was nothing Maximus would not do for his country or for his family. He defended Caesars, rescued senators, and fought in multiple wars for his country, all the way until his death, in battle, while defending Rome in the war with Iudea. He died the way he would have wanted to, fighting for what he believed in, to the very end.

Proculus closed his eyes and looked away for a moment. When he returned to the audience, he had to blink away moistness, but continued in a hoarse voice.

He was the epitome of honor, a loving son and father, and more recently grandfather, and he was... my friend. We shall all miss him more than any of us can articulate and the world without him is… diminished.

Proculus bowed his head in silence. All joined him. They understood it was the passing of a great man who deserved their respect and admiration. After a few minutes of silence, Proculus walked to Curia's right side since Quinn was on her left. She picked up a torch, lit it on fire, walked to the platform, and ignited the pyre for her father.

She was somber with silent tears streaming down her cheeks.

The crowd watched the fire burn in silence. The flames engulfed the platform as ashes floated delicately away. When Maximus and the platform were consumed, they quietly departed. Once they were all gone, Curia turned to leave. Proculus asked, "Where is Servius?" Curia continued looking at the path in front of her.

Quinn answered, "With his wife. She just delivered twin boys."

"Interesting." After a few more steps he added, "What are their names?"

"Primus and Secundus."

"Very interesting," he mumbled.

* * *

The next day, Curia heard that Titus was on his way to Rome with vast treasures from Judea. Vespasian announced that he would meet his son in the outskirts and they would ride into the great city, on chariots pulled by ten horses, together.

The siege, the attacks, and the pillaging that happened afterwards had destroyed the Temple and most of Jerusalem. Curia wondered how many hundreds of thousands of people had died. She had heard that Titus, upon seeing the destroyed Temple, decided to complete the sacrilege and take all of the treasures, including the most precious Jewish artifact, the menorah.

Vespasian said he would use the treasure to begin construction of the Flavian Amphitheater, a massive coliseum, near the center of Rome on land that Nero had taken from the people after the great fire.

They will be remembered in stone, she thought sullenly.

But what of my father?

XX. Departures (71 AD – 72 AD)

"And you who have followed me will sit on thrones, judging the twelve tribes of Israel."

- *The Book of Q (Revised)*

Proculus left Curia alone for a few days knowing she would want to spend them with Servius and Quinn. On the fourth, in late afternoon, she found him. "There is no reason to delay any further. It is time to go see Paul."

"Agreed, however you being there will disrupt the conversation."

"I know, but I want to hear what he says. I will stay out of sight, but within earshot."

Proculus looked at her and realized she was right. *It might be important that she hear Paul's final ideas.* "Then shall we go?"

"Yes."

They headed out of the house towards the jail. Curia was carrying a bag and Proculus asked what was in it, but she replied casually, "You shall see."

When they arrived, Curia spoke to the guard and he arranged to have other prisoners around Paul moved or sent outside for the time being. He also stood guard to make sure nobody interrupted the discussion. The guard handed Curia a chair and she took it into the cell next to Paul's. She pulled papyrus and quill out of her bag.

The guard then walked Proculus to Paul's cell and opened the door. Paul looked up but said nothing. *Did Curia have this all arranged previously?* He sat on the side of the bed since Paul was occupying the only chair in the cell.

Paul looked pensive but didn't appear hostile and that was as much as Proculus could have hoped for. He spoke first, "You know, I understand why you had me jailed and it wasn't even much of a surprise. But restricting me from writing letters to the churches seems counterproductive."

Proculus was a little surprised that Paul was being reasonable. "We could not take the chance that you would discredit Christianity through your letters. You might have taken an extreme view that it is all a sham. You could have damaged it beyond repair."

Paul bowed his head and then answered, "I can see that, and thank you for being honest, but you underestimate me. As much as I think you've manipulated the situation for your own benefit, there is great value in Christianity and I want to see it succeed as much as you do. I just don't agree with your methods."

"My methods could certainly be debated, but they are not the reason I came here and, in fact, are irrelevant at this point since the project is all but complete."

"Then what are you here for?"

This is going much better than I imagined. "A while back you suggested that the next step for Christianity would be to develop stories, or gospels, of Jesus' life and teachings. I could not agree with you more and that seems to me to be the one remaining task I might be able to accomplish for Christianity before I die." He had wanted to bring in the fact that he was close to death to gain some sympathy from Paul and it seemed to work, based on the compassionate look on Paul's face. "I have found a man who used to write plays and is willing to write the first gospel. To make it the most plausible, I would like to hear what you think needs to be included and any oral tradition you know of that might support aspects of the story."

Paul sat back in his chair and contemplated Proculus' request. After a minute, he replied, "This would have been much more comprehensive if you had asked this of me before and then left me papyrus and a quill to write down my ideas. Doing this now, without being able to document it will make it… superficial."

"I understand, and I apologize, but that was not really an option and your superficial ideas on this will still prove to be quite valuable."

Paul grimaced at the flattery. "First, do you have the book of sayings I kept? It was taken from me when I was arrested."

"Yes, we have it and we have made some copies to ensure it is not lost."

"Then that should be the basis for the gospel, that was why I named it *The Book of Q*, but you will need to turn it into an actual story of Jesus' life, from beginning to end." He frowned in apparent pain and added, "Then you should consider destroying all copies. The gospel, or gospels if you end up with more than one, need to stand on their own and they can't do that if this booklet still exists."

Then he relaxed and digressed briefly, "You're fortunate in that I've already been thinking about this. There isn't much to do in here but think, so I've gone through in my mind what might need to be done."

He took a breath and continued, "Any story needs to start with Jesus' birth. There were prophesies of the coming messiah that included signs to tell us when he would arrive. Obviously we missed those signs, but Jesus' birth would have had to shadow those prophesies. You can find those in the Jewish writings."

He pondered that and then added, "There's only one aspect of that I might change. We have been calling Jesus the Christ the *son of man*, but to appeal to a wider, non-Jewish, audience, he really needs to be considered divine - the *Son of God*. Therefore, he wouldn't have been conceived in the normal way. Some of the followers of Judas Iscariot might say that he was a spirit from the divine world who inhabited a regular human body, but that doesn't fit with the theology we are espousing as Christians. Instead, a spirit of the One True God, a holy spirit, would have had to come down and impregnate Jesus' mother. Not only that, but to prove it and to make Jesus as pure as possible, that would have had to occur with a virgin."

Proculus' eyebrow went up at that, "That is quite a stretch from Judaism."

"Not really, there were portents about such an event in some of the old writings. The fact that none of the Jews noticed it during Jesus' time would be the most difficult aspect to overcome. Many of the Pharisees and even the remaining orthodox Essenes will have a difficult time believing it, but Christians probably won't, especially Gentile Christians."

After Paul hesitated, Proculus asked, "What next?"

Paul looked up, irritated. "The second is that I saw Jesus in the vision on the road to Damascus. We've always presented that more like I saw his body as well as his spirit. We could capitalize on that and have Jesus resurrected after he's crucified. When I thought about that idea, I realized that it isn't clear why Jesus was crucified. I know we wanted to use it to blame the Pharisees, but if he was divine, then why did he allow himself to be crucified? There has to be a plausible reason and we don't really have one. I've spent quite a bit of time thinking about it. It has to do with saving mankind somehow, possibly from the wretched existence the Judas followers talk of, but I haven't been able to come up with a cohesive story. You'll need to work on that and you'll need to have someone that knows the Jewish history well, both written and oral."

"That may be difficult after the war. Most of the knowledgeable Jews were either killed or have scattered. Any we might find will not want to help Christians because we did not help them during the war."

"You are acting like all of this will happen right away. These ideas for changes will have to happen over the next few decades. You'll be doing well if you can get a single gospel written that tells an introductory story. It shouldn't and can't include all the changes I'm telling you or it will be unbelievable to people."

"That is sensible."

"Another option to consider is the timing of when Jesus lived. Originally, we based this on The Teacher of Righteousness, but he is so far removed from people that when we spoke of him as the high priest in Jerusalem over a century ago, people tended to lose interest. That was one of the things Maximus and I found during our original travels; we had to imply that he lived more recently and that seemed to make him more relevant in the minds of the people, especially the Gentiles.

"If you remember, we found twelve sects of followers of The Teacher. I would suggest that each of these sects be represented by a single apostle that studied under Jesus the Christ and who represents his best and most devout followers. This happens to correspond well to the prophesied twelve tribes of Israel. That will link the Christians to the Jewish past and provide legitimacy. Some people, of course, won't have anything to do with us and there isn't anything to be done about that.

"Lastly, there is one more area that you will need to research. It's a topic that you will have to be able to answer at some point, but I don't know exactly when that will be. It could be within a few years or not for decades."

Paul faltered, so Proculus asked, "What is it?"

"It has to do with the parousia, the second coming. Many prophesies suggest that the Christ will come back and will become the King of the Jews and will rule over the entire world. That seems unlikely to happen at this point, and people will notice. It's another reason why we have to move Jesus' life to recent times. If The Teacher really was the Christ, then he should have returned to Earth by now and be ruling the world. Moving it to recent times gives you a while to come up with some other explanation.

"That's all I can think of that you'll need to cover in a gospel. Of course, you may need to make some modifications to my letters. You do still have copies of each, don't you?"

"Yes, of course."

"Then you can have this same author, or another one, modify them to show me saying things that match some of these ideas and you can have those copied and sent to churches as readings. That should legitimize the ideas and this gospel."

"That is an excellent idea. Are there any letters besides the ones you gave to me?"

"There are a few, especially ones written in my name by Timothy and others, but you should be able to get copies of those and make the same changes."

Paul seemed to wind down and was looking parched from all the talking. Proculus leaned toward the door. "Guard, would you bring some water for the prisoner?"

The guard disappeared around a corner and then returned with a flagon of water, handed it to Proculus, and returned to his original position where he could keep an eye on both the cell and the approaching corridors.

As Paul was drinking, Proculus said, "I have been pondering the church organization. With what happened in Jerusalem, we need to have a more formal organization for the Christian church, but one that is not so centralized."

"What do you mean what happened in Jerusalem?"

Proculus looked up at Paul, startled. *Does he not know? This could be difficult.* "Most of Jerusalem was destroyed in the war. As was the Second Temple." He stuttered a little in feigned anguish, "I… I assumed you knew."

Paul leaned back in his chair, his face drained of all color. Proculus tried to soften the blow, "That was where Maximus was killed."

Paul looked up at Proculus, eyes glassy and unfocused. "Maximus," he whispered. "I had heard he died from a guard who went to the funeral, but he didn't tell me about Jerusalem." Tears fell from an eye as his head shook slowly. He held up his hand to forestall any more conversation. "I… umm… will you… give me a few minutes? This is… difficult." He trailed off as his eyes shut.

Proculus felt empathetic and did not want to push him. *He has been so cooperative.* All he said was "Of course," and he stood up and left the cell.

He went down the hall to where the guard was and stood talking with him quietly to give Paul some privacy. Curia joined him, but did not speak above a whisper. After a sufficient amount of time had passed, Proculus guessed more than half an hour, he returned to Paul's cell. He could see that Paul had been crying, but he did not object when Proculus came back in and sat on the bed again. Curia had quietly returned to the cell next door.

Paul stammered, "You were saying something about church organization?"

"Yes. We need to develop a formal church hierarchy; one that manages the central tenets and theology for all Christians. Ultimately, we have to have centralized authority for Rome to deal with directly. As it stands today, no single entity represents Christianity. However, we should not, at least yet, have a central location for the leadership or it can be easily destroyed." He started to add "like Jerusalem," but decided that might be a distraction.

Paul answered, thinking as he spoke, "Hmm, that makes some sense. You would need to appoint presbyters over collections of churches and at some point have a single head of the church, a church pater, that can be shown to have authority passed down to him from Jesus the Christ directly. That would mean it has to come through one of the apostles."

"Or from you?"

Paul considered the notion, but shook his head. "No, as much as I might like that, it doesn't make sense because I'm more of a historian and traveling preacher and not one of the twelve apostles. The intuitive choice would be Peter, but you would need to find someone that, previously, succeeded him since he is no longer with us.

"You can also speak with James in Jerusalem and have him be the presbyter there."

"Um, Paul, I am sorry to say this too, but James was executed a number of years ago. There was a dispute with the Pharisees and they were not being moderated by the Romans, so they took the opportunity to accuse a number of Christian supporters of blasphemy and James was one of them." He waited for a response from Paul who seemed numb. He added, "I am truly sorry, Paul."

"You should memorialize James as one of the apostles," Paul offered.

There was an uncomfortable silence while Proculus waited to see if Paul had anything else to say, but he still seemed so bothered by the news about Jerusalem and now James that it was obviously difficult to concentrate. Proculus stood up to leave and made it halfway to the door when Paul stopped him. "There's one more thing you should prepare for." Proculus turned to listen, but didn't return to the bed. "There are already heretics out there trying to use these new ideas in strange and, in some cases, nefarious ways. These need to be fought, and fought hard. The best way is with this centralized leadership of the church that can define doctrine. However, you'll continue to need travelers to preach the word and to counter the heretics. The only way this can work is if there is one standard doctrine for all to follow; otherwise it will break down into various small sects that show little in common."

"I understand. We will take care of it. Is there anything else?"

"No. However, since I've answered your questions and have done what you wanted, I have a few questions for you."

Proculus' eyes narrowed, concerned about where those questions might lead. Then he realized that Paul deserved answers and he sat back down on the bed.

Paul leaned forward in his chair and looked deeply into Proculus' eyes. "Will I ever get out of here?"

Proculus' shoulders slumped. He replied, "It is doubtful. You are too much of a danger to us and to Christianity. In fact, I am sorry to say, you will not be allowed writing materials for the same reason."

"I thought as much. As difficult as that is to hear, I appreciate you being candid. Now, tell me about Jerusalem. What happened?"

"That is a long story, but I can try to summarize." He considered what to say and then continued, "After the fire in Rome, persecutions of Jews began occurring around the Empire. Some events were quite offensive to the Jews in Judea and they fought back. Eventually that led to a full rebellion of the province and General Vespasian was assigned to…"

Paul interrupted him, "I'm sorry, but I know what happened up until Vespasian became emperor. The guards do talk with me sometimes, so I hear things."

"Well," Proculus thought aloud, "Vespasian appointed his son Titus to complete the conquering of Jerusalem. They laid siege to it for many months and were finally able to break through the outer two walls. They struggled with the inner wall and during the period they were trying to break in, the legions laid waste to most of Jerusalem and pillaged indiscriminately. Then, they found the tunnel that leads under the south section of the inner wall and broke in at night to open the gate. The legions flooded into the Temple Mount and destroyed everything. They took the treasures out of the Temple and set fire to it. The intent, I understand, was to make sure Judea did not rebel again and the best way to do that was to destroy their seat of power."

Paul sat back face ashen. "The Jews must truly have lost their way for God to allow such destruction. Maybe Christianity really did have the new covenant and Judaism should fade."

Then he looked up quickly. "Were you the cause of any of that?"

"That is difficult to know. We did encourage strife between the Romans and the Jews and that was some of the impetus for the war, so in a way, yes. However, I was not in Jerusalem and was not directing the specifics." *He does not need to know any more.*

"But Maximus was there, did you give him orders to have the Temple destroyed?"

Proculus looked at Paul in silence. He shook his head slowly. "We are done here." He stood up to leave, walked through the door, and looked back to see Paul with his head in his hands, weeping.

* * *

Curia joined Proculus where the guard still stood. She saw Proculus glance at the sheaf of papyrus in her hand and she said, "I do not have the memory you do for superfluous religious minutiae, so I wrote down his ideas."

Proculus smiled and walked on towards the exit of the jail. Curia pulled a thick braided coil of rope slightly out of the bag. "Wait one moment, please." To the guard she said, "If he has not used this by morning, then help him out." She leaned forward and looked intently into the guard's eyes. "You understand me?" she asked in a grave tone.

He replied, just as serious, "Yes, my lady."

She put the rope back into the bag and walked to Paul's cell. He extracted his head from his hands and looked up with swollen eyes. Curia noticed he looked to her left instead of at her eyes. She said, "What are you looking at?"

"There is a butterfly flitting around behind you, just like..." He stopped and visibly closed his mouth.

She glanced back, but saw nothing. *He's seeing things.* Her eyes squinted at Paul and then she dismissed the vision. She placed the bag on the floor. "You may have use of this."

As she began to leave, she noticed a T drawn on the wall behind Paul. She nodded towards it. "What is that 'T' for?"

Paul glanced back. "It isn't a 'T,' It's a cross and a symbol for Christ's death."

"Interesting." *Coincidence?* "I saw it as representing *Tamdiu*, a name I was considering for our organization."

Paul asked, "Such a long time?"

"Yes, it could mean that or it could be applied to something that will be around for a very long time. It was just a thought." *An even better one now.*

Paul continued glancing at a spot behind her and above her left shoulder. She looked back again, but still saw nothing. "Is it still there?" she asked.

"Yes. It truly is beautiful."

* * *

When Curia met Proculus on her way out, she saw his large eyes and his mouth open to speak. She interrupted him, "Do not start with how valuable Paul is. I agree, he is very valuable, but he is also extremely dangerous. He is the only person alive who could utterly ruin us with his knowledge and his writing ability. We cannot take the chance and we have what we really need from him."

Proculus' lips tightened. He said, "I am not sure it is wise to lose such a valuable resource, we should be able to contain him."

"Maybe, and maybe not. It is time to move on from a dependency on one man anyway."

Proculus' head cocked and then he seemed to accept the idea. "What about the possibility of him being a martyr?"

Curia's voice rose slightly and she straightened up further. "He still could be. If we need to, we can make up a story about how he died at the hands of the Pharisees. Honestly Proculus, there is nothing to be gained by keeping him alive, at least not enough to warrant the risks."

With a sigh, he asked, "You planned that all along?"

Curia walked as she answered. "It depended on what came up in the conversation. I figured if the details of what happened in Jerusalem came out then he would be in the right frame of mind, so I suspect Paul will take care of the problem for us."

* * *

Five weeks later Proculus arrived at his house in Antioch. As soon as he walked in, he knew something was wrong. It was too quiet. He saw the note on the table just as one of the servants walked by. When she saw him notice the note, she looked awkward and walked quickly away.

He went over to the table, picked up the note and read.

> *My Dearest Proculus: I've loved you like no other in all my life. You have a regal quality about you that is more than alluring. You have and are the most honorable person I have ever known, and the most intelligent, and your ability to visualize a different, better future, and then work to make it happen is astonishing.*
>
> *However, what you have wrought upon the Jewish people is unforgivable and I find I cannot reconcile the man I love with the atrocities he has committed and I cannot fathom being with a man who could do such things. Easier to consider him dead, as if*

he had died in that horrible war, preferably fighting on the side of us Jews.

I will always remember you as the stalwart leader of men and defender of the Jews to the Romans. A man of two worlds who tried to combine them to improve both.

Please don't follow me. I'm leaving for the one refuge the Jews have left standing. There is no way for the Romans to breach the fortress at Masada. I'll spend the rest of my days praying for your soul and for God's forgiveness for what you have done.
With much love,
June

Proculus went to his back porch that looked out on the woods behind his house. He went to the rocking chair he had had built years ago, sat down, and read the letter over and over and over. Tears stained the papyrus. *Was it worth it?* He could not contemplate how it could be. He looked into the hills towards his coveted bench behind Lake Yosef with distaste. *Was it worth it?* His best friend was dead and the woman he had loved so dearly for so many years had left him, never to return. *Was it worth it?* The bench called him, but he could not go. *Was it worth it?* How could it be? *Who am I without June, without Maximus?* The pain in his chest and the hole in his stomach persisted.

His mind jumped from image to image. Meeting June, making love, laughing with Maximus, Curia as a baby, speeches with the Senate, marrying June, a tender moment here and there, the night of drinking with Paul, the long road of propositum.

He was finding it difficult to concentrate on any one aspect. Then, as more and more of the images centered on the plan, on their accomplishments, his thoughts settled on the church he had created out of vague stories, ambition, and a dream. And possibly out of the spiritual need of a society. He recalled what that church might mean to the future of Rome. It was set on a course that could ultimately cause it to become the state religion of a reformed Republic, and maybe, just maybe, that might turn the Roman government back to being one *of the people* and *for the people.*

But was it worth it?

Tamdiu
A Sequel

Follow the continuing story of Proclus' plan through Curia and her grandchildren, Primus and Secundus, in Tamdiu. The second book in the series dramatizes the creation of the gospels and two more wars between Judea and Rome. Will propositum come to fruition in Tamdiu? Do the wars destroy the nascent plan Proculus envisioned?

Find out in the tumultuous sequel to Propositum, *Tamdiu*.

Humanism for Parents
Parenting without Religion

A book by Humanist Celebrant Sean Curley,
Exploring parenting without reliance on religion.

By some estimates, over 1 billion people in the world are non-religious (humanist/secular/atheist) yet we base many of our parenting techniques and traditions on religion. There are books available on parenting around each of the major religions, but few discuss parenting in a Humanist household. This book outlines how non-religious parents can have rites, rituals, and practices needed for a healthy, spiritually-fulfilled family.

CPSIA information can be obtained at www.ICGtesting.com
Printed in the USA
BVOW081412200912

300562BV00002BA/1/P

9 781600 477621